"What would happen if I were to lay you down on the cushions here and now, Nell, and cover your body with mine?"

He leaned in, close enough now that she could see the lushness of those black lashes, the chiseled grooves bracketing the wide mouth. He smelled faintly of spiced orange and leather, looked like sin in a kashmir coat.

"I would fight you," she whispered.

"Would you?" He smiled, a slow, sultry grin that hinted at everything Donne wrote and Nell could only imagine. "I won't do it then."

In an instant, his hands were on her arms, lifting her from her seat as if she were weightless. Nell gasped, and then lost her breath altogether when his mouth came down hungrily on hers.

Then as quickly as he had taken her, he let go.

"I will be back tomorrow at noon. Don't make me chase after you again, Nell. I will find you, be sure of that. . . ."

By Emma Jensen
Published by The Ballantine Publishing Group

CHOICE DECEPTIONS
VIVID NOTIONS
COUP DE GRACE
WHAT CHLOE WANTS
ENTWINED
HIS GRACE ENDURES
BEST LAID SCHEMES
FALLEN
MOONLIT

Books published by The Ballantine Publishing Group
are available at quantity discounts on bulk purchases
for premium, educational, fund-raising, and special
sales use. For details, please call 1-800-733-3000.

MOONLIT

Emma Jensen

IVY BOOKS • NEW YORK

An Ivy Book
Published by the Ballantine Publishing Group
Copyright © 2002 by Emma Jensen

www.ballantinebooks.com

ISBN 0-804-11956-2

Manufactured in the United States of America

First Edition: January 2001

10   9   8   7   6   5   4   3   2   1

For my mother,
who read me a thousand stories,
made me believe that writers were as important
to the world as any doctor, architect, or astronaut,
and who shares my deep love
for princely frogs.

And for my son,
who especially loves a good Dr. Seuss story,
and who prefers turtles.

Tá mé i ngrá libh.

PROLOGUE

County Wicklow, Ireland, 1797

"Nell. Wake up, Nell! 'Tis time."

"I'm awake." Had never gone to sleep, actually. Nell threw back the covers and, careful not to wake any of the four girls who shared the bedchamber with her, crept into the hall, shoes in hand.

Kitty was waiting there, lit candle stub in hand. The flickering light lengthened her nose, made tendrils of her rioting red curls. Nell thought she looked like a witch just then, an opinion the vain and pretty Kitty Cleary wouldn't have appreciated in the least. But it was true, and appropriate, Nell thought, considering what they were about to do.

"Will you hurry yourself, Nell!" Kitty hissed as she led the way toward the stairs, nimbly avoiding the creaky step third from the top and another second from the bottom. " 'Tis nearly midnight."

Nell shivered as they slipped into the moonlit Wicklow night. She had gone to bed fully dressed, prepared for this midnight excursion. But she had forgotten a shawl in her excitement. For an instant she debated running back inside. She abandoned the idea as quickly as it had formed. She had neither Kitty's grace nor confidence. She would get caught, no doubt about it.

She always did. And punishments were stern and severe at the Horgan School for Girls. The eminently respectable and generally ill-liked Right Reverend Mr. Ferrall and his wife, who ran the charitable institution, did so with admirable zeal and no humor whatsoever. Nell had felt the lash of both tongues countless times, that of the reverend's birch switch almost as many. She would do nearly anything to avoid a lashing of either sort this night.

"Have you the mirror?" Kitty demanded.

Nell nodded, the carefully wrapped hand mirror clutched tight in her fist. There would be hell to pay if she broke it, but the lure of adventure had been worth taking the chance.

The two girls followed a rough path away from the school and through the neighboring field. It was a cold walk and a muddy one. It had rained hard all day, leaving Nell in anguish, half-terrified and half-hoping that there would be no moon at all. But the skies had cleared as if by magic and the moon shone above, full and bright.

"This will do." Kitty halted as they crested a rocky rise. "Give me the mirror. I'll go first."

Nell handed her precious bundle over with shaky hands. Kitty whistled as she unwrapped it, carelessly tossing the wool scarf aside. At sixteen she was fearless and pretty, and sure of her goals. Nell, plain and quiet at fourteen and possessed of no ambition save leaving Horgan's far behind, envied and admired the older girl desperately. Perhaps Kitty spoke a bit too loudly and swung her hips a bit too lively when young men were about. Perhaps she was a little too familiar when she spoke of the local squire's family, and perhaps her tongue and wit were sharp enough to draw blood. But those were all part and parcel of who Kitty was and Nell no more thought poorly of her for it than Kitty did of Nell for the circumstances of her birth.

"Ready, then?"

Nell nodded, tongue-tied in her excitement.

"Good." Kitty tossed back her hair, raised the mirror toward the moon, and chanted,

> *"Moon, full moon, give to me*
> *a view of who my lover will be.*
> *Will he be handsome, will he have gold?*
> *Show me his face, let his name be told!"*

Then she lowered the mirror and peered eagerly into its silver surface.

Nell hugged herself tightly, giddy and eager to know what her friend was seeing. She waited what seemed an eternity before offering a timid, "Kitty?"

The other girl snorted, shrugged, then thrust the mirror in Nell's direction. "A pretty face, but one I see every time I look in a glass. Your turn. I already know who I'm to have anyway."

Kitty was convinced she would be married to Kevin Keenan within a few months and settled nicely on his little farm. She'd already cuddled with him on countless nights, after all. Tonight's exercise, as far as she was concerned, was a mere formality.

Nell hesitantly lifted the mirror. *Please,* she thought as she tried to remember the words of the old incantation, *just let me see someone's face other than mine. Please.*

With Kitty's impatient prompting, she said the words. Then, heart in her throat, she lowered the mirror. And immediately dropped it on the rocky earth, where it shattered into a dozen pieces.

"Oh, *Nell!*" Kitty snapped. "Well, now you've done it. Seven years bad luck and no lover at all!" She prodded the broken china handle with her toe. "Did you manage to get even a *little* peek before you went ham-handed?"

Mute with terror, Nell could only shake her head.

"Ah, well." Kitty gathered her shawl about her shoulders and turned back toward the school. "Heaven help you when Mrs. Ferrall finds her mirror gone."

Heaven help her, indeed. And it wasn't the broken mirror on Nell's mind as she lay shivering in her bed hours later. It was what had been reflected in its moonlit surface. She couldn't have told Kitty what she'd seen if she'd tried. It had been too awful.

For in that brief instant before the mirror had slipped from her hands, a face had looked out at her. A man's face, fierce and frightening, viciously scarred.

As the first fingers of dawn appeared, Nell prayed silently. She asked forgiveness; it had been a sin, surely, engaging in an old Irish charm. And she asked, too, that God make hers a useful sort of life to someone, as she knew now she would never be any man's wife.

Connemara, County Galway

The boy's ribs burned like fire. He gasped quietly, taking in as little air as he could. It hurt even to breathe. He could smell the crushed forget-me-nots, feel them under his cheek.

Above him, his father snarled and grunted like a baited bear. One fist clenched and unclenched rhythmically. The other had an iron grip on a horsewhip. "So, you think she loves you, do you?"

The boy did not respond. Instead, he wiped the trickle of blood from his lip and squinted up through one rapidly swelling eye.

"You will not look at me!" Richard Robard, Viscount St. Wulfstan, lashed out at the boy's ribs again, his booted foot connecting with a sickening thud.

"Father . . ." Trevor groaned, writhing in pain. This time the boot clipped his jaw, all but knocking him senseless.

The viscount kicked at the scattered flowers. "You are a brainless fool," he hissed. "How could you possibly think that any woman could care for you? How could *anyone* feel anything but revulsion at what you are?"

He jerked away as Trevor stretched out a trembling hand.

"Father . . ."

"Silence!" Richard knocked Trevor's arm aside, then walked around his prone form as if looking for an unbattered inch to strike next.

This wasn't the first beating—the viscount had always been a harsh man—but it was by far the worst. And it had come from nowhere. Trevor had returned from a ride, winded and merry, a bunch of early-blooming forget-me-nots for his mother swinging in one hand. He had whistled his way out of the stable and into the brutal, unexpected smack of his father's fist against his jaw. Even as he had gone down, head striking the hard earth, he had felt the surprise more than the pain.

He could have struck back at any time. He knew that. At fourteen, he had been as tall as his father. Now, at sixteen, he was several inches over Richard's six feet, and at least two stone heavier. Not to mention more than thirty years younger. But he would never strike back, not at his father. Richard knew that.

"Why?" Trevor managed, trying yet again, desperately, to understand. Something had happened while he had been galloping home over the bleak Connemara heath, something important and dire. He'd waited with every blow to learn what it was. "Father . . ."

Richard had come to a stop at his head. Shaking with disgust and unrestrained fury, he crouched and spat deliberately into Trevor's face. "You are naught but the spawn of Satan. She doesn't care for you. No woman will ever care for you. Doubt me, and you are as stupid as you are despicable."

With that, he strode from the stable yard, leaving his battered heir to sob quietly into the dirt.

CHAPTER 1

London, 1813

"They call her Mrs. Nolan."

Trevor Robard, Viscount St. Wulfstan, gave the object of his inquiry a long, appraising look. She was seated in a small alcove across the room, half-concealed by a filmy drape the same dull white as her dress, a colorless figure at the edge of a peacock-bright crowd. "Is she any more attractive when viewed up close?" he asked.

"I could not say." At the viscount's side, Edgar Rickham swung his quizzing glass in a lazy arc. It was, Trevor noted, suspended on a long ribbon made of braided titian hair. According to rumor, the man cut thick strands himself from the lovely head of whichever woman he had in his keeping. His jewelry box boasted raven, red, and countless shades of blond, the ribbons changed at his whim.

"I believe," Rickham continued, his nasal drawl nearly as annoying as the back-and-forth, back-and-forth swing of his glass, "I will have La Belle Balashova introduce me. Apparently Clonegal scarce left his bed during the several years Mrs. Nolan was under his protection."

"Clonegal died in his bed," Trevor said drily.

"Precisely," was the tart response. "Just my point. With a smile on his face, no doubt."

From what little Trevor knew of the late duke's death, it had been prolonged and not at all a smiling matter. But that was neither here nor there. He didn't care how the man had died. He was, however, intrigued by his peers' unsuppressed interest in Clonegal's mistress. Demireps were common as fleas in London, hopping from expensive bed to bed on lithe legs. They were invariably greedy, usually shrewd, and more often than not rather beautiful.

This Mrs. Nolan, as best he could tell from this distance, was not even pretty. Yet a steady stream of men begged introductions from their hostess, the glorious Anastasia Balashova who, in her heyday some twenty-five years earlier, had been the most famous and sought-after cyprian in England. Certainly approaching fifty now, La Belle Balashova was still lovely, still fiery of wit and temper, and still reliable for a lively party. She had outdone herself tonight. The grand salon of her elegant Bruton Street house was crowded with London's elite: Society's men and the Demimonde's women. The room pulsed and glittered under the lights of countless candles.

Wellington had been known to tip a glass in this room, as had Palmerston, Rievaulx, and several of the king's lusty sons. The lovely Dubochet sisters, Harriette Wilson among them, had held court within these walls. Anastasia Balashova was responsible, albeit indirectly, for the depletion of countless fortunes, two marriages—for not every gentleman insisted on marrying respectability—and one very scandalous divorce. Entrée into her soirees was coveted more than invitations to Almack's. There was no question that the lady took devilish delight in entertaining on the very same night as Almack's weekly Assembly. The multitude of black knee breeches and white waistcoats attested to the fact that a good half of the men present had left those hallowed, deadly dull halls—probably at a sprint—to revel at La Belle Balashova's.

Trevor thought he might have seen Brummell and his circle lounging in one corner. A trio of French opera dancers fresh from Paris had arrived on Kildare's arm and were as colorful and loud as an entire flock of parrots. There was a country dance going at one end of the room, a lively game of five-card loo at the other. The Earl of Haddley's recently discarded mistress appeared to be emptying the pockets of that man's young heir. And in the midst of it all, their hostess glowed like a jeweled Russian samovar.

The center of attention, however, was seated all but in the shadows. Trevor had never known La Belle Balashova to play procuress. She entertained lavishly, of course, throwing these famed soirees where the most exclusive courtesans and the *ton*'s gentlemen rubbed shoulders, elbows, and whatever other body parts they so desired. She had arranged the introduction between many a wealthy man and his next mistress. But she had never brought a cyprian out for perusal.

It appeared she was doing just that with the still, quiet woman in the alcove.

"Well," Rickham murmured, "it seems Poole has passed the test."

So it did. Madame Balashova was guiding Henry Poole to the alcove. Poole bowed, his ludicrously tight coat parting to display a portly bottom. Trevor saw

Mrs. Nolan raise a pale hand. Then the rest of the tightly encased Sir Henry blocked her from sight.

Their hostess glided back to her own settee. Hopeful men: Walcott, Carmody, and Lord William Paget among them, hovered nearby like lurkers at the Pearly Gates.

"So who in the hell is this Mrs. Nolan?" Trevor demanded, finding himself reluctantly impressed when something the courtesan said sent Poole skulking away with a flush that glowed even on the bald spot atop his head.

"Good God, man," came Rickham's drawl, "where on earth have you been? Any gentleman who has come within a quarter mile of St. James's these past weeks has heard of the notorious Mrs. Nolan."

Trevor bared his teeth in what he knew the other man would not mistake for a smile. He wondered what sort of effect the truth regarding his recent whereabouts would have on Rickham. It sat grimly enough with Trevor. The infernal war dragged on, and he was not finding his brutal, clandestine part in it as easy to live with as he used to.

He drained his glass before saying, "I do not come anywhere near the St. James clubs if I can possibly avoid it."

"Of course. I forgot to whom I was speaking. Careless of me." Rickham gave his own parody of a smile. "*Sin Wulfstan*, scourge of all things polite, despair of the respectable matron. Tell me, did Rotheroe really threaten to have your eyes on a skewer if you so much as looked at his sister again?"

"No," was Trevor's bland reply.

"I did not think so. Walcott is always so desperate to be considered a wit that he is forced to create the bulk of his tales. I will roast him most soundly—"

"It was Benning, not Rotheroe. Speaking of his wife, not his sister."

"Oh. Well." Rickham shrugged. "Still hardly worth—"

"And it was not my eyes he vowed to skewer."

He saw Rickham wince, one hand sneaking down to hover briefly below his waist. There was no question of the man not believing the tale. Rickham swallowed such gossip like air, countless such anecdotes followed Trevor like a dirty shadow, and this one was absolutely true.

"Hardly worth the effort, Lady Benning," Rickham muttered. "Closed up tight as an oyster."

Trevor saw no reason to report that he regarded Lady Benning as perhaps his most impressive conquest, a steady and persistent crusade and a glorious pearl ultimately. Rickham was a toad and the fact that he had clearly had a go at the young wife of the choleric old Benning—just as clearly unsuccessfully—would ordinarily have called for a bit of smug crowing. But Trevor held his tongue. Scruples had little to do with it; he possessed few. He simply couldn't be bothered.

Trevor cared for Rickham as little as Rickham cared for him, probably less. But it was an animosity dulled somewhat by their hostess's excellent wine. As Trevor had been curious about this shrouded mouse in the corner and Rickham was never happier than when displaying his superior knowledge on any subject, they had formed a very temporary and not particularly cheerful accord.

"Tell me about Mrs. Nolan."

Rickham twirled his glass. "No one knows much, actually. She's from Ireland—" that said with a faint sneer, then, "Oh, I do beg your pardon. So are you."

"So I am." Trevor could easily have taken offense. But he'd been accustomed to slights against the place of his birth since his first days at Eton. He'd blackened eyes and bruised ribs over it then. Now he ignored it. After all, his being Irish was only part of what so many of his peers disliked about him. "She's Irish . . ."

"Illegitimate daughter of some lordling's younger son and a maid, rumor has it. Came over with Clonegal when he returned last year. They say she's been in a sort of mourning for him and is now looking for a new protector."

"An entire eight weeks of mourning," Trevor murmured. "Ah, how the need for money has a way of trampling sentiment into the dust."

"And damned fortunate for some happy fellow." Rickham smiled his reptilian smile. "I can afford her."

Trevor didn't doubt that. Rickham's money was perhaps his only recommendation to the world. He simply wasn't certain why the man had settled on this particular extravagance. The room was full of stunning women who could be bought. Trevor himself had been eyeing a raven-haired opera dancer. He was an admirer of a lush and limber form.

"This ought to be amusing," Rickham drawled.

Mrs. Nolan was entertaining a new admirer. Lord William Paget, usually a loud and eloquent fellow, actually seemed to be stammering as he bent over her hand. Trevor's mouth thinned. He rather liked young Paget. Not yet five-and-twenty, the fellow was altogether too cheerful and enthusiastic in general, and had an impressive habit of showing up just when Trevor had ordered an expensive bottle of something or other, but he was entertaining enough company.

Beyond that, Trevor had served in the same elite military corps with Paget's brother, the Marquess of Oriel, a bond that was firmer and more enduring than Trevor would have liked if given the choice. For some reason, that loyalty seemed to have extended itself to Oriel's brother.

Trevor knew William had neither the funds nor the experience to maintain a mistress of Mrs. Nolan's ilk. She would eat the boy alive in a matter of weeks.

It seemed Rickham agreed. "Young idiot," he announced as he fingered the ridiculously ornate arrangement of his cravat and tweaked several pale curls into their Byronic places. "Should know better than to try his hand at a man's game. I believe it is time for me to demand my introduction."

Like recognized like, Trevor mused, even as he tipped glass and eyebrow in what Rickham would no doubt take as encouragement. *Idiot.* No one demanded anything of Anastasia Balashova. More often than not, one begged.

Trevor wasn't about to do any such thing. But he was going to trundle young William out of harm's way. And he was going to meet this Mrs. Nolan.

Deftly depositing his glass on a passing footman's tray, he struck purposefully across the floor. People scattered like chickens. They always did. From the corner of his eye, he could see the queue of men at La Balashova's side watching him as he bypassed their ranks and neared the alcove. He heard one muttered, *"Arrogant lout!"* Walcott, Trevor thought with amusement. Like recognized like.

Then he was standing behind Paget. Mrs. Nolan was totally obscured by her young swain. Trevor tapped the younger man on the shoulder, and announced,

"Tick tock, puppy. Move along and let the rest of us inspect the display."

". . . uncertain about the Golden Ball," Paget was saying. He turned at the interruption, handsome face in an uncustomary scowl. "I say, Wulf—"

One slight lift of Trevor's brow had him sighing, then turning back to bestow a comically gallant kiss on the lady's hand. Trevor saw the top of a glossy head, heard the soft murmur of farewell.

Paget turned back hopefully. Trevor gave a single quick jerk of his jaw and the younger man slouched off to sulk. And Trevor got his first good look at the notorious Mrs. Nolan.

As usual, his first impression had been faultless. She wasn't beautiful at all. Below the neat coronet of brown-blond hair, her face was small, pale, and possessed of perfectly ordinary features. Her brows were straight and dark, her nose unexceptional, her lips neither thin nor plump, wide nor rosebud. Seated, her figure seemed much the same: neat, average, everything where it should be but nothing either elegantly angular or seductively abundant. An ordinary Irish girl like any of a thousand others.

Then she lifted her gaze, which had been directed somewhere near the vicinity of his knee, and something clenched hot and hard in Trevor's gut.

The beauty which nature had withheld elsewhere was there in her eyes. The stormy grey of the sea in winter, they were large, widely spaced, and fringed with dark lashes long and lush enough to sweep the clouds from the sky. There were shadows there, ghosts of experience, and wells of secrets so deep and alluring that a man could be lost in them in the space of a heartbeat.

There was also an expression of utter horror.

It was gone in an instant, replaced by a lack of any emotion whatsoever. But the revulsion had been there, no question. Trevor was not surprised. Not even an experienced whore like Mrs. Nolan would be able to prevent herself from flinching at that first sight of him. He was well used to it. He was long past caring. Long past, of course. He'd learned years ago to wait for the second glance, and the third, and the twelfth . . .

"Mrs. Nolan."

"Yes," she said simply.

Oh, those eyes. They were fixed on his, and for a crazed, fleeting instant, Trevor misplaced his brain.

"I am," he began, and found himself scrambling for the words. It was wholly unexpected, this lapse, and unthinkable. It was also gone as quickly as it had overcome him. He closed his mouth into a thin smile and deliberately pulled his gaze from hers, sliding it into a tip-to-toe examination of her person. "I am St. Wulfstan," he said finally and, when she coolly lifted a hand, bowed most cursorily over it.

There was no ring on her left hand, but he wouldn't have expected there to be one. Most courtesans fashioned themselves *Mrs.*, a silly nod to respectability. Trevor wondered why they bothered. A whore was a whore, whatever she called herself.

"You are very bold, sir," this one remarked in a voice like the best whiskey: smooth and rich and quietly Irish. "Anastasia did not arrange our introduction."

Trevor grinned and insolently propped himself against the arch of the alcove. "Catholic, are you?"

"I beg your pardon?"

"No moves made without the approval of your abbess."

"As it happens, I am not Catholic, sir, but . . . Oh!"

A sudden blush stained her cheeks. It was soft, rosy, and rather disarming. Trevor would have expected a seasoned demirep to catch his jest immediately. The use of "abbess" to denote a woman who manages prostitutes was hardly new or obscure. Yet it had taken Mrs. Nolan a moment to recognize it. Refreshing, he thought. A harlot with a literal and tidy mind.

At the moment, she was staring at him with the cold disapproval of a true nun. "You will not speak of Anastasia so in my presence, sir."

Yes, there was something prim and unyielding in Mrs. Nolan as she sat ramrod straight, hands folded tightly in her lap. Something amusingly at odds with her chosen situation. Trevor wondered what she would do if he were to slide one booted foot under the hem of her gauzy white dress and lift it.

"Will I not?" he murmured.

"She is doing me a kindness by . . . by . . ." Clearly the lady did not know quite how to phrase the sentiment. *Introducing you to your next mattress,* sprang to Trevor's tongue.

Instead, he offered, "Narrowing the field?"

He might have imagined the spark in her glorious eyes. She lowered them quickly to stare at her unmoving, neatly linked fingers. "Narrowing the field. Yes, I suppose that will do. She is a very good judge of character, after all."

"Canny as a fox," Trevor murmured.

For some reason, the lady seemed to take further offense at that. "You seem to take this as sport, sir," she said icily.

"And you preach to the choir, Mrs. Nolan. I am one of Madame Balashova's many admirers. She is indeed a woman worthy of respect."

Beyond that, he expected a good portion of polite society would rather have Anastasia Balashova in its drawing rooms than he himself. Of course, given the choice of three options, the female residents of those drawing rooms would probably rather cavort with pigs, but in a competition for the lesser of two evils, the retired courtesan might well win over the dissolute viscount.

Mrs. Nolan was still regarding him with distaste.

"I am certain," he pressed, "that Anastasia will tell you I am an admirable fellow in my own way. Perhaps precisely what you are looking for."

She stared past him now, toward the crowded room. "I am not looking for an admirable fellow, sir."

Curious, Trevor thought.

"A contemptible rogue, then? I daresay nearly everyone *other* than our hostess would attest to my being just that." Had he been expecting a smile in response to that, he would have been severely disappointed. As it was, he got no response whatsoever.

He wasn't entirely certain why he was suddenly so determined to have this woman. The thrill of conquest, perhaps. Life, after all, had become painfully dull in the months since his military unit had been officially disbanded and he'd been called home from the Peninsula. Or perhaps it was simply to get in first—ahead of the wriggling, panting pack of dogs who were chasing her for no reason other than the fact that she had somehow become the fashion among the Fashionable Impures.

There were two activities in which Trevor took great pleasure during his civilian days. Baiting his peers was the second.

"Come now, Mrs. Nolan. What have you to lose?

Stroll with me in Madame's lovely gardens. Gaze at the moon. Ascertain for yourself just what sort of man I am."

She sat before him, still and pale as a statue and, in that moment, seemingly just as lifeless. Then, suddenly, without moving a muscle, she changed completely. Her magnificent eyes went dark, opaque with a sadness that Trevor felt uncomfortably beneath his skin.

"Mrs. Nolan?"

It seemed an eternity before she answered. Then, "I think not, Mr. St. Wulfstan," she said quietly, firmly. "Good night, sir."

Another time, he might have stayed right where he was. She certainly wasn't moving. But Trevor hadn't survived his part of the war through arrogance alone. Sometimes a tactical retreat was the best way forward.

He was not, however, going to let this woman have the last word.

He bent down and, without her permission, touched her—placing a single finger beneath her jaw and lifting. He felt her flinch, saw the thick lashes drop to obscure her gaze.

"That is Lord St. Wulfstan to you, madam. At least for tonight."

Then he released her and, turning smartly on his heel, walked away.

Undaunted, intrigued, and more than a little aroused, he settled himself against a far wall to watch. He wasn't certain, but as Mrs. Nolan turned her face toward the waiting queue, she seemed a shade paler than she had before. A good sign, Trevor decided, a confident smile spreading across his own face.

That smile disappeared some quarter hour later when

Mrs. Nolan rose gracefully from her alcove seat, arranged several yards of gauzy fabric, and left the room on the arm of Edgar Rickham.

CHAPTER 2

Try as she might, Nell could find nothing appealing about the man in her arms. She remembered reading in some deadly dull philosophical treatise that the beauty in things exists solely in the mind which contemplates them. Ergo, she decided wryly, she really ought to put a little effort into the matter. It was in her character to find beauty in most things—and most people, but she was completely thwarted in this quarter. Lord Rickham looked, quite simply, like a languid, sun-warmed lizard, and no amount of philosophical contemplation was going to change that.

Not that it mattered, Nell scolded herself. After all, she had accepted the man's advances for his situation rather than his looks. She would not have complained had he been handsome, of course, but his other qualifications had made him acceptable. When governed by somewhat restrictive precepts, one could not afford to be too particular.

It was true that he looked far better in repose. Nell pulled her arm from behind his shoulders, tipping him back against the cushions and allowing her an unimpeded view. With his small, narrow-set eyes closed and his thin-lipped mouth slack, he looked younger than his years and thoroughly peaceful. He was sprawled over the settee, his pale blond hair almost silver against the azure silk. She patted his cheek, then again with more force.

All in all, the matter of his attractiveness, or lack thereof, was a moot point. Rickham was alive, but out cold. And he would quite probably have both the sore head and temper of a bear once he awakened. Which was not going to be in Nell's home if she could possibly help it.

She withdrew her hand and sank back into her chair. Allowing herself a single, despondent sigh, she contemplated the fate of the man who had been, until very recently, braying, posturing, arrogant, and potentially extremely useful.

It was quite simple, really. He had come in contact with the hard edge of the fireplace poker. And, in doing so, had become a large nuisance.

Perhaps had Nell waited a bit longer, trusted in some vague providence, she might have ended up with someone other than Rickham. A pleasant man, perhaps, or at least a less offensive one. She did not ordinarily consider herself naive, but she had envisioned something quite different. She had not once imagined herself soliciting a man she would be forced to smack with an iron stick before they had even gotten properly acquainted.

The Golden Ball was so very important to her. Rickham hadn't understood that. He'd been surprised by her request, then amused. He'd laughed heartily. And when he'd finished with that, he had lunged. No preamble, no warning, not a second's hesitation. Nell hadn't expected him to move quite so fast—or to be quite such a boor. Now, after four months in London, living on the fringes of not-so-polite Society, she decided she really ought to have known better.

Well, hindsight was notoriously keen, and her un-lizardly expectations were neither here nor there. Now she would have to begin again with another man, and perhaps another, and another. "You have left me in a very awkward position, my lord," she addressed the silent figure, "and I really haven't the slightest idea what I am to do about it."

Not surprisingly, Rickham offered no advice on the matter.

A soft tap came at the door. When Nell answered, it opened to reveal the craggy countenance of her butler. With his perpetual scowl and tufted grey hair, Macauley was even less handsome than the recumbent baron. He was, however, a far more welcome sight.

"Ye rang, ma'am?"

"Yes, Mac, I did." Nell gestured wearily toward Rickham. "I am very much afraid that I . . ."

"Clouted 'im, did ye?" Macauley's frown deepened, if such were possible, as he stepped over the poker, adding new creases to his already weathered face. "Can't say as I'm surprised. Looked the sort to deserve it, 'e did, just walking in t'door, and I'm scarce wrong 'bout such things."

"Yes, Mac, you are very wise." Nell twined and untwined a loose curl around one finger. Rickham's grasping hands had gone straight for her hair, making a mess of her careful arrangement. "Now, what are we going to do about him?"

The elderly retainer eyed the baron's limp form with misgiving. "Don't suppose 'e's kicked t'bucket," he said hopefully.

"No. He's very much alive."

"Ah. Aye. Well, I s'pose I could try to carry 'im . . ."

Mac tipped his head first one way, then the other, and flexed a scrawny arm as if contemplating the best way to heft the baron's limp form off the settee. Nell nearly smiled. "He's not as light as he looks. It took me ten minutes to get him up off the floor." She sighed. "I'd expected him to wake up by now. Oh, dear. I suppose I hit him rather harder than I'd intended."

"Not 'ard enough, if ye ask me," was Mac's dour pronouncement.

The two pondered the matter for a silent minute. To Nell's grim view, Rickham looked ready to smack his lizard lips together and roll over in his sleep. She rather wished he would. Then she could simply let him hit the floor again and roll him right down the stairs and onto the street, and let him find his own way home.

It was such a nice thought.

"Well, why not?" she mused.

"Eh?" Mac tilted his grizzled head so his good ear was closer. "Speak up there, missy. Can't understand ye when ye're mumbling." Nell explained. Mac grunted and eyed the distance. "I s'pose it'll work. But t'window's closer."

"The door will do." She sprang to her feet. "Come now, Mac, cease your scowling. I do not like this, either, but one must be as practical as possible when dealing with a man one has attacked with an iron poker. Now, if you please . . ."

The butler leaned over the settee, grumbling something about damned impulsive females under his breath. Nell did not berate him as she grasped one of Rickham's arms. Her choice of the baron had been unfortunate but expedient. She would do better next time.

"All for one simple ball." She sighed. "I suppose I'd best send a message to Madame Balashova."

The butler shook his head as he contemplated his task. "Ye've capped it wi' this one," he said gloomily.

"Yes, well, had I known his lordship would complicate matters so, I would never have solicited him. Pull, please."

Mac muttered something about damned fool quests, and pulled.

An hour later, the baron had been sent off in a hackney, still unconscious and destined to wake up somewhere in Clerkenwell. Mac had taken his creaky self back to bed. And Anastasia Balashova was draped over a brocade settee, looking extremely beautiful and good-tempered for someone who had been woken from a sound sleep and summoned across the better part of Mayfair.

She had made Nell repeat the story twice and was still shaking her head over her tea. "Honestly, darling," she said, the faint Russian accent gone completely in favor of the Yorkshire lilt with which little Ann Baker had been born. "Rickham of all people."

"Not of all people, Annie. Of six. Though I must say my optimism about the remaining four is fading rapidly."

"Oh, that list! You insist on grieving me with it!"

Nell gripped her own cup. "I am sorry you feel that way. You know it wasn't my intention."

The celebrated cyprian looked up, her bold features softening into familiar fondness. "I know, my dear. You are a sweet child. I simply cannot accept that you have chosen this path for yourself."

"I will be thirty come January. Hardly a child. And the path, as you call it, has chosen me."

"Hmph." The older woman pursed her rosebud

lips. "You don't need the money. Clonegal saw to that."

It was a familiar refrain, and Nell answered automatically. And sadly. "The duke was more than generous."

"Yes, he was." The two women shared a moment of silence for the kind man who had been the heartbreak of one and savior of the other. "You won't have the same situation with another gentleman, Nell. Not here."

"No. No, I know I won't. I am not quite so naive."

"I have no idea how you have managed to remain naive at all," came the gentle response. "But it suits you and, I think will serve you well. If I cannot persuade you to change your mind . . ."

Nell appreciated the woman's solicitude. It was lovely to be cared about, but such niceties served little purpose now. "I need to attend Routland's Golden Ball. And since the host is hardly likely to proffer an invitation, I need to find an escort. I have now handily eliminated one member of his little circle, and since we both know I cannot approach the new Duke of Clonegal, I trust you will arrange an introduction to one of the remaining four."

Anastasia tapped a fingertip against the Wedgwood saucer, part of the late duke's legacy to Nell. "Since you have mentioned the matter, Lord William Paget was rather smitten. He's a sweet boy, Nell, second son to the Duke of Abergele. He does not hack off the hair of his conquests or—"

"Annie," Nell interrupted, "Lord William is not on the list."

"But he is such a delightful young man. He might actually marry you."

It was very hard indeed to be severe with her friend,

especially when she employed her round, guileless blue eyes. She was doing so now, and Nell was heartily tempted to throw up her hands and say oh yes, she would meet the delightful young second son to the Duke of Abergele, who might actually marry a demi-rep. Instead, she steeled herself, and replied, "I am certain Lord William is the very paragon of desirable manhood. But I am not looking for a husband and he is not on the list."

He also clearly had no plans to attend the Golden Ball.

Anastasia actually did throw up narrow, heavily beringed hands. "Rickham, Montmorency, Walcott . . . You could not have chosen less appealing specimens. Scoundrels and fools all. Of course, there is Seaton. He is not so very terrible—if one does not object to constant drunkenness."

"Now we have been through this before . . ."

But Anastasia was not finished. "By all means, let me throw you into the clutches of Montmorency! He has gone through three mistresses in a year, and the fourth was not looking at all well when last I saw her." She wilted visibly. "You have managed to settle on . . . let us see now . . . five of the worst degenerates in the *ton*, and that does not even include Routland." Under the dark curls with the streaks of silver she refused to hide, her brows met in a frown. "I must have missed one." She ticked the names of the notorious sextet off on her fingers. "Routland, Walcott, Montmorency, Seaton, Rickham . . . Oh. Oh, Nell. Not Carmody. I cannot. Will not help you in any way as far as he is concerned. You will have to find someone else!"

Nell was tempted to ask what this Carmody had done to make Anastasia dislike him so, but held her tongue. The Earl of Routland was the worst sort of man: a liar, a scoundrel, and a thief. And, like birds of a feather, he surrounded himself with men of the same ilk. That wasn't surprising. What was surprising was that Society flocked to his yearly ball. Like more birds. Hens, perhaps, or widgeons.

Nell set down her cup and folded her hands tightly in her lap. "I don't know what else to do, Annie," she whispered. "I don't know what else I can possibly do."

"You could try to forget," came the quiet reply.

"Anything but that."

"Nell—"

"No, Annie. And if this were any other matter, you wouldn't even suggest it. Not you. You've taught me more about truth and honor than all of my Horgan's lessons and Sunday sermons together. No. I cannot let this go."

Anastasia reached over the arm of the settee and grasped Nell's hand. "Of course you cannot. I know that. And I would never tell you to walk away from a matter of honor. I just hate watching you go through this." She squeezed gently. Then suddenly harder. "I have it!"

"What?" Nell looked up, hope swelling.

"You will ask St. Wulfstan."

Nell's fingers clenched painfully. *That face. His face.* "No. Oh, no."

Perhaps had she seen him approaching, she could have done something. Moved away or kept young William Paget by her side or even just steeled herself somehow. But he had appeared so suddenly, his imposing form filling her alcove and her vision completely and sending every inch of her body into acute awareness.

St. Wulfstan. His name was St. Wulfstan. Or, rather,

she thought, remembering his parting shot, it was his title. Not that it had mattered. All of her concentration had been on his face. *That face.*

It appeared to have been carved from stone. From the angle of his strong jaw to his sharp cheekbones and straight, strong nose, he seemed all corners and granite planes. His hair—thick, an auburn so dark it was almost black from a distance—and swept carelessly back from his proud brow, had the glossy sheen of polished marble. Even his eyes, cobalt blue and fringed with impossibly thick lashes, were almost brutally hard.

But none of that came close to the impact of the scar.

The right side of his high, broad forehead was bisected, viciously, by the scar. It curved like a scythe from his hairline, all the way down to his eyelid. It was bold, livid, and had the dramatic effect of holding his eyelid at half-mast while drawing the black brow upward in a fixed arc. When taken with his dark hair and flashing, mocking smile, it made him look just that little bit diabolic.

"*Nell?*" Anastasia's voice broke through the powerful image in Nell's head. Her gaze, when Nell met it, was concerned. "Are you ill?"

No, Nell thought. *Just terribly shaken. Again.*

She didn't think she could explain that to her friend. She didn't know if she even wanted to try. There was so much else to discuss. Her reaction to one man on one night wasn't important. She wouldn't let it be important. So, summoning some of the inner iron she had forged over the years, Nell managed a calm smile. "I'm not ill. Tired, perhaps."

"Mmm." Anastasia's brows drew together in a fleeting frown. "None of this is good for you. My soiree, Routland's coterie, London."

No, London hadn't been good for her. She'd lost her beloved duke and found herself in a world for which she just wasn't prepared. "I'll go home," Nell said softly, "to Ireland. When I can."

The older woman huffed out a breath, but didn't comment. Instead, she pressed, "St. Wulfstan? He so obviously wished to meet you. He ignored protocol entirely." Spoken, Nell thought, like a true patroness of an elite assembly.

"Yet you are encouraging me to encourage him?"

"I am trying to help you find a way into Routland's ball. You have only a sennight, after all. Time is of the essence. I am not certain I would put any woman in St. Wulfstan's path ordinarily, but he will certainly have been invited to Routland's and might attend."

"Even with a cyprian on his arm?" Nell couldn't help asking.

"*Especially* with a cyprian on his arm," came the tart response. "That is St. Wulfstan, or better, *Sin* Wulfstan as they call him here. Deservedly so. He is not a polite member of Polite Society. He is careless, unsociable, and probably genuinely dangerous. But he is also titled, wealthy, and, I expect, rather fascinating to many of his peers."

Nell knew she shouldn't care, but couldn't keep herself from asking, "How did he get the scar? Was it at war?"

"No one is quite certain of what St. Wulfstan did in the war," Anastasia said with a shrug. "The rumors are not pretty. But no, the scar came many years ago. I don't know how or where. No one seems to." She clasped Nell's hand again. "I suggest him because I believe he can help you achieve your goal. But he is hardly a shining knight."

Nell shook her head with a wry smile. "A shining

knight wouldn't be of any help to me, more's the
irony."

"Then St. Wulfstan might be your man."

"No." Nell shivered with the memory. "No, he
most certainly isn't my man."

She rose to her feet and, pulling the soft sunshine
yellow throw from the back of the settee, wrapped it
around her shoulders. It was one of the few things she
had brought with her from Ireland, one of the few possessions from the days before she had met the Duke of
Clonegal. It had brightened the duke's massive bed in
his Wexford manor house, a bit of the country among
the expensive velvet and linen. It had seemed less
bright somehow as he lay slowly dying upstairs in this
very house, but then, so had everything else.

Nell rubbed her cheek once, quickly, against the
soft wool at her shoulder, and crossed to the windows.
Like the house, the sitting room wasn't very large, but
it was graceful, inviting, and it was hers. The duke had
seen to that. Now, as she stared out over Davies Street,
silent and pearly under the bright moon, Nell allowed
herself to wonder, just for an instant, where she would
be now had she never accepted Clonegal's offer and
moved into his home.

Poorer in spirit, she thought, chin rising, and in experience. And she would still have gone after Routland.

She caught a glimpse of herself in one of the windowpanes. She lifted a fingertip to the reflection of her
pale face. "I am beginning to fear," she said, turning
away from the image to meet Anastasia's kind gaze,
"that I am not at all suited to be a London *fille de
joie.*"

Anastasia gave a half smile. "Who is, my dear?"

"I am not beautiful," Nell said, pragmatic rather
than self-pitying.

"You are perfect."

"Oh, Annie. Really. I am not even especially pretty."

"Neither is Harriette Wilson," Anastasia shot back. "Nor the Marchioness of Oriel, but they have both done exceptionally well for themselves in their respective ways."

"Well, perhaps you will introduce me to Miss Wilson, then, at your next soiree. I expect there is rather a lot she could teach me."

Anastasia's mouth thinned at that. "Harriette's charm and great success aside, I would sooner have you taking lessons from Salome." She set her cup aside, forcefully enough that it clattered harshly against the saucer. "It isn't too late, Nell. There is no reason for you to continue as a demirep."

"Annie—"

"You can live a respectable life. Marry some pleasant young man, have happy little children—"

"No," Nell said, shaking her head. "No."

"You are Mrs. Nolan, sweet girl from County Wicklow—"

"I am Mrs. Nolan," Nell interrupted, quiet but emphatic, "formerly kept by the Duke of Clonegal, Irish, and so plain that my charms clearly must be of the boudoir. That is who I am now, to the people who even deign to notice me." She crossed back to where her friend sat, braced both hands on the hard carved back of the settee. "Oh, Annie. Please. Just help me find a way into the Golden Ball. After that . . . Well, after that, nothing matters so very much. I'll decide who, what I am to be then."

Anastasia reached up and cupped Nell's set jaw with a motherly hand. "I cannot change your mind."

"No."

"Well, then. It is time for you to advertise as all the

finest cyprians do. You will come to the opera with me on Tuesday. We will find you a gentleman there."

Soon after, Nell settled herself at her dressing table to prepare for bed. The curtains and windows were open, a habit she had brought along with her Wicklow wool throw from Ireland. As she unwound what remained of her careful braid, the glint of moonlight in glass caught her eye. Slowly, she turned her gilt-backed hand mirror so it rested facedown on the little table. The moon wasn't full, she knew, but only a fool tempted fate.

CHAPTER 3

Trevor paced the foyer of the King's Theatre like an impatient cat, back and forth on the fringes of the crowd, ready to snarl if the wrong person approached him. The whole place was full of wrong people, overflowing the lavish foyer during the intermission. At least the other attendees had thus far given him plenty of space in which to move. He was in a foul mood. Bad enough that he'd been made to wait; he was vastly annoyed at having been summoned in the first place. He did not like being summoned. Nothing good had ever come of it, from his boisterous days at Eton, where a summons had more often than not involved an encounter with a birch switch, to those not-so-distant days in the military, when he had usually been called upon to spill blood.

And then there were the harsh demands for his presence from old Richard, which had ultimately been the worst of all.

Trevor's head snapped around at the sight of a towering dark head. A Paget, yes, but the wrong one. Lord William had seen him, too, and appeared to be threading his way through the crowd. It was not an encounter Trevor wanted to have just then. The puppy would want an explanation and an apology, and Trevor made a point of never giving either.

He knew better than to try to hide in the crowd; his sheer size prevented that. But he had ample experience in evasion. He doubted young Paget had ever evaded anything in his life, save perhaps his apoplectic sire. So Trevor slipped in the opposite direction, around a plaster pillar, and in seconds was fifteen feet behind the still-advancing Lord William. Now all he had to do was evade this Paget until the other bothered to appear.

"St. Wulfstan," said a voice at his shoulder. A very clipped, English voice, which was mildly amusing as it belonged to a member of what Trevor's mother had always smilingly called "the Irish Roguery."

He turned with no great speed to greet Carmody. The elder Carmody, as it happened. Trevor hadn't seen the old man in several years and found him shorter, greyer, and redder of face than before. The son, who had been waiting so eagerly for an introduction to Mrs. Nolan at La Balashova's was but a younger version of his sire: diminutive, red-faced, nose perpetually in the air. Trevor didn't care for either of them.

"Carmody," he muttered.

"Wouldn't expect to see you here," the man sniffed.

It was the same greeting he had dispensed for thirty years—at Irish weekend parties when men and women alike still wore powdered wigs and Dublin still had a Season; at parental visits to Eton, where the young Carmody had done absolutely nothing of distinction save bully every boy smaller than he; during the rare sessions in Lords that Trevor actually attended and where he and old Carmody sat in opposition on every issue.

Since Trevor had never cared much where he was expected—or unwelcome—he merely bowed curtly to the rest of the group. Irish Roguery indeed. It was a pitifully tame lot, all more English than not, all as pinched and primped and padded as the rest of the *ton*. And it was more his generation than his mother's now, the children of those peers who had happily voted Ireland into a union with England, dissolving the Parliament and making Dublin a social wasteland during the Season. Young Carmody, Ballyclare, Killone.

Trevor remembered the elder Ballyclare and Killone, both dead years now, as being, like Carmody, close versions of the current peers. The late Lord Ballyclare had been an avid huntsman, vital and stupid; Killone the dilettante poet, soulful and talentless. Killone the Younger lifted a languid hand now, as pleasant a greeting as Trevor ever received from this group. Behind the man, the Dowager Lady Killone stood stiff and disapproving. Never an attractive specimen, she became more prune-faced whenever she saw Trevor. He usually ignored her. This time, however, he flashed her his best roue's grin. She blanched slightly, and flinched.

Bitter old bag, he thought.

It amused him, the fact that they still gathered together, generations of intermarriage and excessive wealth. With the possible exception of Killone, Trevor considered them a waste of good air.

Young Carmody gave Trevor an unpleasant smile. "Are you in attendance for the music or the view, St. Wulfstan?"

As usual, the man was drunk. Trevor supposed still being under the thumb of one's papa at five-and-thirty would be enough to make any man drink. For that papa to be Lord Carmody would encourage most to exchange their whiskey for hemlock.

"Why, for the fine company, to be sure," Trevor

drawled, deliberately taking on the West County brogue that so irked these unwilling Children of Eire.

Carmody did not take the bait—or the sarcasm. He merely leered again. "There is quite a display in one of the third-tier boxes."

"Is there indeed?" Trevor was back to scanning the crowd for Oriel.

"Russian sable and Irish marten. Rather costly, of course, but so marvelous to the touch."

Trevor's expression did not change at all, but he felt the thrill of the chase sparking in his blood. So Mrs. Nolan was here, was she? In the age-old courtesan's ploy of putting herself on display in a place where she would be well seen. Perhaps when his business was done, he would go have a word with her. He wasn't a patient man, and he had already wasted days since their first meeting.

Bloody well about time. He spied the Marquess of Oriel making his way across the foyer. As always, the man moved with power and ease, belying the fact that he relied heavily on the ebony cane in his fist. As they did for Trevor, people moved out of the marquess's way. For this man, however, it was out of respect and some degree of awe. So be it. Oriel had always been the noble fellow of the corps, principled and austere. It suited him. Much, Trevor thought, as the mantle of indecency suited himself.

With another deliberate grin for Lady Killone and a careless bow for the rest, he turned to meet the one man for whom he would appear upon request.

"I say, St. Wulfstan." Carmody again, slurring his words. Trevor glanced back over his shoulder. The man was hardly worth the consideration of turning. "You must have a look at Rickham's new glass ribbon. Tell him I sent you."

Trevor merely lifted his unscarred brow and continued on his way. Carmody was baiting him, no more than that. It was too soon for Rickham to have taken that particular trophy, to have fashioned a cord from a whiskey brown plait. If Mrs. Nolan were anything like the courtesans Trevor had met—and there had been more than a few—she wouldn't have committed herself quite so soon. If she were half as intelligent as most of the courtesans Trevor had met, she wouldn't ally herself with anyone like Rickham at all.

Somehow, though, he mused as he made his way across the floor, he was convinced Mrs. Nolan would not slide comfortably into any pigeonhole he chose for her.

"Vile, presumptuous beast," came from behind him. Lady Killone, Trevor decided, saying absolutely nothing he hadn't heard a hundred times before. It had all become altogether too familiar and more than a little tiresome.

"This," he muttered as he reached Oriel's side, "is a damnable place to meet."

The marquess smiled. "It is the perfect place to meet. Come along."

Only a trained eye would see how much he depended on his stick as they climbed the stairs to the expensive boxes. Just as only the merest handful of people knew that his eyes had been damaged as well as his leg. The Marquess of Oriel might not see everything, but he missed almost nothing.

"I assume it is a woman," he commented, as they entered the empty box.

"Hmm?" Trevor's eyes were already sweeping the third tier.

"I can feel your impatience from here. For God's

sake, man, sit down. Whoever she is, she'll keep the
sheets warm for you."

Trevor grunted and sat. "You are only half-dangerous
tonight."

"Ah. Only half-right, then? Which half?"

"One bed," Trevor drawled. "Two women." Then,
"Where is your wife?"

Oriel stretched his long legs over the carpet. "I
should probably take offense at your mentioning
Isobel in that breath. I won't. And she is here somewhere, chattering with my sister, most likely. She will
join me after the next act."

"Steering clear of me, hmm? A pity she doesn't like
me. I find her rather delectable."

Yet again, Oriel took no offense. He never did,
Trevor thought with a wry smile, curse his complacent
hide. "As it happens, Isobel thinks you a splendid
fellow, and well you know it. She simply knew we
needed time to talk."

"You could have invited me to your home for a nice
dinner."

"Come to my home for a nice dinner tomorrow,"
Oriel invited.

"No, thank you," Trevor replied.

"See?"

"Perhaps next week."

"As you wish." Oriel leaned his stick against the
brass rail and rested his elbows on the arms of his
chair. "I knew you would be here tonight."

"Did you really. Taken to sorcery, have you?"

"It is Mozart. You never miss Mozart."

Trevor sighed. He had no idea how Oriel had come
into possession of that little fact, but it was true. Unless he was crouched in a dark, distant clime with a
knife between his teeth and gun in his hand, Trevor

never missed a Mozart opera. He didn't particularly like Oriel for knowing that.

"You wanted to talk," he growled. "I am here. So talk away."

And Oriel did. "Graham's troops have crossed the Douro into Spain . . ."

There had been so many conversations like this one over the past decade, in odd places and hushed tones. Trevor and Oriel were among the few surviving members of an elite military intelligence corps so secret that it had been known only as the Ten—and even then only to each other. Now, as Oriel relayed the news from the Continent, Trevor listened carefully, coldly, storing each detail for future use. When his next task became clear his jaw clenched, along with his fists, but he gave no response other than a quiet, "I'll see to it."

"Good man," Oriel murmured. "I would not ask, Wulf, you know that. But there is no one else with the experience and the stomach for it—"

"I'll see to it."

Oriel nodded and said nothing else. They sat, side by side in the expensive box trying to forget about violence for a time, while much of Society flitted and twittered around them. Then, just as the bells rang, signalling the imminent beginning of the next act, Trevor spied Rickham lounging in a nearby box. The man was sporting a new hair arrangement this evening, the fair mass brushed almost comically forward into his face. Taking fashion to its lamentable extreme, Trevor thought, then changed his mind as he noted the livid bruise just visible at the edge of the contrived style. Apparently Rickham had walked into something very hard. Trevor rather hoped it had been someone's fist. Then, as he watched, Rickham met his gaze, gave a faint salute, and lifted his quizzing glass. Rather than putting it to his eye, however, he let it slide through his fingers until it dangled from its cord, swinging gently back and forth.

Trevor had very good vision. Even from this distance, the cord was clearly a sleek dark blond.

He dragged his gaze away. And found himself staring straight at Mrs. Nolan. She was indeed with Anastasia Balashova, seated right at the front of their box. Behind them, around them, nearly sitting atop them, were more of the *ton*'s male finest. William Paget was there, although he appeared to have been edged off to the side of the box by the Astor twins. Worcester, a mere pup, was leaning altogether too intimately over Mrs. Nolan's bosom. Heatherington appeared to be holding one of her gloves. Several more gentlemen were crowded into the back of the box.

For her own part, Mrs. Nolan sat in the midst of her admirers, glossy head turning from one to the next as they clearly vied for her attention. She was in white again, looking very much the same as she had before. Still pale, still far from beautiful. But damned if Trevor didn't feel that same insistent tug as he watched her.

"I am leaving," he muttered.

"But the opera—"

"Devil take it." He levered himself from the chair. "By the by, tell your brother he really must learn when to cut his losses. He is beginning to look foolish."

Oriel raised a dark brow. "I assume he will know what that means."

"Knowing William, perhaps not. But try anyway."

With that, Trevor quitted the box for the hall beyond. He was going to go home and avail himself of a stiff shot of Ireland's best whiskey. After that, he was going to change his stark black attire for something starker and blacker and spend what might well be a fruitless and frustrating several hours lurking near Covent Garden with Oriel's information and the image of Rickham's new trophy to keep him company.

It was hardly the first time Mozart had been spoiled for him. He simply didn't care to contemplate just how long it had been since he'd sat, content and undisturbed, as the music flowed from beginning to end.

Unfortunately, he was trying to leave just at the time when everyone was returning to their seats for the second act. Trevor stepped from the quiet box into a thick, persistent stream of people coming up the stairs he needed to go down. Neither his size nor his scowl seemed to have much of an effect. A few people did cower a bit and try to scuttle out of the way, but it still took him far longer than it should have to reach the fast-emptying foyer.

Mrs. Nolan was just settling herself in one of the little alcoves off to the side.

Trevor paused and stared at her. He couldn't help himself; he wondered if she were now under Rickham's protection. Her hair was in the same tight coronet, but now with a few short curls framing her face. Fashion or necessity, he had no idea.

He'd thought better of her. Without knowing her at all, he'd thought better of her.

Thought better of a woman who traded sex for money. That really ought to have been amusing, he decided. But then, he'd known his share of whores and his share of gentle ladies and every single one had had her concept of honor and her price. All things considered, he preferred knowing the cost of things up front.

He took another step, ready to make his way out the door and into the street. She looked up and their eyes met. In that instant, Trevor saw a sadness so profound that he felt it like a blow. Then the lady blinked, and it was gone, replaced by cool wariness. But by that time he was already striding toward her. He couldn't have done otherwise.

"Mrs. Nolan."

She sighed. "Lord St. Wulfstan."

"You are running contrary to fashion," he murmured, gesturing to the retreating backs of those last persons returning to their seats.

"So, it seems, are you."

He shrugged. "An ordinary state of affairs."

Yes, Nell thought as she looked at him. He would buck fashion, or at the very least pay it no mind. His very presence defied it. In a place full of indistinguishable, polished men, he was bold, vital, and a bit rough. His clothing was simple black and white, unrelieved by the colors and fussy accessories so popular now. His hair was just that inch too long, and flowed defiantly back from his brow. His smile hinted at things best not mentioned in polite company.

He was not a polite member of Polite Society, Annie had said. Of course he wasn't. A man who radiated such careless vitality would be an affront to anyone who believed society ought to *be* polite.

At the moment, Nell wasn't certain just where she stood on the matter.

"You will miss the second act," St. Wulfstan said conversationally. His voice suited the rest of him: deep, resonant, and, Nell thought, deliberately unpolished.

"I will return eventually. I needed . . ." She didn't care to tell him, as she had Annie, that she was making a visit to the ladies' retiring room. Among other things, it wasn't true. She'd needed a few minutes of peace. She was no closer to attending the Golden Ball than she had been a sennight earlier, and the effort of entertaining the constant stream of gentlemen had left her with a headache.

"You needed to escape."

She blinked, glanced up into very blue and very canny eyes. St. Wulfstan's perception, she decided, was every bit as unsettling as his large presence.

"I did, too," he added simply.

Nell didn't know what to do with his candor. She wasn't used to it. As far as she was concerned, most of what came from the mouths of London's gentlemen were fibs and flattery.

"You don't care for the music?" she heard herself asking.

He smiled—a real smile, she noted, brief as it was. "As a matter of fact, I am rather partial to the music, but that has absolutely nothing to do with attending the opera in Town."

No, she thought, it didn't. One attended the opera to see and be seen and chatter loudly enough to make the performance itself unimportant. She found herself wondering why St. Wulfstan had come. If Annie were to be believed, the man did nothing out of sociability. He did not care for Society; it cared as little for him. How lonely that sounded, remaining solitary in the midst of the group to which one ostensibly belonged.

Lonely, and very familiar.

Nell decided it was time to return to her box. She gathered her wrap and started to rise. "If you will excuse me, sir."

He didn't move. "There isn't anything for you in there, you know."

She was standing nearly chest to chest with him. He

was tall enough that she had to tilt her chin up to look into his ravaged face. His scarred brow, she noted, was lifted even higher than usual, his smile complacent. He looked very sure of himself.

"You are wrong," she informed him.

He had to be wrong. Her entrée into Routland's home was waiting for her inside. It had to be. She had three days left. Only three days.

"It certainly isn't Rickham."

"Rickham?" Her breath caught. She'd heard nothing of the baron, from the baron, since their ill-fated encounter. "What of him?"

"He is not the man for you."

True enough, Nell thought, relaxing slightly.

Then St. Wulfstan added, "What has he offered you?"

"I beg your pardon?"

"Carte blanche? I doubt that. He isn't known for his generous nature."

Nell's jaw had gone a bit slack. "Really, sir—"

"Whatever it is, I will give you something far better."

Now she was gaping at him. His eyes narrowed suddenly, and yet again, he touched her, lifting her chin to look closely into her face.

"*Have* you accepted him?" he demanded.

Nell found her voice. "That is not a proper question, sir!" she snapped, jerking away from his grasp.

"I make no pretension to propriety," was his easy retort. Then, "Come with me."

She closed her eyes for a moment. Conversation with this man was dizzying. "Where?" she asked wearily.

His reply was immediate and husky. "Anywhere."

It had been a very long time since a single word had made Nell's pulse skitter. She promptly quashed the sensation. Without really knowing this man at all, she knew he was dangerous. Simply standing near to him was dangerous. She was too close to her goal, to regaining some part of the peaceful life she'd once had, to allow St. Wulfstan to distract her.

"Why are you doing this?" she demanded.

"I should think that would be perfectly obvious." His gaze was warm now, carnal. Nell shivered.

"You don't know enough about me to want—"

"I know precisely enough to want you." He cupped her jaw again, this time bringing his fingers to rest at the point on her throat where her pulse beat fast and thready. "What of you, Mrs. Nolan? What is it you want? I know there is something. I can see it in your eyes."

She was running out of time. And here was an answer to her prayers, misguided though they might be. She would do what she had to do and then she would go home. To Ireland. It could, if she were very, very lucky, be as simple as that. All she had to do was place herself for a short time in the hands of Sin Wulfstan.

Heaven help me, she thought desperately.

Defeated, more tired suddenly than she could remember being in a very long time, Nell sighed and said, voice small, "I want to attend the Golden Ball."

Whatever St. Wulfstan had been expecting, it clearly wasn't that. "Routland's bash?" he demanded, letting go of her.

"Yes."

"You want to go to Routland's bash."

"Yes."

"God." He blew out a breath. "Why on earth would you want to do that? It's a ghastly affair. The company is dull, the food unpalatable, and the music even worse."

"Be that as it may, I want to go. Will you take me?"

He gave her that fiercely blue, searching look again. "This is important to you."

"Yes."

"You want to spend the evening at one of the Season's least interesting events."

She gave a small smile at that. "Oh, I don't think I will require the entire evening. An hour should more than suffice. Less, I hope. Will you—?"

"Absolutely."

Something sad and hopeful at the same time sparked in her chest. "Thank you."

He shook his head. "Don't. Not yet. I have a price."

"Ah." Nell nodded, sadly. How naive she was, finding it so easy to forget that everyone had a price. "What is it?"

St. Wulfstan leaned down so his face was close enough to hers that she could feel the warmth of his breath. "I will give you your Golden Ball for the evening. You will give me the night." There was no question of what he meant. Nell could almost feel his hands on her already, sliding beneath her clothing. "Do we have an agreement, Mrs. Nolan?"

No. No, I cannot. I just cannot . . .

"Yes, Lord St. Wulfstan," she replied, voice cool and steady. "We do."

CHAPTER 4

From the roof of a dirty, ramshackle building that had once been a school, Trevor watched as a man known appropriately as the Roach stepped from the tavern across the street. Even in the dim evening light Trevor could see the slightly unfocused smile on the man's narrow face. The Roach had clearly been indulging his opium habit. A small boy, ragged as too many of London's children were, scuttled up, a folded paper clutched in his grubby fist. The Roach accepted it with the tips of two fingers. The boy stood, waiting for a coin. What he got was a sharp cuff across his face and a laugh for his frustration.

The Roach scanned the missive, then dropped it, open, into the gutter. He took a step toward the street, then stopped, eyes slewing back to the door he had just exited. *Just a few more puffs before you go?* Trevor asked silently. The Roach shook his head as if in answer. *You think there will be ample time—and more money—after.* Trevor inched forward on his belly until he had a clear view of the street in all directions.

On an average day, Gamaliel LaRoche peddled old gold lifted from the better side of London and young girls, often fresh from the countryside. On other days he parleyed information from Whitehall to agents for Napoleon. And he did it for the money, nothing more.

At Oriel's best estimate, the man was responsible for the deaths of half a dozen good men in England, at least twice that on the Continent. And in the past fortnight he had wormed out certain secrets about a pair of high-ranking members of the War Department. One had given in to the blackmail, handing over invaluable intelligence to the enemy. The other had gone to his supervisor and admitted all. Then he had gone home and put a bullet in his head.

It wasn't known yet who La Roche's London source was. But Oriel was confident the man's identity would be uncovered soon enough. Trevor would deal with that information if and when it was given to him. For now, he would deal with the Roach. It had taken him a day, only a day, to find the man. Arrogance and opium had made LaRoche sloppy. Even his clothing was slovenly, despite the fact that it was clearly expensive. But the velvet coat was visibly soiled, the silk shirt more grey than white as he turned once again toward the street.

Now. Trevor narrowed his vision and pulled his finger steadily back. The gun beneath him bucked and the Roach slumped into the gutter, his shirt a blossoming red.

In a matter of heartbeats Trevor was over the far edge of the wall and on his silent way to the alley below. Once in the street, he walked briskly toward the crowd that was already forming in front of the tavern. With the gun hidden beneath his massive, rough coat, battered hat pulled low over his brow, he looked like any of the area's rougher denizens. No one noticed as he plucked La Roche's missive from the gutter in a single, smooth motion and continued on his way. In a matter of minutes, he was a dozen streets away.

He thought dispassionately of the scene as he skirted

Covent Garden. By now the dead man's pockets would be empty, the coat stripped from his back. By the time the watch arrived, if it did, there would be nothing left save the heap of garbage that had been Gam LaRoche and a bloody shirt. There was every possibility that the street urchin had been the first with his hands in the velvet pockets.

Trevor moved quickly, calmly. As he went, he flicked his hat into a dark stairwell. He shucked his coat in a single smooth motion, turning it—gun inside, into a neat bundle which he tucked under his arm. At St. Martin's Lane he ducked into a small tavern. Its patrons, a far better-heeled lot than those Trevor had just left behind, spared only the briefest glances at the elegantly clad gentleman who strode through their midst.

Without a word, he approached the bar. The tavern keeper left the taps just long enough to take Trevor's bundle and tuck it smoothly out of sight. With an equally smooth move, he handed over a high-brimmed hat, expensive greatcoat, and gold-tipped walking stick. Then he was back to filling tankards and Trevor was through the rear door. Only when he'd reached the alley that would take him back to St. Martin's Lane did he stop. He carefully set his belongings on an upended crate.

Then, bracing himself against another, he vomited into the shadows.

When he was done, he levered himself away from the crates and, with a shaky hand, drew a handkerchief and flask from his coat pocket. He wiped his mouth, took a long draught of brandy, and waited for the last tremor to leave his hands.

He flagged down a hack in Pall Mall and gave the

direction of Anastasia Balashova's Bruton Street town house.

Nell stepped back from Anastasia's bedroom window when he descended from the hack. He was late. A mere quarter hour, but those minutes had dragged like an eternity. Now she let out a heavy breath and walked toward the door. The sound of the heavy brass knocker carried up the stairs.

"Make him wait, dear," Annie said mildly from her seat on a velvet chaise. "Always make them wait."

Nell stopped and perched tensely on the edge of the bed. "Am I doing the right thing, Annie?"

"Which? St. Wulfstan or Routland."

"Either. Both." Nell closed her eyes for a moment. "Yes. I am. It has to be done."

"That sounds like conviction to me."

"Tell that to my stomach."

"Butterflies?" Annie asked with a gentle smile.

"Bats."

The maid appeared. "Lord St. Wulfstan for Mrs. Nolan, ma'am," she informed her mistress.

"Tell him Mrs. Nolan will be down shortly."

The girl bobbed a curtsy and disappeared.

Nell pressed her hands to her stomach. "Oh. Oh, Annie."

Her friend rose and crossed the room. "Deep breath," she commanded, pulling Nell's hands free and clasping them in her own. "Look at me." Nell did. "Good. Now you will be fine. Just remember: You are Mrs. Nolan. Not just a confused girl from the green fields of Ireland, but a woman of the world, with strength and importance and destiny. Never forget that."

"Yes." Nell drew a deep breath, lifted her chin. "I am Mrs. Nolan."

"Now go make use of your tarnished knight."

Nell stood and gave her friend a quick, grateful embrace. Then, shoulders squared, she went to meet St. Wulfstan.

He turned from the sitting-room window when she entered. And smiled. For an instant it was a true smile, wide and surprisingly charming. Then, in a flash, it was his rogue's grin again, and his briefly handsome face was once more a scarred, careless mask.

"Lord St. Wulfstan."

"Good evening, Mrs. Nolan." He didn't bother with subtlety as he let his eyes roam from the top of her head to her toes. "You are looking well."

She wasn't and she knew it. What little color she had in her face was from Annie's deft hand with paint and powder. She had allowed her friend to coax her into an embroidered crimson wrap—*Play the part, dear, always play the part*—over her white dress, but had drawn the line at a profusion of red-ribbon-threaded curls. Her hair was in its customary topknot, with only a few curls to frame her face.

If she were to remember who she was, who she really was, she needed to recognize the face in her mirror.

"Thank you," she said, and nearly returned the sentiment.

He did look well in his evening black. Tonight there was a pin in his cravat, something small and gold and discreet. He wore no other adornment with his stark black and white. He needed none, Nell found herself thinking. Just as he obviously needed no padding to fill out his coat and pantaloons.

She dragged her eyes away from their perusal of his anatomy to find him watching her watching him, scarred brow arced toward his hairline. "Finished?" he murmured.

Nell turned away to hide her blush. "We should go."

"By all means." He was beside her in an instant, hand warm on her elbow as he guided her out the door. "Let the evening begin."

Nell allowed him to help her into the carriage. She settled herself on the forward-facing seat and was immediately forced to slide to the side when he came down heavily beside her. As the carriage began to roll, she moved to take the opposite seat. St. Wulfstan's lightning grip on her wrist held her where she was.

"Humor me," he commanded, amusement in his deep voice.

To have the next hour or so go as planned, Nell would have gladly humored the devil himself. She stayed in her seat, but tugged her arm free of his grasp to fold her hands in her lap. He was too large for the space, she thought, took up too much of the air around them. She deliberately evened her shallow breathing and tried to relax.

One might just as well try to relax when sitting next to a tiger, she decided. Or a wolf.

St. Wulfstan stretched out his long legs as best he could. One of his hard thighs pressed against hers. He gave a faint chuckle as she tried to move away. There really wasn't anywhere for her to go. "You know, Mrs. Nolan," he said after a time, "I have found myself preoccupied all day with a certain thought of you."

Nell gave a vague hum. She had a very good idea what that thought had been. Lustiness radiated from St. Wulfstan like warmth from the sun. She didn't need to hear the words. Either they would be crude or romantically, inappropriately poetic and she could do without either.

Not for the first time, he astonished her completely. He announced, "I have been wondering about your name."

"My name," Nell repeated.

"I don't know it, you see."

"It is—"

"Ah." He held up a hand, silencing her. "Since I do not know it, I have spent the day naming you."

For some reason, that idea made Nell smile. And relax, if only ever so slightly. "And what did you choose?"

"Well." St. Wulfstan propped his feet on the opposite seat and crossed his arms behind his head. "I'd all but settled on Ophelia . . ."

"Ophelia? Good heavens, why?" she demanded. And was thrown once again when he replied,

"Because there is such an air of sadness about you."

"Oh." She had no idea what to say. "Oh."

He carried on from her silence. "Then I thought perhaps Galatea."

That name was vaguely familiar. "I . . . I know that story." She thought hard. Then, "The statue—who was brought to life by Aphrodite after the sculptor fell in love with his creation."

St. Wulfstan nodded. "You are well-read, madam."

"No, I am not. But the duke used to read to me and he loved the ancient myths."

Nell could see Clonegal now, propped against the pillows, cheerfully demanding that she listen while she, curled exhausted by his side, wanted nothing more than to sleep. Often she had slept, missing whatever clash or love affair of god and mortal he'd chosen.

Now she would have given nearly everything she possessed to have those nights back.

"Galatea." St. Wulfstan broke into her memories. "The ideal woman. Designed and constructed by the man she would marry."

"I do not believe I care to be named for a sculpture," Nell informed him tartly.

"No, I did not think you would." He smiled. "And ultimately, it was not what I chose. Not every man is convinced he could create a better woman than Nature does." When Nell said nothing, he pressed, "Aren't you curious as to what I finally named you, Mrs. Nolan?"

Of course she was. "Not especially."

"Liar. I named you *Róisín*."

It rolled soft and rich off his tongue. *Ro-sheen*. Little rose. The old Irish name tugged at her heart, made her think of the trellis that had stood near her gran's door and the fragrant white roses that had bloomed with every summer.

"Why Róisín?" she asked, almost afraid that his answer would be blithe or even cruel.

"Because it was the name of the first girl I ever wanted to kiss," was his easy reply. "And I thought it suited you."

The tight fist that had been clenching in Nell's stomach since afternoon unfurled like petals.

"So, Mrs. Nolan"—St. Wulfstan fixed her with lazy cobalt eyes—"what is your name?"

"Helen," she replied with a sigh. A serviceable name. Plain. Suitable.

"Helen. 'Was this the face that launched a thousand ships? And burnt the topless towers of Ilium?' " He grinned lazily. "How very apt."

Secretly, unwillingly flattered, she murmured, "I do not have a face to launch a thousand ships."

She was brought back to earth with a sad thump when he shrugged, and replied, "I could not help but think all women of your status and profession ought to be named Helen. Men fighting over fair hands, little kingdoms falling." When Nell did not respond, he asked, "Do you not think it an admirable observation, O Helen?"

She answered through stiff lips. "I . . . I could not say, sir."

"No? Well, do you know the next bit of the Marlowe poem? No? 'Sweet Helen make me immortal with a kiss! Her lips suck forth my soul: see, where it flies!' Fits the William Pagets of the world, does it not?"

"Does it?"

"To be sure. Calf-eyed, romantic young fools handing themselves over heart and soul to the fair cyprian Helens of the world. It happens all the time. But we are wiser than that, are we not, Mrs. Nolan?" It was not really a question.

Confused, hurt, Nell quietly demanded, "Why are you telling me all this?"

He levered his legs from the opposite seat. "Just making conversation. Ah, we are here."

The hack rolled to a stop at the end of a queue. Ahead, well-dressed ladies and gentlemen streamed from carriages and through the doors of an impressive Palladian town house. St. Wulfstan sprang lithely to the street. Nell sat frozen.

"Your Golden Ball, madam, as promised."

He extended a hand. For an instant, Nell thought to refuse it. Then she remembered why she was there. *I am Mrs. Nolan,* she reminded herself firmly. Different, perhaps, than the Mrs. Nolan St. Wulfstan saw. He saw the mistress, the elevated whore, and was treating her as such. It stung. It made her angry. But it didn't matter, really. She was Mrs. Nolan, a woman with strength and importance and destiny, and she had a task to complete.

She took his hand and allowed him to help her down.

Instead of guiding her toward the steps, however, St. Wulfstan was leading her away from the house. "What—?"

"Come along," he commanded. They turned the corner and Nell soon found herself walking down a dark alley. St. Wulfstan stopped at an arched wooden door and rummaged in one of his coat pockets before reaching for the door handle. "Now, a moment, please . . ." He deftly slid something metal into the lock. Less than a minute later there was a faint click. The door swung inward and St. Wulfstan gestured Nell ahead of him, into the lanternlit depths of a garden.

Ahead, Nell could see the lights spilling from the house, saw a scattering of well-dressed ladies and gentlemen on a stone balcony, heard the strains of an orchestra coming through the open French doors. And she suddenly understood.

"You were not invited," she announced.

"No," came the blithe reply as he tucked whatever it was back into his pocket. "I was not."

"But you said—"

"I did not. You never asked if I had an invitation. You asked if I would bring you to Routland's fete and we based our agreement on that. I have done so. Now, shall we go join the festivities?"

Nell opened her mouth to argue, to scold. But she realized there was nothing she could say. He had agreed to get her into the Golden Ball. Unless they were summarily hustled out—even if they were—he had indeed done what he said he would. She was on Routland's premises. The rest was up to her.

"You might have told me," she muttered as she started up the path toward the house.

"Why?" he shot back.

She really had no answer.

Trevor smiled at the sight of her rigid back as she stalked away. So she was displeased. Too bloody bad. He'd held up his end of the bargain. He was very much looking forward to her doing the same. An hour, she'd said. She would need an hour at most for whatever she needed to do here. After that, she was his for the rest of the night.

He'd prepared for that. There was champagne ready at his house, with strawberries and plump figs, and crisp sheets on his bed. He planned to enjoy himself immensely. He planned to enjoy *her* immensely.

They slipped through the open doors into the crowded salon, just two guests returning from a stroll in the gardens. As always, people stepped aside as he approached. He had no idea how many of the gentlemen recognized Mrs. Nolan, but most of the guests knew him. There were a few frowns, a few mouths opened in surprise, a handful of coldly averted faces.

Routland's annual Golden Ball unfolded before them.

More opium, Trevor found himself thinking wryly. There was no other possible excuse for such a display. The *ton's* passion for the Eastern and exotic was frequently absurd and usually excessive. The Prince Regent's palace at Brighton was a woeful example. The Routlands' ballroom was even worse. Everything not moving was draped in emerald-and-gold striped satin. Strange mythical beasts with both wings and gills leered from gilded pedestals, and an odd assortment of very English trees had been hauled inside and festooned with what Trevor could only assume was wax fruit. The concept of purple-spotted apples was too disturbing for immediate contemplation.

Footmen rushed about in shimmering caftans serving champagne collected from a bubbling fount. It was a wonder indeed that they did not trip, since each was wearing a pair of shoes the toes of which curved outward and up like ram's horns. But then, it would be difficult to fall in such a crush.

The ballroom was packed to the point of discomfort, though no one seemed to mind overmuch. The assembled revelers were clearly delighted to be in this overblown paradise, poking and pinching bedamned. Lady Routland herself was holding court off to the side. In her gold tissue gown and bejeweled turban, she resembled nothing so much as a dissipated pasha, right down to the moustache. She had never been a ravishing creature, her appeal always having centered mainly on her father's immense fortune, but she had certainly not improved with a half-dozen years of marriage.

Of course, that many years with Routland could have sent Helen of Troy herself into ruin.

Tucking Mrs. Nolan's—he just couldn't think of her as Helen—hand through his arm, Trevor escorted her through the thick of the crowd and onto the fringes of the dance floor. "Well? What now?"

Her glossy head swiveled back and forth as she scanned the crush. "I . . . I need to find . . ."

"Yes?"

"I need to find Lord Routland. I do not know what he looks like. Will you find him for me?"

That had not been part of the deal. Trevor would sooner have pushed her in the direction of Rickham. "May I ask why?"

"No," was her quick response. Then, "Please don't."

He was ready to refuse, but the set of her jaw told him it would be futile. If he didn't point out their unwitting host, someone else would. So he, too, scanned the crowd. His eyes settled on his quarry just as hers did. She gave a quiet little gasp.

And no wonder, Trevor decided. She might not know Routland, but she would certainly recognize several of the men around him. Carmody was there, as was Walcott. And Rickham, familiar sneer in place, quizzing glass held to one eye. The golden brown cord glowed gently in the candlelight. Trevor felt Nell stiffen at his side. Was it the sight of Rickham, he wondered, or the man next to him? For at the baron's left stood the new Duke of Clonegal, all unpleasant six-odd feet of him.

It was no secret that the late duke and his son had not been close, united only in the chains of heredity and mutual dislike. The late duke's mistress would know that. She had undoubtedly met the son, if only over the father's deathbed. This would not be a happy encounter. But it would be hard to avoid. The new Clonegal was a dedicated member of Routland's obnoxious set. In order to get to Routland, Mrs. Nolan would have to face the toadies as well.

"That is Routland in the center," Trevor informed her. "The fat one with the shiny gold waistcoat and the veined nose."

She nodded, and again. "I will . . . I must . . ." She

took a step forward. Trevor grasped her arm, stopping her.

"Shall I come with you?"

There was an iron set to her jaw, a fire of determination in her wonderful eyes. "No," she said firmly. "I shouldn't require above a half hour or so. I will find you when I am ready to depart."

He didn't much care for that response, but it wasn't worth arguing over. Whatever she needed to do in that half hour was her business. If he decided he needed to know what that was, there was no question that he could get it out of her. He was very good at such things. For now, he would let her do what she'd come to do. He would find the liquor and a rigidly respectable matron or debutante to discomfit.

"Go on, then." He jerked his chin toward Routland. "I will be about. If you need me," he added softly.

For an instant he felt that crushing sadness again, saw it swell in her eyes. It was gone as quickly as it had risen, however, wiped completely away. "Thank you," she whispered, and was gone, slipping into the crowd.

She didn't look back.

I am Mrs. Nolan, she was repeating silently as she went. *I am Mrs. Nolan.*

Then, too soon, she was standing in front of the man who had been a harsh thorn in her side for eight long years. He didn't look at her immediately and she took the opportunity to take his measure. He was only as tall as she, paunch and red nose testifying to too much drink, weak-chinned and pig-eyed. His pink scalp showed through thinning fair hair. He looked swinish, Nell decided. As swinish as he was.

He noticed her, then. Gave her a quick look that was as dull as it was dismissive. It was only when the man she'd known as Lord Tullow—now the Duke of Clonegal—let out a low whistle that Routland focused on her at all.

"Well, well," the new duke drawled. "Look what we have here. My father's little bit of fluff. In your house of all places, Rutty."

Routland's small mouth pursed in confusion.

"Good evening, Lord Tullow." Nell used his former title like an insult. He was not the Duke of Clonegal to her, wasn't half the man his father had been. Then she dismissed him entirely. To the slack-jawed, red-faced man nearby, she gave an equally disdainful, "And to you, Lord Rickham."

Rickham's mouth opened and closed for a moment. One hand darted up, stopping just short of his brow where a faint bruise still showed through the elaborately arranged hair. "Mrs. Nolan," he managed at last, sounding very much as if he had treacle filling his throat.

At the sound of her name, Routland blinked and gave an audible swallow. "Mrs. Nolan?"

Nell lifted her chin and looked him straight in his piggy eyes. "Yes, Lord Routland. I am Mrs. Nolan. Do you wish to speak to me here, or somewhere more private?"

For a moment she thought he was going to try to bluster his way out of the situation, pretend he did not know who she was. She could see him weighing the options in his mean little mind. Apparently he was just clever enough to realize she would not be put off. He cleared his throat.

"Of course, yes, yes. Private. Of course." To his uniformly befuddled comrades, he muttered, "Gentlemen, if you would excuse me. I must . . . Mrs. Nolan and I . . ." Floundering, he flapped soft hands. "Mrs. Nolan, if you would come this way."

Head high, she walked with him, past countless curious faces and away from the ballroom. Neither she nor Routland said anything as they walked down a long hallway. But as soon as he had shown her into a dim, lavishly appointed library and closed the door behind them, she rounded on him.

"Did you think I had given up?" she demanded coldly. "Yes, I expect you did."

"Really, madam, I have no idea what you—"

"Don't," she said sharply. He flinched. "What a coward you are. I see that hasn't changed." She watched him cross the room to a loaded table, choose a bottle from among the dozen there. He poured a large measure of amber liquid into a glass tumbler. He didn't offer her either a drink or a seat. "You have done well for yourself. A rich wife, I suppose. Thomas's letters made you out to be as empty of pocket as head."

"I say, Mrs. Nolan, I cannot allow—"

"But that is the way it works, is it not? Your title somehow allowed you to wiggle into a lieutenancy while my husband, who hadn't the blue blood, was forced to suffer your command. Do you even remember my husband, Lord Routland?"

When he merely continued to gape at her, she took a steadying breath and continued. "He was Thomas John Nolan of Wicklow. He was twenty-one years old when he signed on to Nelson's *Victory*. It was a brutal place to serve, especially when so many of the officers were like you, but he gave it his heart and soul because he believed in the cause and because every crew member on board shared in the spoils from captured ships.

"Do you remember him now, sir? He served under

you for nearly two years. He was twenty-three when he was struck by a lead ball at Trafalgar. You were by his side when he died."

Routland tossed back another shot, eyed her narrowly. "What is it you want from me, Mrs. Nolan?"

"The same thing I asked for in each of the nine letters you ignored. I want the three hundred seven pounds, two shillings Thomas was owed when he died."

"I have no idea—"

"Three hundred seven pounds, two shillings," Nell interrupted, calmly, icily. "I know the exact amount because three—*three*—of Thomas's fellow sailors came to visit me after he died. They each separately told how, as he was dying, he begged you to see that his money came to me. Each told me how you agreed." She stalked toward Routland, hands clenched at her sides. "But you know all this already. I wrote it into *nine* letters. Now I want what is due to me."

There was a long silence. Then, "I am not giving you a penny," Routland squeaked, cheeks and nose alike flushed a violent pink. "Get out of my house, and if you ever come near me again, I will have the law on you!"

Dutch courage, Nell supposed. He'd made himself a temporary backbone of whiskey.

This was what she had expected. It was, after all, her word against his. Poor Irish widow-turned-courtesan against Peer of the Realm. She'd expected it, and in the end, didn't really care. In the end, she hadn't come after him for the money. She had written to him for the money; all nine letters had been sent during those days before she'd met Clonegal, when she'd needed each and every pound desperately.

She didn't want the money now. She wanted the satisfaction of watching Routland squirm.

"*Amadán,*" she intoned. As she spoke, she reached into her reticule and withdrew the paper twist she'd placed there earlier. Raising her arm, she dashed the paper to the floor at Routland's feet, where it broke, dusting his shoes with dirt and ash. "*Muc. Cam stile. Cladhaire!*"

Routland paled. "Wh-what are you saying?"

"It is an Irish curse, an ancient and powerful one," Nell replied coldly. She certainly wasn't going to tell him the truth, that she was merely calling him a few insulting names and that she had gathered the ash from her parlor hearth. Nell wasn't about to toy with curses; it wasn't in her nature to invoke evil on anyone. But she knew even the pretense would have an effect on a fool such as Routland. "I should stay away from sharp objects and flame if I were you. Not that it will make a difference, of course."

She saw his eyes darting from the collection of swords and daggers mounted on the wall to the low-burning hearth. Then there was a sharp crack and he gave a pained yelp. He had knocked his glass against the hard edge of the drinks table. A thin line of blood ran from the palm of his hand. The florid color drained from his face.

Nell was quite finished and ready to go. She glanced down to close her reticule. In that second, Routland lunged.

"Make it stop!" he wheezed, grabbing her arm with one hand, waving the other, the bleeding one, in her face. "Damn you, make it stop!" Nell bit back a cry as his fingers bit viciously into her arm.

Then, abruptly, he released her. As Nell watched, wide-eyed, he went up onto his toes for an instant before the large fist gripping his throat gave a heave and sent him flying sideways. Routland hit a bookshelf with a hollow thud, then slid to the floor.

St. Wulfstan stood, not two feet from Nell, and she had neither heard nor seen him arrive.

"My lord," she began, but he held up a hand, silencing her.

"Get up," he commanded Routland. When the other man made no move to obey, St. Wulfstan stalked over to where he sat, seized him by the coat collar, and hauled him to his feet. "I told you to get up." Routland whimpered. St. Wulfstan shook him as a wolf would a chicken. "Where is the safe?"

"What safe . . . ?" Routland broke off as St. Wulfstan shook him again, harder this time. "There." He pointed to a standing globe. This time, when St. Wulfstan released him, he merely went to his knees.

As Nell watched, jaw slack, St. Wulfstan stalked to the globe. He ran his large hands quickly over its surface. In a matter of seconds there was a faint click and he was lifting the top away on a hinge. Nell couldn't see what was inside, but after rummaging for a minute, he came up with a handful of banknotes.

"Three hundred seven, was it?" he asked her over the top of the globe.

"And two shillings," she managed. "But I do not want—"

He let the globe close with a snap. "I have collected the interest for you as well." He paused on his way back across the room to loom over the cowering Routland. "Now you will apologize to the lady." Routland croaked something unintelligible. "Again. Louder."

"I . . . I apologize, Mrs. Nolan."

When Nell said nothing, St. Wulfstan gave an unpleasant smile. "It appears your apology is not accepted. Pity for you, Routland. Best stay on your guard against sharp objects and . . ." He turned to Nell. "What was it again? Fire?"

She nodded. "Flame."

"Flame." Still smiling, St. Wulfstan reached over Routland to the table. He chose a half-full bottle and, with a single flick of his wrist, sent it spinning into the fireplace. It shattered, sending shards of glass flying and sending the flames leaping wildly. Routland ducked and covered his head. St. Wulfstan left him where he was and returned to Nell's side.

"Are we finished here?" he asked as he steered her from the room without a backward glance. "Good. Your part of the evening is complete. I am ready to begin mine."

CHAPTER 5

Trevor decided they would go through the front door this time. He wanted to get Mrs. Nolan—widow, he now knew, of Thomas John Nolan of County Wicklow—out of Routland's house the speediest way possible. He was eager to get on with the rest of the night. And he didn't especially care for her pallor. Never a raging palette of color, she was at present the same shade as her dress.

He guided her down the hall. "We'll find a hack outside and go to my home. I think we could both use a shot of something Irish and fiery." She didn't answer. "Mrs. Nolan? Helen?"

"Nell."

"What?"

"Nell," she repeated, almost inaudibly. "I go by Nell."

"I am very glad to hear that. Helen doesn't suit you. Nell. Come along. This place is worse than Almack's, although I must say you certainly livened it up."

She said nothing as they reached the ballroom and its familiar, dull occupants. Trevor had seen members of the so-called Roguery: Ballyclare, Killone and his sour mother. Carmody, of course. He hadn't had time to go in search of anyone with whom to amuse himself; he'd decided instead to follow Nell. And now he couldn't care less who was present. Apparently, however, the assembly had become very interested in his presence—and Nell's.

This time, when heads swiveled their way, Trevor saw as many eyes on Nell as on him. As before—as usual—the crowd parted before them. The orchestra was between dances, for there was no music playing. As he and Nell made their way toward the exit, Trevor heard the first of the whispers. They rose in volume and number until certain words became clear.

St. Wulfstan. Irish. Clonegal. Whore.

He knew Nell heard them, too. She stiffened at his side. When he looked down, however, her chin was in the air, expression cool and composed. *Good girl,* he applauded her silently, and pulling her arm more firmly through his, forged ahead.

They had nearly reached the foyer when a figure blocked their way. Trevor had had precious few dealings with the man who was now the Duke of Clonegal. But what he'd had was more than enough. The new duke was a bore, a boor, and, Trevor suspected, generally angry as hell.

At the moment, he was leering at Nell. "Departing so soon, Mrs. Nolan?"

"I have done what I came to do," she replied icily.

The duke eyed Trevor, glanced at Nell's hand on his arm. "Indeed, I expect you have. An interesting choice, madam."

Trevor felt Nell's fingers tighten on his sleeve, a clear message to let the matter go. Pity. He should have liked to send the other man sliding down the garish marble hall on his posterior. It seemed that pleasure would have to be deferred.

"I believe I hear Routland calling you, Clonegal," he muttered. "Run along. We are leaving."

It seemed Clonegal was not so stupid as to take the bait. He did flush a dull red. "I would take care if I were you, St. Wulfstan."

"If you were me, we should all have good reason to take care. Good night, Clonegal."

"Mrs. Nolan." The duke reached out a hand to stop her, pulling it back quickly when Trevor gave a quiet growl. "There are several matters we need to discuss. I will be paying you a visit soon."

"You will not—" Trevor began, but Nell's hand tightened again.

"It's all right," she told him softly. Then, to Clonegal. "Come as you will. If I am at home, I will speak with you." Then she stepped around the red-faced duke, Trevor at her side.

"Nell," Trevor began. She silenced him again.

"Please. I don't wish to speak of it. Of any of it."

He raised a brow. "I was merely going to ask if you wished to wait inside while I arrange for a hack."

"Oh. Yes. I will wait just inside the door."

"As you wish."

He left her there and pushed his way through the steady stream of people still entering. As he sent one of Routland's beleaguered footmen for a hack, he seethed quietly. The sight of Routland's hands on Nell had spurred him into action, almost pushed him beyond control. Up to that point she had done splendidly on her own, right down to her dramatic little curse. Not for the first time, Trevor wished he knew some Gaelic. He would have liked to understand exactly what she'd said. He didn't believe in such things, but had a healthy respect for superstition. On a weak mind, it could wreak amazing results. It had certainly had a notable effect on Routland.

Something would have to be done about Clonegal.

Trevor hadn't liked the way the duke's eyes had roamed hungrily over Nell, liked it even less that she had agreed to see the man. If he had anything to say about it, there would be no meeting between the two of them. If she objected, too bad. He was not going to have the son trying to step into the father's place in bed as he had into the ducal coronet.

Trevor was also going to have a bit of a chat with Nell about her past. The husband had been a surprise. Trevor didn't care for surprises.

He had to get to the bottom of the Rickham matter as well. If there had been no arrangement between Nell and the baron, well and good. If there had, she was simply going to have to forget it. There were two things Trevor never shared. A secret was one. A woman was the other. Until he'd well and truly tired of her, Nell Nolan was his alone. Perhaps their bargain had only been for the one night, but he was confident there would be many more.

With that thought filling his mind and tightening his body, he went to fetch Nell. The hack waiting for them was large and looked relatively well-appointed. A couple could engage in some very pleasant foreplay in a decent hackney. In a good vehicle, the possibilities could go on for hours.

It took him thirty seconds to discover that Nell was not where he had left her.

A half hour later, temper under careful control, he arrived at Anastasia Balashova's house only to be informed by the little maid that Mrs. Nolan was not there. He didn't believe that. At first. After looming over the terrified girl for a long minute, hearing her faint insistences that Mrs. Nolan did not live in the house at all, was simply a frequent visitor, he knew she was speaking the truth. He then demanded to see

Madame Balashova and was told she was not present, either. He didn't believe that at all, but short of shoving the maid out of the way and tromping through the house, there was nothing he could do.

He started to head for home. The memory of what awaited him had him changing his mind. His bedchamber was laid out for seduction. In his present frame of mind, he had no desire to face the bottles of champagne, the fruit, the carefully arranged sheets.

Turning back the way he had come, he set his course for Watier's. There he would find something stronger than wine and perhaps a few hands of cards. After that, he would go home, settle himself in his library, and make his plans for Nell Nolan.

He was furious, certainly. He was also grudgingly impressed. For the first time in a very long time, someone had gotten the best of him. Nell had used him to get what she wanted, then she had scarpered, debt unpaid. He found himself wondering just how many men had done the same to her. More than one, he guessed. But that was not his concern. She'd chosen her path in life. She had also chosen the wrong man to play false.

Retribution, Trevor decided, would be sweet. And if Nell were lucky, it would be rather nice for her, too.

"So you crept back out the way you'd come." Anastasia shook her head with a wry smile. "Resourceful, dearest, but I cannot like the idea of you wandering about alone at night."

Nell shrugged and helped herself to another cup of chocolate. She had not been able to sleep the night before and had waited impatiently for a decent hour to arrive so she could visit Annie. As it was, she had waited until after eleven and still caught her friend at breakfast.

"As you see, I survived the evening unscathed."

"Did you?" Annie murmured. "It could not have been easy, facing Routland."

In truth, facing Routland had not been so bad. Nor had Rickham or Tullow—Nell still would not, could not give him his father's title—done more than disgust her. What had not been easy was St. Wulfstan.

In between those moments when he'd made her feel like a cheap trollop, he had made her feel like a queen.

Precious few people had ever made her feel valuable. Certainly no one had ever come to her rescue as St. Wulfstan had, arriving like a vengeant knight to flatten Routland as easily as one might swat a fly. She knew, too, that he would have done the same to Tullow had she not held him back. He would have fought for her honor.

Her honor. She gave a wry smile as she wondered what he thought of her honor now.

"Nell?"

She glanced up to find her friend studying her closely. "Hmm?"

"What are you going to do about St. Wulfstan?"

"I hate when you do that," Nell sighed.

"Do what?"

"Look into my sorry mind. I was just thinking of my ignoble flight last night."

"Yes, well. What are you going to do about it?"

"Nothing," Nell said flatly. "I am going to pack my belongings, sail away, and forget my time in London as best I can. This has not been a happy place for me, Annie. I am going back."

The older woman's gaze was sympathetic but direct. "Back to what, dearest? If I remember correctly,

Thomas's family wanted nothing to do with you after his death."

No, Nell thought sadly. They hadn't. They had blamed her for his death, convinced she had pressed him to join the navy in search of wealth. She'd never tried to explain how she had begged him not to go. How she would have been more than happy with a simple life on the Nolans' large farm. But Thomas, young and foolishly daring, hadn't listened before his death. His parents, staid and bitter, wouldn't have listened after.

Widowed at twenty-two, penniless and with few skills, Nell had been near desperation when she'd found the situation that would ultimately be her salvation. The Duke of Clonegal's former mistress lay dying of a lingering fever. She needed care; Nell needed employment. So she had joined the duke's household, persuaded as much by his kindness to the woman who had left his bed years before as by necessity. The bonds that had quickly formed between them all had been unexpected, sweet, and stronger than iron.

Anastasia Balashova had recovered eventually and, with her former lover's blessing, returned to England. She had never cared for Ireland, had always missed the noise, the parties, the simple chaos that was London. The duke had hidden it well, but his own health was slowly, inexorably failing. When Annie left, Nell stayed. For seven years she cared for the wonderful man who had become her father in all but blood. Finally, when the creeping cancer had ravaged all but his mind, Clonegal, too, decided to return to London. His affairs would be settled, his family summoned.

He'd tried to protect Nell from the inevitable gossip. She hadn't cared what was said of her. If London wanted to think her his mistress, so be it. She wasn't going to leave his bedside. She had no plans to marry again; respectability was a mantle she would gladly shuck.

Now Clonegal was gone. He'd made certain she would never want for anything. He had left her the house and more money than she needed. Now that she had faced Routland, her last demon, she could go back to Ireland. She would keep the London house, at least for now, and she would buy herself a little cottage. In Clare, perhaps, near the wild cliffs of Mohr. There she would just be Nell Nolan, widow, with a home and roses growing on a trellis and nothing to do but walk in the soft rain.

"Will you come stay with me, Annie?" she asked. "Come visit for a bit in winter when life here has gone quiet?"

Her only friend reached across the table, took her hand. "I will. Of course I will. I'll miss you too much to do otherwise."

Just then, the door knocker clacked, startling them both. A minute later, the maid appeared in the doorway. She looked a bit pale and pinched.

"Lord St. Wulfstan for Mrs. Nolan again, madam." The girl blinked miserably. "He said he knew she was here this time. Of course, I didn't say aye or nay . . ."

Annie looked at Nell. Nell pressed a hand to her jittery stomach and shook her head. Annie's brows went up, but she told the maid, "Inform his lordship that he was mistaken. There is no one here to see him." When the maid had left, she turned back to Nell. "You are going to have to face him sooner or later, you know."

"No," Nell replied shakily. "No, I will not."

"Men like St. Wulfstan do not simply go away, my dear."

"Perhaps not, Annie, but women like me do."

* * *

Trevor was feeling reasonably cheerful. He had a good meal in his belly, a glass of his host's best port in his hand, and the location of Nell Nolan's house tucked comfortably in his mind. All he'd had to do was follow her home from Anastasia Balashova's that afternoon.

"A woman again?" Oriel asked from his place in the opposite chair.

Trevor grimaced. "What is it? Is one of my silences more eloquent than another? Or are you just very lucky with your guesses?"

"Perhaps I've just known you too many years. Who is she?"

It was so very tempting, Trevor thought. He could tell Oriel the whole sorry story, get another man's take on it. But that meant opening a door into the more private aspects of his life—something he did as rarely as possible—and admitting he'd been thwarted in his pursuit thus far. Beyond that, Oriel was almost nauseatingly happy in his marriage. It seemed indecent somehow to bring the issue of common lust into the Oriels' blissful home.

To hell with that, Trevor decided.

"She is a cyprian, as it happens," he announced, "an expensive trifle who has taken my fancy. Nothing more."

"Ah. The infamous Mrs. Nolan."

"Good Lord, man, how—"

"William," Oriel explained. "He was really rather angry with you over that expensive trifle."

"She is an experienced, enterprising whore," Trevor shot back. "She would twist your nice little brother into a human plait within a fortnight."

"William insists she is gently spoken."

Perhaps. When she was not arguing like a fishwife or spouting malevolent Gaelic curses.

"And quite kind."

Trevor hadn't seen much evidence of Nell's kindness. But it would be a lie to say he hadn't sensed it in her—a gentle warmth flowing beneath her cool surface.

"You sound as if you approve of William's pursuit," he growled. "I am telling you now, Oriel: I have my eyes on this one—"

Oriel's grin cut him off mid-warning. "As it happens, Wulf, I think you are absolutely right. William does not need to get himself involved with the Mrs. Nolans of the world. And I must say, it is refreshing to see you so passionate on a subject. One would think you hadn't a care in the world most times."

"One would be right."

"Bollocks."

Trevor grunted. "You are becoming a bore, Oriel."

"According to you, I have always been a bore. Tell me about this cyprian. If William is to be believed, she is a cross between Aphrodite and Helen of Troy."

Trevor started to smile at the image. He caught himself, and snapped, "Your brother is a fool, and you may tell him I said so. She is merely a woman who is blessedly too disreputable to wed and just enticing enough to bed. Tell me about the Roach's contact."

There was a long moment of silence. Then Oriel sighed. "Ah, Wulf . . . Fine. We know now there are two: a mole in the War Department and someone with money and enough social status to rub elbows with men like the Duke of York."

If there were a subject Trevor loathed more than the Prince Regent, it was the prince's host of dismal siblings. "The Duke of York is a buffoon."

"Precisely. A military buffoon with a notoriously

loose tongue." Oriel shrugged. "I am not concerned. We'll flush out the rats soon enough."

Yes, that had been Oriel's job, and his skill. He'd called himself a rat-catcher, the one who discovered spies and traitors when everyone else had failed.

"I assume you'll let me know when you do," Trevor said.

"Or perhaps I will see to the matter myself."

"No. You'll need me. You couldn't strike water if you fell from a bloody boat."

"True enough," Oriel replied, unoffended, "but you have done more than your fair share of . . . what you do. We've relied on you too long, Wulf. Let someone else take on that burden."

Again, so tempting . . . God, he'd wanted out so many times, wanted to go back to some ordinary life. Only the realization that there was no ordinary life waiting for him—nothing waiting for him at all—had kept him attached to the Ten. To what little remained of it.

"It's what I do." Like Oriel, Trevor didn't put a label on it. "You'll let me know when you've found your rats. Now"—he set his empty glass aside—"I am leaving. Thank Isobel for feeding me and tell her the south side door to my house is seldom locked. She can make use of it when you eventually begin to bore her, too."

"Tell her yourself," Oriel said easily. "She threatened to take my cane to my posterior should I let you leave without saying good-bye."

Trevor tapped the man's sturdy ebony stick with a fingertip and gave a blithe whistle. "Should make for a lively night. I've always had my suspicions about those Highland Scotswomen."

Then, ignoring his friend's good-natured growl, he

stepped through the French doors and into the London night.

Nell sat back on her haunches and rubbed at her back. She'd only been through a single bookshelf and was aching already. True, she had spent the better part of the day upstairs sorting her possessions into piles and packing crates, but the books had done her in. The duke had had so many, and new ones, fresh and fragrant in their leather-and-gold bindings, had arrived nearly every day Clonegal spent in London. Housebound, often bedridden, reading had been his last great pleasure.

Nell's eyes misted as she lifted a slender volume of Donne's poems. They had been the duke's favorites—and hers: lyrical, romantic, and often lusty. For Clonegal, the poems had brought back memories of his younger days. For Nell, they had brought a soft, wistful longing for the sort of devil-take-all love she'd never known.

This book would go into her valise. When she was finally ready to leave London in a few weeks, when the last crate was packed and the last piece of worn furniture covered, she and her most precious possessions would make their way to Ireland and not look back.

She jumped at the unexpected sound of the bell. Macauley would send whoever it was away. She had made it clear she was not to be disturbed and had already declined the company of the Astor twins, Lord William Paget—twice, Carmody, and a Lord Killone—whom she didn't think she had even met. As flattering as the attention was, it was unwelcome, too, and now nothing more than a nuisance.

She looked up at the sound of pounding footsteps on the stairs.

"And I'm telling ye," she heard Mac's rapidly rising voice as the doors to first the sitting room and then the dining room slammed open, "ye can't just be barging in wherever ye please. She's not at ho—"

The library door opened with enough force to make the fire leap in the hearth. Lord St. Wulfstan stood framed for an instant before striding into the room. He had a large bunch of wild-looking roses in one hand and Macauley attached like a crab to the tails of his coat.

"Sorry, ma'am," the retainer gasped as he skidded along in the viscount's wake. "I tried . . ."

Nell set the Donne aside and tried to still the suddenly rapid thumping of her heart. St. Wulfstan didn't look particularly friendly, but then again, she reasoned, retribution seldom started with flowers.

"No matter, Mac," she murmured as she rose to her feet. "You can let go now."

Macauley looked doubtful, but released his grip on the viscount's coat. "Aye, well, I'll be in shoutin' distance if ye need me."

Nell nearly smiled at the image of the diminutive man tackling St. Wulfstan, who was twice his size and probably half his age. "Thank you, Mac." When he'd stomped out, leaving the door conspicuously open behind him, she turned to her uninvited guest, who was now leaning against the mantel, arms crossed over his formidable chest, flowers sticking out from beneath his elbow.

"Are those for me?" she asked, pointing, unsure of just what to say under the circumstances.

St. Wulfstan glanced down and seemed almost surprised to see the roses. He uncrossed his arms and stuffed the bouquet into the ornate Chinese vase decorating the mantel. Little roses. Nell didn't miss the significance. *Róisín.*

"I try not to arrive at a lady's home empty-handed," he commented, voice giving her no hint as to his mood.

"That is very . . . courteous."

"Shall we discuss courtesy, Mrs. Nolan?"

"I . . . ah . . ." Feeling herself blushing, Nell tried to remind herself just how far from polite and refined their erstwhile bargain had been. She waved shakily toward a chair. "Would you care to sit?"

"No."

She did, perching on the edge of the leather sofa. "Tea?"

"No."

Nell sighed. "You are not making this easy on me, sir."

His scarred brow rose. "I was not aware I was meant to. I am not the one who went haring off into the night."

"True. You are not." Nell found herself twisting pleats into her dust-smudged skirts. A faint *tap tap tap* had her looking up. St. Wulfstan was drumming his fingers against the mantel. Other than that, he was the very picture of calm. "I . . . Thank you for not being angry."

"I am furious, actually."

"Oh." Nell dared a look into his eyes and wished she hadn't. The anger was there after all, banked perhaps, but fiery blue. "I'm sorry."

"Are you? For which bit? Scarpering? Refusing to see me after? Breaking a promise? That's the one I find bothers me the most. I expected better of you for some reason, but that is neither here nor there. Tell me this: Did you have any intention of honoring our agreement?"

She hadn't. For the very first time in her life, she had made a promise she'd had no intention of keeping.

Even as she'd done it, spoken the words, it had left a bad taste in her mouth. Nell had no idea when the lines had gotten so fuzzy—when it had become acceptable to play the courtesan but think ill of the men who treated her as one; when it had become acceptable to make a devil's bargain but not keep her side of it.

To lie and not answer the consequences when the lie was exposed.

She decided not to answer at all. "Have you come to collect?" she asked quietly, afraid of the answer but needing desperately to know what was going on behind that stony mask.

He eyed the generous sofa, both brows lifting now. Nell's pulse began its nervous dance again. Then he turned his attention to her, his gaze doing that familiar roam over her body.

"The thought did occur to me." He came away from the mantel, moving so quickly and smoothly that she barely had time to gasp before he was looming over her. "What would happen if I were to lay you down on the cushions here and now, Nell, and cover your body with mine?"

He leaned in, close enough now that she could see the lushness of those black lashes, the chiseled grooves bracketing the wide mouth. He smelled faintly of spiced orange and leather, looked like sin in a kashmir coat. So completely, dangerously unlike any man she had ever known outside of her dreams.

"I would fight you," she whispered.

"Would you?" He smiled, a slow, sultry grin that hinted at everything Donne wrote and Nell could only imagine. "I won't do it, then."

In an instant, his hands were on her arms, lifting her from her seat as if she were weightless. Nell gasped, and then lost her breath altogether when his mouth came down hungrily on hers. His lips were hard, demanding, slanting again and again over hers with the potent confidence of a man without fear. Nell tasted the heady essence of fine wine, felt the fierce heat of him from their joined lips to thighs, and saw shattered light behind her eyes. Then as quickly as he had taken her, he let her go.

She slid inelegantly, bonelessly back into her seat.

He straightened, shrugged his coat back into its severe lines. "I'll go now, but I will be back tomorrow at noon. Don't make me chase after you again, Nell. It will only make me cranky. I will find you, be sure of that, and you don't want me cranky when I do."

Then he was gone, and all Nell could do was sit right where he'd left her, trying to regain her breath.

CHAPTER 6

Trevor's mood wasn't tremendously improved the following morning. The post had contained a letter from his steward. According to George O'Donnell, assuming Trevor had deciphered the whiskey-spattered scrawl correctly, a substantial part of the west wing's roof had collapsed into the attics. And if that weren't bad enough, not a single workman from the area would come in to fix it. There had also been a fire in the empty stable block—the third outbuilding fire in as many months—that Trevor doubted was an accident.

He had a very good idea what was happening. There was no money in the estate's coffers to pay for repairs. Or any of the amenities his tenants expected. What little went into the accounts went right out again into two sets of pockets: the meager domestic staff that remained, and the steward's. Trevor had begun to suspect that O'Donnell was leeching money some months past. Now he was certain of it.

In the ordinary scheme of things, only a very stupid man would steal from Viscount St. Wulfstan. But O'Donnell had been clever enough to realize that Viscount St. Wulfstan was not likely to notice a few discrepancies in his Irish estate's accounts. Trevor had turned his back on Ireland ten years earlier, with his mother's death. He'd been back once since, to make certain the report of Richard's death was true and that the man was six feet under the peaty earth.

Ireland was as famous for its absentee landlords as it was for its beautiful land. Trevor was but one of many peers who all but ignored their property there. He wasn't proud of his disinterest, but he'd never bothered to change it. And now his tenants were making their displeasure known.

O'Donnell's letter had sent Trevor on a wholly unpleasant errand. The meeting with his solicitor had not gone at all well. The man, regretful though his sentiments had been, had passed on the same bad news he had been dispensing since Trevor had inherited the title and lands eight years before.

Richard's bitter and brutal decrees stood firm, impervious to the desperate circumstances. The former Lord St. Wulfstan had tied up every possession, every pence so tightly that Trevor could not sell so much as a table knife to pay for repairs to the table. Richard had possessed some small affection for the property. In fact, he had not once set foot off the estate during the last two years of his life. Whatever affection he'd felt, however, had apparently not extended to keeping up with repairs, and his animosity for the next viscount had all but guaranteed that the stones would crumble around that viscount's ears.

The familiar, hated twinge of sorrow had Trevor cursing anew. It had been more than fifteen years since Richard's fatherly pride had turned to vitriol. Yet still it hurt. Trevor had been condemned by the man he'd loved for a very human indiscretion, one imprudent flare of passion between a hot-blooded man with few responsibilities and a starry-eyed woman with too many.

At sixteen, Trevor had been typically wild, careless, enjoying the pleasures of life to the fullest. In the months following Richard's vicious assault, Trevor had earned himself the sobriquet "Rogue Robard." *Scurrilous bastard!* Richard had screamed. *Disgrace. Filthy devil.* And Trevor, aspiring to be as dutiful as possible, had proven him correct. It had taken the *ton* less time than Richard needed to grow cold in his grave to label his son "Sin" Wulfstan. Trevor had accepted the nominal alteration with the expected roue's grin, and set out to seduce the first woman who had dared breathe it to his face. She had warmed his bed, then given him the cold shoulder each time they met in public.

He had done a very good job at showing how very little he cared. And soon, he had stopped caring at all.

"*Sláinte,* Father," Trevor saluted grimly now as he skirted St. James's Square, using one of the mere handful of Gaelic words he had ever learned. He thrust fisted hands into his empty pockets. "Are you content now, you sanctimonious brute?"

There was little satisfaction to be found in querying a dead man, especially when that ghostly figure had everything to be content about. Trevor had taken on precisely the coarse character Richard had decreed, and was completely at the mercy of his iron-fisted Last Will and Testament. London didn't know, had never guessed, that Sin Wulfstan lived from his skill at gambling, and the stipend he received from the War Department for doing the jobs no one else wanted to do. He played cards well enough to keep himself; he would find a way to keep Nell Nolan. But his Irish property was falling into ruin and would fall farther. There was no St. Wulfstan fortune; there hadn't been in a very long time.

Trevor crossed Piccadilly, entered one of the tidy rabbit warrens of streets that held Mayfair's smaller houses. He spied Nell's ahead, bright and cheerful with its set of shiny marble steps. He wondered if the massive marble monument Richard had commissioned for his grave was worth anything. Perhaps it could be broken into pieces and used to repair a wall or two. . . .

He shoved the depressing thoughts from his head as he waited for Nell's troll of a servant to answer the door. Ireland would wait. Not for long, perhaps, but it would wait. He needed this time with Nell first. God only knew why, but he needed just to be in her presence. It had occurred to him that she might very well have disobeyed him and run. She'd been surrounded by piles of books and several packing crates when he'd arrived the night before—perhaps only to clear space or tuck away memories, or in preparation for a move.

He would soon find out.

Nell peered down into the street. He was there, filling her doorstep. As she watched, he removed his hat and ran a hand through his hair. It was the first time she had seen him in daylight. The sun, weak as it was, brought out the fiery sheen of the thick, auburn mass and lit the blue of his coat—dark but not, as she'd expected, black. She couldn't see his expression at all.

Drawing a deep breath, she went down to answer the door.

His fierce scowl disappeared as soon as he saw her. He smiled, fleetingly as always, but as always, Nell was startled by the difference it made to his face. In that instant, with his jewel blue eyes, sun-touched skin, and flashing grin, he took away the breath she'd so determinedly drawn.

Then he was looming over her, scarred and saturnine once more.

"I don't suppose you let the old coot go," he offered as a greeting.

Nell sighed. "Macauley isn't well. I thought it best if he keep quiet today."

"Apoplexy?" came the wry guess.

"Rheumatism," Nell said mildly. Severe enough to make the man's normally ruddy face pale. She didn't think he'd needed an encounter with the viscount. "Will you come in?"

He didn't. Instead, he propped one shoulder against the doorframe. "You come out."

"But . . ." This wasn't at all what she'd expected. She'd been ready for him to fill her sitting room with his potent presence. Ready to explain why, in carefully rehearsed lines, she wasn't going to invite him into her bed.

She'd been ready to dodge his large hands and mobile mouth. She wasn't ready for him to kiss her again. The first time had been too unsettling.

"Come out," he repeated. "Get something to put on your head and one of those ridiculous, endless frothy things you seem to wrap yourself in, and come out for a walk with me."

Speechless, Nell gaped at him. Then common sense took over. If they were outside, he couldn't very well pounce on her. Or at least she thought he would not. With men like St. Wulfstan, one never knew.

"Very well." She stepped back. "Will you wait inside?"

"I'll be right here."

She nodded and turned to hurry back up the stairs. He stopped her with a quiet, "Nell."

"Yes?"

"Thank you. For not making me come after you."

Speechless again, she could only nod once more and go off in search of hat and shawl.

Five minutes later, she was walking by his side down Curzon Street, arm threaded tensely through his. He was whistling softly, swinging his stick in his free hand.

Nell waited as long as she could before asking, "Where are we going?"

"You'll have to wait and see."

"I don't much care for surprises."

"Well, that's unfortunate, isn't it?" was his bland reply.

Nell irritably shook her right hand free of her wrap. She didn't care for surprises, and this man seemed to have an endless supply of them. "Really, sir, I must insist—"

"No, you mustn't." He glanced down at her, expression unreadable. "You are not currently in a position to insist upon anything. Remember?"

She certainly didn't want to be reminded. "Are you trying to make me anxious, my lord?" she demanded. "Or angry?"

There was a long moment of silence. Then he lifted a brow—a familiar act and one, she was beginning to think, he'd perfected in lieu of showing any particular emotion—and murmured, "Am I to take it then that my efforts to make you weak with desire have fallen somewhat short?"

She felt her jaw go slack. "I . . . I cannot . . ."

He winked at her. Actually winked, a brief flick of his scarred eyelid, paired with that devilish, flashing grin. "Close your lovely mouth, Nell, or put it to some better use."

She remembered the kiss and promptly blushed.

She'd never met anyone with half this man's nerve or total unconcern. "You are very hard to like," she heard herself announce. And wondered when she had become so prunish, so very prim.

"I never mentioned anything about liking, Mrs. Nolan," he shot back, and returned to whistling.

They turned into Park Lane. As much as she hated to admit it, Nell couldn't help but always be impressed by the grand houses there, one after another, sitting in massive, solid elegance like well-heeled Society matrons. She'd never been inside any of them, never expected to. So she was startled when St. Wulfstan guided her off the street.

"Is this yours?" she whispered.

He gave a short laugh. "No, but it appears I would have better luck at stimulating your desire if it were."

She couldn't tell if he was jesting this time. Either way, the comment rankled. "I assure you, I do not equate a man's merit with the size of his home."

"Clever girl. You should put much more store in the size of his . . . Ah. Here we are."

Instead of going to the front of the house, they walked around the back, stopping at what appeared to be a large coal shed. St. Wulfstan shoved open a door, walked straight into the ill-lit space.

"What . . . ?" Nell began, then gave a quiet little gasp when her eyes adjusted to the light.

The large room was filled with stone. Some was mounted on the walls, more stood on the floor, a few pieces were propped against walls and each other. There were fragments of statues and complete friezes, horses and men and strange mythical beasts. Every single one looked ancient.

"What is this?" she asked breathlessly, staring at a trio of reclining stone maidens who were garbed in classical, drapey gowns. All were incomplete, missing head or limbs, but the carving was so precise, so delicate, that Nell could almost feel the wind blowing their vestments.

"This," St. Wulfstan said, "is the Earl of Elgin's collection from Greece." He pointed to a single, lush female figure, little more than a torso, but so lovely that Nell was once again breathless. "Galatea."

"Is she? Is she truly?"

He shrugged, smiled. "Probably not, but there is no one to prove it one way or another."

Charmed by the man, awed by the display, Nell walked along a row of fragments. She ran a hand reverently along the broken tops as she went. It didn't matter that some pieces were little more than shards with unidentifiable lumps on them, nor that her glove was now filthy. St. Wulfstan had given her something no one else had, something she had longed for so many times: a journey to another time and place.

For countless minutes she wandered silently through the marbles, examining a finely detailed sweep of drapery here, reverently stroking the back of a centaur there. St. Wulfstan, she noticed when she looked up, was looking at her rather than the sculptures. He was leaning almost insolently against another reclining female figure. One of his arms was looped over a stone shoulder, his hand resting on a breast. Nell promptly swung her gaze back to the matter nearest to her hand, which turned out to be the formidable haunch of someone or other.

"Are these all from the same place?" she asked.

"Most are from the Parthenon. The greatest temple of ancient Athens." St. Wulfstan patted the hip of his statue. "This one is likely an attendant to Athena.

Your bottom there probably belonged to a god. Does it feel divine?"

Nell flushed and removed her hand. She scanned the room. Everywhere she looked were body parts: breasts, thighs, shoulders, wrists. Male and female. She'd never seen anything like this display, could never have even imagined it. In that instant, it all seemed rather beautiful. And somehow a bit amusing. She fought her smile, but couldn't help remarking, "Your knowledge is quite frightening, sir."

He laughed, then replied, "And there is so much more I am willing to share."

Nell knew she was ankle deep in fast-rising water. A courtesan would know how to take St. Wulfstan's bawdy banter, would know how to answer. Nell was already well out of her depth.

She opted for a cowardly retreat.

"Will you thank Lord Elgin for me when next you see him?" she asked, wandering a few feet to study a helmeted warrior. "This is all so marvelous. I would like to express my gratitude for the experience."

"You'd be thanking the wrong man, then, wouldn't you?" St. Wulfstan came away from his stone lady to stand just behind her. "Allow me to experience your gratitude."

He was too close. Caught between him and the stone soldier, Nell felt enclosed, overwarm suddenly.

"This is his display," she offered, pressing herself back—into unyielding marble. "His invitation . . ." She blinked. "Did he invite you? Us?"

St. Wulfstan shrugged. "He isn't overly particular about who sees the marbles."

Something in his voice had Nell studying him through narrowed eyes. "Would he be particular in this instance?"

"He might. I once sent him a crate full of copies of Byron's *Childe Harold*."

"Poetry? Why would that make him dislike you?"

"Have you not read *Childe Harold's Pilgrimage*?" he demanded.

Nell shook her head. "The duke wouldn't allow Byron in the house, called him a vulgar upstart."

St. Wulfstan, she decided, really had a lovely laugh: deep and rich and completely untempered—at least for those fleeting seconds when it rang out.

"I would imagine Clonegal's forefathers said much the same of Donne," he announced. "Well, in the work, Byron lambasted Elgin for removing the marbles from Greece and made sport of the fact that Lady Elgin had a bit of a problem with fidelity. It sold brilliantly. The twenty copies I sent were a mere drop in the bucket."

Nell tilted her head and regarded him. "Do you agree with Byron on the matter of the marbles?"

"Oh, I never formed much of an opinion about that."

"So you sent the books because . . ."

"Because Elgin very publicly accused me of being one of his wife's *problems*. I don't care for that sort of display."

With that, he stepped in close enough that his thighs brushed Nell's skirts, close enough to completely fill her vision and block her view of the shadowy room. Her heart bumped a quickened beat.

"He must have been very angry," she managed.

"He was."

"A wife is not like a statue, after all, to be shared. I would imagine Lord Elgin believes that."

St. Wulfstan's mouth curved. "Elgin is a fool."

"For being upset that you bedded his wife?" Nell demanded.

"For a great many reasons, actually, but his careless handling of his treasures is certainly among them. One thing you should know about me, Nell: I don't share."

"No," she whispered as he reached for her. "No, I imagine you don't."

Glad they understood each other, Trevor clasped her waist and lifted her. Her eyes widened in surprise and she grasped his shoulders. If she meant to push him away, he didn't give her the chance. He covered her mouth with his, swallowed her little gasp. He settled her atop the stone figure she had been examining and, with his now freed hands, roughly cupped her face, holding her still so he could have his fill of her.

For a few moments she sat, unmoving. Then, in the space of a heartbeat, she was kissing him back. Trevor growled low in his throat, instantly and completely aroused. He coaxed her lips apart, deepened the kiss. Her fingers dug into his shoulders; he lowered one hand to her knee, pressed until she opened just enough for him to step between her thighs. He spread the other hand around her ribs, feeling the slight weight of her breast above his fingers. Nell gave a quiet hum but didn't break the contact of mouth against mouth. She smelled of honey, tasted of it, and was just as tempting.

This, he thought vaguely, reveling in his conquest, was why men through the ages had sold their souls for the favors of courtesans. In the arms of such a woman, a fellow could be lost to the world, to his duties, to sense, and never give a damn.

Then suddenly Nell was pushing at his shoulders, dragging her lips from his. He waited, blood raging, while she stared at him. Her mouth was kiss-swollen, her eyes shadowed. Then, "Please," she said shakily, lashes sweeping down to cover whatever emotion lurked there, "let me go."

Not if the devil himself demanded it, Trevor thought. But he stepped back and lifted her down. The moment was gone.

"We'll go," he said gruffly.

"Thank you."

She carefully arranged her wrap around her shoulders, then walked ahead of him toward the door. She stopped just short of the threshold and reached out to touch a centaur's jaw with a fingertip. Trevor waited for her to speak, and was surprised when she asked, "Have you been there? To Greece?"

"I have."

"What is it like?"

He studied her pale profile. No lofty goddess, this. Not even close. "The heat gets to a man's head," he replied finally, "and makes him forget who he is."

She nodded, as if she understood, and walked out into a day that had turned cool and cloudy.

They walked back to her little house in silence.

Yes, he'd been to Greece, and Italy, even Turkey. He'd lived them all in a blur of strange liquors, lushly patterned cushions, and spiced foods. For more than two years he had wandered from locale to exotic locale, leaving each place when what little money his mother could send him ran out, or when he was no longer welcome at local gaming tables or at the dinner tables of men with pretty wives and daughters.

He'd done a very good job of forgetting who he was, or rather, who he had once been.

The matter of who he would become was just as handily settled. He had just been not-so-politely asked to relinquish the hospitality of a Pyrenee merchant and had nowhere to go, no money to get him to his next destination, no one calling him home. But his skill at long-range shooting had caught the attention of another young Anglo-Irishman named Oliver Marlow. Just as clever, seemingly just as devil-may-care as he, Marlow had paid the bills for the drink and rooms, and had told tales of valor and near escapes that not even the best Connaught bard could have topped. Within days, Trevor had accepted passage back to England for training and a place in the covert group that would come to be known as the Ten.

Marlow was long dead now, shot down on a dusty Spanish road. The Ten had become four: Oriel, Rievaulx, Rotheroe, and St. Wulfstan. They were a decade older than when their activities had begun and, in more than one case, aeons harder. The memories were mostly grim, some just too painful. . . .

Trevor blinked to find himself staring at Nell's front door. She fumbled for her key. He saw she was chewing on her lip when she'd managed the lock and turned back to face him. "Are you . . . Did you wish to come in?"

Yes. Oh, yes.

"Thank you, no." He saw the surprise in her eyes. "Not today. But I will, Nell. Be sure of it."

"I . . ." She broke off and shook her head. "I do not know what you want of me, my lord."

"Yes. You do."

In an utterly feminine, if hesitant gesture, Nell raised a hand to smooth her hair, touch the point on her throat where her pulse beat. "Well, I don't know what to say to that."

He shrugged. "Don't say anything. Just be here when I come for you. You may pack up as much of this house as you so desire, but you will be here. We have matters to settle and I won't wait forever."

She flushed, the delicate pink that made her almost beautiful. If she'd been thinking of disappearing again, she'd best think again. He would know. He had his ways of keeping an eye on her. If she made a move to leave Town, he would know.

"When?" She was toying with a corner of her wrap, a nervous and somehow charming gesture.

"Not tomorrow. The following night. I will be here at seven o'clock. Be ready." He suddenly recalled the small parcel in his pocket. "Ah. I nearly forgot. I cannot visit empty-handed, after all." He removed the palm-sized leather pouch and held it out.

For a moment, he thought she was going to refuse it. Then she held out a hand. "What is this?"

"Open it when you like and find out." Trevor tipped his hat. "Until next time, madam." Without waiting for her response, he spun on his heel and walked away.

She called out to him before he'd taken a dozen steps. "Lord St. Wulfstan." He stopped. "It really is none of my concern, what you do with ... other women, but I have to ask ..."

He turned and gave her a wicked grin. "No."

"No?"

"No, I did not bed Lady Elgin."

She stood, a pale figure against the rich red brick of her house, glossy head tilted. She was still holding the unopened pouch. "I see. But I was not going to ask about Lady Elgin."

"Who, then?" The possibilities, if he listened to gossip, were endless.

"Róisín."

"Róisín?" In his mind, Trevor saw sunlight on mahogany hair and wind-kissed cheeks. A lifetime ago. "What about her?"

This time, Nell's fingertips brushed her soft lips. "Did you ever kiss her?"

"I did. Once."

"Why only once?"

"Because I couldn't understand a single word she yelled at me as I was running away after."

That clearly surprised her. "You ran away?"

He smiled. "I was nine and she spoke only Gaelic."

"Oh." Nell nodded, and stepped halfway through the door. "Do you know Gaelic now?"

"I haven't learned a word since that day," he replied, swinging his stick in a careless arc before tucking it under his arm. "But I haven't run away from anything, either."

"Oh," Nell said again, and disappeared into the house.

Trevor whistled all the way home. He wanted Nell Nolan, and was going to have her, soon, warm and willing beneath him. There was no question of that. He whistled as he climbed the steps to his door.

He had his hand on the doorknob when he heard the faint buzz and felt the bite. "Damn mosquitoes," he muttered, waving his hand near his cheek. The things were a blasted nuisance. This one hurt.

Once inside, Trevor raised his hand to his ear. When he pulled it away there was blood on his fingers. Quite a bit of blood, actually. Outside, he had been too pre-occupied with his pleasant musings to think intelligently. Now his mind was working with standard precision. There were no mosquitos to be found on his London doorstep. In fact, he had not seen a mosquito since his last visit to the Peninsula.

Mutely, he crossed the hall to look into the tarnished mirror. There was blood on his collar. In fact, it

had run down to leave a dark patch on the shoulder of
his coat. Turning his head slowly, he stared at his ear.
An inch-wide section near the top of the lobe was still
bleeding and there was an angry-looking red stripe
below his temple.

Trevor walked back to the door. He found the
mosquito almost immediately. Embedded in the polished wood of the doorframe, right at ear level, was a
mangled bullet.

CHAPTER 7

Nell sat in one of Anastasia's parlor chairs two days later, St. Wulfstan's pouch in her lap. "What am I to do with this, Annie?"

"Do with it? Why, spend it, I suppose. What else does one do with money?"

The four hundred pounds sat far more heavily in her hands than a sheaf of banknotes should. "I cannot keep it. It is payment for . . . for . . . services."

Her friend raised delicate brows. "If I am not mistaken, dearest, you have provided no services. And the money is yours, retrieved by St. Wulfstan from Routland's tight little fists."

So it was. Still, it felt like ill-gotten gains and it made Nell uneasy. "I am being very silly," she sighed.

"Could it be perhaps that you are feeling guilty?" was the shrewd response. "I know you, Nell, and I rather think you are struggling not with what is in your hands, but what you felt you needed to do to get it."

"I'll give it back to Lord St. Wulfstan," Nell muttered, not very pleased with herself for being deliberately obtuse. "I don't need money."

"Neither does he. Nor would he be agreeable, I imagine, should you try to return it to him. It isn't the favor he expects."

"He expects me to share my bed with him."

"Yes, I imagine he does. You said you would, after all."

Nell blinked miserably at the older woman. "One would think you were taking his side over mine."

"Oh, please, Nell. You know very well that I am doing no such thing. I—" Annie coughed harshly, a sound that had Nell staring at her with concern. She hadn't noticed before, caught up as she was in her own troubles, but she noted the pallor of Annie's cheeks, broken by two small, vivid patches of color.

"Annie, are you unwell?"

"I am fine. A small cold. Nell." She shook an admonitory finger. "I won't have you worrying. I am fine."

Nell wasn't convinced. She had seen her friend ill— very ill—before and that single cough had triggered old memories and a strong unease. "Annie . . ."

"A cold. Nothing more. Now, tell me, have you made firm plans for leaving London?"

"Clonegal's man of affairs in Dublin will find a suitable place for me to stay while I search for something permanent. I need only give him a fortnight's notice."

"So you may leave at any time."

Yes, Nell thought, she could. And she had intended to be gone as soon as she could post that letter to Dublin and arrange passage. But now, seeing for the first time that Annie had grown thinner even in the past sennight, watching as she stifled another cough, Nell smoothly changed her plans.

"I shall stay until the end of the Season." Then, if her friend was still unwell, she would extend her stay again. And again and again until she was no longer needed. She couldn't even conceive of doing otherwise. "I will get my fill of fine theater and opera while I can."

"Oh, I am glad. I will miss you terribly, you know."

Not nearly so much, Nell knew, as she would miss Annie. The pain would be every bit as fierce as that she'd borne on losing the duke. Fighting off the sadness, she managed lightly, "Yes, well, if I'm to stay, something will have to be done about my gentlemen callers. Poor Mac is up and down the stairs like an India rubber ball, the larder is forever bare, and something gets broken every time the Astor twins visit. Of course I cannot scold, as I still am unable to remember which is which. Do you know Lord Killone? He has called twice and I cannot recall having been introduced to him."

"He has attended several of my soirees. I certainly know no ill of him."

"I do," Nell jested. "He has an appalling sense of the correct time to pay a visit. Today it was before noon."

"And Clonegal?" Annie demanded, cutting slickly through the levity.

Nell sighed. "He continues to call. Mac turned him away again this morning. Along with all the other eager young swains I simply could not face."

She had meant to see the new duke, steeled herself for it. But when the moment came, she had lost her resolve. Suddenly cowardly—perhaps because she did not have St. Wulfstan's massive form by her side—she'd had Mac send him away. Rickham had called, too, cursing the butler and his *whore mistress* when he'd been informed she was not at home. Nell had heard the vicious words all the way up the stairs. They had chilled her.

"The men will continue to come, dearest, as long as

you remain unattached. The elusive Mrs. Nolan has become the fashionable challenge of this Season."

"How utterly ridiculous!" Nell snapped. "Then I will continue to turn them away, I suppose."

Annie toyed with a delicate tea cake. "There is a solution, you know."

"Decamp for the wilds of Eire?"

"Accept St. Wulfstan."

Nell bobbed her cup. "Annie!"

"Well, why not?"

"Why not? Correct me if I am mistaken, but I recall you saying that he was not a lady's best choice. Beyond that, I have absolutely no need of any man's financial protection."

Her friend hummed vaguely. "I find my opinion of St. Wulfstan has changed somewhat since you have told me of his behavior during your times together." Then she smiled. "And there are reasons other than money to accept a man's suit."

Nell blushed. She couldn't help it. And remembered Thomas with a soft affection that was not quite sufficient to overcome the simple truth that nothing they had shared in the marriage bed had been so spectacular as to make her long for more. But then, St. Wulfstan's embrace . . .

"Would it be so very bad?" Annie demanded gently.

Would it? Nell recalled his kisses almost guiltily. Those had not been so bad. They had not been bad at all. In fact, the simple touch of his lips, of his hands on her, had warmed her in unfamiliar and not particularly welcome ways.

She had so little experience with desire. She had loved Thomas, loved him with all her heart. But they had been so young, so callow. This quick spark and tingle she'd felt in St. Wulfstan's arms was more than a little frightening. As was the thought of just giving herself to any man, body without heart. And to this man: a rogue, a self-styled reprobate . . .

"Nell, I would never tell you to do something you did not wish to do. Stand by your principles."

"How easy that sounds. But I haven't thus far, have I? I made a devil's bargain that I am refusing to keep."

Annie shrugged. "Needs must," she said philosophically.

Unwillingly, Nell found herself remembering again. St. Wulfstan's hands, alternately hard enough to be frightening and gentle enough to make her feel like the most fragile of glass.

She shook her head briskly. "No. Bargain or no, I will not be his . . . be a . . ." She broke off, glanced apologetically at her dearest friend, who had spent her life as a courtesan.

Annie did not look angry. She simply looked unwell. "Oh, Nell," she sighed. "What bothers you more? The fact that he was willing to trade his aid for time in your bed, or that you accepted?" She shrugged, set aside the teacake and wiped her fingers on her napkin. "You will decide how best to deal with St. Wulfstan. Did you not say you were seeing him tonight?"

"I am." Nell glanced at the mantel clock and wondered where the afternoon had gone. She would have to face St. Wulfstan altogether too soon. "I must go."

Annie embraced her at the door. "Needs must," she repeated softly. "You simply must decide what it is that you need."

The problem, Nell realized as she made her way back to her own house, was that she'd been so clear on what she needed to do for eight years. Now that she had faced Routland and finally laid both the ghost of her young husband and her own sad demons to rest, she had no idea at all of what she needed.

It wasn't St. Wulfstan. She knew that much. When he arrived, she would tell him. She would apologize for her lack of honor. She would appeal to his if she had to, but then, she didn't think he would try to claim his reward by force. There was no doubt that he was a man of action, of violence, even. But Nell knew somehow that he wouldn't hurt her. He would be angry. She had ample experience with angry men, with bitter, hurtful words. She would weather whatever storm arose. Then he would leave; she would stay in London only until she was certain Annie didn't need her. After that, she would be free to go home to Ireland—and the precisely nothing that awaited her there.

Trevor arrived on her doorstep at seven o'clock. Early, perhaps, for the expected Season evening, but he paid little heed to what was expected. Beyond that, he was tired of his own company and had been craving Nell's since the moment he had left her two days before. He had firm plans for the night and wanted to begin as soon as possible.

The scowling gnome was back on duty. He barely grunted a greeting before turning on his heel and somewhat creakily stomping off, leaving Trevor to follow him up the stairs. The parlor door was open, candle and firelight glowing from within. The butler didn't bother to announce him. Clearly he was expected.

Trevor paused in the doorway. Nell was seated by the fire, book in her lap. Gone was the familiar, unflattering white. Instead, she was wearing a dress of muted yellow, plain and unfashionable, and it made Trevor think of sunlight in autumn. She lifted her eyes to his and he was struck yet again, even from across the room, by the pull of that sea grey gaze. He stepped toward her.

She stared at the bandage. "What have you done to yourself?" she asked softly in lieu of a greeting.

He lifted a hand to the narrow strip of gauze that wound once around his head. "My horse kicked up a stone."

"Ah."

She accepted the explanation without comment. Of course she did. As far as she would know, Trevor wouldn't be dodging bullets on his own doorstep. He could only imagine what she would make of the truth—and of the fact that he wasn't overly concerned with having been shot at. It was hardly the first time. Either an irate husband of some past affair was out for blood or someone was taking exception to Trevor's clandestine activities outside the bedroom. Odds were even. He expected an answer eventually. For now, he would simply be a bit more on his guard than usual. All in all a familiar state of affairs.

As Trevor watched, Nell's marvelous eyes flickered to his other hand, to the small parcel he carried. She glanced away almost immediately, pretending not to be interested in the gift he had brought. She soon spoiled it by taking another quick look. Trevor found himself charmed by this small display of sheer, feminine eagerness.

"Would you like to open it?" he asked.

"Open what . . . ?" Realizing how ridiculous it was to play innocent, she gave a wry smile. "Yes, I suppose I would. But I think perhaps we should talk first."

He had a very good idea of what she intended to say. He would listen. To every carefully planned, eloquent, silly word. Just not now.

"I don't think so," he replied easily. "If we talk, we shall be late and I do not care to be late. Fetch a wrap."

"What?" She blinked at him.

"A warm one. There is a chill in the air tonight. And a hat. You may open your present in the carriage." When she didn't move, he jerked his chin toward the door. "Well, go on."

And she did, rising, brow furrowed, to walk past him into the hall. She smelled, he noticed, like honey and cloves.

"Where—?"

"Oh, leave off, Nell, and find something to wear. I have a hackney waiting."

She actually made it to the stairs before stopping. "I cannot go out with you."

"Whyever not?" Trevor gave a silent groan. He was in no mood to parry her inevitable excuses as to why she was reneging on their bargain.

She took him by surprise when she brushed a hand down her skirts and commanded, "Look at me."

He did. To his eyes, she looked like sin and salvation wrapped together in a sunny package. "Yes?"

"I am not dressed to go out. This is an old dress and not at all suited—"

"Ah. You would prefer to stay in, then?" He could see images of pan to fire in her gaze and nearly smiled. "As it happens, I wish to go out. So, for the last time, go find something to cover your old, unsuitable dress and stop making me wait." He waved the parcel in front of her. "Well?"

She glowered—quite prettily, really. "I will not be bribed!" But she disappeared for several minutes, returning with hat and wrap.

He helped her into the carriage, shaking his head in

exasperated amusement behind her back when she immediately took the rear-facing seat. "Oh, Nell," he murmured and, settling himself into the opposite seat, pulled her efficiently to sit beside him. "Here."

She took the paper-wrapped gift but did not open it. "Where are we going?"

"You'll see."

"Hmph. And what is this?"

"Open it and find out."

He heard her huff out a breath. "You are a veritable font of information this evening, are you not?"

He grinned. "And you are charming. Open it."

She did, undoing the string and peeling back the paper with the slow care of someone not accustomed to receiving gifts. Trevor found himself wondering just what sort of men she'd known in her time as a courtesan. Careless ones, he decided. No man who had seen the expression of awe on her face as she lifted the last corner of paper would have been able to resist showering her with presents.

"Oh," she breathed. "Oh, it is beautiful."

The little stone figure of Venus was not beautiful, not really. It was ancient, worn, and worth almost nothing. Which was, of course, why Trevor still had it in his possession—the last remnants of a once-impressive collection. It was a piece he had bought himself rather than the purchase of one of his forebears. He had found the little Venus in a dusty shop in Rome and had gladly handed over his food money for the day to possess this small fragment of graceful history.

"I cannot accept this," Nell was saying, even as she traced a reverent fingertip over the stone head.

"Why not?"

"Because it is too much—"

"It is a trifle."

"—and it signifies something I cannot—"

"It is just a small gift, Nell," Trevor said with a sigh. "Say 'thank you' and be done with it."

"Thank you. It is truly lovely. But I will not accept it." She pressed the thing into his hand. "Please don't argue with me."

He sighed again, but tucked the Venus into his coat pocket. "You are a difficult woman, Nell Nolan."

"I have never meant to be," was the quiet reply.

They sat in silence for the remainder of the ride. Only when the carriage pulled up at the entrance to the pleasure gardens did Nell move. She pressed her face to the window. "Is this Vauxhall Gardens?"

"It is."

He saw the smile before she hid it. "I have never been here. Why did you bring me?"

"Because," he said simply as he climbed out and helped her down, "I thought you would enjoy it."

As they strolled down the Grand Walk, he studied her studying the spectacle that was Vauxhall. She gaped at the crowds of loud, loudly dressed young men, gazed wistfully, Trevor thought, at the dresses of some of the ladies, and smiled as a corps of drunken soldiers marched by in cheerful, clumsy formation.

There was music in the Grove, a full orchestra playing a lively tune, and Nell stopped at the sight and sound. Her hand tightened on Trevor's sleeve. "How wonderful!" she breathed. He quite agreed, and she was every bit as much of the picture as the musicians.

"Come along. I have arranged for a supper box."

She kept up her perusal of everything as they made their way to the box, craning her neck so far around that Trevor was certain she would do damage to herself.

"You will be able to see everything from your seat," he informed her amusedly. "Nell."

"Hmm?" She reluctantly dragged her gaze from a man walking a trio of beribboned geese on leads.

"Sit. Eat."

And they did. There was the famed fare of ham and tiny roasted chickens, little mince tarts and country cheeses, braised leeks and miniature colored marrows. In front of them, the orchestra played and revelers strolled by. Behind, painted on the box's wall, merry maidens frolicked in a spring garden.

Trevor poured Nell a glass of wine. *"Sláinte."*

"Sláinte," she replied. "I thought you said you knew no Gaelic."

That hadn't surprised her, despite the fact that he had been raised in Ireland. The Anglo-Irish aristocrats seldom bothered to learn the native language. It had been firmly discouraged at Horgan's, too, but Nell had learned from her gran as a small child and had quietly, defiantly been careful never to lose a single word.

"I know *almost* no Gaelic," was St. Wulfstan's response. "I daresay you are proficient." When she merely hummed, he pressed, "Fluent?" She nodded. "Interesting. Do you miss Ireland?"

Her answer was quick and fervent. "Every day."

"Ah. You were happy there."

She sipped at her wine. "Not always. Life was difficult after my hus . . ." She stopped abruptly.

"After your husband died," Trevor completed the phrase. "I know you had a husband, Nell." He found himself wanting to ask if she had been happy in her marriage, if she'd been very much in love. But he didn't particularly want to hear the answer, so instead he asked, "Where were you raised?"

"County Wicklow. And you?"

"Galway," he said gruffly. "Connemara. Tell me about your Wicklow home."

In the torchlight he could see her eyes go blank. "I grew up in a charitable school."

"I see. I imagine that was unpleasant."

"It was . . . not so terrible. Not really."

Trevor heard the lie in her voice and found himself silently cursing whatever wastrel aristocrat had been her father. It was obvious that Nell Nolan had had little luck with the men of her young life. Abandoned by one, widowed by another. "How long were you there?"

"When I was seventeen I ceased to be a pupil and was allowed to teach some of the smallest girls. Soon after, I met Thomas. He . . . had a farm."

He had a farm. So very simple.

"I expect your upbringing was as different from mine as land and sea," Nell remarked—with more interest, he thought, than self-pity.

Yes, he supposed his youth had been altogether different. He'd been spared the poverty—until he'd left home, at least. And he'd been spared the stigma of publicly acknowledged illegitimacy.

He shrugged. "I scarcely remember my younger days."

"Oh, I cannot believe that. You are hardly aged. Come now, you must recall—"

"Nell," he said warningly.

She tilted her glossy head. "Ah, I see. When you said you had no memories, what you really meant was that you have no intention of sharing any of them."

"You are very wise, my dear."

"No. I am actually very foolish. But that is neither here nor there. Am I allowed to ask any personal questions of you, my lord?"

Trevor reached for the platter of fruit between them and chose a plump strawberry. He imagined he was paying a penny for each one. Criminal. But he'd done well at the tables the night before. Not well enough to repair a roof, but enough to see a few shillings spread out in the form of overpriced fruit.

"What is it you wish to know?" he demanded finally.

He watched as Nell toyed with a cherry, felt the familiar tug of desire.

"How did you get the scar?"

"Of course. The scar." He leaned back in his chair, twirled the stem of his wineglass between his fingertips. "Tell me this: Have you bedded Rickham?"

"Sir!"

"Not willing to answer that?" he asked. Even in the candlelight, he could see the high spots of color on her cheeks. "Very well. If you—"

"No," she said, so quietly that he barely heard. "No. I didn't."

He nodded. "I am very glad to hear that, Mrs. Nolan."

She met his gaze again. "The scar . . . ?"

"No," he said.

"I beg your pardon?"

"No," he repeated, and reached for the bottle. "I don't think you should ask me personal questions."

She colored anew. "But that is hardly fair—"

"Hush." The strains of a Haydn symphony swelled through the air. Trevor refilled his glass. "This is why *I* come to Vauxhall."

So they sat, silent, as the orchestra played. Nell watched as he listened. She wanted to be angry, to be offended by his conduct. And she supposed she was. Only, as she saw his eyes drift shut for a moment with a particularly poignant melody, she couldn't hold the anger.

He was an enigma, this man with the ravaged face and rogue's tongue. And the longer she knew him, the less she understood.

He turned, caught her staring. He lifted his scarred brow, then tipped his glass in a slow, languid salute. Disconcerted, Nell reached for a strawberry. She gasped, nearly dropping it when his free hand shot out, impossibly quick, to grasp her wrist. There was little she could do as he drew her hand toward him across the table. When she'd reached as far as she could, just before she would have had to either lean toward him or resist, he lowered his head and took the berry between his teeth. Then he grinned at her, a carnal smile that had her hackles rising and pulse leaping in the same instant.

She tugged; he held on. "Stop fighting me, Nell," he murmured, lips against her tingling palm.

And then the sky erupted above them. Nell jumped as the fireworks burst through the sky, brilliant white stars falling into embers. There was another burst, this time a shower of jewel colors. The crowd gasped, then cheered. The orchestra played on, the cymbals crashing with the lights overhead. Nell had never seen anything like it, and she knew it was a memory she would carry with her for a very long time.

It wasn't until the display had ended that she realized St. Wulfstan had released his grip on her wrist. In the excitement of the moment, she hadn't pulled her hand free. She had gripped his fingers tightly with hers. She flushed and withdrew her hand now, linking it with her other in her lap.

He grinned at her across the table. "That," he announced, "is why I brought you here. I thought you would appreciate fireworks."

"It was perfect," she said, unable to hide her unso-phisticated pleasure. "Beautiful."

"Yes," he agreed, eyes on her. "Beautiful. Come along."

"What . . . ?" But he was already pulling her to her feet. She managed a last look at the wonder that was Vauxhall Gardens over her shoulder as he hustled her toward the gate.

Within minutes, they were back in a carriage, heading toward Mayfair. Nell could still hear the fire-works echoing faintly in her ears, could still feel the subtle humming of her blood. Of course, she thought tensely, that could have been the fact that St. Wulfstan had once again refused to sit opposite her, and had one of his hard thighs pressed against hers.

"I . . . thank you," she said as they skirted the southern corner of Hyde Park. "That was my first time."

"For?"

"Vauxhall," she replied. "And fireworks."

"Well, I am delighted to have participated in your first something," he murmured, voice dry.

The carriage was dark. Nell could just make out his wry smile. She sighed. Something had changed the mood of the evening, had changed his mood. And she didn't think it was simply her mention of his scar. He would be used to people's response to his face—accustomed, too, to the question. If he chose not to answer, that was his decision. No, there was some-thing more, and she didn't know what it was. In her life, no one had ever kept her so off-balance as St. Wulfstan. It was disturbing, of course, but it was also that little bit intriguing.

The carriage rattled to a halt in front of her house. Nell allowed St. Wulfstan to help her down. His hand lingered at her waist, rested lightly against the small of her back as he escorted her up the stairs. She unlocked the door with slightly trembling fingers. He followed her into the foyer. There was a single taper burning on the side table, casting his face into planes of shadow and light.

This was it. This was the time for her to say what she needed to say.

"My lord," she began, voice determinedly steady. "I do not know precisely what you expect of me, but I—"

"Nell." He lifted one large hand, brushed a fingertip quickly over her lips to silence her. "I know what you intend to say and I find I just do not have the stomach for it. I will go, but first give me this . . ." He tossed his hat onto the table. Then he drew her toward him, tilting her face toward his.

"Wait, I don't think you underst—"

"Be quiet," he growled, and kissed her.

Nell felt the spark all the way to her toes. His lips were hard, the kiss angry, she thought. But wonderful all the same. No one, she knew, had ever wanted her so much that he'd had to keep his passion tightly controlled. And St. Wulfstan was. She knew that, too. He could crush her with ease, could make her malleable by sheer force. But he didn't.

"My lord . . ." Nell shoved at his shoulders. "Please. Stop."

He released her abruptly and she wobbled for an unsteady moment before regaining her balance. Above her, his face was stone-hard, taut, his eyes dark and shuttered.

"Very well, madam." He stepped back, started to turn. "I do understand. I will leave you."

"Don't." Startled by her own boldness, Nell reached

out, clasped his clenched fist in both hands. "I need you to listen to me."

He remained half-turned away from her, his hand unyielding in hers. "Dammit, Nell, I told you. I am not in the mood for more of your excuses and explanations tonight."

"That's fine," she said softly. "I don't intend to offer you any."

"No? What, then?"

She took a deep breath. "I am offering myself."

"*What?*"

She released his hand, clasped both of hers tightly at her waist. "I am inviting you to stay with me tonight."

His eyes were narrowed as they studied her face. "Why?"

Why? She hadn't had time to answer that for herself. She had made up her mind only as they climbed the stairs to her door. *Why?* For the reasons Annie had given, Nell supposed. And because she had nothing to lose. Her reputation was long gone, her virginity even longer. Because she had made a devil's bargain.

"I believe in matters of honor," she said quietly, eyes lowered.

And I want this, she couldn't say aloud. *Oh, I want this.*

She gasped as he jerked her face up. There was fire in his eyes now. "Is that enough for you to do this, Nell?" he demanded harshly. "Honor?" She would have nodded had he not been gripping her jaw with iron force. Ultimately, it didn't matter. "Oh, to hell with that," he growled. "It's enough for me."

He released her face, grasped her by the waist, and lifted her until they were eye to eye. He kissed her again, quick and hard, then set her back on her feet. "Lead me, Mrs. Nolan."

Nell started up the stairs on shaky legs. She could feel St. Wulfstan close behind her, feel the heat and vitality emanating from him. He would fill her bedchamber, her bed. Her.

She was as terrified as she was eager.

Bang. The sound of the door knocker made her jump and nearly lose her footing. *Bang.* Heart pounding, she stopped and turned. St. Wulfstan, scowling, stomped down the stairs.

"Expecting a caller, Mrs. Nolan?" he demanded over his shoulder. "I told you I do not share."

"I am not . . ." She watched as he stalked toward the door. God help any man who stood there. Killone again? Young Lord William Paget? St. Wulfstan hauled the door open.

Nell had never seen the man who stood there. Large, handsome, he had the gold-tipped stick of a wealthy man and the hard bronze eyes of a lion.

"Oriel," St. Wulfstan said before the man could speak.

"I'm sorry, Wulf." There was a moment of hushed conversation, then, "If I could, I would . . ."

"I know." St. Wulfstan was already halfway up the stairs. "Nell. I have to go."

"I . . ." Something in his eyes told her not to ask questions beyond, "Will you come back?"

His grin flashed. "I dare anyone to try to stop me. But it won't be tonight."

"Ah." Nell nodded briskly. There was no use in being disappointed, certainly no reason to show that she was. "Fine, then. Another time."

He came to stand on the step just below hers. "You could slay a man with that indifference, Mrs. Nolan." Then he pressed his lips to hers, pulling back just as she leaned in. "Dream of me."

And he left, sweeping his hat from the table and closing the door behind him with a resounding thump. Nell lowered herself slowly to sit on the stairs. Her pulse was still going like thunder, her breath shallow. So close. So very close. She could change her mind now, could creep away after all to Ireland and avoid the risk of being singed by the very heat of this man. She could.

Her gaze settled on the flickering candle. Beside it on the table stood the little stone goddess.

CHAPTER 8

Trevor stalked over the carpet in Brooks's club, ignoring the surprised looks his presence generated. He had little use for the place, maintained his membership only for times like these, and to irk those members who would gladly have seen his privileges summarily revoked. But London's elite gentlemen's clubs were full of fools and reprobates. It took more than questionable character to have a man expelled.

The entertainment value of watching the Duke of Abergele's face grow apoplectically red as he passed aside, Trevor was in no mood to be there. But as a matter of fact, he was there to see the duke's son. When Oriel asked, Trevor appeared.

He found the marquess in a quiet corner, sitting firmly upright in a leather chair, untouched glass of wine at his elbow, eyes dark in inner contemplation. Trevor stopped a few feet away and studied the one person he knew he could call a friend. Oriel had suffered in the war: a badly damaged leg, impaired vision, and scars that Trevor knew no eye could see. But Oriel had done well on returning home, had found a wife and enviable peace, and now had a small son. If Trevor hadn't had a deep respect and equal if unwilling liking for the man, he might have hated him for his luck and his complacency in it.

"So tell me, Wulf, how do I look?"

Trevor growled as he dropped into the facing seat. "Do I smell?"

"No. And what does that have to do with how I look?"

"All about you, is it?" Trevor gave a resigned sigh and wry smile. "It simply makes me doubt my skills at skulking if I cannot sneak up on a blind man."

"You approached with all the stealth of a raging bull." Oriel gestured to the bottle and empty glass near his. "Help yourself." Then he efficiently cut to the core of the reason for their meeting. "I assume it went well."

"Well enough." Trevor didn't want to discuss the details of the night before. And he knew Oriel wouldn't expect him to. He poured himself some wine, stared into its ruby depths. "One more link gone from Bonaparte's chain."

Oriel nodded. "Thank you. His Majesty thanks you."

Trevor grunted. "His Majesty wouldn't know a matter of importance if it bit him on the arse." Then, "Don't thank me. It's what I do."

"Ah, Wulf. Fine. Allow me to apologize, then, for dragging you from Mrs. Nolan's bed."

"You didn't."

"But—"

"You interrupted me on my way into Mrs. Nolan's bed, as it happens."

"Even worse, I am afraid."

Oh, yes. Much worse. Had he been dragged from Nell's bed, sated and lazy from lovemaking, Trevor thought it might not have been so bad to be thrust out into the night with a knife cold where it was tucked into his waistband and a grim task heavy on his mind.

"You can always say no," Oriel said quietly.

Trevor shrugged. "Someday I will. Soon, perhaps. There is still one of the Roach's contacts out there. You'll ferret him out and I might not be here to see to the rest. I am going to Ireland."

Oriel looked as surprised as if Trevor had announced his intention to make a pilgrimage to Jerusalem. "Are you serious?"

"Deadly, as it happens. I need to visit the Tombs."

More than one Viscount St. Wulfstan had tried to change the name of the estate. But the ancient burial mounds had been on the land thousands of years before the first Robard, and would be there long after the last had gone to his own grave. Local residents had smirked at efforts to rename the towering stone house. It was the Tombs and the Tombs it would remain. So the name stood fast and, for his part, Trevor found it highly appropriate.

"I can't ignore it any longer," he said. "The place is crumbling and my tenants are ready to burn what hasn't already fallen."

"Yes, well, it can be difficult to manage an estate from across a sea," Oriel remarked. Then, "Wulf, you know you only have to ask—"

"No," Trevor said more sharply than he knew was warranted. The offers to lend him money were made with all the discretion and goodwill of friendship but they still pricked at his pride. If he could have kept the knowledge of his distressed finances from Oriel, he would gladly have done so, but the man's ability to ferret out information went well beyond his work with the War Department. "No. Thank you."

Oriel nodded. "I understand. Well, a length of time at home might do you good." Trevor saw no reason to correct him on either count. It wasn't home and he couldn't see what good could possibly come of visiting, but that was neither here nor there. "When will you leave?"

"Within the fortnight. Unless you know you will have need of me."

"Go. You've done more than enough here."

Trevor drained his glass and rose slowly to his feet. God, he was tired. He wanted to go to bed. With Nell Nolan. And not get out again until he'd spent himself thoroughly, slept like the dead for a while, and spent himself again.

"Come for dinner tonight," Oriel offered.

"Why?"

"Perhaps because we would like the pleasure of your company?" When Trevor snorted, his friend continued, "Isobel's family has descended on us."

"And that is meant to be appealing incentive?"

"They are lively. You are too much alone."

"Well, thank you for that paternal insight." Trevor returned the disapproving scowl of a doddering old gentleman across the room. "I do not intend to be alone tonight."

"I was thinking of company better than that of a whore—"

"You will not refer to Mrs. Nolan as a whore." Trevor's voice was low and cold.

"Wulf, she is—"

"You will not."

Oriel was silent for a long moment. Then he dipped his head in acknowledgment. "I apologize. That was careless and uncivil of me. But the invitation stands."

"I'll keep that in mind. You found Mrs. Nolan's direction last night; you know where I will be should I be . . . needed." Trevor turned to go. "By the way, you look like hell."

He headed for the door, Oriel's words echoing in his ears. *Better than a whore . . . a whore . . .* Whoever, whatever Nell was, he knew, it was far better than a simple whore, even as he reminded himself that she was, in fact, a courtesan, a woman paid for pleasuring men. He hadn't paid her. Yet. And there was no escaping the truth that his past was every bit as dirty as hers. He knew what he'd become. If that didn't bother him, and of course it didn't, there was no reason to think Nell's past bothered her.

He wondered if Nell was indeed ever tormented by her choices.

Just inside the door, two figures were handing their hats to a footman. Too late, Trevor recognized them. Carmody turned, spied him, and gave an unpleasant smile.

"St. Wulfstan. I wouldn't expect to see you here."

"And you, Carmody," Trevor replied, his own smile bland, "become more and more like your sire every day."

Indolent, stupid, useless.

Carmody's companion turned then. "Speaking of sires, I confess I have been most curious on a matter. Did mine leave a comfortable bed?"

Trevor's expression didn't falter. The new Duke of Clonegal was even more of a waste of good tailoring than Carmody. He wasn't stupid, which made his lazy uselessness worse. But then, Trevor mused silently, perhaps Clonegal wasn't so intelligent after all. A truly intelligent fellow wouldn't bait someone who was a few years older, a good two stone heavier, and who knew nine ways to kill a man with nothing more than his bare hands.

"It's tearing at you, isn't it, Clonegal?" he murmured. "That curiosity. Did you think she came with the title, part and parcel of the ducal holdings? But you are hardly your father, sir. How unpleasant it must have been to have her refuse you. I would offer my platitudes, but you see, I have absolutely no idea how it feels."

He gracefully shouldered his way past a red-faced Carmody. One of the club's ubiquitous footmen was already waiting with his hat and stick. "If you gentlemen would excuse me, I find myself most weary. I believe I will go to bed."

"St. Wulfstan."

He spared Clonegal a glance as he fished in his pocket for a few coins. "Yes?"

"Don't make yourself too comfortable."

"Ah, advice." He handed the footman a shilling. Then he flipped a penny to the duke, who caught it with a reflexive jerk. "Worth precisely what one pays for it. Good day, sirs."

He whistled as he stepped into the street, but it was through clenched teeth.

Nell had always loved Piccadilly. The broad street, with its lively, colorful traffic and shiny storefronts, was the best of London. Cheerful young men flowed in and out of their apartments at the Albany on their way to their clubs or Lock's. One, clearly no more than eighteen, emerged from the hatter's as Nell passed, youthful face aglow with the joy of his first purchase from the elite establishment. A peer's son down from university, Nell speculated, or fresh from a country estate. In a few years he would probably be a bored, overdressed dandy or worse, a complete rake like those who leered at any woman bold or careless enough to stand in front of a gentleman's bastion like Lock's. Nell had had her share of leers as she made her way along the street. But this young man gave her a clear, charming smile as he stepped back to let her pass.

Ladies did most of their shopping elsewhere, in Oxford Street or Leicester Square where many of the better dressmakers and milliners were to be found. There was little for a woman in lively, palpably masculine Piccadilly. There was Hatchard's, the marvelous booksellers, where Nell had frequently come to pick up this slender volume of poetry or that new collection of critical essays for the duke. She had enjoyed those visits, appreciated the rich wood paneling, towering shelves, and appealing smell of fresh paper and leather.

She had been even happier sitting quietly in St. James's, Christopher Wren's gem of a church nearby. Clonegal had tried to tell her about the stylistic grandeur of the galleries, the mathematical precision of the colonnades, but what Nell appreciated was the simple coziness of this pretty little church. She always made a point of stopping there, especially now, for a few minutes of prayer and thanks for the kindness of one generous and wholly decent man.

She'd strolled in Green Park earlier with Annie, then visited St. James's to light a candle for the duke. Then she'd sat and tried not to ask for guidance. Not when the path she'd very nearly taken was so impious. And her mind was still far from resolved on the matter. So she'd sat and tried not to think of St. Wulfstan, of his hands and lips and cobalt eyes, at all. In the end, she'd crept almost guiltily from the church.

Now she was on her way to her favorite shop in the street. She tucked the paper-wrapped parcel Annie had given her under her arm and pushed open the door to Berry's. She paused for a moment to breathe in the medley of wonderful aromas—clove and tobacco, rich coffee, and Nell's purpose there: tea. Quietly thrilled with anticipation, she surveyed the row upon row of painted tin cannisters and decorated jars. She would buy orange pekoe and some smoky souchong. Perhaps some coffee, too, just to have it in the house.

The place was not busy; there were maybe a half dozen gentlemen present, one settled happily on a set of massive scales, having his weight measured. All turned to watch as Nell crossed the floor. She paid them no mind. She knew it was bold for a lady to shop there alone, knew, too, that in doing so, she was declaring herself unconcerned with her reputation. True enough. She was.

A flustered-looking young clerk hurried to assist her. She gave him her list calmly, taking pleasure in the words: *pekoe, souchong*. She added *assam* just for the enjoyment of saying the word. Tea was perhaps her greatest indulgence. Long gone were the days when all she could afford was common bohea or green leaves.

She'd chosen her coffee and was debating indulging in cinnamon bark when she felt a presence at her elbow. She turned to find a man standing there. He was not familiar. And he was just distinctive enough that she knew she would have remembered him, if only because of his head of tousled red hair. He was tall and lean, pleasant of face without being overly handsome. He was clearly a member of the *ton*. Ginger hair aside, he looked like any number of wealthy, idle gentlemen who lounged their way through the London Season doing small mischief and no real good.

Nell drew herself to her own full height and steeled herself for the encounter she was certain would come. In the past weeks, she had lost the blessed anonymity of her days with Clonegal. Now it seemed that nearly wherever she went, some man recognized the elusive Mrs. Nolan and felt the need to speak to her. Some pleaded for an audience. A few of the comments were flattering. More were lewd.

"Mrs. Nolan," this one said.

Nell sighed inwardly. "Do I know you, sir?"

To her surprise, he appeared slightly abashed. "You do not," he replied, gripping his expensive felt hat between his fists. "And I apologize for being so forward as to approach you in this manner."

Behind him, there was a low whistle, followed immediately by another, louder. "Well, forge on, man!" the fellow on the scales encouraged. Another called, "Don't think you can afford the goods, sir!"

The clerk handed over her purchases just then, and Nell turned to leave. Her precious foray into Berry's had been spoiled and she scolded herself for not having expected it, not having known better. She felt the faint prick of tears behind her eyes and was determined to be well away from the place before a single one fell.

The gentleman reached for the parcel. "Please, Mrs. Nolan. Allow me."

Nell was ready to snap at him, or to simply shrug him off and hurry out the door. Then she remembered who she was. *I am Mrs. Nolan. A woman of the world.* She lifted her chin and gave her best cool smile. "Thank you."

The whistles and wolf calls followed them out the door. Once in the street, Nell promptly reached for her purchases. The man did not relinquish them. "Please," he said again. Then, "Grace me with a moment of your time."

Nell had a very good idea that he would ask her for more grace and more time after that. But she was deft enough at discouraging unwanted attention—with a fireplace poker if necessary. So she waited, a falsely unconcerned smile on her face, foot tapping against the ground.

"Allow me to be so bold as to introduce myself. I am Killone."

"Ah." Nell nodded. "You are very persistent, sir."

"I expect that is the Irish in me." He gave her what might have been a winning smile had she not been thinking that he probably had as much Irish in him as the China tea in his hands. "I have lands in County Clare and used to summer in Bray."

So did a great many of the Anglo-Irish gentry. Nell offered a bland, "How nice. Have you been calling on me in order to discuss Ireland, sir? Or do you believe a shared tie to a country will improve your chances?"

"My chances?" He blinked at her. "I . . . oh. I believe you mistake my intentions, Mrs. Nolan."

"Do I?"

"Well." Killone cleared his throat. "I would, of course, be honored to have a deeper acquaintance with you, and am certainly at your disposal should you—"

"You do not know me," Nell interrupted sharply. She'd had enough. "I do not know you. And I am not presently looking for the sort of deeper acquaintance to which you refer."

"I understand. Best turn to the other matter, then."

"And that is?"

"Quite simple, really. I believe I knew your father."

Nell felt the blood rushing to her head, heard the sealike roar of it in her ears. She was weak-kneed, suddenly, and cold. Sheer force of will kept her steady on her feet. "I . . . I beg your pardon?"

"I have spent a good deal of time in and near

Dublin, Mrs. Nolan. I believe I had the pleasure of meeting your father there."

Nell swallowed. *How could he know? And why in God's name would he care?* She pressed her nails into the palm of her hand and felt the chill subside. "I suppose that is possible, sir. I could not say."

"Yes, well, that is why I called on you in the first place. I hoped we could discuss the matter and you could put my curiosity to rest."

"No." Nell glanced around, looking desperately for a hack. In a perverse twist of fate, there did not seem to be a single one in Piccadilly. "No, I do not think so. I—" She stepped away, gasping when she felt a hand at the small of her back.

She spun. In that instant, for that instant, she felt a relief and safety that rocked her. St. Wulfstan stood there. He was in his customary dark colors, wearing his familiar dark expression. To Nell's eyes, he was dazzling.

"Good afternoon, Mrs. Nolan," he said. He did not smile, but Nell was close enough to see the spark in his eyes.

"Good afternoon, my lord." She blinked and nearly sighed when he dropped his hand from her back.

"Killone." His attention was on the other man now, his mouth hard.

"St. Wulfstan. I was just speaking to Mrs. Nolan about—"

"I can imagine. You are wasting your time."

As Nell watched, Killone seemed to lose some of his diffidence. "Your certainty is impressive, but then, it always was."

St. Wulfstan gave a thin smile. "We have known each other a long time, haven't we? What would you say? Twenty years?"

"More, probably. We move in small circles."

"So we do. And you should well know that I have a temper."

"Actually," Killone murmured, "if memory serves, you were a perfectly cheerful boy."

"I grew up," St. Wulfstan said harshly. "Now certain things make me quite angry. Seeing another man making an attempt to take something that is mine happens to be one of them."

Nell heard the words, heard the arrogant possession in his voice. She would have been annoyed, but was far more intent on his anger. He was warning the other man off, to be sure, but there was something defensive in his mien. Something Nell had a feeling she would not understand.

Killone's ginger brows went up. "I don't suppose it would serve much purpose to tell you that all of this is unnecessary. Nor to suggest that after twenty-odd years of acquaintance, you do not know me half so well as you think." He shrugged. "No matter. I will say, though, that this little display was most interesting." He turned to Nell. "I hope you will not take offense, madam, when I say that you have made peculiar choices."

"I—" Nell began.

"Am I being too subtle?" St. Wulfstan demanded. "If I were to say *stay away from her if you value your freckled hide*, would that be too subtle as well?"

Killone flushed slightly, obliterating those faint freckles that did pepper his cheeks and brow. "Someday you might regret saying such things to me."

"Unlikely," St. Wulfstan muttered.

A carriage rolled up to the curb, then. Thinking it might be a hackney, and more than ready to be away from this unpleasant scene, Nell turned toward it. It wasn't a hack at all, but a small town coach with an ornate coat of arms painted on the side. As Nell watched, the near window came down and an older woman's face appeared. Beneath fading blond hair it wasn't a pretty visage, and the scowl that appeared at the sight of St. Wulfstan did not improve the picture.

"What *are* you doing, Killone?" the lady demanded. "We are expected at Lady Castlereagh's for tea. I do not wish to keep her waiting."

"Of course not, Mother." Killone's expression was wry as he handed Nell her parcel. "Good day, Mrs. Nolan. I trust we shall meet again."

There was a hiss from inside the carriage. The lady, Nell noted, had not looked at her at all. In fact, she had very deliberately averted her pinched face. It didn't matter. Nell would gladly let the matter pass. She didn't expect anything but the cut direct from the Society ladies whose paths she occasionally crossed. She didn't want their acknowledgment.

Had she known what St. Wulfstan intended, she would certainly have stopped him. But by the time he spoke, it was too late.

"A good day to you, Lady Killone," he was saying, an audible and insolent West County brogue slipping into his voice. "Off to see Lady Castlereagh, are you? Give her my best, so, from a humble member of the Irish contingent."

Lady Killone's thin lips were pressed tightly together. It appeared she was not going to respond. When she finally did, it was with a clipped, "I am not your messenger, St. Wulfstan."

"Ah, well," was his blithe reply, " 'Tis Lady Castlereagh's loss, then."

He sketched a brief bow. It was abundantly clear that Lady Killone wanted nothing to do with him.

Nell thought he was going to leave the encounter at that. Even knowing him as little as she did, she realized she should have known better. Casually goading this pinch-faced matron was impertinent. What he did next was outrageous.

"I don't believe you ladies have met," he announced, stepping aside so Nell was in full view of the carriage. Beside them, Killone took an audible breath. Lady Killone's jaw dropped. "My lady, allow me to introduce Mrs. Nolan, another fair denizen of Ireland. Mrs. Nolan, Lady Killone."

The matron's mouth opened and closed silently. Her face, merely sallow moments before, was now a brilliant crimson. For the longest moment, no one said anything at all. Then the lady let out a strangled, *"Killone!"*

Her son leapt into action. He dragged open the carriage door and climbed inside. Before he had even settled himself in his seat, his mother rapped her parasol against the roof and the vehicle rolled away.

St. Wulfstan turned to face Nell, scarred brow lifted in an insolent arc, a smug smile on his face. He was clearly waiting for her to respond. She had a very good idea that he expected a smile in return, if not outright praise.

She waited until she was certain her voice would be steady. Then, "I cannot believe you did that."

"Neither can she," was the self-satisfied reply.

Nell felt the twine binding her Berry's package digging into her clenched fingers. "How *dare* you? How *could* you?"

His smirk faded. "How could I what? I just put that insufferable old harpy in her place."

"You did no such thing." The heat of anger rose

and roiled in Nell's stomach. "You slapped me into mine!"

"What in the devil is wrong with you, Nell? You are being ridiculous."

"Am I? Objecting to being treated like a . . . a . . ." She couldn't bring herself to say the horrible word that pounded in her head. ". . . a common doxy?"

His eyes narrowed above her. "What I did was introduce you to a member of the *ton*. You are complaining because I treated you like a lady? Would you rather I treated you like a . . . what was it? Common doxy?"

"How stupid, how naive do you think I am?" She felt the tears again, behind the fury.

"What sort of question is that?" he demanded, his own annoyance showing. "You are far from stupid, Nell. And as for being naive, I have yet in my life to meet a naive . . ."

He broke off. Nell finished for him. "Whore?" she said, very quietly. Then, "You made no introduction. You very deliberately insulted a woman you do not like by forcing her to acknowledge—no, simply *look at* your whore. You knew precisely how she would respond, and you got precisely what you wanted. Even better as far as you are concerned, you insulted Killone as well without having to exert yourself by saying another word to him."

St. Wulfstan jerked off his hat and ran a hand roughly through his hair. "Oh, for Christ's sake, Nell—"

"I am not your whore. I am no man's whore. You think you can treat me as you like—demand my presence, my company, then disappear without so much as a word of explanation . . ." She realized she had strayed from the matter at hand and was allowing feelings about the night before to show. Feelings she hadn't even been aware she possessed.

She shook her head angrily. "I don't think you meant to insult me just now with that godawful display; that was simply your carelessness. Nor do I think you intended to hurt me. But you did, and that is unforgivable. I have no idea what is between you and Killone, but I will not be a part of it. And I will not be used."

She gave a soft cry when he grasped her by both shoulders. Her parcels thudded to the ground. She felt his wrath through his hands, knew he could break her so easily if he chose. Above her, his face was dark, the angry grooves beside his mouth deep enough to look painful. His scar stood out, ugly and livid.

"Hear me well, Nell," he growled. "You would be wise to think twice before accusing *me* of using *you*. I always intended to give every bit as much as I received. As for last night, I regret that. More, no doubt, than I should. But I have responsibilities, and beyond that, I have no need to answer to you for my behavior. Any of it."

He tightened his grip, lifted her until she was standing on her toes, the buttons of her spencer brushing against his chest. She could feel the raging heat of him through the fabric. "Let's be done with this, Mrs. Nolan. Give me what I am owed and we can go our own ways. I will find my next *lady*; you will be free to move on to your next gentleman." He lowered his face until Nell could see how very deep the fire in his eyes went. "Tonight, Nell. We can finish it all tonight."

Nell's anger was no match for the hurt. It swelled and twisted within her, making her catch her breath. She breathed in painfully, then again, deeper. "Let go of me," she said dully. He did, as if she had suddenly burned his hands. "I will not be home if you come."

Through the thin glaze of tears, she saw a heaven-sent hackney depositing its passenger at Lock's. She clumsily gathered up her belongings and waved to attract the attention of the driver. She didn't look back as she left.

CHAPTER 9

Trevor was drunk. He'd been drunk for the better part of the last twenty-four hours. In fact, he had very few memories of the previous night. But as he had awakened in his battered wing chair in his own cold library, morning light filtering through the windows and an empty scotch bottle wedged uncomfortably against his hip, he assumed he hadn't done anything which he needed to remember.

He had sobered up just long enough to gather the formidable collection of papers relating to his estate and spread them over his desk. The resulting headache, not helped by the night's overindulgence, had driven him to open another bottle. The state of his finances and the Tombs had him refilling that first glass. The fact that Nell's face kept imposing itself on his papers eventually sent him staggering out of the house and into a hack, bottle in hand.

He had ended up at the Red Hollow in Tavistock Street, a gaming hall he had frequented for years. It had once been dirty, dangerous, and filled with an equally dirty and dangerous clientele. It had been discovered by cleaner, wealthier men, and had spent a dismal year as a ridiculously fashionable spot. Now, much to Trevor's approval, many of the gentlemen had departed and a few of the original characters had returned. The combination suited him perfectly; there was plenty of money to be won and not an overabundance of fellow former Etonians.

Trevor was drunk, but not very drunk. In the hour he'd passed at the Hollow, he had forgone whiskey in favor of the watered-down plonk the proprietor passed off as wine. Among the few matters he took seriously, gaming was near the top of the list. He didn't gamble for entertainment; he did it purely for the money. A reasonably clear head was necessary if he was to win. And win he did. There was a tidy pile of coins and bills in front of him, more tucked into his pocket. He estimated that he had taken nearly a hundred pounds from his first opponent, the careless son of a rich baronet. The man wouldn't miss it. To Trevor, it was a much-needed gift from somewhat south of heaven.

His current opponent was an equally rich but far less complacent merchant whose wares were uncertain and quite probably illicit. He had lost fifty pounds to Trevor, and judging from the narrowed eyes and tight mouth, was becoming unhappy with his luck. Trevor was as smart about playing his opponents as he was the cards. For the next quarter hour, he was careful to lose just enough hands to keep the man satisfied while still coming out another thirty-odd pounds ahead. With the fellow aristocrats he didn't bother, but with the rougher opponents it was wise to keep from appearing too successful. Otherwise, one might leave the establishment only to end up in a nearby alley with a knife in the ribs and empty pockets.

Trevor didn't think this one would take another lost hand well. So, after deliberately surrendering ten precious quid, he sat back in his chair with a rueful smile, and announced, "I fear my luck is changing. Time for me to take a few quiet minutes with Monsieur Burgundy." He tapped the half-full carafe.

His opponent stared from him to the wine with an expression that was less shrewd than greedy, then nodded. "As you wish. Perhaps we'll have another round later."

"Perhaps." And perhaps they would. Clearly the man thought he would stand a good chance of winning back all of his money and more once Trevor finished the bottle. Not bloody likely. "Now, I will leave you the table . . ."

Trevor wobbled a bit as he pushed back his chair and stood. Better to appear more cup-shot than he was to whoever was watching. And someone was watching; he could feel it. Let them think him drunk. He would take any advantage he could get. He tucked away his gains, grabbed glass and bottle, and wandered into the smoky depths of the hall. There was a trio of loud, gaudily dressed dandies at a far table. Sheep for the fleecing. They were playing commerce, one of Trevor's specialties. He was tired of *vingt-et-un*. A change would be pleasant and very probably profitable.

He was halfway there when raised voices nearby caught his attention. One was woefully familiar.

"Are you saying my word, my marker is not good enough?" the voice was saying, more desperate than offended.

"I don't take markers from toffs," came the guttural reply. "Ain't worth the trouble of trying to collect. Your sort scarpers rather'n paying up. I'll have my money here and now."

"But I . . . But I don't have . . . Here now, that isn't necessary . . ."

Trevor saw the glint of a blade as he wearily changed directions and headed for the table. He could knock the knife and the arm holding it halfway across the room with a single kick. But he had a feeling there were more weapons at the ready. He wasn't in the market for more scars. The unfortunate loser didn't have any and Trevor had a feeling the man's mother would blame him should her son acquire one. The Duchess of Abergele had a low enough opinion of the Viscount St. Wulfstan as it was.

"Good evening, gentlemen," he said smoothly as he reached the table. "Will."

The relief on young Paget's ash-pale face was palpable. "Wulf. Thank God."

Trevor quirked a brow. "Correct sentiment. Wrong recipient."

William gave a convulsive swallow as his eyes darted between Trevor and the hulking, glowering tough standing across from him. The knife had disappeared for the moment, but the fellow was big as an ox, looked like a troll, and appeared angry enough to squash the younger man with the tabletop.

"Perhaps you could explain to this gentleman that I am worth every penny," Paget pleaded. "If he would but take my marker—"

The behemoth's growl was enough to frighten William into silence. There was a scuffling of chair legs and feet and suddenly two more trolls were looming behind the first. One was actually paring his thumbnail with a vicious little stiletto. Trevor sighed.

"How much does he owe?" he asked.

"Seventy-two quid, six shillings," was the response. The brute was eyeing Trevor with the same mixture of distaste and respect he was receiving. Like knew like, Trevor mused with irony, when it came to violence.

"How much do you have?" he demanded of Paget.

"S-seventeen pounds." The young man poked a shaky fingertip among the coins he had taken from his pockets. "Three shillings, a sixpence, four pence . . . and two half-pence."

"The devil take it, William!" Trevor snapped. "What on earth were you thinking, gaming with little more than lint in your pockets?"

Young Paget wilted further under this scolding. "I didn't . . . my marker . . ."

"Isn't worth the paper you would write it on at this moment." Scowling, seeing a few sumptuous meals and a new pair of boots vanishing in his mind, Trevor dragged a handful of banknotes from his pocket. He grimly separated fifty-five pounds, then dug in his waistcoat pocket for a guinea. "Your money, sir." The troll took it with a grunt. "Come along, William."

Paget didn't move. He was staring in pale misery at the scattering of copper coins left on the table.

"*William!*" Trevor got a grip on the back of the younger man's coat collar and hauled him up from his seat. "Move."

"But my friends . . ."

Were nowhere to be seen, whoever they were. No doubt they were there somewhere, having taken themselves safely out of harm's way. Trevor's mouth thinned. He let go of Will's collar and merely prodded him in the back as they wove their way between the tables on their way to the door. He would gladly have given the young idiot a good kick on the arse with each step, but decided to spare some of the fellow's pride. Bad enough to have to be rescued, far worse to be frog-marched out the door.

However, Trevor was furious, both at the loss of the money and at William's foolishness. He snapped, "I would dearly love to knock some sense into you here and now, but I am certain your father would shoot me for having done it first."

"Oh, God," Paget moaned, missing the bottom step and stumbling as they climbed toward the door. "My father. He will have my head. I'll have to ask him for the money. I haven't fifty pounds until next month."

"What a bloody shame," Trevor muttered with no sympathy whatsoever.

As Will leaned miserably against the banister, only halfheartedly trying to get his right arm into his left coat sleeve, Trevor took the opportunity to turn back and scan the cavernous room. He'd felt eyes on him for several minutes. He was curious as to who was so very interested in his movements.

More than a few gazes slid away under his perusal: the trolls', the baronet's son, a few more disapproving members of the *ton*. Nothing out of the ordinary. A movement in a far, smoky corner caught his attention. All he could make out was a turning back in what appeared to be an expensive coat. The man's companions weren't clearly visible, either. Shrugging, Trevor looked back to where Will, now decidedly green of face, was struggling with his hat. One quick shove had the younger man up the stairs. The glowering behemoth of a doorman already had the door open. He pulled it shut after them with a heavy *thunk* before Trevor could announce that he wasn't leaving.

Will staggered a few feet, then rested his forehead against a convenient brick wall. "I believe I am going to be ill," he said with impressive clarity.

"Fine. Mind your shoes."

Trevor walked a few feet away to wait. The street was dark despite the moonlight and deserted, a scattering of sounds drifting down from nearby Covent

Garden. A man's laugh carried faintly, followed by a feminine one. Trevor imagined the pair heading toward an alley or dingy room, streetwalker and her customer, deal made. A man could buy whatever sort of pleasure he fancied in Covent Garden. Trevor knew it would be but a matter of a short walk and a few shillings to tend to the persistent ache in his loins. But it was Nell and Nell alone that he wanted, curse her soft hide. Considering how they had parted the day before, it was more likely that hell would freeze over than that he would get his satisfaction there.

He hadn't wanted to contemplate the finality of that awful encounter. Now he had to. Her anger had been too fierce, her eyes too cold. They'd had their chance; they'd lost it. And for what? Some carelessness on his part, deliberate misunderstanding on hers.

"Damn you, Nell," he hissed into the shadows. "Damn us both."

He'd grown so good at not allowing himself to *want*—to want something so simple as the welcome of a woman's sincere smile and open arms. He'd had fifteen years to hone his indifference. But now, as he remembered her small hands gripping his fist the night before, keeping him from walking out her door and away from her, the indifference wasn't there. He couldn't quell the bittersweet conviction that Nell Nolan might have banished some of the chill that, hard as he tried to deny it, had gripped him for nearly half his life.

He ran a hand that wasn't quite steady over his brow. "Oh, Nell."

He turned at the sound of shuffling steps. Apparently Paget's stomach was stronger than his brain. The fellow hadn't been sick, and was rejoining his grim

rescuer. "Thank you, Wulf," he offered. Trevor grunted.
"I will repay you, you know."

"Yes, you will."

"When I can . . ." Paget scuffed a foot against the
cobblestones. "I don't understand how it happened. I
was winning."

"Of course you were," Trevor muttered.

"Up a tenner, then twenty, then fifty . . ."

"Of course you were."

"And then, all of a sudden, the fellow started
having the devil's own luck."

"Of course he did." Trevor knew the game well.
He'd played it himself countless times. He didn't want
to hear about it now. He hadn't had time to don his coat
before leaving the Hollow. He pulled it and his walking
stick from where he'd tucked them under his arm.
"You'll pay me when you can—"

"I will ask my father tomorrow."

"There's no need for that." Trevor knew the Duke
of Abergele, knew his temper was every bit as fierce as
his love for his children. The money would send him
into red-faced sputtering. The knowledge that his
younger son had been gaming with amoral, lethal ruffians in the Red Hollow would give him a fit of the
heart. "Next month is fine, or the one after."

"Thank—"

"Don't," he interrupted harshly. "You did an idi-
otic thing, Will. I won't be there next time."

He couldn't see the younger man's face in the darkness, but imagined it was now flushed a dull red. "No
need to rub my nose in it, you know."

Yes, there was. Trevor remembered just enough of
his more innocent days to know that a young man felt
untouchable, invincible. At Will's age, he'd already

had a good half dozen debauched years. But before that, he'd been just as blithe, just as careless.

A hackney bounced down the street and stopped in front of the Hollow. When its passengers had descended, Trevor all but shoved Will inside. He dug in his pocket for another precious guinea and shoved it into Will's hand. Then he slammed the door closed on the unwanted thanks, gave the driver the Abergele direction, and watched as the vehicle rattled off.

For the first time, he noticed that the moon was full that night. He stifled the powerful urge to howl at it.

Muttering vague invectives, he thrust one arm into his coat sleeve and headed down Tavistock Street toward Mayfair. He didn't relish the mile walk home, but he didn't want to part with another penny and knew the night air would do him good. He could have gone back into the Hollow, he supposed, and found another game. But he knew his edge was gone. Better to quit while he still had a decent sum in his pocket.

The blow came from nowhere. Perhaps had he been contemplating anything other than his cursed poverty, he might have avoided the first strike between his shoulder blades. As it was, his cheek was bouncing off the cold brick of the closest wall, a cut opening in his chin, before he even realized he was being attacked.

A second blow struck in the same spot as the first, hard enough to make his knees buckle briefly, not powerful enough to make him fall. He smelled dank odors of the docks wafting from his attackers' clothing. From the corner of his eye he saw at least two figures, one whose arm was lifting to strike yet again. A guttural command turned into a pained grunt as he struck out with his own foot.

The excessive amount of rotgut he'd consumed over the past twenty-four hours was not helping his speed

or balance. But the training and covert activity of
so many years was as much a part of him as his
name. Working on instinct, he kicked again, this
time making contact with one assailant's knee. Even
as the man was falling back, Trevor spun about and,
with a sweeping uppercut, sent him thudding onto the
cobblestones.

Something unyielding, a sap or iron bar, glanced off
his shoulder. He slammed into the wall again, saw
stars behind his eyes, and felt the recent wound at his
temple reopen. His second arm and walking stick
were tangled in the folds of his greatcoat. Cursing
himself for not having fastened the bloody thing properly, he spun away, struggled to set himself to rights,
and sized up the remaining attackers. Only two, he
thought, and well practiced, as they shifted around
him, dark as the shadows. He thought he saw the dull
glint of steel. At least one more figure remained motionless and cloaked in the shadows.

One-armed still, he came away from the wall,
kicked out, and felt flesh give. A second man went
down, clutching at his gut. The other lunged at the
same time. A right hook sent him stumbling back, but
the first was back upright and in Trevor's face in an instant, the sharp tip of a knife pressing just below his
chin. Trevor went very still.

"Say g'night, guv," a rasping voice commanded.

The man pulled the knife back slightly, shoved
Trevor backwards, toward the black maw of a tiny
alley—just as Trevor got his stick clear.

"I think not," he announced, and twisted the ornate
silver handle.

"Wha'?" The blackguard glanced down at the soft
snick, dropped his own hand as he spied the lethal

blade glinting from the base of the cane, poised perfectly between his legs. "Holy Mother o' . . ."

He windmilled backward, fighting for balance on the slick cobblestones. In that instant, Trevor had pulled his custom-constructed, fist-sized pistol from the depths of his coat pocket and cocked it. The two downed ruffians struggled to their feet. One stumbled away; the other took a brief, considering look at Trevor. Then he, too, vanished into the shadows of Tavistock Street.

Breath burning in his lungs, Trevor put his back to the wall again and trained the gun in the direction of the silent figure who had not participated in the attack. There was no sound, no movement. Then he heard the unmistakable clatter of heels against the cobblestones. Trevor knew that by the time he reached the end of the street, the man would be long gone.

His cuts weren't deep; years of experience had taught him to gauge such things easily. But they stung and he smelled the warm copper of his blood. His shoulder was numb, his head pounded, and there was a faint ringing in his ears. Other than that, he was right as rain. He retracted the blade of his sword-stick with a deft twist of his wrist.

Then, groaning quietly, hand to his head, he lowered himself onto the cold stones.

Nell sucked at a knuckle she'd scraped against the edge of a packing crate. She didn't plan to take much with her to Dublin, but she couldn't bear to leave the cheery blue-and-white Wedgwood china on which she and the duke had had so many pleasant meals. That, her clothing, some books, and a handful of cherished knickknacks would come with her. The rest would stay. Perhaps she would come back to this house

someday; perhaps she would just leave it for good
with all that remained inside. There wasn't anything
for her in Town now. It was time to leave. Soon.

Annie seemed better. She hadn't said as much, but
Nell suspected there was a new gentleman in her life—
or, just as likely, an old flame from her past. There was
never a shortage of men at Annie's door or in her
parlor, some who had been faithful friends if not
lovers through the years.

Nell wished her friend all the happiness—and
pleasure—life could bring. She smiled, a bit sadly, as
she recalled the gift of the day before. It was an ornate
ebony box, delicately carved and inlaid with ivory. Inside rested a collection of small sponges and a bottle
containing a special vinegar-based liquid. It was, Annie
had said, an intelligent woman's key to the gates of
unencumbered pleasure. Such a poetic turn of phrase,
Nell thought, for such a practical matter. And an unintentionally saddening gift for a woman who had once
longed so poignantly for children that it had been a
physical ache. But there had been no baby for her and
Thomas, and she had long since accepted the fact that
there would never be one. The box, a necessity of the
courtesan's trade, made no difference there, but it had
been a reminder.

For less than an hour she had thought that she
might use it. That she might have need of it when St.
Wulfstan came to call. But a mere few minutes had
ended that possibility. Even now, a full day later, the
pain hit her sharply in the chest. His cavalier behavior
had made her angry. The fact that he hadn't understood what he'd done had hurt her—more deeply than
she could have imagined.

She had arrived home, chilled and then numb, and
tucked the box away in her dressing room. Tried to

tuck her feelings away with it. It hadn't worked. She still ached inside.

"Enough!" she hissed aloud, scolding herself and the pain, too, as if it were a live and malicious creature.

She'd known from the first meeting that St. Wulfstan was not a man to be taken lightly. In hindsight, clear as hindsight always was, she knew he was not a man to be taken at all. He was too cold, too careless. How could she have thought that she could share her body with someone so unconcerned with what was inside? She couldn't even bear to think how she had let him touch her emotions. As much as she had struggled to harden her soft heart over the years, it still could be touched by the right words, a gentle gesture. A night of fireworks and a little stone statue. The Venus stood next to her bed. It just seemed to belong there.

The standing clock in the hallway chimed eleven times. Nell placed the last carefully wrapped plate in the crate and rose to her feet. She wasn't tired, but knew that if she let herself, she would stay awake until dawn. Then she would be weary and sluggish all day. Not that she had anything planned other than more preparations to leave, but she hated feeling heavy and slow.

She tightened the belt of her dressing gown as she left the pantry. Macauley and the rest of the meager staff had long since retired, leaving the house quiet. Nell recalled one of the duke's beloved collections of classical mythology that she had not been able to bring herself to pack away yet. The rich, gold-embossed leather cover was worn smooth, and the pages smelled faintly of the cherry-scented tobacco he had favored. It would be a comfort just to hold the book. It might even dispel some of the pervasive loneliness. And the reading would occupy her mind. She would choose a tale—of war, she thought, rather than love or lust—and read until she could sleep.

She stopped in the library to fetch the book from its place on the shelf. Her eyes lit on the desk and the little leather pouch resting there. It was St. Wulfstan's, still holding the money he had taken from Routland. Nell had left it there. She hadn't felt right using the money, regardless of what Annie said. Now she thought she might donate it quietly to some charitable home for young women. One better, kinder than the one in which she had been raised. There must be one in a city the size of London. Annie would know. Nell would ask her.

She silently scolded herself again for becoming up-set at the sight of something so silly as a leather pouch. She had been disappointed—wounded—by men be-fore. This one wasn't the first and Nell couldn't change what had happened between them. She could, how-ever, work hard at keeping herself from being hurt again. The widow Mrs. Nolan who would soon settle in the west of Ireland would be a far different creature from the one leaving London. She would be incon-spicuous in all ways, proper and serene. She might even take up embroidering altar cloths for the local church. It hardly mattered that her stitches tended to resemble chicken scratchings. She would have all the time in the world to practice.

Nell located the book and left the library. She had just reached her bedchamber and closed the door be-hind her when the door knocker banged below. The sound was so unexpected, shattering the stillness of the silent house, that she dropped her book. It fell against the hard floor where the carpet ended and the spine broke. Nell gasped, heart thudding, startled into immobility. The knocker clacked again, hard and insistent.

She was able to move then, and struggled to reopen the door. By the time she'd gotten her fingers to cooperate and bent to gather up the broken book whose thick cover got stuck under the door, she heard Mac moving below. She hurried down the stairs and stopped him before he'd reached the stairs to the foyer. She winced at the sight of the ancient pistol in his hand. It had belonged to a long-ago Duke of Clonegal, a novelty the last duke had kept out of sentiment and the fact that he'd liked the way it looked against the paneling in the library. After he'd died, when Nell had been able to enter the library at all without weeping, she had tucked the gun away deep in the dining-room sideboard. She loathed guns, couldn't countenance deliberate violence.

"Put the gun away, Mac," Nell commanded. God only knew when he'd found the thing. And if he'd loaded it. Old pistols were notoriously unpredictable. She didn't want him blowing off his own toes.

"Now, ye stop right there, missy," he grunted at her, as she pushed past him.

She ignored him and hurried down the last flight of stairs. She had a very good idea who was waiting. And she was going to say a few terse words and close the door again smartly—before he could speak or Mac could try to shoot him.

The sight that greeted her had the hot words dying on her lips. St. Wulfstan stood on the stoop, illuminated by the light of a full moon. His coat was torn, there was blood on his cravat and face. But what had her pressing a hand hard against her own mouth was the expression in his eyes. Even in the moonlight, she could see the desperation. And the desolation.

"Nell," he said simply, voice low and ragged. "Please, Nell . . ."

She didn't pause for an instant. "Come in," she said softly, and held the door wide.

CHAPTER 10

Trevor followed her back up the stairs. Her butler waited at the top, scowling fiercely and holding a gun that looked more ancient than he was. Nell didn't stop. "Go back to bed, Mac," she said firmly. The fellow grunted something unintelligible, but obeyed.

Trevor expected her to stop at the parlor door. She didn't. Instead, she continued up another flight of stairs. Hope blooming faster than any of the bruises he knew he would sport in the morning, he stayed close behind her. Her sweet, subtle scent wafted down to him with each ripple of her soft white dressing gown. With her coronet of glossy hair, gold in the muted candlelight, and white gown, she was angelic, and for once he didn't mock himself for such a thought.

He followed her along the hall and through a doorway into what was obviously her bedchamber. His body tightened at the very sight of the tidy bed with its neatly turned sheets. In the next instant, he took in the simple pair of armchairs in front of the fire, the austere furnishings, the prim white of the bed hangings, and realized this was not the master bedchamber. This wasn't the room or the bed she would have shared with the duke. And Trevor wondered why she slept here now, if out of respect or the sadness of memory.

Then he saw the little Venus next to the bed. Something that didn't feel entirely like lust swelled within him.

"Nell—"

"Sit," she commanded, gesturing to the chairs. "Take off your coat. I'll be back." Then, in a waft of pale flannel and honey scent, she disappeared back out the door.

He took off his coat but didn't sit. Instead, he wandered around the room, taking in the little touches that were Nell. The pair of silver-backed brushes on the dressing table, handles carved in a delicate Celtic knotwork pattern. The small porcelain dish of hairpins beside them. The slender, much-worn book of Donne's poems on the table between the armchairs. There were no mementos that he could see, no portrait miniatures or silly little bits of jewelry.

The room was simple, practical, and so unexpectedly inviting that Trevor sighed with it. There was a vase of daisies on the windowsill, a sunny yellow wool throw tossed over the back of one chair. He lifted it to his face, smelled Nell in the soft folds. Then, realizing how filthy and battered his hands were, he reluctantly returned the throw to its place. There was neither water pitcher nor basin in sight, so he lowered himself into a chair to wait. He wasn't certain just why she had brought him there. Oh, he had his ideas and they were warm, delightful ones. He wanted desperately not to be wrong.

She came back a few minutes later, basin of steaming water in her hands, a cloth folded under her arm. He started to rise and she shook her head, keeping him in his seat. As he watched, tongue-tied suddenly, she set the basin and cloth on the little table, then came to stand between his bent knees. His pulse flared and he was certain she could see the unmistakable sign of his desire. If she did, she gave no indication. Instead, she dipped the cloth in the water and began gently to clean his face. He ignored the sting. In truth, he barely felt it.

"Should I ask?" she queried softly.

"Would you mind not?"

"No. I don't mind." She clucked her tongue at the worst of the cuts and scrapes. "How does the other fellow look?" she demanded, turning his hand in hers and surveying his abraded knuckles before plying the cloth there.

Trevor couldn't help it; he answered her gentle humor with a smile. "Worse."

"Good," she said, handing him the cloth to clean his other hand. "Now, if you'll excuse me again . . ." She disappeared through a door into what was probably her dressing room. She reappeared briefly, just a pale, serene face around the doorjamb. "There is brandy in the Chinese cabinet in the room down the hall. If you would fetch it . . . Take a candle from the mantel." Then she was gone again.

Curious, Trevor followed the direction of her vague wave and found himself in the master bedchamber. He lifted his candle, studied the very masculine decor. It was a man's room, an aristocrat's room, elegant and expensive, heavy with precious mahogany and dark silk. There wasn't a sign of Nell anywhere and Trevor couldn't imagine her there at all. Then, disgusted with his efforts to picture Nell in the bedchamber of another man—and grateful that she hadn't brought him here—he opened the lacquered cabinet and, as promised, located a bottle and two glasses.

He returned to find Nell seated neither on the bed nor a chair, but standing instead in front of the fire, facing the flames. He set the brandy on the table. She didn't turn. "Nell?"

"Why do you want me?"

He blinked, surprised. "I beg your pardon?"

"What is it about me, my lord? Is it the challenge? The fact that other men have tried and failed? Are you thumbing your nose at the Society who thinks ill of you? I have been trying for weeks now to understand you, and admit that I have been wholly thwarted."

"For God's sake, Nell—"

"I need to know." She turned from the fire then and faced him, face cool and composed but hands clasped tightly enough at her waist that he could see the whiteness of her knuckles. "I am not beautiful, nor even exotic. I am not accomplished or witty or terribly clever. So I need to know why you have pursued me."

Trevor felt indecision and rejection hovering in the air. She was ready to withdraw, to send him away in the next breath. There was no time to come up with the pretty, convincing words that always worked so well. So he said precisely what came into his head. "I don't know all of it, Nell. But I realized earlier that if tonight were my last on earth, there is nowhere I would rather be than with you."

"Oh," she said, and opened her arms.

He was across the room in an instant, telling himself to be gentle even as he crushed her to his chest. The wanting was too fierce for much gentleness. He heard her gasp, but didn't give her the chance to speak or even breathe in before he covered her mouth with his. Heat and hunger speared through him. He filled his hands with soft flannel, tugged, and felt her arms drop to let the dressing gown slide to the floor. Then she reached for him, twining her arms around his neck, her fingers in his hair.

"God, Nell," he murmured against her lips.

Through the thin muslin of her nightgown, he could feel the warmth of her skin and the gentle curve of her hips. He hauled her even closer, not caring that his arousal was pressing hard against her. It was delicious torture and she didn't seem to mind. She hummed low in her throat and held him more tightly.

Then he was lifting her, turning away from the fire. "I meant to go slowly," he growled, as much to himself as to her. She felt feather-light in his arms; the bed was only a few steps away. "I meant . . ."

"No," she whispered, pressing her face into the hollow of his shoulder. "No, this is as it should be."

And that was it. He crossed the room in three strides and laid her against the sheets as gently as he could manage. He waited only long enough to look, to take in the deep rose of her kiss-swollen mouth, the dark circles where her nipples showed through the white muslin. Then he was tugging at his own clothes, tearing a button from his waistcoat, another from his shirt in his haste. When at last he was naked, the last item joining the pile on the floor, he turned back to Nell.

She was propped on her elbows, eyes wide and stormy grey, fixed intently on his bare skin. His blood leapt in response and he hardened more, more than he thought possible. He knew what she was seeing: the battle-hardened muscles, the scars—and there were more than a few of them. But there was no revulsion in her expression. He saw some surprise but he saw heat, too, and he concentrated on that as a seaswept sailor would on blessed land in the distance.

He came down, half-atop her, bearing her back onto the sheets with his body. He braced one arm above her shoulder, used the other hand to draw her nightgown up. Her legs were warm and silken against his.

"My lord—"

"Trevor." He gave a pained smile when she stared at him blankly. "My name, Nell, is Trevor." He slid a knee between hers, opened her to him, shifted until he was between her thighs. His breath was shallow; he could feel every muscle straining, cording. She was all moist heat and honey scent. "Say it. Please."

"Trev—" was all she managed before he joined them with a single, sure thrust.

There was nothing gentle about the way he entered her, filled her, but Nell wanted nothing to do with gentleness. She wrapped her arms around his ribs and knew she was marking him with her nails. But she didn't care and knew he wouldn't either. She gasped as he thrust deeply, moaned as he withdrew and thrust again. Each stroke set a trail of sparks within her. Not knowing where the daring or the impulse came from, she dropped her hands from his back, clenched them on the hard muscles of his buttocks, and urged him to move faster.

"Yes," she panted. Sheer sensual instinct swept away all the years of celibacy and inexperience, urging and guiding her. Nell wrapped her legs around Trevor's hips, her breath coming in short, sharp pants that matched the rhythm of his thrusts.

She could never have imagined this, imagined the intense pleasure of speed and unrestrained power. When his hands closed over her breasts, hot and hard, her back arched. More. She wanted more. As if readng her mind, Trevor drew back, almost leaving her entirely, then surged forward, going so deep that she was convinced he was touching the very center of her.

"*Trevor!*" she cried, as sensations fierce as a tempest battered her.

Nell was no stranger to storms. She had been raised in Ireland, had been married to a sailor. She had known the pounding assault of sorrow and helplessness. But she had never known anything like the storm that swept through her now. Glorious and wrenching at the same time, she felt it stealing her breath, stealing every vestige of self-control she had built so carefully over the years. And all she could do was surrender to the violent wonder of it.

It wasn't until the last wave had subsided, leaving her trembling and tingling in its wake that she realized Trevor had gone completely still. She opened her eyes. His face was so close to hers that she could feel each short breath on her skin. His eyes were dark and fathomless, mouth unsmiling. It was a mask as hard and stunning as any from an ancient stonecarver's hand. Only the pulse beating visibly beside the scar and the lines bracketing his wide lips, deepened by strain, told her that he was struggling for control, had waited for her pleasure without grasping his.

She had no idea when she had stopped seeing the scar, but she saw it now. And she could only imagine how it felt, going through life with such a mark. Wordlessly, she reached up and cupped his hard jaw between her palms. She pulled his face down to hers and placed a single, soft kiss on the rigid line bisecting his brow.

There was a moment of utter silence. Then he

growled, a hard, harsh sound, and seized one of her hands. In that instant, she wondered if a gesture of tenderness had been a mistake, if she had crossed a forbidden line. Then he twined his fingers with hers, held on tightly as he gave a last, miraculously deep surge and spilled himself within her.

They lay motionless for countless minutes after, still joined. Eventually, Nell felt her pulse slow, heard his breathing grow even. His hair was damp and silk-soft against her brow. The rest of him was hard, even in relaxation. He was heavy, of course he was, but she wanted to protest when he pulled away to lie beside her, one arm under her head, the other thrown over the tousled sheets. Then he pulled her to him so her cheek rested on his chest, and she was content.

"That should have killed us."

"Hmm?" she murmured, breathing in the enticing scent of his heated skin.

"Not many people can go up in flames like that," he said gruffly, "and live to tell the tale."

Nell smiled against his chest. *"Is furasta deagadh ar aithinne fhorloiscthe."*

"What was that?"

"An old Wicklow proverb that says a smoldering ember is easily sparked." She glanced up at him. "This was burning well before tonight. For both of us."

His face was so intent, his long frame so still beside her. Then, so fast that it stole Nell's breath, he flipped her onto her back. He braced his elbows on either side of her shoulders and took his weight onto them. He covered but didn't crush her. When he grinned, Nell felt it to her toes.

"Come to Ireland with me."

"What?" She blinked at him, certain she hadn't heard correctly.

"To Connemara, to my estate there. Come with me."

"I . . . you are serious."

"Of course I'm serious. I need to leave within the sennight. I assume you can be ready."

Nell squirmed beneath him but he didn't budge. "I cannot simply pack up and go . . . back."

"Whyever not?" His splendid mouth curved. "You have already put half of this house into boxes and crates, haven't you?"

"Well . . . I . . ."

"Thinking to run from me. You really should have known better, my dear. Where were you going to run to, Nell?"

She debated lying, but had a feeling he would know. "Ireland."

"Home. And now you can, without being concerned that I was hot on your heels."

He was hot on her thighs, on her stomach. It banished some of the chill that the mention of *home* had brought. She shook her head. "I don't really think I can . . ."

"And I am not really asking," was his arrogant reply. "You'll come with me, Nell. I need you."

"Oh," she said, and knew in that instant that she would swim to Ireland if he asked it of her.

"I need someone with me who knows the culture."

She came back to earth with a sad little thump. "The culture," she repeated dully.

"Mmm. And the language. I suppose I could hire someone with those qualifications, but with you I won't have to. I need someone I can trust to be honest."

Nell gave a silent sigh. Trust was something, she reminded herself. And scolded herself for having read more into three simple words. A man like St. Wulfstan wouldn't need her. He would need the services she could provide.

Trust was something, after all. So, too, was the way he made love to her.

"You belong to me now, Nell," he murmured, bending his head to scrape his teeth lightly along the line of her throat. She shivered with the sensation. "You do know that, don't you?"

"I—"

"There will be no one else. Not here and not in Ireland. I've told you before that I don't share what's mine."

Saddened that he would even feel the need to mention such a matter, that he would think for a moment that she held herself so cheaply as to lie with anyone else, Nell replied, "There will be no one else. You don't need to speak on the subject again."

"Good. Now I suppose we ought to discuss compensation. I could pay you—"

She couldn't bear to even let him finish the thought. "I don't want your money," she said dully. "I don't need it and I don't want it."

"No?" He stared down at her, expression unreadable. "You are a curious sort of . . . woman, Mrs. Nolan. But very well. I'll just have to make certain you are compensated in another way." He levered himself off her to stand beside the bed, the very sight of him in his naked glory making her tingle even through her heavyheartedness. "Time to remedy a wrong."

He grasped her wrist and pulled her to her feet. Then he turned her to face away from him. She could feel the hard heat of him against her back and leaned back instinctively, pressing herself as close as she could. She couldn't help herself; the lure of him, of what she knew he could do to her was too strong. Behind her, Trevor gave a harsh growl and dug his fingers into her shoulders.

Then his fingers were gliding up her neck, sending delicious shivers down her spine. The touch moved higher and she was vaguely aware of the pins being removed, one by one, from her hair. Moments later, the thick braid came loose from its tight coronet, falling to rest heavily between her shoulder blades. Nell felt the gentle tug as Trevor threaded his fingers through the thick strands, separating them to flow unrestrained over her back.

The sensation was comforting and erotic at the same time. Nell closed her eyes and relished the rhythmic tug of his fingers in her hair. Then, suddenly, his hands were on her thighs, kneading her flesh through the crumpled linen. From there his touch drifted upward, over her stomach to her rib cage which jittered now with her shallow breaths. He paused there and Nell squirmed against him, wanting more. He obliged her.

He slid his fingers up the sides of her breasts, the teasing touch driving her wild. Then he joined his fingertips over her heart. In the second before she reached up to guide him, he swept his hands downward, rubbing his palms over her straining nipples. Her breath coming quick and thready, Nell arched her back, thrusting herself toward his touch. Every inch of her seemed to be on fire, and his hands only covered so much. Twisting about, she wound her arms around his neck and molded her body full against his.

"Ah, ah," he admonished. Instead of embracing her, he placed his hands on her hips. "Slowly this time."

Nell felt his fingers clenching against her skin, expertly drawing her nightgown up her calves, her thighs. She needed no coaxing to lift her arms. Trevor lifted the soft fabric over her head before tossing it aside. When he stepped back to see what he had bared, Nell felt no embarrassment. "You are exquisite, Mrs. Nolan," he murmured, and in that moment she believed him.

When he laid her back on the bed, she twined her limbs around him, reveling in the contact of skin against skin, drawing him with her. He looked down at her somberly. "I didn't pause to talk of this before and I'm sorry for that. We . . . I can take precautions against conception. There are French sheaths, but I don't have one with me. I didn't think—"

Nell placed a finger over his lips. "I have taken care of the matter."

"Have you?" His smile spread, wicked and lazy. "Well, then . . ."

His kiss had none of the fierceness of past times, but all the power. Nell sighed when he lifted his mouth from hers, then hummed when he whispered a thrilling path down her throat to the valley between her breasts. She arched against him, a silent plea. When he complied, she nearly came off the bed. His touch was masterful, his lips and tongue impossibly clever as they surrounded, pulled, teased the sensitive nipple into a taut bud. When he lifted his head eventually, Nell moaned her displeasure. She vaguely heard his chuckle before his mouth closed over the other peak.

When he turned his head a few moments later to brush his cheek over her breast, she did not complain. Instead, she gave a throaty cry, arching again as his whisker-shadowed jaw rubbed over her fevered skin. She ran her hands over the hard curve of his shoulders. His skin there was taut, smooth, unmarked. Her fingertips tingled as they explored. The rest of her sparked under his touch.

At last he slid upward until they were jaw to jaw. "I want to be inside you, Nell Nolan," he said huskily.

She opened for him in eager response. She felt herself stretching to accommodate the glorious length and breadth of him. Then he was sheathed fully within her and Nell found herself wishing he would never withdraw.

It was a very long time before he did. This time was slow, careful, and blessedly prolonged. They moved together, hips rocking, hands stroking, for countless minutes until Nell's climax rolled sweet and potent through her. Trevor followed, burying his face in her throat with a quiet growl. When he did pull away, she followed, and he tucked her firmly against his side.

For that moment, there was nothing Nell needed to say. Talk of the next day, or the next, or of Ireland would wait. As she watched through heavy eyes, the fire and candles guttered, the light of the full moon cast its silvery glow on the room. Beneath her cheek, Trevor's chest rose and fell gently with his breath. Nell smiled and closed her eyes.

When she woke in the morning, the sun had risen and he was gone. Nell stretched stiff muscles and recalled with pleasure how they had become that way. And it would happen again. She smiled. Trevor's waistcoat hung from the dressing-room doorknob. It wasn't a gift, at least not in the usual sense. But the message was clear. He would be back.

CHAPTER 11

He didn't return for three days. The first had been spent in the seedier parts of the city in search of answers. Over the years, he had built up a network of sources who were invaluable when it came to knowing the dealings of London's underworld. Mysteriously—or perhaps not so very—not one seemed to have anything to say to him. He'd rattled a few doors and teeth, used his fists to gain entrance to several spots that made the Red Hollow look like the queen's drawing room. In the end, he'd come away with a few more bruises to add to those he already sported, and no answers. Whoever had hired the thugs to attack him must have possessed very deep pockets. Trevor had never been able to pay much for information, but he'd become very good at scaring it out of his quarry. This time, no one was talking.

After that, he'd spent two less dangerous if equally unpleasant days in the saddle. Back in London, he was stiff, sore, and certain he smelled like something come back from the dead. He supposed he could have waited to visit Nell. But he hadn't wanted to. He'd managed to arrange comfortable passage for the two of them to Ireland—a last-minute effort and an expense he could scarce afford—in another two days' time and there was much to do in the interim.

She made him wait. He cooled his heels in her parlor, mildly amused by this display of pique. The first ten minutes could have been a matter of fashion, the next fifteen a matter of primping in the looking glass. By the time he had been waiting a half hour, Trevor decided Nell was annoyed with him for not having informed her of his departure from London. To be fair, he'd made her wait three days. He ought to be able gracefully to accept a half hour.

"To hell with that," he muttered to his unshaven, decidedly disreputable-looking reflection in the parlor mirror. He stalked out of the room and took the stairs to the next floor two at a time.

He didn't knock, merely shoved the door to Nell's bedchamber open. As expected, she wasn't engaged in any activity legitimate enough to keep him waiting. She was seated on the edge of her bed, hands clasped neatly in her lap, feet swinging slowly to and fro above the floor. Her mouth opened soundlessly at the sight of him, but before she could speak, he was on her, hungry lips and hands taking their fill of her. She thumped once against his shoulders with small fists, then she went limp, allowing him to bear her back onto the mattress. When he finally released her, her tidy topknot was askew and her eyes were vague. He grinned; she sighed.

"Who taught you your manners?" she asked wearily as she sat up, poking ineffectual fingers at her hair.

"A pack of wolves," he replied cheerfully. When she leaned a little closer and wrinkled her nose, he chuckled. "I have been paying them a visit, as it happens."

Nell shook her head at him. "I don't suppose I am allowed to ask where you have been."

Trevor flopped over on the mattress, crossing his arms behind his head. "Ask away."

"Oh, no. I'll not fall for that again. I'll [ ] you'll refuse to answer."

"Fine. Don't ask."

He could see her indecision. Apparently some misplaced sense of pride won out, because she slipped from the bed to cross the room. She stopped behind one of the little armchairs, gripped the top with both hands. This, Trevor thought, did not bode well for his hopes of a quick bath and slow exploration of her body in front of the fire. He sat up.

"Nell?"

She stared in the vicinity of his knees. "I have spent these past several days thinking."

This didn't bode well at all. "About?"

"About Ireland. About going with you."

"I see. And . . . ?"

"And I have accumulated countless reasons why I should not."

Trevor stifled a groan. He didn't have time to sort out the intricate Gordian knot of Nell's thought processes. He'd intended to use what time he could spare in making them both cross-eyed with pleasure. But he knew that if he tried to run roughshod over her concerns, it would take twice as long to mop up the resulting mess.

"Give me one reason," he commanded.

"One reason is that you are most domineering," she shot back, and he couldn't help but smile.

"I will make an effort to be less so. Next."

She raised a brow, but continued, "You are developing a regrettable habit of distracting me from important matters by . . . kissing me."

"You don't care for my kisses?" he queried, enjoying the immediate rosy flush that stained her cheeks.

"I didn't mean that. Of course I enjoy . . . very

much . . . I simply will not have you thinking you can end serious conversations by pouncing on me."

"Fine. I won't think that." Trevor levered himself from the mattress and stalked across the room. "You see, my dear, we are quite in accord. Now, come here . . ."

She sighed as she sidestepped his outstretched hand and retreated to dubious safety behind the other chair. "I am not finished. I am my own mistress here, of myself and of my home—"

"And so you shall be mistress of me and mine there."

"Ah, my lord—"

"Trevor."

She blew out a breath. "Trevor. Do you have any idea how difficult a man you are to understand? Or how I am to go about doing so?"

He had no answer whatsoever for that one. "What is so very important for you to understand?"

That appeared to flummox her, if only for a moment. She stood very still, mouth compressed and eyes thoughtful. Then, softly, "I suppose I need to know what to expect from our . . . arrangement. I am to be mistress, helpmeet, translator. I can do all those things, certainly."

He was becoming impatient. "Then what is the problem?"

"The problem is that it sounds so feasible, so tidy now. But no doubt there will come a time when you will no longer have need of me in one capacity. Or in all. No, perhaps I *do* know what will happen then. The same that always happens between women like me and men like you. But in Connemara, should you set me aside as men do their unwanted mistresses . . . or should I wish to leave, I will not be able—"

"Nell." Trevor ran a weary hand through his hair. He really was not in the mood for this. "Ask me where I have been these past three days."

"I will not. You will only—"

"Ask me."

She huffed out a breath. "Very well. Where have you been, sir?"

He propped a foot on the seat of the chair in front of him. Ignoring her disapproving look, he casually leaned his elbow on his raised knee. "I have been chasing a representative of the Archbishop of Canterbury halfway across the southwest of England. Go ahead; ask."

This time, she merely rolled her eyes before complying. "Why were you chasing a representative of the Archbishop?"

"Why, because the Archbishop himself refused to see me, of course. No great surprise there. I said some rather unflattering things about him several years ago . . ." He grinned at Nell's exasperated frown. "Come here and get your answer." He spread his arms wide.

She eyed him warily. "No."

"I will not pounce on you, Nell." He gestured to the open flap of his greatcoat. "Now come here."

When she gave a stubborn shake of her head, he sighed and withdrew the folded paper from his pocket himself. He tossed it onto the little table. Nell stared at it for a long moment. Then, rather like a mouse snatching cheese from a trap, she reached out and quickly seized the paper before retreating again. Amused, Trevor watched her unfold it. Then he lowered his foot to the floor and headed for the door. He needed a drink and there was no sign of the brandy decanter he had retrieved from the duke's chamber days before. He would simply have to go help himself again.

Nell stopped him as he was halfway out of the room. "What is this?"

"Can you not tell?"

She was staring at him, brow furrowed. "I have not read—"

"So read it. I will be back in a minute."

Grinning, anticipating a very warm reception on his return, he went in search of his refreshment. The small thump that came from her chamber while he was rooting among the late duke's splendid collection of bottles made him chuckle. The second, louder, had him lifting his head. He grabbed the decanter nearest to hand, deciding they could share the single glass he'd found, and headed back down the hall. The door to Nell's bedchamber was closed. Trevor balanced bottle and glass in one hand and turned the knob.

The door to Nell's bedchamber, he discovered, was locked.

"Nell? Open the door."

"No!" came muffled but emphatic through the wood.

"Nell . . ."

"I was going to say yes. To Ireland. To going with you."

"Splendid. Now open the damned—"

"But you've changed everything!"

This was not at all what he had expected. "Nell," he said very slowly, "do you understand what that paper is?"

"Of course I do. I am not stupid. It is a special license."

"It is. We can be married tomorrow—"

"No."

His patience was vanishing fast. "What do you mean 'no'?"

"I mean no, we will not be married tomorrow. You have lost your mind!"

Trevor closed his eyes, counted five. "Nell, I am very sorry if you would have preferred flowers, pretty words, an elaborate wedding, but there is no time. Now, I am getting very tired of talking to the door." He knew he could break it down with a single thrust of his shoulder, but he was already stiff and sore enough as it was. And he didn't think Nell would much care for his demolishing bits of her house. "Now, open—"

The door swung sharply inward. Nell stood there, two bright spots of color on her cheeks and tears in her eyes. "Go home, Lord St. Wulfstan."

"Nell, I said I was sorry."

She shook her head. "You really don't understand, do you? This isn't about pretty words or flowers. This is about the simple fact that you didn't *think*. You cannot marry me. I am not what you want. Or need."

He was beginning to comprehend. "I can do anything I want," he said gruffly. "And you are precisely what I want. And need. Is this about what you fear people will say?"

"In part," she admitted. "Oh, for God's sake, Trevor. Bad enough what the *ton* will have to say about a peer marrying a courtesan, but you intend to go back to Ireland. Just imagine what your tenants, your neighbors there will say. Bringing your . . . your . . ."

"My *wife*." He reached out, snared her chin before she could move out of his reach, and tilted her face up to look fully into his. "I have bloody little to give you, Nell." God, the truth was painful, but he couldn't hide from it, not now. He gestured to his scarred brow with a sharp wave of his free hand. "This I cannot conceal, but there are other matters less obvious. My fortune is not—"

She jerked free of his grasp, eyes wide and accusing. "Do you think me so shallow that a scar would make you any less beautiful to me? Worse, do you honestly believe it matters a whit how wealthy you are? You may be rich as Croesus for all I care."

"Nell, you misunderstand—"

"*You* do not understand. Even you, with who you are, cannot make people accept me."

"I have precious little to give," he repeated slowly, "but my name will be enough. You will hardly be the first mistress to become a wife in London Society. And to hell with what the *ton* says regardless. I need you with me in Ireland, and believe me, my tenants will accept you as my wife without a qualm. They wouldn't have had anything to do with my mistress. I did think, Nell. I thought long and hard and this is the only answer. Does that make it any better?"

He had no idea what to make of her quiet response: "And I didn't believe it could be made any worse." She sighed then. "I will be your mistress, Trevor, but I won't be your wife."

"Yes. You will." He was angry now, and helplessly pained, but took great care to hide both. "I am going to go now," he informed her calmly, coolly. "There are some matters I must attend to, but I will be back later. We'll talk then."

"I—"

"Shh." He bent and kissed her once, as gently as he could manage. "Until later."

Trevor kept his step firm and his posture erect as he walked away from her, until he'd turned the corner that took him out of sight of the house. Then he stopped and let out a breath in a long, low hiss, feeling himself folding inside like a sail without wind.

For more than fifteen years, from the hour that Richard had pounded him with vicious fists and words until the moment he'd decided to marry Nell, Trevor hadn't thought of marriage, of having a woman forever by his side. He'd simply, unquestioningly accepted that there would never be one. And until that instant mere minutes ago when Nell had uttered the single word *no*, he hadn't realized how much he'd counted upon her *yes*.

He rubbed a hand roughly over the spot high on his chest as if he could eradicate the ache within. Then he stiffened his shoulders again.

He made his plans for the rest of the day, emotionless and pragmatic. He would have to have his bath at home. Then he would pay a visit to Oriel. It was time to tell the marquess about the attacks, and about his fruitless search for the culprit. After that he would go to Watier's. Like all of the gentlemen's clubs, Trevor avoided it whenever possible. But he needed money and there was plenty of that spread among the members who gathered around the gaming tables there. Gambling at Watier's tended to resemble shooting fish in a barrel; there was no sport in it. But he had to have full pockets when he reentered the Tombs.

As he strode down Brook Street, he resolutely wiped the image of Nell's face from his mind. He wouldn't think. He simply wouldn't think. Wouldn't have her eyes haunting him. Nell's eyes, the grey of the sea in winter, the same as the very first time he had seen her: stirringly beautiful and unbearably sad.

Nell sat in the library several hours later, watching the afternoon light fade outside the windows. She'd come there as soon as Trevor left, and sat now on the floor near the hearth, legs pulled up to her chest, chin on her folded arms. The only sound was the soft hiss of the flames. It should have been restful. It wasn't.

The first sight of the marriage license had made her heart jump, a quick and hopeful little leap. To *belong* again—to someone, someplace. To perhaps, just perhaps, have that second chance at having a child. Oh, it had been glorious, that brief instant where it had seemed possible. Where it had suddenly, magically seemed to make all the sense in the world.

Moon, full moon, give to me a view of who my lover will be . . .

Common sense had followed too quickly. She couldn't marry this man. Nell didn't think she could marry any man, but especially not this one. It was one matter, putting her body into his hands. They were, after all, such talented hands. And even that, something as simple as shedding some clothing and inhibitions, had been such a difficult decision to make. Putting her future into his hands was another matter entirely. He was the same careless, arrogant, untouchable rogue he'd been before she had made love with him. He continued to confuse her as no one else ever had, even if he did pleasure her as Thomas certainly hadn't done. But he also continued to hurt her—unintentionally, perhaps, but hurt her all the same.

He needed her for certain ends. He didn't love her.

Moon, full moon, give to me a view of who my lover will be . . .

Once, so long ago that it seemed another lifetime, she had wished on the moon. So long ago that she could almost deny what she'd seen in the mirror. She was a woman grown now, with too much hard-earned knowledge to trust in fate or the vagaries of her heart. She couldn't allow either to matter to her.

She would trust Trevor with her body. She couldn't possibly trust him with either her future or her heart. Neither mattered to him.

She was crying again. Nell sniffled and groped in her pocket for a handkerchief. There wasn't one there; she'd left it in her bedchamber after her crying spell there had ended. Clonegal had always kept fresh handkerchiefs in a desk drawer. They were long gone. Nell had used them, one after another, in the days following his death. The Duke of Clonegal had loved her—in his sweet, fatherly way. And he had cared enough about her future to make sure she would never want for anything. Anything monetary, at least. That sort of care made all the difference.

She rubbed her nose on her sleeve. Then she rose to her feet and stretched stiff muscles. Sitting and feeling sorry for herself served no purpose. She wasn't certain just what she would do, but she needed some busy work. She strode to the door and nearly flattened Mac, who was just outside.

"Ye've a visitor," he grumbled, holding out a little cream-and-gilt calling card.

Nell hadn't even heard the door. She took the card and blinked in surprise. It bore the name of the Marchioness of Oriel. Oriel, she recalled, was the name of the dark, grim-faced man who had come for Trevor on the night of Vauxhall. She wondered what his wife could possibly want of her.

The answer came quickly. If the marquess had been able to track Trevor here so easily, his wife had probably done the same. It was more than likely that she suspected her husband was having an affair with the notorious Mrs. Nolan.

The impulse to have Mac tell Lady Oriel that she wasn't at home was strong. Nell didn't have the energy to defend herself against the anger of a jealous wife, especially one whose anger was mistaken—or at least misdirected. Facing one more cold, condemning society matron was one more trial than she thought her weary head and fragile pride could bear. But she wasn't a coward, had worked very hard for her bravery. So she straightened her shoulders and told Mac to bring Lady Oriel into the parlor.

She was completely taken aback by her first view of the Marchioness of Oriel. The lady who strode into the room in a blaze of brilliantly red hair and emerald wool was young—certainly younger than Nell herself—and she appeared neither cold nor haughty. She certainly wasn't a beauty; under the flaming hair, her nose was just that shade too broad and her mouth too wide for beauty. But she had a pleasant face, one that bore no signs of anger.

"Lady Oriel . . ." Nell began.

"Mrs. Nolan." The woman actually held out her hand. Nell shook it, bemused. "Please forgive my rudeness in arriving unannounced and uninvited. I am not usually so mannerless."

"I . . . ah . . ." Nell found herself stammering. "Will you sit? May I offer you some tea?"

At this, Lady Oriel smiled, then continued in her musical Scots brogue, "And you so polite. Now I really feel I ought to be ashamed of myself. Aye, I will sit." She did, settling herself on the brocade settee. "But there's no need for tea. I won't stay long. I expect you're curious as to why I've come."

It would be so easy, Nell thought, to be charmed and disarmed by the frank friendliness. But she had just enough experience with the *ton* to know better.

Gathering her composure, she took her own seat and murmured, "Curious and surprised, certainly. I cannot imagine your husband or your peers in Society would look kindly on your paying me a visit."

Lady Oriel blew out a dismissive breath. "Ach, I couldn't care less about Society. 'Tis a flock of silly hens and billy goats for the most part. And my husband wouldn't mind. He'd rather like to meet you, too, I expect." She glanced around the little parlor. "Pretty room. I like the painting of the sea."

So did Nell. It reminded her of Ireland. "Lady Oriel—"

"Turner, is it? He'll be very famous someday. Nathan has several of his paintings and keeps them to himself in his library. Silly man. Ah, but I don't suppose you want to hear me talk about men and paint." The marchioness fixed Nell with vividly green eyes, suddenly all cool seriousness. "I came because I wanted to see the woman who has our Trevor all but running in circles after his tail."

Nell blinked.

Lady Oriel was giving her a thoughtful and not so patently friendly perusal. Then she said, bluntly, "He intends to marry you."

Nell didn't respond. She owed this woman nothing. And if Lady Oriel had come to list the myriad reasons a viscount shouldn't marry a whore, she would have to introduce the subject herself. Nell imagined she could add a few lines to the list, but she wasn't going to be so helpful.

So when the marchioness announced, "You must be an extraordinary woman, Mrs. Nolan," Nell felt her jaw dropping.

"He has few friends," Lady Oriel continued, "and fewer people he actually likes. 'Tis like trying to reach the heart of a pine tree, getting to know him. Few can stand the constant jabs to the eye." She leaned forward, eyes locked on Nell's. "We care for him, Nathan and I. We care for him a great deal. It grieves me something fierce, but I believe we are the only ones who do," she said on a sigh, and Nell softened.

"I care for him."

"Aye, I'm sure you do. You'd have seen the back of him long before he'd think of marrying you if you didn't. How much do you care?"

"I . . ." Nell knew she should be telling this woman to mind her own concerns, that this wasn't among them. She found she couldn't. "Enough that I know I cannot marry him, I suppose."

"But not enough to do so?"

In another time, Nell mused, had circumstances been just a bit different, she and Lady Oriel might have been friends. She knew she would have enjoyed that. It was so rare to meet someone whose intelligence matched their compassion. "It doesn't appear so, does it?"

Lady Oriel sat back and drummed her fingertips on the arm of the settee. "He needs someone."

"Perhaps, but it isn't me."

"Hmm. Perhaps it isn't. Well." The marchioness rose gracefully to her feet. "I'll be off then. I've said my piece, for what it is, and won't be taking up more of your time."

Nell rose, too, and before she could change her mind, asked, "How did he get the scar?"

Lady Oriel gave a small smile. "I don't know. My husband doesn't know. Does it bother you very much?"

Nell's answer was immediate and heartfelt. "It doesn't bother me at all. It never really did."

The other woman nodded once, then started for the

door. "I'll see myself out." She paused in the doorway. "There are more reasons for marriage than love or convenience, you know."

Nell didn't answer. She gestured Lady Oriel ahead of her into the hallway, walked with her to the top of the stairs. "May I ask you a very impertinent question, Lady Oriel?"

"After the passel I've asked you? To be sure you can."

Nell rested a hand on the newel post, felt its unyielding solidity. Everything else in her day had felt so unreal. "What do you hold most dear in your life?"

"Ah." If the lady thought the question either crazed or rude, she gave no indication. "My son," she said emphatically. "My husband. My family. And my pride. In that order."

Nell nodded. "Thank you."

"I won't ask you the same. You've answered enough of my questions already."

Nell couldn't really recall having given a straight answer to anything, but it didn't matter. She and Lady Oriel wouldn't be meeting again. She was curious enough, however, to ask, "So, will you tell Lord St. Wulfstan?"

"Tell him . . . ?"

"That you paid a visit to his . . . to me? That I am indeed unsuitable for marriage? You should."

The lady smiled gently. "I didn't come to pass judgment on you. 'Tisn't for me to do so. And I can't be telling him anything about your heart. That isn't for me to do, either. Good night, Mrs. Nolan, and good luck to you."

Nell stayed where she was until the door shut soundly behind the marchioness. That, she thought, was per-

haps the strangest audience of her life. She didn't
know what to make of it. But neither did she think she
would forget a word.

Tired, feeling the beginnings of a headache coming
on, she retreated to the library. She'd lost the desire to
do anything useful. Instead, she wanted only to wrap
herself in her yellow wool throw and stare into the
fire. She hadn't been there for more than five minutes
when Mac appeared in the doorway. His face was red
and he was scowling fiercely.

"There's another one here. I've put 'im in the front
room. Wouldn't take no for an answer." The elderly
retainer jerked an indignant chin toward the hall.
"I'm sorry, miss. I couldn't stop 'im."

Nell sighed. "No, I don't imagine you could. It's all
right, Mac." She rose wearily to her feet and went to
face the dragon.

But it wasn't Trevor who was waiting for her in the
parlor. The new Duke of Clonegal turned from the
same painting Lady Oriel had admired not half an
hour before. He didn't greet Nell. Instead, he commented, "My father always did go for the lesser talents. Unfortunate. I daresay he paid well for this one,
too."

Nell faced him squarely, arms crossed, chin lifted.
"Why are you here, sir?"

He raised a dark brow. "I thought we'd had an understanding, Mrs. Nolan, that we would have a nice
coze. But I've found you impressively unavailable."
He smiled and Nell wondered how a mouth so like his
father's could have none of the warmth. "Did you
think you could avoid me forever? That was careless
of you."

In that moment, she wanted to hurt him, even if it
was just with small jabs at his pride. She knew it was

unworthy; there was no place in her life for deliberate unkindness. But he had hurt his father, repeatedly and deeply over the years. Nell wanted to wound him for that. She shrugged. "I must indeed confess to carelessness. I didn't think of you at all."

His face twisted for a brief instant, turning harsh and ugly. There was no resemblance between father and son in that moment and Nell was glad of it. Then he was smiling again. "Perhaps I deserved that, Mrs. Nolan. But I am not here to spar with you."

"No? Then why are you here?"

The duke didn't answer immediately. He crossed the room, drew his watch from his waistcoat pocket, and checked it against the ormolu clock on the mantel. Then he took a leisurely look around the parlor. "Do you know how this house came to be in my father's possession, Mrs. Nolan?"

Nell didn't know. Nor did she care. But she had a very good idea that he had a reason for telling her, and wasn't going to leave until he had done so. "I have no idea."

"It belonged to a whore," the duke said smoothly. Nell couldn't hide her wince. He smiled thinly. "My maternal great-grandfather's whore. I rather suspect that my grandfather installed his own bits of fluff here once or twice. Ironic, perhaps, that he would include it in my mother's dowry. But then, he was rather fond of my father—delighted with the match. And he never cared much for his own daughter."

He wandered around the room then, touching a china ornament here, flicking a fingertip at a chairback there. "I wonder if he intended for his son-in-law to follow in family tradition. And so my father did. I don't think my mother has ever set foot in this house. The Clonegal town house is far grander, of course, and in a much better location. And they always had their separate lives. Mother has always had her Society events, her charitable acts. Father had his women."

He turned to Nell, expression perfectly pleasant now and slightly expectant, as if he'd commented blandly on the weather and was waiting for an equally bland response. Nell's hands were clasped tightly at her waist; she could feel the pressure of bone against bone. It was, she thought, holding all of her together.

Voice tight, she demanded, "Is there a point to all this, sir? Or did you simply want the satisfaction of insulting your father's mistress?"

"Now where would the satisfaction be in doing that, my dear? My father was a man of his times. He made his choices. You were simply one of them."

He walked over to Nell and boldly lifted her jaw with a fingertip. She stepped out of his reach, cool and composed even while her heart was jittering and her legs felt like jelly. In that instant she wished with all her heart for Trevor to walk through the door. She wanted to see that awful smile wiped abruptly from this man's face.

"No," he continued, turning away from her to collect the hat and stick he'd placed on the side table. "I came to see if I wanted to bed you myself." He tucked his stick under his arm and gave a mocking bow. "As it happens, I don't. Good day, Mrs. Nolan."

And he was gone.

Nell stood where she was in the middle of the parlor for several long minutes. Then she crossed the room on shaky legs and settled herself at the beautiful little writing desk the duke—*her* duke—had given her on her last birthday. She drew two sheets of paper from their drawer and began to compose the two letters she wanted to send. When she realized she didn't know where exactly to send either one, she carefully set aside the dry pen.

Then she rested her head on her folded arms and cried.

CHAPTER 12

Trevor studied the familiar Connemara landscape with disinterest. This was where he had been born, where he had taken his first steps, then learned to run and leap. And it was the place he had eventually fled at a gallop.

As far as he could tell, nothing had changed. There was rumor of a wealthy D'Arcy scion building himself a colorful village to the south, but here was still the stark tapestry of bogland and rocky road, the Twelve Bens a distant and jagged silhouette behind them and the sea a wash of grey ahead. They passed the occasional squat stone cottage with its requisite thatched roof and sheep pen.

The carriage rolled into the little village of An Cloigeann. Little there had changed, either. It was still tiny, untidy with its heaps of fishing nets and sails, and salt-scoured. But it was picturesque in its own way; the doors to the few cottages were painted brightly and children played among the tackle.

The only change Trevor could see was a round Martello tower squatting on the headland, one of dozens of such lookouts that had been built along Ireland's shores. He shook his head at the sight. If Napoleon decided to launch an invasion of Britain from this spot, he would have a mighty struggle ahead of him.

Even if his troops managed to get through Connemara without sliding into the bogs, they would still have the entire width of Ireland to cross. And the Irish were heartily tired of being invaded. While English rule was tolerated—if barely—the little Corsican would no doubt be summarily tipped right back into the sea.

The fishing boats were in for the day and most of the village's population was out sorting the catch. Everyone looked up as the carriage rolled by; visitors were rare in Cleggan. As the curiosity on some faces turned cold, Trevor resisted the urge to sit back from the window. He stayed where he was, fully visible. Everyone would know he was back soon enough. It might as well be now. And there was no question that he would be recognized. If the *ton* had long memories, the rural Irish had eternal ones. The passage of time and the scar had changed his face, but it wouldn't matter. The people of the area would recognize the face and would probably see the scar as a sort of divine retribution for his sins. So be it.

He hadn't expected a warm reception. So the glares and averted gazes came as no surprise. He was not so prepared to see an older woman, bent and thin, spit on the ground as the carriage passed. Then she made the sign of the cross on her chest and forehead. He couldn't hear what she hissed as they rolled by, but he could imagine.

"Do you know her?" came the gentle query from beside him.

He had nearly forgotten that he had not come home alone. He had come home with a wife.

His wife.

Nell had summoned him back to her comfortable little house in Davies Street and calmly, civilly accepted his erstwhile proposal. Even as he'd cursed himself for not leaving things be, for giving her any opportunity whatsoever to question that decision, he had been asking her what had changed her mind. He'd had to know.

She had smiled, a bit sadly he'd thought, but with the innate warmth that was so much a part of her, and said, "I found one more reason to accept than to refuse."

"And that is?" he'd demanded.

"I would miss seeing your face," had been her quiet reply.

The hollow ache had disappeared from his chest. All that had mattered then, as he'd lifted one of her small hands to his lips, all that mattered now as he studied her pale face, was that she'd said *yes*. Nell Nolan had accepted him, simply and warmly. As no other woman had ever done.

"Do you know her?" she repeated now, nodding toward the old woman outside the carriage.

"It doesn't matter," he said wearily. "She knows me."

"She is very angry." Nell spoke without censure or audible curiosity. Just the simple statement of a woman who had known her own share of scorn. Only, Trevor thought, she hadn't deserved hers.

He shrugged. "I haven't been a good landlord. In a sense, the village is my responsibility. I've made their lives harder by my absence."

He hadn't been much good before he left, either. He had no idea why this particular woman hated him so, but he assumed she had her reasons, and valid ones. It could have been her poverty. It could just as likely have been a daughter with whom he'd carelessly flirted or a son he'd flattened in one of the senseless fights that had erupted during his last days in Connemara. He had a great deal to atone for, and he had only the vaguest idea of how he was going to do it.

"You're back now. You'll make things right."

Nell's quiet confidence would have amused him if it hadn't been completely misplaced. Trevor smiled humorlessly. The methods of making things right that he had perfected over the last decade weren't going to help him here.

The road rose gently from the village. The mile went more quickly than Trevor remembered. As a child, when one of the greatest treats had been to come into the village with his nursemaid to watch the fishermen unloading their nets—waiting each time to see if one would relent and let the lord of the manor's son help—the journey had seemed to take forever. This time it went far too fast. His mood had grown increasingly more grim as they'd traveled north from Galway City. This was not a joyous homecoming.

The carriage drove through a pair of standing stones, the white quartz reminders of civilizations that had been gone for millennia. The fourth Viscount St. Wulfstan had altered the road to wind through the stones, an act that the seventh viscount thought arrogant and careless. No one was certain what the purpose of the markers had been, but Trevor was reasonably certain that building a road between them had broken an ancient line. He wasn't superstitious by nature, nor did he have much of an interest in any of the great white rocks dotting his land. But he had a respect for history, especially for the proud, fierce people who had become the Celts, and now wondered if moving the road again would be anything other than a foolish extravagance.

They crested a low rise and suddenly there was the Tombs, spread in moldering splendor before them.

Trevor ignored the pleased flutter in his gut at the sight of the ancient pale stone facade, the five sets of graceful gables that ended in spearing points, like a star. He looked only at the visible hole in the roof of the west wing and the crumbling edges of the eastern gable.

There was a scattering of missing windowpanes. He imagined there were even more on the seaward face. There were gaps, too, in the old sea-buckthorn hedge, and his mother's hard-fought flower beds had vanished altogether. The fountain cherub had collapsed—or been knocked—to the ground, where it was almost lost to scrubby grass. As the carriage pulled around the uneven rocky sweep that had once been a grand drive, Trevor saw that part of the marble stoop was missing; both of the decorative urns that had flanked the door were gone.

"Well, my lady," he muttered through a tight jaw to the still and silent figure beside him, "welcome to your new home."

Nell allowed him to help her down from the carriage. She took in the wreck of the house before her without a word or even a wince. Her fingers tightened warmly on his. "I can smell the sea air. How lovely."

She hadn't complained once—about anything—since they had left England.

Trevor tucked her arm through his. He could feel the hard circle of the ring through her glove. She hadn't complained about the hard journey. She hadn't complained about the rushed wedding ceremony, performed by a seedy-looking clergyman in a dark, wharf-side church that backed onto a tavern. She hadn't so much as flinched at Trevor's rough, slightly desperate lovemaking while the waves rolled angrily beneath their berth. She had opened her arms, welcomed him, and he had eventually been able to sleep, confident in his possession of her.

His wife.

"The sea is just beyond the rear of the house," he said gruffly. "Would you like to see it?"

She shook her head. "Later. Show me the house now."

A scrawny adolescent hurried toward them. He tipped his cap in a brief jerk, muttered something in Gaelic, then grabbed the first of the meager baggage from the carriage. He spun about when Nell spoke to him, a musical stream of words that meant nothing whatsoever to Trevor but nearly had the boy dropping Trevor's portmanteau onto his foot. Wide-eyed, he said something in return. They conversed for a moment, then Nell smiled, nodded, and the boy went back to unloading the bags—with, Trevor noticed, just a bit more care.

"His name is Peadar and it appears he is a quarter of your staff."

Trevor scowled. According to the steward, O'Donnell, he had been paying eight people to maintain the house. One more lie. "Did he tell you who the others are?"

"Names," was Nell's cheerful reply as she deftly avoided the broken step, "not positions. But I'm sure we'll have it all sorted out soon enough."

The massive oak door swung slowly open. A tiny figure appeared in the maw. Trevor blinked—and again. Not possible . . .

"Mrs. King?"

The walnut face lit like a candle. "Master Trevor! Oh, I beg your pardon . . ." Beneath soft white hair, his old nursemaid's eyes were faded but shining. "Lord St. Wulfstan. Welcome home to you."

"I . . . You are still . . ."

The old woman held the door wide. "Alive or here?" She smiled. "And where else would I have been going? Come inside now. Bring your lady and leave the wind."

Trevor followed Nell into the massive hall. It was just as he'd left it, from the ancient trestle tables and chieftans' chairs to the huge fireplace that offered as much warmth as an icicle in January. The same faded tapestries lined the stone walls; the same tattered Robard standards hung from the gallery above. He was home.

"Nell," he interrupted her wide-eyed perusal of the shabbily grand hall. "This is Mrs. King, the . . . house-keeper?" He raised a brow in the old woman's direction and she shrugged and nodded. "My wife"—the word still felt strange on his tongue—"Lady St. Wulfstan."

Mrs. King made a creaky curtsy. "Welcome to the Tombs, my lady. We've been after waiting a long time for you. Now, I've a fire laid in the east parlor. We didn't know when to expect you, my lord, but it won't take but a moment to have a tea ready."

While Nell gaped at the ornate ceiling, Trevor drew the older woman aside. "O'Donnell?" he asked quietly.

"Gone," was the grim reply, "and with the second-best silver in his pockets." As Trevor was thinking re-signedly that the man must have had very deep pockets, Mrs. King said with prim pride, "Sure and I hid the best three years ago. I knew you would come back and set everything to rights.

"We're a bit shorthanded," she went on. With more regret than censure, Trevor noted. "Just me, Cook, and her two: Peadar and Muirne. You call on me should you need to speak to them. They've no English."

"That won't be a problem. Lady St. Wulfstan is from Wicklow. She speaks Gaelic."

"Does she now? Well, that's handy, isn't it?" Mrs. King smiled—with something that looked very much to Trevor like pride. "You've done well by yourself, my lord. And you'll do well by what's yours to tend."

And that, apparently, was that.

Mrs. King trundled off. Trevor led the way to the parlor. Nell followed, craning her neck to take in every detail. And there were details aplenty. The Robards had been collectors from the days they had been brutal Connemara pirates stealing from English and Spanish ships alike. Then one aging member of the family had decided it was time to retire in some sort of style. He had cleverly delivered the contents of the next Spanish galleon to the Queen of England. He would just as gladly have done the opposite and handed over an English ship to Spain, but he'd had no great desire to move to Madrid and had surmised, too, that Elizabeth was more likely to be generous in her reward.

He'd been right. The queen had granted him an earldom, which she had then promptly taken back when he, tiring early of retirement, had gone after one of her ships. Upon its intact deliverance, she had summoned him to London where she had scolded, threatened, and given him a regal swat on the figurative posterior by only returning him to a viscountcy. She might have done worse had she known that he lifted a set of jeweled candlesticks on his way out of the palace.

Those candlesticks were still in the house somewhere, unless O'Donnell had taken them, one more old, glittery bit of Robard greed and history that Trevor couldn't use. And couldn't sell. He sighed as

Nell admired a set of sterling wall sconces, again when she stopped to examine a dark little painting that happened to be a Hals. He got her into the parlor eventually and left her to admire its slightly shabby opulence while he lit the fire.

This had been his mother's favorite room. He remembered her cautions against running near the Chinese vases and putting muddy heels on the blue-silk upholstery. The silk, though faded and torn in spots, was still there. So was the very faint purple streak on the sofa where his enthusiasm for a jam tart had outweighed her gentle warnings.

Within minutes, a young maid had scuttled in with the tea service on its familiar silver tray. The sugar bowl and creamer were missing, replaced by more old china. O'Donnell again, most likely, Trevor thought and regretted that he would have to wait to toss the blackguard headfirst into Ballinakill Harbor with the second-best family silver weighing down his pockets. There was no provision in Richard's will preventing Trevor from throwing away the house's contents, after all.

He would catch up with O'Donnell eventually. The money was gone, but revenge was sometimes indeed a dish best served cold. For now, he would concentrate on mopping up some of the mess he had made of his bittersweet inheritance.

Several hours later, after a plain but decent meal and mostly silent walk with Trevor along the beach below the house, Nell stood in the center of her bedchamber. Like the rest of the house it showed signs of neglect: the curtains and bed hangings were faded and frayed at the edges, the carpet worn. But there was a serene beauty, too. The furniture was fine, the moldings graceful and clearly done by a master hand. And when she opened the curtains, she was delighted by the sweeping view of the sea.

Nell had been surprised and awed by the beauty of the land through which they'd traveled. She had never been to Connemara, the region that made up the western section of County Galway. She had always heard that it was a rough place—which had certainly proven true—and a lawless one. Countless generations of wild Gael lords, often smugglers and pirates, had lived here. From the eastern county of Wicklow where Nell had been raised, Connemara had seemed like the wild end of the earth. And it was that. But it was also the most breathtakingly lovely place she had ever seen.

The Tombs was an extraordinary house in an extraordinary land, and Nell held close to her heart the spark of conviction that she could be happy here.

She clenched her hands on the windowsill. She *had* to be happy here. This was her home now. A new place, a new life, full of all the hope and promise a new beginning afforded. She had made her choice, coming to this beautiful, desolate spot so far from anything and anyone she'd known in her nearly thirty years, wife to a man she'd known for such a short time. She had married Trevor for three simple reasons, based on simple dreams, and one reason that had nothing to do with dreams or logic or anything that had ever motivated her.

She had wanted a home, a place where she belonged. Not a town house in London, but a home where she could walk outside and breathe fresh air, greet neighbors as they passed in the road. She had wanted a purpose. Inactivity had weighed on her after the duke's death. Nell needed work, good work. And she had wanted a child—a little hand to hold in hers as she walked along the hedgerows, looking for bramble berries, a warm and sleepy body in her lap as she sat by the fire in the quiet evenings.

Those were the logical, rational reasons, the sort she had always followed. But it was the fourth that had sent her to her desk to write the note that would call Trevor back to the house in Davies Street. She had accepted his proposal for three rational reasons and the inescapable fact that, no matter how calmly and clearheadedly she had tried to convince herself otherwise, she had known that she couldn't walk away from him, or let him walk away from her. The tie between them was like a ribbon of moonlight through a window: too real to be denied and too ethereal to be broken.

Moon, full moon . . .

Nell pressed her forehead to the cool glass. She had known. She had somehow known her destiny was irrevocably entwined with St. Wulfstan's from the moment he had stalked into Annie's party with his cool arrogance and scarred face.

She stared out over the water to the darkening horizon where the moon was just beginning to appear. She wondered where Trevor was now in his glorious ruin of a house. His mood had darkened with each mile that brought them closer to Connemara and had not improved upon arrival. He had been somber, face hard, all evening. Nell imagined the mantle of responsibility was weighing heavily on him. She hoped she could help. She wanted so much to help.

There were no sounds through the connecting door and, when she peeked through it, she found only a dark and empty bedchamber. Trevor's valise was there, but he was nowhere to be seen. So she returned to her own room, quickly unpacked what little she had brought, and went in search of him.

She got lost twice, following two hallways that ended in locked doors. She speculated on what was on the other side: complete wings with room after once-impressive room. When she ended up in what was clearly a ballroom—certainly not grand, but lovely with its towering mirrors and wide expanse of floor—she allowed herself to imagine what could be. Parties at Christmas and at the harvest, the house full of light and music and people. It could be done. It could be . . .

Carefully closing the ballroom door behind her, she wandered until she found a staircase that led her down to the floor below. She eventually discovered Trevor in the library. There was no fire in the hearth, and the waning light coming through the salt-sprayed windows did not reach his face. She could, however, clearly see the features of the portrait he was examining so intently. It wasn't a handsome face that stared down from its place above the mantel. It was long-nosed and weak-chinned beneath its elaborately curled wig, and there was a hardness to the eyes and mouth that hinted at cruelty.

Trevor didn't turn at the sound of her approach. Nell stopped at his side and squinted to read the tarnished plaque set into the portrait's elaborate frame. "Richard, sixth Viscount St. Wulfstan," she read. "Your father?"

Trevor grunted an affirmative.

Nell studied the unappealing face above. "I see no resemblance."

Trevor grunted again, then, "A comment both he and I would consider a great compliment. Venomous old wretch."

The hatred in his voice startled her. She'd grown

accustomed to seeing Trevor as a man of little emotion. Such vitriol was surprising—and a bit frightening. She hadn't known what to make of his earlier bleak mood. It was much worse now.

"Trevor . . ." She laid a tentative hand on his rigid arm. His head snapped around.

"What a legacy he left," he said bitterly. "An heir he loathed so much that he was prepared to destroy the name and estate he cherished. This bloody place is ready to crash down around our heads with the next sea breeze. God only knows the state of the outbuildings, let alone tenant lands. May you rot in hell," he muttered to his father's face, but Nell heard more weariness suddenly than rancor.

"It's all right," she said softly. "Some money and a bit of hard work will repair the house, the—"

His harsh laugh cut her off abruptly. "Is that all it will take? How very simple. Thank you, madam, for enlightening me." Nell stepped back, stung. Trevor hissed a breath through his teeth. "You didn't deserve that. I'm sorry. I was flagellating myself and my beloved papa quite comfortably before you came in." He ran a hand through his hair, sending it into sharp little peaks. "There isn't any money, Nell. Or at least not much."

He fixed her with a hard gaze brimming with anger and challenge. Anger at circumstances, she thought, and a challenge to her to react. To rail at his deception and manipulation. To cry, perhaps, and add one more burden to his shoulders.

She nodded. "I thought there might not be."

"*What?*"

"You hide it well, my lord. But I have lived most of my life practicing economy, and a very small part of it among people who practice none at all. I know the signs of both."

"Nell, I tried to tell you . . . once. After that—"

"It was a matter I was content to leave unspoken, at least until it couldn't be any longer. I said once that I didn't care what you had. I still don't. I have money. More than enough to make a good start on your house and lands."

His eyes darkened above her. "I won't have you thinking I lied in order to take anything from you. I don't want your money."

She smiled. "I seem to recall saying much the same to you." Then she sobered, brushed her fingertips lightly over his clenched fist. "You didn't lie and I'll certainly not fault you for what wasn't said. But you'll have to trust me now, if we're to go on from here. And the money is there, ready to be put to good use."

His hands moved whip-fast to wrap around her upper arms. Nell bit her lip, half-expecting him to thrust her away from him. Instead, he pulled her to his chest, wrapped his arms around her, and rested his chin on top of her head. She could feel his sigh on her hair.

"Oh, Nell. You have no idea what you've taken on."

"Maybe not," she said, rubbing her cheek against the fine wool of his lapel, "but I'm not afraid of it."

She couldn't afford to be afraid of the coming days—or years. There was nothing left for her anywhere else. For good or ill, she'd made her bed. She would lie in it.

As if reading her mind, Trevor murmured, "Come upstairs with me. Now."

She could feel the evidence of his arousal, felt herself warming. "Yes."

In seconds he was ushering her from the room, guiding her quickly down an empty hallway and into the echoing hall. Clumsy in her own haste, she tripped on a worn spot in the stair's carpet. She would have gone down had not Trevor, with an impatient growl and chuckle, hauled her upright and into his arms. He kissed her once, firmly, and carried her the rest of the way. Nell laughed, thrilled, when he kicked the door to his bedchamber open and launched both of them toward the bed.

They landed in a tangle of limbs and spent countless minutes rolling across the mattress in a delirious scramble of questing hands and lips. By the time Trevor rolled off her, Nell's hair was a tumbled mass around her shoulders and her heart was going like thunder. He ran a warm hand up the inside of her thigh and cupped her. Her breath hitched audibly, and he grinned, lazy and impatient at the same time. "Go on," he urged huskily.

"Hmm?" She felt the insistent press of his fingers and nearly came up off the bed.

"Go get your little coffer. I need to be inside you."

Nell shook her head to clear it. "But, I thought . . ."

"What?"

"Well . . ." She was floundering and didn't know why. "I . . . we are married. I did not think there would be a need . . ."

Suddenly he was not touching her at all. "You left it behind."

"No. No, I have it, but I thought . . ."

He sat up abruptly, shifting the mattress and rolling her away from him. "I don't want you becoming pregnant," he said flatly.

Nell tried to ignore the knot of certainty forming in her stomach. "You don't want me becoming pregnant . . . Now, you mean? While we have so much to do . . . ?"

"I don't want you becoming pregnant. Ever."

She didn't understand. She didn't understand at all. They were married. She had married him, come to the ends of the earth with him, and brought with her all the fragile dreams she had tried so hard to abandon over the years.

"But your name," she whispered. "Your title."

"Will die with me. I am the last St. Wulfstan." He scowled down at her. "For God's sake, Nell. Don't tell me you expected . . . I thought you . . . I've never encountered a courtesan who . . . Ah, hell."

He turned away to stare at a wall that Nell hazily noted bore a painting of a family: a father, two small sons, the mother in powdered wig and panniers. "I come from a cursed family," he said, cold and resolute. "I will not be responsible for putting another blighted generation on this earth."

"I see."

Trevor felt Nell sitting up, sensed her pulling away from him. When he looked, she was perched at the end of the bed, one pale hand wrapped around the canopy post, the other pressed to her waist.

"Perhaps I should have said something before. It just didn't occur to me that you might have some foolish, young girl's desire for—" He barely caught her when she slipped from the bed, his fingers just closing around her wrist. "Don't run away from me, Nell," he growled. "Don't ever run away from me."

She looked from his face to his hand gripping her wrist. "I was going to find the box," she said quietly, and waited for him to release her.

He let her go. She returned a few minutes later, garbed in her nightgown, hair captured neatly again in a tight braid. She said nothing. He opened his arms, ready for her to refuse. But of course she didn't. She came to him, soft and fragrant and warm, as she had each time before. If she was a bit quieter than usual as he ran his hands over her body, she was still welcoming and responsive and he could feel the quickened beat of her heart when he covered her breasts with his palms.

He eased into her slowly. She was ready for him and the sensation of her closing around him from within had him groaning softly. He resisted the urge to move hard and fast, to make them both wild. Instead, he eased forward—until he felt the faint but unmistakable barrier of the little sponge. Only then did he begin his steady strokes within her while he stroked her brow, her hair, the curve of her neck with his fingertips.

When he heard her soft gasp and felt the gentle tug of her release, he allowed his own to shudder through him. Nothing in a very long time had felt as right as spilling himself into Nell. Their lovemaking on the boat had been fiery, satisfying, but he'd forced himself to pull out at the last second. He'd come to her too quickly and hungrily for her to prepare herself. This time she had, and in his moment of release, Trevor felt there was nothing on earth that could touch him as long as some part of him was touching Nell.

Spent and sated at the same time, he rolled onto his back and twined an arm with hers. When she gently pulled away, he turned. "Nell?" He realized she hadn't said a word since returning to the room.

There was a long moment of silence. Then she whispered, "You didn't have to check. You could have trusted me." And she turned away from him.

Trevor knew when she finally fell asleep. Her rigid body relaxed beside him. He'd been staring at the ceiling, trying to find something to say, something that was an apology and a caution in one neat phrase. He couldn't tell her the truth. That was a secret too deep and jagged to be shared. He couldn't tell her, even though he had a feeling she might understand. And might not condemn him. Others had, and for something over which he'd never had control.

He would be the end of two centuries of Connemara lords. Even while Richard had been battering him all those years ago, cursing him to a bleak future, Trevor had vowed to be the last. Curses couldn't be broken; they weren't real. Poisonous familial lines were and could.

CHAPTER 13

Trevor was already gone when Nell woke the following morning. She lay for a few minutes, one hand resting in the indentation his head had left on the pillow. Then she sat up and reached for her dressing gown, which was draped over the foot of the bed. The maid, she thought, until her eyes lit on the bedside table. There was a bunch of wildflowers there, shoved a bit haphazardly into a water glass. Unable to help herself, she sighed and reached to touch a pale blossom. She saw celandine and little violets, early purple orchids and forget-me-nots.

How very like him, she thought, to manage an apology and a command without saying a word. The glass was set directly in front of her sponge box.

She pushed back the covers and climbed from the bed. There was warm water in the ewer—Trevor, again, she supposed—and she washed quickly, removing the last traces of him from her thighs. As she did, she allowed herself the single, piquant thought that perhaps he would change his mind. That after they had been together a while, worked and made love together here, he would change his mind. For the moment, she would simply tuck away those old longings yet again and do what needed to be done.

She had married him for a home, for good work,

and for a beloved family of her own. Two of three, she told herself now, was far better than what she'd ever had.

She supposed she could have wished for a charming prince. Once she had. But she'd given up that dream many years ago. Princes were rare; men were only human. She had gone into her first marriage naive and hopeful. She'd entered this one practical. And hopeful. Trevor was a good man at heart; she didn't doubt that for a second. And there was a tenderness behind the rock-hard shell. She'd caught glimpses of it. Oh, she knew that marrying Trevor didn't guarantee a happy ending. She knew he would, like so many men of his station and appetites, probably leave her behind at some point to return to the whirl of London, leaving her to miss him, if only for a time. She'd known that, but hadn't cared. If he left her, it would be in Ireland, with a home and work.

And a child . . . Nell blinked hard. She wouldn't cry. There was no reason to cry. Two of three was fine. Better than fine.

As she dressed she mused—more philosophically than she was inclined so early in a day—that life was a series of lessons learned the hard way. She replaited her hair and pinned it securely atop her head, donned sturdy shoes, found a soft wool shawl to ward off the cold of an Irish morning and the old stone house. There was too much to be done to wallow in disappointment. Or to waste time. She strode purposefully to the door.

The sadness caught up with her there. Closing her eyes tightly against the tears she could feel rising fast, she leaned her forehead against the comfortingly solid wood and let the sorrow engulf her. She couldn't fight it, not this time. So she stood, shoulders shaking, until the tears receded and she could no longer imagine the empty ache in the very center of her, where no baby would ever grow. As soon as she was able, she took a deep, steadying breath, opened her eyes, and continued on her way.

She only went wrong once on her way to the dining room. Trevor was there, empty plate pushed to the side and a large array of papers and ledgers spread halfway down the table. He was leaning on one elbow, hand fisted in his hair as he read from a ledger.

"Good morning," Nell said from the doorway.

He started, then scrambled to his feet. "Good morning."

Their eyes met. In his, Nell saw regret and wariness—but not before she'd seen simple, unmistakable pleasure. No one had ever brightened at the sight of her in the morning. And for the moment, that was enough. She smiled and took a seat.

Trevor lowered himself slowly into his. "Nell," he began, "I am concerned that I have ... damaged something ..."

She shook her head to stop him. "Don't." The fine linen tablecloth, soft and yellowed with age, needed repair. Nell traced a pull in the fabric with a fingertip as she continued. "I understand what you need of me. I don't think I quite did before."

"Nell—"

"No. It's a good understanding. Necessary." She looked up, held his gaze squarely. "There's no shame in needing help. Or companionship. The weight of responsibility is heavy enough," she said softly. "I wouldn't wish solitude on anyone." Then, chin up, she gestured to the papers. "What is most pressing?"

"Nell."

"Please." She felt her jaw tremble and resolutely hardened it. "I would like to help."

After a long moment he nodded. "Very well. I . . . thank you. I suppose the best place to start will be with a tour of the estate. I need to see what has fallen down. Or been burned down," he added grimly. He located a large, curled paper among the piles and unfolded it. When he jerked his chin at the seat beside him, Nell came around the table and slid into it. Content, heartened, she allowed her bent arm to rest against his and studied the map he was tracing. "Here is the house. There are tenant farms here, here, one there . . ."

By the time they rose from the table, the morning fog had lifted. Nell carried a cup of tea to the window and looked out over the overgrown lawns where they sloped down to the sea. A tern swooped low, plucking its breakfast from the water. She could see strands of red dulse on the sand, tangled with darker Irish moss. One of her very first memories, perhaps the only one of happier days when she was very small, was of collecting seaweed in Wicklow Bay with her grandmother. She remembered struggling with the slippery plants and the heavy basket, Gran laughing as the dulse slopped over the edge and onto Nell's feet.

That was how Nell saw it in her mind, looking down at sturdy little shoes almost covered with red seaweed. She'd been three, perhaps four, thinking only of the sweet her grandmother would make later. She hadn't had dulse pudding in many years, and her gran had been gone even longer. But there was something about the sight of the beach now that brought comfort and a warm glow. She thought she could be happy here on the edge of Connemara. She thought she could make a home for herself.

She turned from the window. "May I make a suggestion?" she asked Trevor.

"Of course."

"You want to make repairs to your tenants' homes before this one, correct? I agree with your belief that local men will be more amenable to the work if it begins on their own holdings. But I have an alternative to your appearing unexpected on each farm. Even visits made with all good intentions aren't always welcome."

Trevor wearily swept a stack of papers to the side. "I have to begin somewhere."

"So you do. I suggest you take the bull by the horns, so to speak."

"And?" he demanded.

"Go to the village first. With me."

"Christ. Nell—"

"Trust me," she said firmly. "Now, I'll need fifty pounds . . ."

An hour later they were bouncing along the road to Cleggan. Nell watched Trevor as he drove. His hands were sure on the reins. The horse was ugly and ill-tempered, the open tilbury had seen better days. But Nell was far less concerned with being tossed into the road than with what lay at the end of it. Her reticule felt heavy in her lap. Inside was a portion of the four hundred pounds that had been plaguing her for weeks. Only now she had a plan for spending it.

She had noticed the shabby look of the village the day before. But then it had been busy, filled with people. This morning, the boats were still out; the main street was nearly deserted. Now Nell saw the flaking paint on most of the buildings, the frayed ropes and bits of net lying in piles around the dock. A small girl darted through a dark doorway and scam-

pered down the street. She wore a much-mended dress
that, judging from its size, was intended for a much
larger child.

Trevor pulled the horse to a stop. Nell climbed down
without waiting for his help. She saw a curtain twitch,
and then another. As she approached the child, a
woman appeared in the doorway, broom in hand. Tool
or weapon, Nell thought wryly. Odds were even.

"Dia dhuit ar maidin," she greeted the little girl,
who was watching her with wide eyes. *"Cad is ainm
duit?"* When she got no response, she crouched down
and smiled. *"Nell is ainm dom. Tá mé—"*

"We know who you are," the woman said from the
doorway, eyes cold on Trevor. The girl rushed back to
hide behind her drab skirts. "I'd be asking why you're
here."

Nell knew that Gaelic words and accents varied
greatly across Ireland. She had no trouble understanding, however, or missing the bitter suspicion in
the woman's voice. She kept her smile firm and
friendly. "I am Nell Robard—"

"From Dublin, are you?"

In another time and place, Nell might have found
the scorn amusing. If this woman thought ill of her for
being a Dubliner, thought ill of Trevor for marrying a
fancy girl from the great city, heaven only knew how
she would react to the truth.

"Wicklow," Nell corrected. As if it mattered. "But
this is my home now. I need assistance. Perhaps you
will help me, Mrs. . . ."

"O'Hehir," came the grudging response.

"Mrs. O'Hehir. I am very pleased to meet you."
Nell thought the responding grunt carried just a bit
less hostility than before. "There are so many things
we'll be needing at the house. Staff, supplies—"

"And you think to find them here?"

"I thought I would try here first. There is a shop . . . ?"

"There is, aye, but you'll not be finding much at all. If you're after buying fancy silk and ribbons, you'd best be taking yourself to the city."

Nell winked at the child, who dared a quick, dimpling smile before disappearing again behind her mother. "I've little use for silk." She gestured to her own tidy but plain dress. "What I need is far more basic. Food, mostly. Candles. That sort of thing. And someone to repair what won't be replaced."

The woman's eyes narrowed. "O'Donnell had everything up from Galway City."

"Yes," Nell sighed. "I'm sure he did. But Mr. O'Donnell is no longer in Lord St. Wulfstan's employ and I will be relying on local service. Can you help me?"

For a long minute they faced each other. Nell thought Mrs. O'Hehir would be her own age, perhaps younger, and had certainly once been much prettier. But the difficult life had etched lines around her mouth and hardened her eyes. Nell wondered if things had worked out differently, if Thomas had lived and they had settled on his farm, whether she herself would have looked so worn at thirty.

Perhaps. But perhaps, too, she would have had a daughter tugging at her hands and skirts.

She glanced up from the little girl to find Mrs. O'Hehir studying her with unreadable eyes. Then, with a quick jerk of her head, the woman stepped from the doorway. "You'd best be talking to Aine Egan. She used to work at the house, before the old lord died, and runs the shop now."

Nell followed her to a weather-beaten door. The woman who answered it was just as careworn, and just as suspicious. At her neighbor's quick explanation, she lifted a brow and demanded, "Are they thinking any hereabouts will be in a rush to lift a finger for them? Good riddance, I said, when the old one died. And now the young one's back, thinking to belong. God should have left him wherever it was he went."

Saddened, hoping the surprise wouldn't be too unpleasant, Nell murmured, "I am sorry for your troubles, Mrs. Egan. My husband wants only to put things to rights."

The woman's eyes widened at the sound of her own language. "Well, I suppose I should be begging pardon—"

"Please." Nell shook her head. "There is no need. If you would just listen to why I am here. Decide, then, if you can assist me." She pulled a sheet of paper from her pocket and began to read its contents aloud.

Several other women crept in, spurred by curiosity, Nell thought, and by the possibility of change. The group listened to her list, nodding at some items, raising their brows at other. "I've no idea where we're to find six girls—" Mrs. Eagan said.

"My sisters will be glad of the work," Mrs. O'Hehir cut in. "And the Lullys have the two. 'Tis a start. As for men, Kern's eldest has been off the boat for nearly a year now. He'd be grand in a garden. Seamus is still one-handed, but he has a way, he does, with horses . . ."

Trevor watched from the doorway. Nell, shoulder to shoulder with the other women, was the picture of quiet efficiency. At one point, she said something that drew reluctant laughter from the others. Trevor had no idea what she was saying, only that her words and soft voice were working wonders. The very air had changed. It was filled now with rising cheer and anticipation.

Deciding he would leave her to her gentle magic, he strolled back toward the docks. There was a lone figure there, a man with one arm in a sling, patched coat thrown over his shoulders. There was something vaguely familiar about the face and absolutely no mistaking the expression.

Loathing and scorn blazed from the fellow's narrowed eyes. Trevor couldn't understand any of the torrent of words aimed at him, but the message was clear. His return was not a cause for celebration.

Suddenly Nell was by his side, speaking quietly to the man. She was answered with a snort, a hiss, and more angry Gaelic.

"Well?" Trevor demanded.

Nell sighed. "I won't translate most of it."

"Fine. What does he want? Other than my speedy demise, that is."

"Yes, well, I believe your demise would make him quite happy. Oh, now, Trevor, please." She got a grip on his sleeve when he started forward, fists clenched. "Offer him a job."

"*What?*"

"All of them—this place—need money desperately. It appears your steward was very dedicated about collecting rents, but not nearly so quick to pay for the few services he demanded. This is Seamus Lully. He hasn't been able to fish since March. The bone in his arm has been slow in healing. He needs work."

Suddenly Trevor remembered. Lully was perhaps a year older than he, with quick fists and a quicker temper. "What sort of job am I supposed to offer him?"

"You need grooms—"

"He'll only torch the stable, dammit."

"Then we'll build another one," Nell said softly. "And another, if necessary."

She was right. He knew she was right. Annoyed, but impressed nonetheless, he nodded. "Fine. See to it."

A half hour later, Nell was showing him a list of names and an empty money purse. "I paid for what I could in advance."

"And you honestly think you'll see what you paid for."

Her quick, brilliant smile almost had him dropping her as he helped her into the carriage. "It will come. They'll come."

He shook his head in wry admiration. "You bewitched them."

"Nothing of the sort. I paid them." When he'd settled himself on the seat and gathered up the reins, Nell reached over and briefly grasped his hand. "They're angry with you, Trevor. I know you don't blame them for that. But I believe they understand what brought you back. It might take a while for the trust to come and for the anger to go, but it will. Now, I do hope you like fish."

Trevor slapped the reins and turned the horse toward the end of the village. "I like fish well enough. Why?"

"Because," came the cheerful reply, "we are to have it for dinner tomorrow."

"Fine."

"And the day after."

Trevor lifted a brow. "And . . . ?"

"The day after that, too." Nell busied herself with the buttons of her gloves. "We must support local endeavors, after all."

"We must indeed." Trevor sighed. "For what it's worth, I don't care for mutton."

"Oh, dear. With all the sheep farms about." Nell patted his shoulder. "Well, you shall have ample opportunity to develop a taste for it, my lord." Then, "Will you show me the area now? We should wait at least an hour before visiting your tenants."

"Why an hour?"

"Because," Nell replied, discreetly tilting her chin toward the end of the street where several women and children were hurrying off, "it will take that long for word to reach everyone."

So they spent the next several hours driving over his lands. He took her to the Cove of the Hags, where she was vastly amused to learn that the place was named not for witches, but for the ill-tempered, noisy green cormorants who nested there. Trevor recalled an old tale of Mrs. King's. He told it to Nell, the local assertion that the birds were actually greedy fishwives who had so harassed their husbands that the poor men had appealed to Mannanán MacLír, the sea god, for help. Unlucky himself in love, the god had been only too glad to comply.

"So he transformed them into cormorants," Nell murmured with a smile.

"Left to squawk at their husbands from afar."

One of the birds screeched irritably in their direction. Nell laughed. "Connemara wives beware."

Trevor grinned at her. "Beware indeed."

She was standing at the edge of a rocky shoal. She'd removed her serviceable bonnet and had her face turned into the salty breeze. Gold-tipped curls blew wildly around cheeks pinkened by the wind. With her untempered smile and bright eyes, she was a lovely picture.

She squeaked as an errant wave jumped over her shoes, wetting the hem of her dress. Trevor tugged her away from the water. "Come along," he commanded, "before MacLír decides to claim you for himself."

"Ah, a typical god, is he? Always chasing other men's wives?"

If Trevor remembered correctly, the sea god had almost lost his own wife to another woman's husband. He didn't say so to Nell. He had neither the reason nor desire to talk about unfaithful wives.

"I hardly think I am the sort to appeal to a deity," she remarked airily as she shook the water from her shoes.

Trevor wrapped a warm hand around her upper arm, keeping her balanced. "You appeal to this mere mortal," he told her firmly, and earned himself a brilliant smile in response.

They walked around Wulfstan's lake, where they watched dragonflies darting over the surface. It was little more than a pond, really. More folly on the part of his ancestors, Trevor thought wryly.

"Ah. A princely frog." Nell crouched down near a rise of turf until she and the creature were nearly eye to bulging eye. "I suppose you want me to kiss you."

Trevor lifted her by the waist and turned her to face him. "That," he informed her, "is a toad, not a frog. Kiss me instead." She did, almost shyly, before slipping off to search a bog bramble for berries.

Eventually, they started their visits to the farm cottages. Trevor had noticed that the larger roads in the area were in appalling condition. The small ones were even worse. Trevor's admiration for his wife grew as he watched her tromping cheerfully over the boggy earth in places where the carriage couldn't go. By the third dismal holding, where she had charmed the

grim-faced tenants with her Gaelic and patient friendliness, he was in awe of her.

He supposed he shouldn't be surprised. He knew
Nell, knew her nature. He also knew that women in
her profession seldom succeeded simply because they
were pretty—or even talented in the boudoir. They
succeeded because they were smart and could bend
themselves to suit circumstances and people. But he
had long since stopped thinking of Nell as a courtesan
and the thought was ugly and jolting now.

She was his wife, a viscountess. Her past didn't
matter. Trevor turned away from where she chatted
with a farmer and his wife. As much as he loathed the
thought, he knew pasts did matter. Perhaps too much.

They had a long walk back to the carriage. Nell was
smiling to herself and ticking something off her fingers. He didn't ask. He didn't want to spoil her child-
like delight in whatever she was contemplating. She
stopped suddenly, pulling him to a halt, and shaded
her face with her hand. "What is that?"

He followed her gaze across the field. A dolmen
squatted solidly on a small rise. It was one of perhaps
a half dozen age-old markers scattered over his lands.
He remembered this one. He had spent one frustrating
but delightful night atop its capstone, kissing a local
girl and trying to coax her into more. She hadn't
spoken much English, but he thought he'd understood
enough. Parish priest and hawk-eyed mother notwith-
standing, she'd been reluctant to relinquish her virtue
on top of an ancient tomb. Trevor had agreed that it
wasn't the most comfortable place imaginable. He
hadn't shared her superstitious nature. He'd been fifteen, concerned only with losing his virginity. The following week he had enjoyed a very pleasant romp

with a housemaid atop a nearly identical dolmen on the other side of the estate.

He didn't think he would share those reminiscences with Nell. He did consider lifting her atop the flat stone and indulging a new and prurient fantasy. Instead, he shoved his hands into his pockets and followed her across the damp earth.

"It's a dolmen," he explained. "The entrance to a portal tomb."

"Ah." She reached the stones and ran a hand over the edge of the top slab. Then she bent to study the three supporting uprights. "I've never seen one. How amazing."

"Surely they exist in Wicklow."

She stood up and shrugged. "I would imagine so, but my world was very small. I was a widow before I'd ever seen Dublin."

Trevor wandered to the opposite side of the dolmen and leaned his arms on the capstone. "Where on earth did you come from, Nell?"

She smiled and propped her elbows on her side of the stone. "A very tiny village near Wicklow Town called—"

His laugh cut her off. "No, no. I suppose I should ask *how* rather than *where*. How does a little girl from a charitable school in a tiny Wicklow village come to be the elegant, sophisticated Mrs. Nolan?"

"The same way Mrs. Nolan became Lady St. Wulfstan, I suppose," was her quiet reply. "Choice, circumstance, and some strange enchantment."

"Strange, indeed. You are a remarkable woman, Nell."

He saw her flush at the compliment. "Nonsense. I am a perfectly ordinary woman in a remarkable world."

Ordinary as a lily sprung from weeds, he found

himself thinking. "Where *did* you come from?" Then, when she merely raised her brows at him, he asked, "Have you any family at all?"

"I have no idea," she said simply, flatly.

"Then why did you come back here?"

"Why did you?"

"Duty," was his terse reply.

"Truly?" she demanded, resting her chin on a bent hand.

"And what else would there be? I couldn't leave fast enough. This is a dismal place."

"Ah, well, I suppose I can understand that. Wicklow—Ireland—doesn't carry the most pleasant memories for me, either. But I still missed it so fiercely while I was gone . . ." She laid a palm flat on the stone and deftly changed the subject. "I wonder who is buried here. Someone very important, I imagine."

"Not important at all, I would say. Forgotten a thousand years."

Nell tilted her head and regarded him with her shadowed, beautiful eyes. "Do you take all of history so very lightly?"

He'd been thinking again about hauling her onto the smooth rock. He chuckled. "You take it seriously enough for both of us."

"Mmm. What of magic. Do you believe in that?"

"As in hags and princely frogs? Spells and curses? Or something else?"

"All part and parcel of the same thing," she replied. "Do you?"

"No. Of course I don't." Before Nell turned away, Trevor heard himself adding, "Not now."

She stepped around to the front of the dolmen, not quite close enough for him to reach her. "But you did once."

He shrugged. "Childhood ends. Now come along. I'm tired of standing in a bog."

She crouched for a minute in front of the opening. "Whoever you are," she addressed the shadowed hollow, "may you have peace and magic." Then she rose and slipped a hand into Trevor's. They struck off across the field toward the waiting carriage. "Do you think the rest of the visits can wait until tomorrow?"

"Certainly. Why?"

"Well, I should get back and warn Mrs. King about the impending arrivals."

"Fish?" Trevor queried dryly.

"Fish," she confirmed, "and, I hope, some more staff."

"To tend to the fishes' needs, I suppose?"

Nell smiled. "To tend to the viscount's needs."

Trevor stopped in his tracks, pulled her to him and kissed her curving lips. "I have a wife to do that. I'll concede the new staff to the haddock and mackerel."

"Whiting, actually."

Trevor sighed. "I am not so fond of whiting."

Nell kissed his chin. "Well . . ."

"Don't tell me. I shall have ample time to develop a taste for it."

"Actually, I was going to admit that I am not overly fond of whiting, either."

He felt the laugh blooming in his chest and something less identifiable unfurling behind it. "Ah, Nell. It is a remarkable world with you in it. Come along. We'll roll out the tatty red carpet for the whiting."

He had another reason for wanting to return to the house, one far more personal than fish or staff or wet feet. He wanted to search for his mother's belongings. He'd summarily cleared what was left of Richard's from the master bedchamber. But a quick glimpse into the mistress's had revealed only Nell's few things.

Here in Connemara, he wasn't worried about someone plunging a knife into his back. He was confident that he'd left those troubles in London. No one would be haunting him with violent intent. Which meant it was time to face the real ghosts.

CHAPTER 14

The weeks passed with dizzying speed. Before Nell's eyes, the house was regaining its beauty. Missing glass was replaced and windows sparkled. The marble floor had been sanded and polished until it gleamed. Mealla O'Hehir, helped by her sisters and friends, had sewn new hangings for the beds and windows. The women had all snorted over the price of the velvet and silk brocade; Aine Egan had been afraid to have it delivered to her worn little shop. Every day, something else was mended or replaced or restored. Even now, workmen were laying down their hammers after a day on the roof of the west wing.

More men were behind the house, layering sticks and hay into a towering pile at the edge of the beach. Nell stood and watched through the dining-room window. Behind her, the much-expanded staff bustled back and forth carrying linen and platters and armloads of candles. In front of her rose the pyre that would become the Midsummer's Eve bonfire after dark.

She had been planning the evening for several weeks, almost from the moment that the first wagonload of supplies and shy young men and women had arrived from the village. If all went as she hoped, the grounds would be filled with people and laughter that night.

She had sent invitations to everyone in the area, tenants and landowners alike. Midsummer's Eve was an important occasion in Ireland. She was determined to make it a grand yearly occasion at the Tombs.

The local parish priest had already arrived. Undaunted by the curt greeting he'd received from the Protestant master of the house, little Father MacDonagh had settled in, plopping himself down in a deep armchair in front of the fire. With an ottoman under his feet and a glass of madeira in his hand, he was happy as a stoat. Later, he would say a prayer at the lighting of the bonfire, the nominal Christian blessing of a very pagan tradition. Until then, Nell was sure he would be content to stay right where he was.

Leaving the final preparations in the hands of her cheerful if not precisely organized staff, she went upstairs to dress for the evening. For this special occasion, she had chosen a special dress. The fabric had arrived, tucked among the upholstery brocade. Mealla and Nell had sighed over it then; Nell sighed as she surveyed the finished product in the looking glass.

It was a simple column of silver-gilt silk. Pale, gossamer lace from a Galway convent trimmed the sleeves and low neck; gilt ribbon bound the fabric beneath Nell's breasts. She had abandoned her tight topknot for once and her maid had threaded more of the ribbon through the curls piled loosely atop her head. Studying her reflection, Nell knew she had never looked as well as she did then. Far from beautiful still, but she was quietly thrilled with the result.

"You look like moonlight." Trevor's voice came from across the room.

Nell spun to find him leaning in the doorway. He had not completed his own toilette and his brilliantly white shirt hung open to reveal a wedge of hair-sprinkled chest. Nell's heart stuttered at the sight of him. As precious as the days had been over the past month, the nights had been incomparable, magical. She warmed with memories, and with the promise of more nights to come.

"You really must stop looking at me like that," Trevor growled, "if you wish to remain in that dress." Nell smiled and dropped her gaze. She toyed with the trim on her bodice. "Oh," came his dry remark, "that's *much* better."

In an instant, he was across the room, his lips brushing over her temple, his hands closing hotly over her breasts. She laughed, then sighed breathily. "You'll muss me."

"So I will," he murmured. "God, Nell, you are beautiful tonight."

"So are you," she whispered into his chest.

He snorted and pulled away. Then he commanded, "Stay here," and disappeared through the connecting door.

Nell wandered back to the window to wait for him. Twilight was descending, the moon on its slow rise. Below, the pyre was nearly complete. Long torches had been lit and thrust into the sand to burn in a merry ring. Nell smiled as she felt Trevor's hands at her shoulders. Then she felt the cool touch of metal on her skin and looked down.

The gold was twisted in a delicate knotwork pattern, subtly Celtic in its design, and linked with countless small diamonds. What had Nell catching her breath was the pendant. It was more spun gold, fragile as a spider's web and worked into a globe. Inside was a pearl, round and shimmering pale, the size of a hazelnut.

"Your golden ball, my lady," Trevor said hoarsely, "with the moon inside."

Tears came to Nell's eyes. "It's beautiful . . . too beautiful . . ."

"It has been a long time since I came to you bearing a gift."

Nell fingered the little globe. "You shouldn't have done this. The expense—"

"Hush. The stones are all from old family pieces. They can't be sold, and I thought you deserved something made just for you. So I had the gems reset in Galway. They suit you. I should have done this before."

"No." Nell could just see the pearl reflected in the window. "No, it's perfect that you did this tonight. Thank you." She turned into his arms and kissed him with all of the gratitude and happiness she felt.

"Wear it tonight," he murmured.

"Of course I will. Did you think I would take it off and tuck it away somewhere?"

He grinned. "I meant later tonight. It and nothing else."

"Ah," Nell said, and smiled back. "Now go finish dressing. The pyre is ready."

She turned back to the window. Trevor peered over her shoulder as the men used ladders to place the last of the kindling atop the stack. "Did they leave a branch or bush in the county?"

"I hope not. They went door to door throughout the neighborhood, asking for wood."

"It appears no one said no."

"It's bad luck to." Nell touched her fingertips to the necklace. "It's a very important night, tonight."

Trevor dropped a quick kiss on her nape. "You are becoming a true Connemara girl."

"Mmm. I'm enjoying learning the traditions. Whatever the people here can teach me . . ."

"They've fallen in love with you, all of them."

Nell leaned back into his solid chest, heart swelling. "What a wonderful thing to say."

Together, they watched the men removing the ladders. More people came down the now-neat lawn to join them. Flasks came out of pockets and were passed around. Several men even tipped theirs in the direction of the house in merry toast. How very different feelings were from a mere handful of weeks earlier. There was still some wariness, especially when Trevor's tenants encountered him. His mood had lifted a bit since their arrival; he certainly was attentive and casually affectionate with his wife. But there was still a formidable reserve, a grim edge to him, and it showed most strongly when he was around the local people.

The fact that he did not speak their language certainly was part of it. But Nell was teaching him a little more Gaelic each day and he learned quickly, so that would eventually change. It was more than language, though. There was ancient history and bad blood Nell did not fully understand, and something else— a shadow over Trevor's presence in Connemara— that she didn't understand at all. Nell still flinched every time anyone turned from her husband, or crossed themselves at the sight of the scar. Trevor appeared not to notice, but Nell knew better. He noticed everything.

He seemed content that the people had warmed to Nell, slowly but surely accepting her as the lady of the manor. And if they were not precisely in love with her, she had fallen very much in love with them.

As she descended the stairs a quarter hour later on Trevor's arm, Nell couldn't remember having been happier. The great hall was clean, bright, decorated with new cloths and summer flowers. Peadar, now a proud footman in a smart uniform, had unearthed two dented and rusty suits of armor from the depths of the attics. A visit from the local blacksmith had restored them to shiny if not smooth glory. Nell had filled the visors with violets, laughing as she did at the diminutive size of the suits.

The St. Wulfstan knights, she'd teased her husband, had not been very impressive in stature. He'd merely raised a dark brow and directed her attention to the size of the codpieces. Both were impressive indeed. Silly male arrogance, she'd countered, then laughed and blushed at his knowing leer. That night he'd taken her breathy retraction with an equal amount of male arrogance and graciousness.

Together they walked through the growing crowd. Mealla's daughter Cait bounced into view, crisp white dress already stained with juice from a pilfered fruit tart. Nell bent down and deftly caught the girl's hands, keeping them off her own dress, but allowing her to pull Cait in for a sweetly sticky kiss.

"Dia dhuit tráthnóna, a Cháit."

The child returned the greeting, then darted a shy glance at Trevor. She went up onto her toes and whispered into Nell's ear.

Trevor listened to his wife's soft laugh. He understood only "yes" in her reply. Nell looked up at him. "Cait says you are very tall and wanted to know if you can catch stars."

"And what did you tell her?"

Nell straightened and patted the child's dark curls. "I told her that I didn't know about stars, but that you've given me the moon and I didn't even have to ask for it. She's very impressed."

So was he. Nell stopped here and there among their guests for a few words, spending as much time with the blacksmith as she did the wealthy Martins and D'Arcys. She slipped easily from Gaelic to English, from gracious mistress to courteous neighbor. She glowed and charmed; countless eyes followed her as she moved throughout the room. She looked up every so often to find him in the crowd, her smile just for him. And Trevor realized in that moment that he would kill anyone who tried to turn that smile away from him.

As darkness began to fall, everyone moved from the house to the rear lawn. A few young men plucked the burning torches from the sand and held them in cheerful impatience near the base of the pyre. The little priest shouted a few jovial phrases in what sounded to Trevor like a drunken mix of Gaelic and Latin. The instant the last word left his mouth, the men plunged the flames into the kindling. The bonfire went up with a muted roar that was lost to the cheering of the crowd.

Trevor remembered Midsummer's Eve bonfires from his childhood. But they had been small and private, lit by the estate's tenants. He had watched from the uppermost windows of the house, scanning the dark land for the little bursts of light, straining his ears to catch the shouting and snatches of song. There had never been a grand party at the Tombs. Even at the end of the harvest, the people had been left to their own celebrations. Trevor imagined former viscounts had provided food and drink, but they had never opened their home.

Now the air was full of music and laughter and some noises that were not nearly so pleasant. Children and adults alike banged on old pots and kettles, a few blasted away tunelessly on horns made from old bottles. People jumped over bits of burning wood; some tossed large twigs upward, then laughingly dodged the falling sparks. From his vantage point at the top of the lawn, Trevor watched as one youth who had not leapt quite nimbly enough and whose rough trousers were smoldering, was rolled briskly on the grass by helpful friends. He was on his feet moments later, grinning and juggling the several tankards people were pressing into his hands.

Nearby, a trio of fiddlers were joined by two *uillean* pipers and several men holding goatskin *bodhrán* drums. They launched into a merry jig and were soon joined by more fiddles and a tin flute. Two by two, men and women skipped into the dance until they overflowed the space that had been cleared. On the edges, single dancers did quick, high-stepping patterns that would have defied all of London's overpriced dance instructors.

Trevor closed his eyes for a moment and just listened to the music. It wasn't a tune he knew, but it leapt and lilted and he thought he could listen all night. When it ended, he opened his eyes. It occurred to him that he could demand the musicians play the song again. They would. After all, he was paying for the celebration. He gazed almost wistfully at the goatskin drums with their carved wood tippers. He'd always wanted to try one and knew he could ask to have a go. But somehow, he didn't dare. This wasn't his evening; it was theirs.

He stood back from the celebration, knowing he wasn't really part of it, content to watch his wife working her own magic in the midst of the pagan revelry. She joined John D'Arcy in a lively reel, laughed and shook her head as Aine Egan tried to teach her a series of quick steps. She caught his eye and gracefully extricated herself from the crowd.

"You look very imposing, standing here," she told him when she reached his side. "Come down and dance with me."

He glanced at the couples enthusiastically hopping and flailing to the music and shook his head. "You come up and dance with me." He jerked his chin at the bedroom windows above.

"Later." Nell grasped one of his hands between hers. "Please. Come be part of things. I hate seeing you standing apart, as if you don't belong."

He didn't. Not to the position, nor to the house. Certainly not among the carefree country folk below. But he couldn't explain that to Nell, much as he knew he should.

"Leave them to their enjoyment," he said gruffly. "I'll take no pleasure in it and will only spoil theirs with my presence."

"Oh, Trevor." Nell sighed and squeezed his hand. "Very well, then. Come with me."

"I am not dancing."

"You don't have to."

She guided him down past the bonfire, stopping to take a torch from the ring before continuing down the beach.

"Where are we going?" he demanded. As much as he had enjoyed surprising Nell in the past, he didn't much care to be on the other side.

"Patience," she scolded.

"There is a breeze out here. You'll be cold."

"I'll be fine. Stop whinging." She tugged him along.

Trevor grunted. He hadn't been accused of whinging in more than twenty years and it rankled. "Nell—"

"There. That is where we are going."

He followed her pointing arm. All he could see was the dark stretch of beach and a small mound. It didn't look like a spot for pleasant surprises or warm trysts. But Nell had struck off ahead, leaving him with nothing to do but follow. When he caught up with her she was already bending over the mound, which turned out to be a knee-high pile of brush and twigs. She set her torch to it and it burst into flame.

"Sit," she commanded.

Trevor discovered a small rug spread a few feet from the fire. He lowered himself onto it. Nell joined him. "What is this?" he asked her.

"Something I had Peadar prepare earlier." She gestured to a prickly-looking pile at their feet. "Choose something and throw it into the fire."

"Nell—"

"Indulge me."

Trevor grumbled as he lifted a bound bunch of twiggy plants. A familiar scent wafted to his nose. "What is this?"

"Rosemary. Throw it in." He did, then watched as Nell chose a circle of oak leaves and tossed that into the flames. The greenery hissed as the fire consumed it. "That's hawthorn," she said of the next group of twigs, "and this is clover. We really ought to have pinecones, but I couldn't find any."

"And why on earth should we have pinecones?"

"Shhh." She placed a finger over his lips, then twined her arm with his and rested her cheek against his shoulder. "Just watch the fire for a while."

The flames were leaping merrily by then, brilliant reds and yellows and faint flashes of blue. Nell knew when the tenseness ebbed away from Trevor. The muscles under his sleeve relaxed and he released his breath with an audible sigh. Twenty yards or so away, the waves flowed rhythmically over the sand and in the distance the big bonfire blazed. The music, the sea, and the crackling of the fire played together in pleasant harmony. When Trevor pulled his arm from hers and lifted it, she snuggled against his chest, smiling as he closed her into his embrace.

They stayed that way, not speaking, until the fire burned low. Near the house, the large fire was little more than a pile of embers. Enough time had passed for Nell to know Trevor had lost—even if only temporarily—the cares that weighed on him, that she sensed but somehow knew better than to ask about. She didn't especially want to go back. This quiet little interlude had been almost unbearably sweet. She knew she should be back at the house when the guests started to leave. She knew, too, that precious interludes had to end sometime.

"Trevor."

"Hmm?" He started and she hoped the thoughts he'd been so lost in had been pleasant ones.

"There should be one oak garland left."

He found it. "Should I put it in?"

"No. Leave it where we've been sitting." She climbed reluctantly to her feet and, when he followed, lifted the blanket. "Put it there." When he had, she bent to touch it lightly with her fingertips. "This is for the fairies."

"Fairies, is it?"

She clucked her tongue at his dry tone. "Careful. You'll offend them and they'll touch us with mischief rather than magic tonight."

"We don't need fairies tonight," he shot back, then, gently, "Another local superstition you've learned?"

Nell tucked the folded blanket under her arm and turned back toward the house. "No. This is something a friend taught me many years ago in Wicklow.

She believed in curses and spells and asking the fairies to make the future bright."

"Did she get her bright future?"

"She died at sixteen," Nell said quietly, seeing Kitty's pretty face in her mind as if it were yesterday. "She caught a cold and died."

"A cold? People don't die of colds."

"They do when they aren't tended. The headmaster and the mistress of the school did nothing when she developed a fever. Kitty was lively, you see. Saucy and a bit wild. They decided the fever was a sign from God, that she would rise from her bed weaker and humbled. She died instead."

"Ah, Nell." Trevor ran a warm hand down her back.

They walked back to the house in silence. The musicians were still playing, softer songs now. People were grouped around the still-burning remains of the bonfire, scooping ashes and embers from the outer edges into tin cups. "The embers will go into their hearths," Nell said as she watched, "the ashes sprinkled on the fields. For luck and good days to come."

She smiled as an elderly woman pressed a little tin cup into her hand. *"Go raibh maith agat,"* she thanked her, then, *"Slán abhaile!"*

As one guest after another took their leave, she wished them safe home, too. By the time the fire was little more than a faint glow and the last of the wine and ale was gone, the embers in Nell's cup had long since been reduced to ash. She shrugged, then sprinkled the cool contents onto the grass.

Trevor was nowhere to be seen. She found him in the front of the house, lifting old Cathal Egan into the plush new tilbury. Six decades on the sea had left the man bent and weather-beaten. His smile was bright, though, if wavery as he gave Trevor a drunken salute.

Then Peadar clicked the horse into motion and they were off, bearing the old man comfortably home.

Nell smiled as Trevor joined her on the stoop. "You've made a friend there," she said.

"He won't even remember in the morning."

"Yes, he will." She held the door wide. "Come inside now. I feel fairies in the air."

"They're not invited," Trevor shot back, grinning, and was through the door in a heartbeat.

The house was still busy, the staff clearing away the remnants of the celebration, as they headed for the stairs.

"Begging your pardon, m' lady." One of the maids was hurrying across the floor, cloth-wrapped bundle in her arms. She bobbed an awkward curtsy as Nell and Trevor stopped. "One of the lads found these in the back of one of the old sheds when he was searching for wood. Peadar and Sean read a bit, but the writing is all in English, so they'd no way of knowing if these are important. They're very fine, so we thought best to bring them to you. They were among a pile of lady's things, all fancy once, but given no care, as if they'd been left as rubbish." She held out the bundle.

Nell took it. She lifted the cloth, uncovering a stack of thin, leather-bound diaries. There were perhaps twenty of them, and beneath the dust and grime she could see that they were very fine indeed. The once-colorful, cracked leather was embossed with gold, the pages edged with the same.

"I wonder what these—"

She looked up, startled, when Trevor seized them from her hands. "Where did these come from?" he demanded. He jerked his chin at the maid. "What did she say?"

Nell explained and watched Trevor's face darken.

"That troll," he snarled. The maid scurried off. "That vile, sanctimonious old troll. May he rot in hell!" He drew a ragged breath and ran one hand gently over the top diary. Then he turned to Nell. His eyes were fierce, but she saw sadness behind the fire. "Go ahead to bed."

"But—"

"Go to bed, Nell. Please. I have something to do that cannot wait."

She nodded, knowing there was no use in protesting. "Very well." She touched her fingertips to his rigid jaw. "Wake me when you're done, if you like. I won't mind."

He gave a jerky nod, then turned on his heel. Nell watched him stalk across the hall and disappear through one of the far doors. Then, trying to ignore the knot of unease forming in her stomach, she climbed the stairs to her chamber.

CHAPTER 15

Trevor set aside yet another journal and stretched muscles that had stiffened in the cool library. He debated getting up to restoke the fire, but couldn't be bothered. He had a great deal more to read. His mother had been a prolific writer, but she hadn't bothered to date her entries. In the past two hours, he had read bits from her debutante days, her early days as Viscountess St. Wulfstan, and the middle years when her biggest concerns had been what clothing to order for the Dublin Season. She wrote of dresses and baubles, of her pair of pretty white horses and shiny tilbury that had put Lady Ballyclare's bays and curricle to shame. She had complained about the Union with England and how the Anglo-Irish aristocracy was decamping family by family for London, leaving Dublin a social wasteland. She made no mention whatsoever of the '98 rebellion, of the Irish lives that had been lost and the dreams that had been dashed then. So far, Trevor hadn't found anything beyond the self-centered, self-satisfied ramblings of a pampered gentlewoman.

That didn't surprise him. Elizabeth St. Wulfstan had been blithe, careless, and vain. He'd never had any misconceptions about his mother's character. But she had been pretty and vivacious during his childhood, ready to sing or play a childish game with her son, and he had loved her. That hadn't changed, even when everything else had. Trevor had forgiven her for her carelessness, for her secrets, and for not protecting him from Richard's brutal fists. Even now, his only anger was that she had died without any sort of farewell.

He poured a measure of whiskey into his emptied glass and lifted the next journal. Perhaps this one . . . He'd looked for them many times since returning to the Tombs, turning out drawers and digging through attic trunks. He hadn't really been surprised when he'd failed to find a single one of her possessions. In the end, he'd assumed that either Elizabeth or Richard had destroyed the journals. It would never have occurred to him that they were moldering in a filthy outbuilding with a pile of the clothes she had chosen and worn with such proud delight.

Trevor wondered when the old man had found the journals. It would have been before Elizabeth's death, certainly. But she had kept writing even after her husband read her secrets. The journal Trevor held had only a handful of entries. The last one began,

Nuala Doyle has promised me a cream for my eyes. She claims it will take away the awful little lines that are spreading like cracks in a glass. I don't suppose I shall put much faith in her words. She is only six-and-forty, a full two years younger than I, yet looks to be an old woman of seventy. Still, I have had such daily good from her sleeping draughts . . .

She had died within a year of that entry. Vain to the end, Trevor mused. But then, he had not been back to visit her since fleeing at sixteen. He wondered if he would have been horrified to see her, face lined and slack from daily use of sedative draughts.

Elizabeth's journals had been an entertaining diversion to her at first, a comfort and solace later. She'd hidden them from her husband from the beginning. *"Everyone must have something that is theirs alone,"* she'd told her son when he had come upon her writing one day. *"One's little secrets."*

She had spilled her secrets to her journals. He'd carried his inside. Oh, he thought now, he had an abundance of things that were his alone, and not an ounce of solace or comfort to be found in them. He had learned at a very early age to keep his own counsel. His mother was too busy or uninterested to listen; he had very little contact with the neighborhood children. By the time he was seventeen, his secrets had become too shameful to share. By the time he'd spent a few years working with the Ten, his secrets had become too grim and unforgivable.

He turned his attention back to his mother's last journal. Like the rest, it had been tossed away like so much refuse. Trevor could only assume the old man had commanded that all her possessions be taken from the house and destroyed. Perhaps they had gone into the shed to wait for the next rubbish fire and been forgotten.

Trevor couldn't stand to read anything further from the last journal. He would come back to it if none of the others gave him the answers he needed. But if his mother's last entry had been about the lines around her eyes, it wasn't likely she'd written anything of import there. He chose another from the stack and skimmed it. More balls, more fripperies, more determined one-upmanship with Ladies Ballyclare, Killone, and Carmody.

The next journal fell open in his hands, its spine broken.

Is it evil of me to accept such happiness when it is found in such faithless acts? In his arms I can almost remember the beauty of the long-ago past, and almost forget the ugliness of the present . . .

Trevor's mouth went dry. He read on, cutting through the florid prose and melodrama, growing colder with every entry. This must have been the first one Richard had found—on that day sixteen years earlier.

Still this illicit love grows, struggling like a flower in the craggy moors, yearning to burst forth into the sunlight but ever relegated to the shadows . . .

Trevor turned the page, and another, and another. Then,

My prayers have been answered. I am at last with child! The good Lord willing, it will be a boy, and St. Wulfstan will have an heir. That the child shall not be a St. Wulfstan at all need never be known . . .

His child grows within me, and I bloom with health, yet I cannot be truly content. I have not seen him in nearly a month, and while St. Wulfstan struts and preens in his supposed triumph, I secretly pine for the true father of my child . . .

We have named the child Trevor, after my father. He is a perfect infant, sweet and healthy. His hair is dark, with fiery lights and his eyes the color of cobalt glass. There is every chance that either will change as he grows older, but even should they not, I anticipate no trouble. Between St. Wulfstan's Norman heritage and my Celtic, there is darkness abounding . . .

* * *

Trevor flourishes even as I feel myself sliding into a bleak chasm. He has not been to see his son, not been to see me. I dare not send messages which might be intercepted. So I pray fervently for a chance meeting, yet it has been so many months now . . .

Under Trevor's eyes, his mother's love affair withered to nothing and, as the journals entered the years after his birth, all references to her lover vanished. He read every entry. He watched himself grow. Elizabeth had been delighted by his talents: his early speech—*St. Wulfstan will remind me that the boy said 'Papa' first, but 'Mama' comes far more often and always with that beautiful baby smile;* his quickness in running to her, his pleasure in collecting wildflowers for her dressing table. *Wild orchids today, violets yesterday to match my dress* . . . Then, years later:

His face—my son's beautiful face where I can see so much of myself—ruined. How very clever of Richard to strike at me in such a way. He would not touch me, but O, a mother's feelings. I will feel that vicious lash of the horsewhip each time I look upon my son, will imagine it on my own pale brow . . .

Trevor viciously crumpled the page. After all these years, he felt the searing pain as clearly as if it were yesterday. And he knew his mother hadn't felt the agony of the whiplash for a moment. She would never have seen it in the mirror. She would have looked at her face—until the first of the lines appeared, at least—and admired its unmarred smoothness.

"Hell," Trevor muttered. "Bloody everlasting hell!"

With a furious sweep of his arm he knocked the stack of journals from the desk. His glass went with them, shattering, spraying crystal shards and whiskey over the carpet. Then, with an anguished moan, he buried his head in his hands.

She had written too many of her secrets, yet not quite enough. She had never given the man's name.

Trevor had spent the last sixteen years carrying the knowledge of his parentage like a splinter under his skin. He'd learned to live with it. But he had always assumed that he would learn his father's identity someday. He had counted on it.

Exhausted, frustrated, and entirely defeated, Trevor kicked the journals into a loose pile near the hearth. Had there been a fire there, he would have burned them. He would—another day. Leaving them where they lay, he stalked from the room.

Had he not consumed half a bottle of whiskey over the past several hours, and had he not felt so wretchedly alone, he would have been better able to handle the fact that Nell was not in his bed. As it was, he was only able to keep the connecting door between their chambers from slamming against the wall as he threw it open.

Nell came awake instantly. Silhouetted against the faint candlelight behind him, Trevor looked larger than ever, larger than life.

Before she could speak, he growled, "What are you doing in here?"

She smelled whiskey and wondered how much he'd drunk. Whatever had been in those journals had clearly affected him—more deeply, certainly, than he usually allowed things to touch him. She could feel the barely contained emotion emanating from him all the way across the room. "What time is it?" she asked softly. Something told her she was dealing with a wounded creature and needed to use the utmost care.

"I have no idea. Late. Early." He stalked across the room to loom over the foot of the bed. "I'll ask again. Why are you in this bed and not in mine?"

She didn't think this was quite the time to tell him that she didn't like the master bedchamber. It was cold, severe, and had shadows in the corners that never seemed to leave, even when the sun was shining through the windows. The idea of climbing into the massive bed without him had been unappealing. She tossed back the covers and swung her legs over the edge of the mattress. "I'll come now."

"You can bloody well sleep with me," he snapped as she reached him.

"I am going to—"

"I won't have you thinking you can hop in and out of my bed. You're not Mrs. Nolan any longer. Don't forget that."

How could she, when he slapped her with it? Nell caught her breath with the physical hurt of his words. He hadn't mentioned her past in a very long time. It was only the whiskey and pain talking, she told herself firmly. And she could help.

She rose and walked to him, ignoring his low growl when she touched his shoulder. "I don't like being in that bed without you," she murmured, "so I waited for you here." She stroked his arm, then his hard jaw. "Will I come now or will you stay with me here?"

He growled again, low in his throat, then abruptly sank to the edge of the bed. "God, Nell," he groaned, then dropped his head into his hands. Nell didn't have to think. She stepped between his knees and cradled his bent head against her stomach. She stroked his hair, the bunched muscles in his shoulders. And eventually his arms came up to encircle her. He held her tightly, his cheek pressed into the folds of her nightgown and slowly Nell felt him relax beneath her hands.

They stayed like that for several silent minutes. Then Nell gently cupped his face in her hands, turning it up to hers. Even in the dark, she could see the bleakness in his eyes. "Oh, darling," she whispered, feeling his torment like an ache around her heart. "Can you tell me?"

He appeared to hesitate for a moment. Then he shook his head. "Not now. Tomorrow."

She nodded, lowered her hands to squeeze his. "Come to bed now. Your hands are cold."

She bent and unfastened his shoes, drew them off. His fingers seemed leaden on the buttons of his waistcoat, so she took care of that, too. His shirt followed. Nell started to undo the placket of his breeches and was startled to feel him full and hard beneath her hands.

"Oh. My."

He chuckled, a pained sound. "I'm drunk, Nell, not dead." Then he snared the end of her braid where it had fallen forward over her shoulder. He tugged, pulling her closer. "Say no if you wish; I'll understand. I've . . . been known to howl at the moon on occasion."

Nell had received better apologies in her life, but few that meant more. This one touched her heart and registered hot and low in her belly. She straightened and undid the row of buttons at her throat. Then she grasped her nightgown and drew it slowly over her head. She could feel the cool air of the room and the heat of his gaze on her bared skin as she let the gown fall to the floor. The pearl pendant rested warmly over her heart. She had expected him to come to her; she'd prepared for it.

She stepped back, beckoned to him. He rose and they stood for a long moment, chest to chest but not quite touching. Then she knelt and unbuttoned his breeches, drawing them down his legs. He stepped out of them and kicked them away. Nell cupped him in her palm, reveling in the power pulsing under the silken skin, pressed a tender kiss to the inside of his thigh.

"No," he growled, taking a step backward. "No. I want this to be for you." He grasped her shoulders and pulled her to her feet. "Tell me what I can do for you." His hands were moving now, sliding down her arms, over her hips. He pulled her to him and brushed his lips over her cheekbones, then over her eyelids when her eyes drifted dreamily closed. "Tell me."

Nell's breath hitched; her heartbeat was quickening. "Just touch me," she whispered. "Don't stop touching me."

"Where?" The rough edge to Trevor's voice coursed over her sensitive nerves, making her shudder with longing. "Where do you want me to touch you?" His fingers were in her hair suddenly, tugging it free of its braid, then threading through it to caress the nape of her neck. "Here?" He traced a tantalizing path down her neck and around to the base of her throat. "Here?"

"Yes," Nell panted. "No."

He cupped her breasts, grazing each nipple with his thumbs. "Here?"

She was too busy concentrating on simply drawing breath into her lungs to do more than nod. When his fingers brushed over the taut peaks, she bit back a whimper. Light and gentle as a breeze, his thumbs circled her nipples, then he pinched gently, tugged. Nell felt the pull all the way to her core. She moaned, her head dropping back. Trevor slid his hands down to her hips again and buried his lips in the hollow of her exposed throat. Nell hummed in protest and in pleasure. Then he was parting her thighs. "Here? Tell me yes, Nell. I want to touch the very center of you."

"Yes," she managed. "Oh, yes."

His fingers delved gently, teasing and stroking. When her knees went weak he held her, lowering her to lie on the mattress. Nell's first impulse was to hold him tight against her. But when she tried to do so, he made a guttural sound, half chuckle and half growl, and pulled away.

"I'll keep touching you, sweetheart, as you want. Where you want. But"—now he was sliding down her trembling form, his breath hot on her already-fevered skin—"I choose the part of me that will touch you."

He knelt on the floor. His hands parted her loosened thighs. Nell felt the moist heat of his mouth and she whimpered. This was a pleasure she had never known before lying with this man and it awed her. Consumed her. She buried the fingers of one hand in the thick silk of his hair, crushed the sheet beside her hip with the others.

Her climax thundered through her, stunning in its speed and power. She cried out, arching her back and tightening her grip, looking for any purchase in the storm as it raged. Trevor disentangled her fingers from his hair. She felt him spreading her arms wide, felt his fingers sliding between hers. "Will this do?" he whispered.

She cried out again, squeezed his hands hard. He covered her with his body, hot and solid, and she suddenly wanted to cry with the simple wonder of what he did to her. He eased into her, filling her completely as the waves were receding, and she knew she would climax again. But he made her wait this time, measuring his strokes to keep her at the summit without tipping her over it. So smoothly that they weren't separated for even an instant, he rolled her over to straddle him. Nell was certain he could feel her heart, he was so deep inside her. She rocked slowly at first, then with a thrilling, desperate tempo. On and on it went, the glorious heat and press of him within her. Each time she neared the peak he stilled, waited that crucial heartbeat, then drove her up again. Only when Nell begged, crying out his name with ragged breaths did he give those final, impossibly deep thrusts that lifted her off her knees and sent them both spiraling over the edge.

She collapsed bonelessly against his chest. Her pulse was thundering in her ears; she could feel his heart pounding against her cheek. She was weak, breathless, and as vitally alive as she could ever remember being.

"Nell?"

"Hmm?"

"I . . . Thank you."

She slung a lethargic arm across his chest and propped her chin on her wrist. "For?"

"For not sending me away tonight. You could have."

"Mmm. I could have," she agreed. "But you needed me. And I wanted you."

He closed his arms around her. "After what I said.
You humble me, Nell."

It wasn't the declaration she suddenly realized she
craved, but it was heartfelt; she could hear it in his
voice.

"I am sorry," he said then, "for . . . what I said. It
was unforgivable."

"More unnecessary," she replied. Then, almost
without thinking, she quietly informed him, "Yours is
the only bed I've ever wanted to share. The only one I
ever will."

His chest jerked beneath her. "Say that again."

She did, then, "And I've only ever given myself to
one other man: Thomas Nolan."

Without tipping her off him, Trevor dragged a
pillow beneath his head. She could see his face.
He looked, she decided, as if she had spoken to him
in old Gaelic. "I don't understand. The others . . .
Clonegal . . ."

"No others. And I was a companion to the duke, a
nurse first to Anastasia Balashova who *was* his mistress, later to him as he was dying. I did what I did,
took on the character I did to gain entrée to the
Golden Ball. After that I intended to come home to
Ireland. But you . . ." She smiled a bit sadly. "You
changed everything."

He didn't respond. Nell waited, then waited some
more. Finally, she murmured, "I thought it was time
you knew."

After another interminable silence, he nodded. "I'm
glad you told me," he said gruffly, and nothing more.

Stung and confused, Nell tried to pull away from
him. Immediately, his arms tightened around her
back, keeping her firmly where she was. She went still,

holding her breath, waiting for him to say anything. He didn't. But he didn't release her, either.

Nell stared into the darkness for countless minutes. He could have said so many things. *Thank God . . . I misjudged you, Nell, and I'm sorry for that . . . I suspected as much all along . . .*

For the first time, she was forced to wonder what he thought about marriage—their marriage. About her. Did he really not care that the courtesan he thought he'd married hadn't been a courtesan at all? And Nell realized *she* cared. Now, when she'd left both Nell Nolan of Wicklow and Mrs. Nolan of London behind her, she cared a great deal. When it all came down to the heart of things, all she had that was hers alone was her honor.

She had given Trevor everything else she possessed: her fortune, her body, her loyalty. Without knowing she was doing it, she'd given him her heart, completely and irrevocably. She had fallen in love with a rogue, with a man who could break her heart as easily as a crystal glass. And he probably would.

She loved him. With all that she was.

"God help me," she whispered.

"Hmm?" Trevor shifted beneath her. "What did you say?"

"A little prayer," she replied, closing her eyes against the ache in her chest. Praying would be of no use. Nell was as certain of that as she was of her feelings for this man. From the moment his face had appeared in a hand mirror on a cold Wicklow night, her fate had been sealed. Faith had nothing to do with it. It had been pure, ancient magic. Enchantment.

And enchantment, she knew, did not always mean a happy ending.

Trevor grunted. "Go to sleep, Nell. You can pray in the morning."

As it turned out, she did. But the fervent words she spoke then were not for her, or even for the man she loved.

CHAPTER 16

Trevor woke from a dream of rain and standing stones to find morning light coming through the windows. It took him a minute to recognize his surroundings—he spent little time in this chamber—and to realize that Nell wasn't in bed beside him. He stretched, lazy with the effects of good sex and a good night's sleep.

Then he remembered.

The flash of anger and desperation hit him fast and hard. His mother's vanity, Richard's brutality . . . The fact that the man he'd loved like a father wasn't his father at all. He'd carried that burden with him for half of his life. He thought he'd gotten past the worst of it years ago—learned to live with it. He could credit the faint ache in his head to whiskey, but the painful tightness in his chest was that of an old wound that had reopened.

He scrubbed his hands hard over his face and reminded himself that he'd gone searching for answers in his mother's journals. He could have left it alone. But he hadn't. He'd needed to know. It shouldn't surprise him that he'd come away with no answers but a fresh supply of grim images he'd worked so hard to forget. He shouldn't have expected his parents to give him anything more in death than they had in life.

Just then he caught a subtle waft of Nell's scent from
her pillow. In an instant, the pain and fury ebbed, returning to being the same burden he'd carried for so
many years, nothing more and nothing less. He could
bear it. And he could, if he chose, share it. He could tell
Nell. If he chose to.

Her nightgown was folded neatly at the foot of the
bed. Her brush and several abandoned hairpins sat
atop her dressing table. The necklace lay nearby,
arranged so carefully that it made a perfect circle on
the glossy applewood. Nell's presence was all around
him, modest and certain and calming . . .

"Oh, Christ." He stared up at the ceiling as he recalled the rest of the night. "Oh, you bloody fool," he
growled at himself. Ten minutes later, he was dressed
and on his way down the stairs to find her.

She was in the breakfast room. The post had arrived, a rare occurrence in this corner of Ireland, and
was spread over the table in front of her. The room
had been carefully restored; glaziers had come from
Galway to replace the broken panes in the stained-
glass panels that topped the tall windows. The golden
light burnished her hair, brightened the yellow of her
dress, and to his eyes she looked like a beam from
the sun. Moon by night, sun by day, Trevor mused,
and found himself smiling. What more could a man
ask for?

Then she looked up and the smile died on his
face. "What is it?" he demanded at the sight of her
vague eyes.

She set the letter she'd been holding carefully down
on the table, smoothed it with her palm. "My father
died," she said quietly.

Trevor didn't respond immediately. He hadn't thought
of Nell as having a father—at least not one whose

death would touch her. At last he managed, "I'm sorry."

"Six months ago."

"What?"

She tapped the missive. "I've just learned now. I wrote to a neighbor in Wicklow weeks ago, asking for news of my parents. She has only just replied."

He was confused. "You . . . knew your father?"

"Of course I knew him. You look surprised."

"I confess I am. I had thought . . ." Trevor spread his hands, not knowing quite what to say. He'd been ready to tell Nell about his own father, what little he knew, assuming she would understand. Suddenly he had the sensation that he might have been wrong.

"You thought . . . Ah. Yes, Annie said there was a rumor about my parentage. A peer? A younger son? And a housemaid, or something like that. I'd forgotten; it mattered so little to me." She shook her head with a wry smile. "The truth is much less interesting."

Trevor sat down across from her. "Tell me."

She nodded, then turned her face to the window. It was clear she wasn't looking at the bright summer day and calm sea. Whatever she was seeing in her mind was less appealing. "My father was the Right Reverend John Ferrall. He was headmaster of the Horgan School in Glanely, County Wicklow, and fixture at all of the finer dinner tables in the area. He was fire and brimstone in the pulpit, but clever enough to tilt his sermons so his rich parishioners saw heaven within their reach." She sighed. "My mother was the suitable extension of his godly arm. Nothing more than that, and rather less, I suppose. She had none of his intelligence or deceptive charm and all of his ignorance. They were both zealous, severe, and cruel."

"A minister's daughter," Trevor muttered as he digested this wholly unexpected information.

"Mmm. And not a very good minister's daughter at that."

"Wayward?" he asked, trying to create a comprehensible picture.

Nell laughed humorlessly. "Hardly. I tried very hard, you see, to be a dutiful daughter, but I always seemed to fall short. I wasn't clever, I preferred local folktales to Psalms, and, worst of all, I wasn't pretty. So I was of no use. None of the moneyed sons would ever be interested in marrying me and boosting my parents up another step in the social ladder.

"I married Thomas because he asked, because he was sweet and eager, and because he would take me away from Horgan's. I became an embarrassment to my parents then, their daughter the farmer's wife. When I joined the duke's household I completely ceased to exist to them." She glanced down then at the letter. "I sent a letter to Horgan's, too. According to Mrs. Livingstone, my mother is still there. She wouldn't even write to tell me my father had died."

"Do you want to go see her?" Trevor asked gently.

This time, Nell's laugh was harsh. "Why? She would only close the door in my face." Then she ran a weary hand over her brow. "I would like to think I would go anyway, out of duty and respect. But I know better. I'm not so noble. For all that they preached of love and forgiveness, they possessed none. I suppose I've forgiven them for their cruelty to me, for the beatings and the insults. But I can't forgive them for what they did to Kitty and dozens of other poor girls through the years."

Her mouth and eyes softened, if only a little. "But now that you know, you can take comfort in the fact that you married a respectable widow of respectable birth."

Trevor leaned back in his chair and crossed his arms over his chest. "And why would I do that?"

Nell shrugged. "These things matter. Perhaps less if there are to be no children, but they matter. What is the expression? Blood always tells? Anyway"—she folded the letter roughly and tucked it into her pocket—"he is gone and may God have more mercy than he did."

Little pieces had begun to fall into place. Trevor had never understood her weekly treks to the Anglican church five miles away, or the little gold crucifix that rested on the table beside her bed but that she never wore. Now he did. Other women might have rebelled against godliness, would have lived wilder, careless lives. Not Nell. She'd simply found her own peace, quiet and firm.

"I'm sorry," she was saying now. "I have ruined a lovely morning and for naught. Shall we take a luncheon basket to the headland and watch the boats?"

"Fine. I would like that."

Nell rose and gathered the rest of the post into a neat pile. "This will wait. Bills," she said, brisk and nearly cheerful now, "and what is most certainly a letter from Clonegal's solicitor, cautioning me against spending my inheritance so rashly. Let's see. This will be the third . . . no, fourth. Silly man." She paused on her way across the room. "Oh. Oh, Trevor, I am sorry."

"For what?" he asked, surprised.

"For not asking about what was troubling you last night. How insensitive of me. You'd said you would speak of it this morning."

He shook his head, managed a smile. "Too much

drink and several hours with memories of my parents. I should be apologizing for my behavior."

"Don't. It all ended well enough."

"Nell . . ."

"I'll go speak to Cook about preparing a basket. Shall we say half an hour?"

"Fine." He watched her leave, knowing he should have said something more. He just didn't know what it was.

These things matter . . . they matter.

He'd kept the circumstances of his birth secret for more than fifteen years. He could keep them secret until he died.

They chose a spot on the headlands with a clear view of the sea and a standing stone to protect them from the worst of the wind. Nell studied her husband's profile as he reclined beside her on the rug she'd spread over the earth. He'd grown a bit thinner in the past fortnight; there were hollows under his jutting cheekbones. It suited him, she thought, but worried her a little. Whatever was weighing on his mind was showing in his face. And she hadn't seen him eat anything the night before, nor that morning. She couldn't make him talk to her if he wasn't ready, but she would fill a plate for him when they opened the basket and make sure he ate it all.

From this side of him she couldn't see the scar. He was beautiful, even more so when he faced her straight on, eyes warm on hers. The sea breeze slipped around the stone, lifting his hair. She brushed the overlong strands back from his brow, then ran her fingertips through the soft waves at his nape that had begun to curl in the damp air. He turned toward her with a faint smile. "I daresay Cook tucked a knife in there with the food. You could have a good hack at this tangle."

"I wouldn't dare." Nell tugged at an auburn lock. "I like it just the way it is."

"Wild?"

"Absolutely."

And she did. There was more than a little of the wild beast about Trevor, and she was beginning to understand that she wouldn't have him any other way.

He reached up and snared one of the neat curls that framed her face. "The night of the opera I thought Rickham had a watch chain made from your hair. He wanted me to think it, wanted me to take a good look."

"Did you?"

"No. I wouldn't have been able to resist the urge to garrote him with it."

Nell sighed when he let his fingers slide feather-soft along her cheek before pulling his arm back to his side. For a man so quick to talk of violence and, she knew, so capable of it, he'd shown her so much gentleness. And silly as these little flashes of jealousy were, they were terribly gratifying.

"He tried," she said after a moment, realizing that London seemed years away instead of just a few weeks. "He came at me with a pair of shears on the first night of our acquaintance." She smiled with the memory. "He actually had them in his pocket. I cannot fathom why."

"His watch chain collection is famous," Trevor muttered. "I imagine he wants to be prepared at all times to take the next trophy."

"Ridiculous."

"Perhaps, but women have been giving locks of hair as signs of favor for aeons." He jerked his chin at the

stone behind them. "Perhaps a couple met here before
he went off to battle a rival Celt clan—or the Vikings
or the Normans or the English—and she sent him off
with a Gaelic blessing and twist of golden hair to wear
next to his heart, letting him know she belonged to
him and would wait for his return."

Nell could easily imagine women a hundred years
before—or a thousand—standing at this point, watching the sea for the boat carrying their lovers home.
"You have the heart of an Irish bard," she told him.

He grunted. "I was raised by Irishwomen with a
propensity for fairy tales."

"And you married another. How fitting." Nell
reached over him and lifted the flap of the basket.
"Ah, there is a knife."

"And?"

"And I'm of the mind to give you a sign of my favor.
What do you say to that?"

He snared her wrist. "I'd say I won't have you chop-
ping away at your hair."

"Not even to prove that I, as you so like to tell me,
am yours and yours alone?"

She caught her breath when he flipped her onto her
back in a single, smooth motion and pinned her with
his warm weight. "You are mine," he said gruffly,
"whether you choose to prove it or not. No knives
necessary."

Nell smiled. "Just as well, then. I was actually going
to grace you with food instead."

They watched the sea as they ate. Mackerel schools
had been thick near Omey Island, so the village's
boats were all visible. She squinted at a familiar blue
hull. "Dónal O'Hehir has changed the name of his
boat. It used to be *Na Corcán Órga*: the *Golden Caul-
dron*. I always thought that perfectly apt for a fishing

boat. But he wasn't having good catches in the spring, so I suppose he gave in to superstition and changed the name for a change of fortune."

"What is it now?"

"*Na Daighear: Fire.*"

Trevor let out a shout of laughter. "Superstitious, bollocks. Your man Dónal has a sense of humor."

It took Nell a minute. "Oh. Oh, goodness. From Pot to Fire." She shook her head. "I imagine Mealla was livid."

"And why is that?"

"One should never mock the sea," Nell said seriously. "One must ask for its blessings very nicely."

"Yes, I suppose one should." As Nell watched, astonished, Trevor cupped his hands around his mouth and bellowed, "MacLír! Mannanán MacLír!"

A gull cried in the distance.

"Hmm. Do you think he doesn't hear me, or just doesn't feel like answering?" Trevor asked Nell.

She shrugged. "I have no idea."

"Oi, MacLír! With all due respect, you're making me look bad in front of my lovely wife here!" He turned to Nell. "I must be doing something wrong. Is it my tone, do you think?"

"Oh, surely not. Might it be that the sea god doesn't speak English?"

"He's a god. He ought to speak Chinese," Trevor muttered. Then, "Very well. *Ba mhaith liom iasc beatha* . . ." Something that sounded like faint laughter carried over the waves. Trevor lifted his scarred brow at Nell.

She suppressed a smile. "You asked him for the fish of life."

"What is the fish of life?"

"I've no idea. Try *uisce beatha*. The *water* of life."

"I'm after asking for whiskey," he shot back with a wink. Then, to the sea, *"Ba mhaith liom uisce beatha!"*

"Agus mé!" came from the distant waves.

"Ah, another whiskey man, our MacLír." Trevor turned to Nell. "How do you say 'long life'?"

"Fad saoil."

"Fad saoil, uisce beatha, agus . . . mo bean mé i bhfarradh le!"

"Áiméan!" came from the sea. The blessing.

"There," Trevor said contentedly. "I did it."

And he had, with dubious grammar, but the words to make Nell's heart twist. *Whiskey, long life, and my woman beside me.* A sudden wind whipped around the standing stone, but she barely felt it.

"You did perfectly," she whispered, but Trevor wasn't listening. He was pulling on the boots he'd shed and grumbling good-naturedly.

"Well, hell," he muttered. "I should have asked him for a horse. And I should have argued when you said you wanted to walk."

Nell sighed. The moment was lost. "Here"—she handed him the wine bottle they'd emptied together—"put this in the basket and we'll go."

He complied, then demanded as he pulled his hand from the basket, "What's this?"

She took the bound cluster of plants from his fist. "It's for my father. Dulse," she murmured, "so he may rest in peace, rue so he may be forgiven his sins, and rowan so that he'll haunt me no more. I thought I would stop by your family cemetery on the way home and place it there somewhere. I . . . haven't been there yet, and it's as close as I'll ever go to his grave." She nodded to the basket. "I made two more. For your parents."

Trevor's head snapped around. "Why?" he demanded harshly.

She shrugged. "It seemed right. Wasn't it?"

"No. No, dammit, it wasn't! For Christ's sake, Nell—" The shock and hurt in her eyes stopped him mid-growl. The fault wasn't hers, nor was his anger. He cursed luridly and ran his hands roughly through his hair. "Ah, hell. I'm not you, Nell. I'm not forgiving. And I won't put a damned thing on their graves."

"I only meant—"

"I know. I know you meant well. That's your nature. It isn't mine." Contrite, he reached out and touched her sleeve. "I'll go with you. Just understand if I won't walk through the gates." He could see tears in her eyes and silently blasted himself for putting them there. "Oh, Nell . . ."

"No"—she hurriedly swiped at her eyes with her sleeve—"no, it's all right. I understand."

"I don't think you do."

She faced him squarely, chin up, gaze direct. "Are you going to explain any of it to me?"

He opened his mouth to do it, to tell her. And found he couldn't. "No. I'm not. I . . . I'm sorry."

She nodded. "I believe you are." He reached for her, but she was already rising. "You don't have to come with me. I can do this alone."

"I said I would come." He pushed himself to his feet, took the basket while she folded the blanket. "We should go quickly. The rain is coming."

It only happened in Ireland, this sudden turn from sun to rain. Soft weather, they called it in the east. Here in Connemara, summer rain lashed the earth, often hard as nails. In the distance, Trevor could see the boats pulling in their nets. They knew better than to stay out. So did he, but he had penance to do for hurting his wife.

The first drops fell as they reached the graveyard. How fitting, Trevor thought, and turned his back to the Irish rain that always seemed to fall at an angle. He didn't enter the hallowed ground. Instead, he stood outside the rusting iron gate and watched Nell move among the stones. She'd pulled her shawl over her head, and looked very much—too much, he decided—like a brokenhearted mourner. He wondered if she'd stood in the rain over her husband's grave, silent and tearful, impervious to the fact that she was being drenched.

Unable to help himself, he wondered if she would do as much for him. And realized he cared about the answer. He would never know, especially if she placed rowan on his grave to keep his spirit from following her.

He blew out a breath, annoyed with himself for entertaining such absurd thoughts. Nell walked slowly from stone to stone, bending to read the older ones that time and weather had worn down. He wanted to call to her to hurry, but found he didn't want to intrude on her solitude. At last she wandered to the far corner of the plot where a massive oak tree stood, its largest branches curving to the earth outside the fence. He started to call out to her, but it was too late.

Nell bent to lay her herbs there, away from the family graves. Then she saw the plaque set into the trunk of the tree and leaned closer. Trevor knew what it said; he'd read it countless times, fascinated, on those Sundays when his mother had forced him to accompany her on her duty visits to the graves of the parents-in-law she'd loathed.

Without, the plaque read, *lyeth the Unchristened babes.*

That was all—a cold, comfortless acknowledgment, not even a half dozen words, written so long ago that they were barely legible.

Nell straightened so quickly that her shawl fell to her shoulders. Trevor saw her lift one hand and press it to her mouth. She stood, frozen, for a long moment. Then she turned and ran. Her rowan bouquet slipped from her fist as she went, landing in the hollow behind a fallen, centuries-old marker.

She didn't stop. Trevor didn't think. He stormed through the gates with a few long strides and caught her before she'd taken more than a dozen stumbling steps. He closed her tightly in his arms and held her while she cried, great tearing sobs that he could feel to the very core of him. He held her, heedless of the rain, and silently cursed every cold, malignant St. Wulfstan who had come before him. He stroked Nell's hair, murmured nonsense to the top of her head. Then, when her sobs had quieted into shuddering breaths, he told her,

"You can't see them from this side; the biggest branch is in the way, but there are rosebushes planted outside the railing. Dozens of them, some nearly as old as the tree. A few will be flowering now; more will bloom in late summer."

Nell stirred against his chest. "The mothers?" she asked, her voice muted and husky.

"Yes."

Generations of mourning St. Wulfstan wives had planted their grief in that spot. Trevor's mother had buried a child there, a stillborn son. He knew this not because she had planted a rosebush or ever visited the site; she hadn't. He knew because Richard had told him.

"I had a son!" he'd raged, while the blood from the whiplash had poured down Trevor's face. *"My son, buried under that godforsaken tree, and damn your soul, it isn't you!"*

Nell was sobbing again. Trevor stifled a roar, swept her up into his arms, and carried her from the cemetery. He didn't put her down when they reached the house, merely slammed his foot against the heavy door until Mrs. King appeared.

"My lord," she gasped. "My lady. What—"

"We were caught in the storm," was all Trevor said. Then he strode past her and carried Nell up the stairs. He didn't put her down until he'd reached her bedchamber. She wasn't crying any longer, but she was shivering violently. He unwrapped the sodden shawl from around her shoulders and started to undo the buttons of her dress. Mrs. King was there suddenly, clucking her tongue and gently batting his hands away.

"I'll see to her. You go get yourself into some dry clothes before you catch your death."

Trevor started to protest. But one look at Nell and he changed his mind. She was ash-pale and holloweyed. Knowing he would only make matters worse, he turned on his heel and left the room. He heard his old nursemaid's soft murmurings as he went. He didn't go to his own room. Instead, he went back down the stairs in search of the whiskey he hadn't consumed the night before.

An hour later, reasonably dry and only slightly drunk, he went to find Nell. She was seated at the little writing desk in her sitting room, wearing a fresh dress and wrapped warmly in a soft wool shawl. She had a letter in her hands and Trevor found himself back in the morning, saw her sitting in the colored light shining through the stained glass.

He would start the day over again. He would kiss her good morning and then try to coax her back into bed . . .

She looked up then, with the same bleak eyes she'd faced him with all those hours ago.

"Nell . . . ?"

"It's from my solicitor," she said dully, indicating the letter she held. "The Duke of Clonegal is contesting his father's will. He is demanding the return of everything his father gave me."

CHAPTER 17

"What was that?" Trevor strode across the room and plucked the letter from Nell's nerveless fingers.

"Apparently he is claiming the house and money and is contemplating demanding that I be prosecuted for my actions. He claims I took advantage of a man not in his right mind."

"Preposterous," Trevor spat.

"Yes." Nell recalled the duke's final days, when even breathing had been painful for him. His body, once so mobile and robust, had wasted away to little more than loose skin and bones. But his eyes had been sharp, even through the pain, and his mind had been even sharper. He'd known precisely what he was doing. "But the courts might listen to him, at least just enough to hear the case. After all, it is the word of a courtesan against that of a duke."

"Rubbish."

"No," Nell said sadly. "It isn't. I know how these matters tend to go. I don't truly believe a court would find me guilty of any wrongdoing. Enough people knew of Clonegal's clear mind before his death. His son does, too. But it could be horrible. Either way, he'll take the money and the house."

"He can't just take them, Nell."

"Mmm. He'll find a way to prove his father had no legal right to leave the house to me." She recalled the new duke's unpleasant visit. Now she knew why he had taken such pains to inform her of the house's history. His words hadn't even been the beginning of the insult. They had been a prelude of things to come. "He'll do it," she said sadly. "I just wish I knew *why*."

Trevor was sitting now on the edge of the bed, reading the letter. "Money is a powerful motivator."

"That isn't it. The Clonegal fortune is immense. The two thousand pounds left to me is but a drop in the pail."

Trevor's head jerked up. "Two thousand? That is all you have? God, Nell, we've spent half that already! If I'd known—"

"Two thousand came to me in the will." She gazed out the window to where people had been dancing and a fire had been blazing not twenty-four hours earlier. It felt like weeks. "The duke set aside a great deal more than that in the year before he died." She wondered how he had known this would happen. "He did the same for Annie—for Madame Balashova. His son can't touch that. He doesn't even know it exists."

"He's doing this for two thousand pounds and a bloody house?"

"So it seems."

"Let him have them."

Nell turned around to face him. Trevor was leaning forward, eyes fierce. She closed her eyes for a moment. "You make it sound so simple."

"It is simple. Give him the damned house. Send him the money with a bow around it. You don't need either."

"No?"

"No. Assuming you are correct about the rest of the money, the two thousand can go with good riddance. You have a home here; I have the London town house should we ever need it. I can't sell or even let the beast, so it will just sit empty until we choose to make use of it."

"What if I want to keep the house I was given?"

Trevor blinked, clearly surprised. "Why in God's name would you? I just said we have two houses. And it's hardly as if you'll be going back to England anytime soon."

Nell knew there was a storm coming, but she didn't know what she could do to divert it. She sighed. "I think I must go back. Soon."

"*What?*"

"This is a matter of honor and principle," she explained. "I must attend to it."

He surged to his feet in a single, powerful move and came to loom over her. "You will not be going back to London to attend to anything, Nell. Do you hear me?"

"Of course I hear you," she said softly. She reached up to touch her fingertips to his set mouth. "I have to do this, Trevor. Try to understand that. And know I would never ask you to ignore something so important to your sense of who you are."

She flinched at his snort, let her hand fall into her lap when he jerked away. "What will you do if I forbid you to go?"

"Are you forbidding it?" She watched as he paced the room like an angry cat. She wasn't quite sure why he was so upset, but she was reasonably certain of his answer.

He gave it. "No. I'm not. I have a feeling you would go anyway."

"I might not, but please don't force me to make that choice."

He stopped at the door. "Fine. You know my feelings on the matter, but I won't ask you again not to go."

"Why does this bother you so?"

"You have to ask?" he shot back.

"Yes, it seems I do."

He crossed his arms over his chest and regarded her coolly. "Perhaps it is simply that this entire suit of Clonegal's is absurd and you'll only fuel the fire by rushing back to London. The matter will have to go through the Prerogative Court. That is the Archbishop's province and tends to move with all the speed of tree sap."

"Even for a duke?" Nell asked evenly.

Trevor shrugged. "Once the Season is over, nothing moves quickly for anyone."

"Well, be that as it may, it isn't enough reason for me to stay. Nor, I think, for you to be so upset. Oh, Trevor." She rose to her feet and started to go to him. The look in his eyes stopped her after a few steps. She spread her hands in a helpless plea. "Can't you tell me—whatever it is?"

"Dammit, Nell, there's nothing there for you!"

She recalled one evening, a lifetime ago, when he had stood in the foyer of the King's Theatre and spoken nearly the same words. But there had been the heat of pursuit in his gaze then, a sensuous drawl in his voice that had brought a warm ripple to her pulse. Now he was just cold; *she* felt cold.

"Do you honestly believe there's any good to be had in going back?" he demanded.

"I don't know. I can't know until I've gone." Nell

stared into his hard face, but couldn't see if the shuttered emotion there was solicitude or jealousy. Or dis-
trust. "Are you concerned for my ease of mind,
Trevor, or yours?"

"Don't turn this around on me, Nell. I won't play."
They faced each other across the room. "I've said my
piece and leave the decision up to you. Make whatever plans are necessary."

Nell knew she ought to be pleased, but it was a
hollow victory. She sighed. "Thank you. I'll send
Seamus to Galway to book passage to London. Will
you come with me?"

Trevor stood in the doorway, face hard as granite.
"I will come with you. But don't expect me to support
you in this once we are in London. I cannot do that."
Then he spun on his heel, stiff and military precise,
and left.

Nell watched him go, fought hard against the urge
to go after him. After several long minutes, she turned
back to the desk, sat down again, and started to pen
her response to the letter. There was nothing else for
her to do.

The next few days were hard. Trevor was grim and
unavailable during the day—always polite, but distant. Only at night did his face lose that cold stiffness.
When he slept, Nell would watch him for long minutes in the moonlight, would gently trace his lips and
the line of his jaw with a fingertip.

She had returned to her solitary bed the first night,
thinking it best, only to have him stomp in several
hours later and carry her into the adjoining room. He
hadn't made love to her then, but she'd woken in the
morning with him curved warmly around her, hands

and legs entwined with hers. Then he'd awakened, left the bed with nothing more than a gruff good morning, and had disappeared for the remainder of the day.

They slept beside each other at night, came together once with a silent intensity that had left her breathless and tearful at the same time, and were all but strangers during the day. Nell felt Trevor was pulling away from her a little more each day. She considered canceling the plans to go to England, let the duke have the house and the money without facing him at all. She might have done so if she'd truly believed it would make a difference. But she knew she'd never really had Trevor in the first place, not all of him. And she had to go, for herself. Until she had, she wouldn't have peace. Then she would be able to deal with whatever it was she and Trevor had—or could have.

She spent the days preparing—packing and touring the estate to bid her farewells to the tenants. The warm welcome she received in each house tugged at her heart. She knew she would be back. She just didn't know when. And she was frightened to the core by the likelihood that those happiest days of her life, spent here in Connemara, were irretrievably lost.

She forced her smiles, reassured people that she and Lord St. Wulfstan would return as soon as possible. That the estate wouldn't be forgotten or neglected again. She promised to bring pattern books back for Mealla O'Hehir, a French porcelain doll for Cáit, and cuttings of English roses for Pól, the gardener. On the eve of departure, she took tea with Mrs. King in that lady's little sitting room. They discussed the running of the house while Nell was gone; Mrs. King promised to keep up the orders for fish, even if they went uneaten into the earth around Pól's Connemara violets.

When the last of the tea was gone, Nell prepared to take her leave. She was starting to rise from her seat when the housekeeper stunned her by asking,

"Has your husband told you how he came to have the scar?"

Astonished by the question, Nell sank back into the chair. "No. He hasn't."

"Ah. I was afraid he wouldn't. God love him, he hasn't the sense to know where he'll find comfort. Nay"—Mrs. King clenched her hands together tightly—" 'tisn't a lack of sense, but experience. How could he know where solace lies when he's had none of it in his life?"

Nell leaned forward. She needed to hear this. "Tell me more. Please. Tell me about the scar."

"Sure and I will. I ought to have done this weeks ago, but I didn't want to seem impertinent or meddling." Mrs. King's eyes lost their customary sparkle. "The old lord did it, when Master Trevor was no more than sixteen. Beat him black-and-blue with fist and foot, then struck him across the face with the lash of a horsewhip. Two grooms had to carry the boy to me, he was hurt so badly. I didn't think his face would ever stop bleeding." She sighed. "The bruises faded and the bones healed, but something inside him stayed broken."

Nell sat frozen, horrified by what she'd just heard. Finally, she managed, "Do you know why his father did it?"

Mrs. King shook her head. "That I don't. 'Twas never spoken of after that day. What I do know is that Master Trevor left the instant he could sit a horse again, left without looking back, and everything within these walls changed. His lordship took to drinking most nights and a good many days, too. Her ladyship moved into the west wing. She would come out to take long walks along the beach—I saw her more than once, sitting on the sand with her eyes on the road above as if she were waiting for something—but that was it. There were no more jaunts to Galway and Dublin, no more deliveries of dress materials and fine foodstuffs.

"They died, the pair of them," Mrs. King said sadly, "years before their hearts stopped beating."

"How awful," Nell murmured.

"Aye, 'twas that. But I'm not telling you this for their sake. I'm after telling it for yours. And Master Trevor's. I'm concerned that your leaving here will do you both ill. He wasn't ready to leave last time, not truly, and I know 'twas hard for him to come back. It took him fifteen years. I'm afraid he won't come back this time, and he needs to be here."

Nell ran a weary hand over her brow. Her own fears were wearing on her. "What is it that I am supposed to do?"

"That part is simple." Mrs. King leaned across the table and grasped one of Nell's hands in hers. "You love him something fierce. Bring that love back home with you, back here where the pair of you belong. The rest will take care of itself."

"How do you know . . . ?"

"That you love him so much? 'Tis in your face. Don't you ever look in a mirror, my dear?"

"Not very often," Nell admitted.

The housekeeper gave a sad smile. "Oh, the pair of you. You don't see and he can't allow himself to believe." She squeezed Nell's fingers. "Make him believe. However you can."

That night, Nell was ready for Trevor when he came to bed. She was wearing her necklace and nothing else. "Well, well," he murmured, and stretched out on the bed beside her. He grasped the pendant between thumb and forefinger and rolled it slowly back and forth. "There's no mistaking this invitation."

"I would hope not." Nell lifted an arm and twined it around his neck, drawing his head down.

His lips didn't meet hers. They just brushed her jaw before settling in the hollow of her throat. He nipped lightly. When he slid one hand around her rib cage, Nell caught her breath. But instead of caressing her, he flipped her away from him so her back was tucked against his. She could feel his hardness pressing insistently against the back of her thighs.

"Trevor—"

"I've accepted the invitation, so let me in."

He lifted her leg and draped it over his as he slid his knee between hers. He entered her with a sure thrust and Nell cried out softly. As he moved rhythmically within her, he stroked her hip, her stomach, the valley between her breasts. Nell couldn't see his face, but she could hear his breath, quick and rough, in her ear. She tried to turn in his arms, to come face-to-face with him, but he held her fast. Then, when he rolled her nipple between his fingers just as he had the pearl, she felt the unmistakable swell of her impending climax.

It washed through her quickly and quietly, too fast to savor, but incredibly sweet all the same. Behind her, Trevor growled as he increased his tempo, leaning into her, his weight bearing her into the mattress. Nell felt the necklace sliding into the hollow of her neck; the pendant caught between her shoulder and the mattress. She knew she would have a bruise there in the morning.

Trevor spilled himself into her with a muffled groan. He was still for a minute. Then he rolled onto his back, his leg sliding from between Nell's. She felt the mattress shift and suddenly he wasn't touching her at all. Confused, still a bit shaky, she turned over and propped herself on her elbow so she could see his face. His eyes were closed.

"Trevor."

"Hmm?"

"I know you're angry—"

"I'm not angry, Nell."

He opened his eyes just enough to see her. With that slumbrous, heavy-lidded gaze and the curve to his lips that was always there after they'd made love, he was breathtaking. Just looking at him made Nell's heart thump. She loved this man. Oh, how she loved him. Even when he was bruising her heart.

She smoothed his hair back from his brow, feeling the ridge of the scar under her palm as she did. She could take him to task for tonight at another time if she really wanted to. For now, she would do what she could for the scars she couldn't see.

"There is something I want to tell you, that I think you need to hear."

"Tell me we're not to be on that boat when it leaves Galway Bay," he demanded lazily.

Nell bit her lip. "No," she said finally, wearily, "that isn't what I was going to say."

"Then I don't need to hear it tonight. Good night, Nell." Trevor turned over, leaving her to stare at his back.

* * *

London was much as they'd left it: crowded, noisy, and dirty. Trevor stared from his sitting-room window onto Curzon Street and missed Ireland. The poignant tug of sentimentality surprised him. And he didn't much care for it. He had always been as content in Town as anywhere. But even his own house seemed unfamiliar. In the less than three days they'd been there, Nell had turned his dark, silent bachelor home into a circus.

He had been content with just the single charwoman who had occasionally run a limp feather duster over the furniture and prepared marginally palatable meals. Nell had moved her staff from the Davies Street house, already managed to acquire more, and now there were maids underfoot, a singing cook in the kitchen, and the cantankerous old manservant Macauley performing butler duties with a perpetual scowl and ongoing complaints about the extra stairs. He stomped by the door now, muttering vague invectives.

Trevor had taken refuge in Watier's the night before. He'd had too much brandy, lost a hundred pounds to Isobel Oriel's fool of a brother, and been restrained by the same fool when he'd tried to throttle George Carmody. Carmody's sly suggestion that Trevor have a look at the club's betting book had started it all. His wager inside: *Mr. GC wagers Lord R £200 that the Duke of C will have a new residence by 1 September* had Trevor seeing red. The one below, written in the same hand, had Trevor wrapping his hands around the man's throat and shaking him like a dog with a rat.

Mr. X wagers Mr. Z £500 that he will possess Irish bedlinen by All Hallows' Eve.

It might just as well have been Nell's name. And there were twelve more similar bets, all regarding either the case or the dispensation of a certain lady's favors.

In the end, Isobel's brother had been the one sporting an unintentionally blackened eye—his own fault, Trevor had grumbled even while he'd paid for an exorbitantly priced beefsteak to put on it, for getting in the way. Carmody, eyes bulging above his reddened neck, had hared off, but not before getting in a final shot.

"You can bring a cow into the house and call it a poodle, but it will still give milk and dream of greener pastures," he'd jeered.

Trevor had gone for him again, but this time three of the club's footmen were ready, and held him until Carmody, yellow-bellied coward that he was, had scuttled out the door. Other members had glanced nervously Trevor's way as he'd shaken off the footmen. He supposed he could take on each bettor with his fists, or call them out for the insult to his wife, but he was too drunk to undertake the former and he knew there wasn't a man in London who would face him on a dawn field. Even two sheets to the wind, he was the best shot in Town. He'd had to satisfy himself for the moment by pinning the betting book to its table with a single thrust of a dinner knife he'd appropriated from a wide-eyed young lordling in the club's dining room.

He didn't think anyone would dare to make further wagers. But that was rather like a barn door closed after the horse.

Trevor nearly snarled at the young maid who entered the room now. She hurriedly handed him a sheaf of afternoon newspapers and ran back out the door.

He tossed the papers into the fireplace, unread. He'd made the mistake of reading the morning editions. Nell's return to Town had been mentioned in all three. And while she had been called Lady St. Wulfstan by each with nominal respect, one had used the adjective *scandalous* and another had referred to her place in society as *clouded*. Nell, who had seen the news first, had merely sighed and turned back to her breakfast.

She looked tired and pale; he couldn't help but notice that, but otherwise was going about her duties as if nothing were out of the ordinary. She'd unpacked cases and crates, arranged meals, sent out a number of messages to merchants and grocers. She was calm, pleasant, and refused, damn her eyes, to rise to any of the unworthy bait he threw at her. Trevor had been spoiling for a fight since the letter had arrived in Ireland. He knew he'd been behaving badly, but so had she. Matter of honor, his arse. Sense of who she was, bollocks. She was his wife. She shouldn't have even considered answering Clonegal's ridiculous suit. It was nothing but trouble easily avoided. If Clonegal wanted the house so badly, he could have it. Nell didn't need it, shouldn't want it, a house she had shared with a dead man. Trevor had given her his home. He had given her his home, his name, a little corner of the Ireland she claimed to have missed so much.

Trevor didn't want Nell to be in London. London was a temptation. *She* was a temptation. They were all here, the men who had pursued her before. And Trevor had no doubt that they would do it again.

A leaden weight settled in his gut. He thumped a fist hard against the wall above the mantel, rattling the mirror that hung there. Years before, a massive wooden escutcheon had been in that place, the St.

Wulfstan coat of arms. He'd removed it the day he'd taken possession of the house, wanting no reminder of Richard or his own wrongful possession of the title within his sight.

What he saw there now wasn't much better. "Bloody everlasting hell," he cursed at his reflection, twisted by the decorative glass.

He didn't believe Nell would betray him, at least not now. Her admission that she'd lain with only two men had affected him, more than he'd shown, certainly more than he would ever have expected. He'd felt shaky in that instant. No, Nell wouldn't go easily or casually into the arms of another man. There was a steadfastness about her, a strength of character that awed him.

It wasn't enough. He didn't want her tied to him by a gold ring and sense of honor. He wanted more. He wanted all of her. And that wanting shook him to his core.

He'd learned his lesson well, all those years ago: that he could not afford to covet a woman's affection. Not if he wanted to remain whole. These feelings he had for Nell battered his stability. Like ivy on a wall, they had crept over him, into him, easing through the little cracks and crevices even he hadn't been able to eliminate, weakening his very foundation.

He had broken, was broken. He had allowed Nell to slip into his heart.

She doesn't care for you. No woman will ever care for you. Doubt me, and you are as stupid as you are despicable.

"Trevor?"

Nell's soft voice replaced Richard's harsh one in his ears. He spun to find her standing in the doorway, hat in hand and a wrap draped over her arm. She'd grown thinner, he noticed. Her eyes seemed larger in her pale face.

"Where are you going?" he demanded, finding some precious steadiness in aggression.

"I am going to visit my friend Annie. I just wanted to tell you I was leaving."

"To see Anastasia Balashova. *Brava,* Nell. Return to London wearing a cloak of outraged respectability, then trot out to visit a known demirep. The newspapers and Clonegal's solicitors should have a field day with that, should they learn of it. Scandalous viscountess revisits her clouded past."

He regretted the words even as they spilled from his mouth, more so when she recoiled visibly. "Ah, Nell. I didn't mean—"

"What are you so afraid of?"

She stalked into the room, cheeks flushed with emotion. Trevor realized it had been a very long time since he'd seen her angry. He'd gotten used to her contagious contentment.

"Tell me!" she demanded. "What on earth do you think you are going to lose by my actions? The money? I told you, the bulk of it cannot be taken from us. Your good name?" Her eyes were stormy now. "Forgive me for saying this, my lord, but you yourself have admitted to being something of a *persona non grata* among your peers. It never seemed to bother you before. So what is it?"

Trevor had spent enough years in the military to understand tactical retreats. But his own emotions had been roiling before Nell came into the room and they spilled over now.

"I am not afraid of a bloody thing!" he snapped, striding forward to meet her in the middle of the room—where his height allowed him to tower over her. "But let me tell you what you might consider anticipating. One"—he thrust a finger toward her face— "you will find yourself in a very unpleasant legal battle that could very easily be avoided. Two, your uncomfortable situation and potential humiliation will be very, very public. That is the way London works.

"And three"—he added a third finger to the other two—"you will find yourself the object of attention of those very men who pursued the mysterious Mrs. Nolan—and ones who didn't, trying to possess you now. Believe me, Nell, they will try, perhaps even more now that Mrs. Nolan has tied herself to the scandalous St. Wulfstan."

He finished with a hiss and waited for Nell to respond. She gaped at him speechlessly. Then she drew an audible breath.

"I am your wife." She said each word clearly, carefully.

"I know that!"

"Well, then, stop treating me as if I were your whore!"

It was Trevor's turn to gape as Nell turned smartly on her heel and headed for the door. It took him a moment to find his voice.

"Dammit, Nell, don't you walk away from me!"

She didn't stop. Instead she quickened her pace. By the time Trevor had stormed out of the room after her, she was running up the stairs, hat and wrap lying in a heap on the floor. He followed, taking the steps two at a time. He found her in her bedchamber, standing by the dressing table. She was deftly unpinning her hair. That done, she unwound the plait, then rummaged in the dressing-table drawer. He saw a flash of silver in her hand.

"What are you doing?" he demanded.

Nell didn't answer. She shook her hair over her shoulders. Then, bending her head, she pulled a thick strand from the middle of the mass and raised the shears.

"Nell, for God's sake, don't . . . !"

The crunch of the blades was audible as she cropped the strand close to her head. It fell over her hand, lush and shiny, easily two feet long. As Trevor watched, dumbstruck, she pulled a length of gilt ribbon from her dressing table drawer. Something flashed in his memory—the image of her standing framed by a window, eyes glowing as she touched a pearl at her throat. She'd had this ribbon threaded through her hair that night.

She coiled the cut hair now and tied the ribbon in a tight bow around it. "Here." She thrust the shining knot at him. "Any jeweler in Clerkenwell can make this into a watch chain for you. You can wave it in front of those men you suspect might have their eyes on me."

Trevor stayed where he was, hands loose at his sides. "Nell—"

"Pursuit," she snapped. "Possession. Is this how all men regard women? It's silly, and very, very sad. But if that's the way it is, so be it." She faced him, eyes bright with unshed tears but chin held high. "What more do you need, Trevor? I made love with you. I *married* you. I am yours. You pursued me and now you possess me—completely. Is that what you wanted to hear from me?"

She pushed past him, pressing the soft coil into his hand as she went. Trevor heard her quick footsteps going down the stairs, then, a minute later, the thump of the front door.

No, he said silently as he tucked Nell's hair into his coat pocket. It wasn't what he wanted to hear from her at all.

CHAPTER 18

"Love isn't always enough."

Nell looked sadly at her friend. "I am beginning to understand that," she replied. "I love him, rather desperately, I'm afraid, but I cannot seem to fit that final piece into the puzzle. He won't *let* me love him, Annie. Not properly."

"Ah. Welcome to the reality of life with men. Silly creatures."

"Perhaps, but tell me this: Why is it that in our fairy tales, love is enough? The girl loves the boy and they live happily ever after. That simple."

Annie smiled gently. "You weren't raised on fairy tales, Nell."

"True." Nell sighed. "I wasn't. But that doesn't mean I didn't wish to live in one. I still do, I suppose."

"Mmm. Just keep in mind that fairy tales usually have a dragon, a scheming stepmother, or a gruesome death somewhere in them."

"True as well. Oh, Annie, I haven't a clue what to do next."

Coming back to this house had been necessary for many reasons. Perhaps the greatest of which was that Nell had known she could spill her woes into her friend's lap, receive sympathy, comfort, and perhaps an answer or two. Annie knew men. She had been an endless font of good advice and basic truths in the past. Nell knew this last one: *Love isn't always enough* was true. She just didn't know what else she had to give.

Annie reached across the tea table to grasp her hand. "You've made a good start. From all you've told me, the two of you were going along fine until it became necessary to return to London."

"It started before then. There's something haunting him."

"So it seems. You need to be in Ireland, Nell, much as I miss you when you are not here. Trust me, there's nothing good for you in England."

"Whatever torments him is there, too."

"Mmm, well, I wasn't necessarily including St. Wulfstan in that statement. My concern is for you."

Nell twisted the gold band on her finger. "He's a part of me now. Odd isn't it that I spent nearly thirty years having no idea who he was, and after mere months I cannot imagine life without him."

Annie sighed. "Odd and very common. I don't know what to tell you, dearest. A man with dark secrets is a woman's *bête noire*. He cannot be conquered."

"I don't want to conquer Trevor. I simply want to understand what haunts him." Nell rubbed her temples. She'd had a headache building since they'd reached London. "I believe it started in Connemara, in that house. But he won't tell me. Or cannot, and I've run out of guesses."

Her friend gazed at her thoughtfully. "Well, what would you imagine would upset him most?"

"Finding Rickham in his bed," Nell said drily.

"Yes, well, that would upset anyone. But seriously, Nell . . ."

She thought for a minute. "I suppose it would have

to do with his father, both his parents. His father hated him."

"Why?"

"I don't know. I don't think he knows."

"That could be it," Annie suggested. "There's little worse than needing answers from a dead man."

"I can't help him there, Annie. I can't resurrect his father."

"No, you cannot. But you can do what his father didn't, and go on loving him."

"I thought we had just agreed love isn't always enough," Nell said sadly.

"We did. But somewhere, sometime, it *must* be. And it's always a good start." Annie reached out and squeezed Nell's hand again, then sat back in her chair. "On the matter of fathers and sons, tell me how you are dealing with Clonegal's pitiful scion."

"I have arranged to meet him tomorrow morning, as it happens."

"Oh, Nell, do you think that's a good idea?"

"It's necessary," Nell replied firmly. "He has agreed to meet in St. James's Park."

"Why there?"

"It's just public enough to keep him from making a scene, with just enough privacy at nine o'clock to keep the scene from becoming public. I can't bear to face him in his father's house, not after the last time. He certainly wouldn't allow me into his home, and you can imagine what Trevor would do should I try to bring the duke into his."

One of Annie's dark brows went up. "You haven't told your husband about this meeting, then?"

"How could I? He would try to prevent it."

"That," Annie murmured, "might not be a bad thing."

Nell shrugged. "I have to do this. When it's done . . . perhaps then we'll be able to go home and begin again." She scanned the familiar, sunny sitting room: the pretty gauze curtains, the scattering of expensive knickknacks—gifts from Annie's admirers through the years—on the mantel. Her eyes lit on the massive spray of colorful lilies nearby. "From your gentleman?"

Annie turned and smiled at the sight of the flowers. Nell was surprised to see her blush as well. "They are."

"You seem happy, Annie."

"I am. I have hopes . . ." She shook her dark curls with a low laugh. "One of the first rules of the trade: Never speak one's dreams aloud. Suffice it to say I am most content and even a bit complacent."

"I'm glad."

And Nell was, tremendously. Her friend deserved all the happiness possible. Annie had not mentioned the man's name, nor given any information at all, save that he was an old acquaintance. Which led Nell to believe that he was very important to England. Or perhaps just very, very important to Annie.

"Ah." Annie dropped her napkin beside the biscuit plate and rose from the table. "We cannot forget . . ." She crossed the room to her writing desk and pulled a sealed letter from within. "You'll be wanting this back now that you've returned."

Nell accepted the letter and tucked it into her pocket. "Thank you for keeping this for me while I was away. I didn't know if the time to deliver it would be while I was in Ireland."

"Are you certain you don't want me to do it now?"

It was tempting, but Nell had already made her plans. "No. No, this is one of the things I must do."

Tired suddenly, daunted by what lay ahead, she propped her elbows on the table and dropped her chin into her palms. "Oh, Annie. Nothing has gone at all as I envisioned it."

The older woman gave her a sympathetic smile. "It seldom does. Even in fairy tales."

"What a shame. Well, I suppose I should go home. We're to attend a musical evening with the Oriels. I don't want to go."

"Whyever not? I don't know Lady Oriel, but I've always found the marquess delightful."

"I don't know the marquess, but Lady Oriel seems kind. It's certainly gracious of them to be seen with me. I believe they are doing what they can to show their support for Trevor while I'm embroiled in this matter with the duke. I'm grateful for that. But I'm not part of their world. I never will be."

"You'll be fine, Nell. Take acceptance wherever it comes." Annie's eyes went distant and sad for a moment. "There is so little of it in this world." Then she shook her head and smiled. "Don't go home right now. Stay a bit longer."

Nell considered declining, but she really wasn't ready to face Trevor. Not just yet. She sighed and threaded her fingers into her loosely bound hair. "Thank you. I will."

"Good," Annie said cheerfully. "Now come here and let me see what you have done to yourself."

Nell walked around the table and parted her hair. "It seemed the right thing to do in the moment," she said ruefully, fingering the short ends.

"Hmm. A dramatic thing, certainly. And, I think, a rather romantic one. Was St. Wulfstan suitably grateful?"

Nell remembered the breeze on the Cleggan headland, and Trevor's relaxed, wonderful face in the shadow of the standing stone. "Shocked," she replied. "But it was he who put the idea in my head in the first place." She told her friend of the basket and the knife and the stone.

Annie regarded her thoughtfully when she'd finished. "Well. I might not have given your husband the credit he deserves. Pity." She lifted an elegant shoulder. "I don't suppose my opinion matters in the least to him. So . . . Ring the bell. We'll have more tea before you go."

Trevor wasn't home when Nell returned. It had nothing to do with anger. Nor was it a matter of running late on his own errand. Rather, he was delayed by the fact that, as he was on his way to see Oriel, he came very close to dying.

He'd needed to get out of the house after the scene with Nell. He'd needed, too, to pay a visit to the marquess. He would have walked, but Macauley displayed his talent of not following orders and doing any number of things he wasn't asked to. He brought Trevor's hat, but no stick. He then displayed perhaps his only other talent—useful but unwanted now—and let out a piercing, deafening whistle. A hackney appeared at the end of the street. Trevor had intended to walk, but it seemed easier now to climb into the vehicle. He would walk home.

He regretted his decision several minutes later when they turned onto Oxford Street. It was one of London's better summer days: pleasantly warm and dry. It appeared that everyone who hadn't already left Town was there in the one street. Trevor grew increasingly impatient as the hack moved at a snail's pace through the snarl of pedestrians and other vehicles. He rapped on the roof and reached for the door handle, cursing himself for not having walked in the first place.

The hackney saved his life.

Had he been on foot, the bullet would undoubtedly have found its target. As it was, it merely shattered the window and lodged itself in the cushion near his shoulder. The sudden explosion of glass could not have been more unexpected. Moving on instinct rather than intellect, Trevor threw himself onto the floor. For a moment, he struggled to get at his coat pocket. But there was no pistol there. He was in a fashionable summer coat, he'd grown complacent in Ireland, and he had left all of his weapons at home.

Seconds later, the driver's face appeared at the window. "What in the name o' God was that?"

"Hailstone," Trevor said curtly. A gold coin precluded further questions. It would more than pay for the window and silence. He climbed down to the street. A few curious faces were turned their way, but there was an eerie normalcy to the thoroughfare's busy traffic. A quick scan of the street showed him nothing—no fleeing figures, no gunman ready to shoot again. Belatedly realizing that he was in a highly vulnerable position, Trevor climbed back into the carriage. He rapped again and they were on their way, turning off the crowded street.

He glanced down at his hands where they were clasped between his legs. They were shaking like autumn leaves. "God," he muttered, and clenched his fists tightly until the shaking stopped.

He'd been shot at countless times in the last ten years; one bullet had actually pierced his chest. He had faced muskets, sabers, and poisonous serpents. None had ever made him so much as break a sweat.

Now his heart was thundering fast and hard enough to burst through his ribs.

The difference, he realized, and it was a terrifying realization, was that in the past, he had never particularly cared if he lived. Now he did. A great deal.

He needed to think. Thinking, he could manage. He had no such illusions about his emotions. So he took a deep, steadying breath and did his best dispassionately to determine how someone had gotten close enough to fire a bullet that had missed his throat by mere inches.

Whoever had fired the shot had clearly been following him, and had taken the opportunity of the halt to aim through the window. He stuck a finger into the hole in the worn leather squabs. It had been a fairly small gun, fired from close range. Trevor's eyes narrowed as he considered how a gunman could have aimed and fired without attracting any attention. People had turned at the sound. There had been none of the outcry that the sight of a leveled pistol would have caused.

The answer came quickly. Whoever had fired had done so from inside another vehicle. Trevor couldn't remember any of the various gigs or carriages that had been alongside them. He hadn't been watching. He did now, but saw only a landau, going the opposite way. When he reached Oriel's house, he looked carefully up and down the street and saw no one at all.

Five minutes later, the marquess let out a low whistle as he handed over a large glass of brandy. "You have more lives than a cat," he commented.

Trevor grunted as he lowered himself into one of the library chairs. "Even a cat's luck runs out sometime. It's time for me to get out, Oriel. I'll help you locate

the Roach's second source, but after that I'm done."
He drained his glass in a swallow. "What?"

Oriel was looking at him strangely. "We tracked
down the second man, a fortnight after you left Town."

"Who was it?"

"A minor undersecretary. The sort of man who
works his way steadily up the ladder, but no one
bothers to remember his name."

Trevor closed his eyes for a weary moment. "Then
who in the hell wants me dead?" He looked up when
his friend said nothing. "Yes, yes. I know. The possibilities are endless. Christ, Oriel, it could be almost
anyone."

The marquess leaned back in his chair and tapped
his fingers rhythmically against his thigh. "Whom
have you annoyed recently? For the moment, let's rule
out old grudges. Very few men have the patience to
wait for retribution. Start with the last six months."

"Don't you think I've done that a dozen times?"

"Do it again," was the terse response. "He almost
got you today."

Three times, Trevor corrected silently as he touched
a fingertip to the tiny nick a piece of glass had made in
his cheek. Too close—three times.

"It all seems to come back to Nell," he admitted reluctantly. "I was on the Continent through winter.
And I don't think I left any loose ends there." He
rarely did. "The first attack was after I'd met Nell—
after I'd decided to have her."

"So I'll ask again: Whom have you angered?"

Trevor ticked off the possibilities on his fingers.
"Routland, Clonegal, Rickham, your brother . . . Yes,
yes, I know," he muttered at Oriel's grunt. "But little
William was none too happy with me on more than
one occasion. Killone," he continued. "At least one of

the Astors. Grunt all you want. I literally rubbed one's face in the mud—I've never been able to tell them apart so I haven't a clue which it was—and they do frequent Manton's. One is a decent shot; the other couldn't hit Carlton House with an elephant."

"You don't think it's an Astor any more than you think it to be William," Oriel announced.

"No. I don't. I think it is someone clever enough to hire out his dirty work and wealthy enough to pay well for it. Whoever shot at me today slipped into the Oxford Street crowd after without causing a ripple."

"Does Lady St. Wulfstan know?"

"That someone is trying to make her a widow for the second time? No."

"Have you considered telling her? She might be able to fill in some missing pieces."

Trevor's mouth thinned. "Unlikely. And answer me this: When your life was in danger not more than a month into your own marriage, did you tell Isobel?"

"Of course I didn't. I didn't want to drag her into the mess."

"Precisely," Trevor replied. "Nell and I don't discuss the past as far back as last week. As far as I'm concerned, it doesn't exist."

"So she doesn't know anything about you?"

"My military *activities*, you mean?" Trevor smiled humorlessly. "My wicked life? I can imagine that conversation: 'Not that I don't daily give you reason to regret marrying me, but I thought you might like to know that I spent ten years of my life killing people. And when I wasn't doing that, I was making a general nuisance of myself.'"

"Secrets destroy marriages—and people."

Trevor gave a harsh laugh. "You know, Oriel, I'm not sure even you know how bloody clever you are."

"I'll choose to take that as a compliment, regardless of how it was intended." The marquess handed Trevor the brandy bottle. "Drink to long life, Wulf. Then start again at the beginning, the day you met your wife . . ."

He remembered every detail. As Nell sat beside him in the candlelit Abergele ballroom later that night, a small orchestra playing Handel before them, he remembered. She had been wearing white, as she was now. She'd been pale, also as she was now. And he had wanted to sweep her into his arms and off to whatever bed he reached first.

He still wanted that, but there was so much more. He wanted to tell her about one day soon after he'd arrived in London. He had been taken in by an Eton schoolmate, which meant he had crept in and out of the house behind the mother's back. One night, she had arranged an evening of Beethoven. Unable to resist hearing music from a composer he only knew by name, Trevor had lurked in the back of the room, eyes closed as the music swelled and flowed around him.

He'd been jolted back into the moment by a lady's terrified screams. A maid, entering the room with refreshments, had seen him in the shadows, seen his scarred face, which had not yet fully healed. He had run from the house, her screams echoing in his ears. He still felt the shame and misery of that moment whenever he heard a Beethoven symphony.

He wanted to tell Nell about wild, breathtaking Donegal, where he'd gone first after fleeing Connemara. How he'd stood on the towering cliffs at Slieve League staring at the waves crashing against rocks far below. He'd thought about leaping. The pain of Richard's words and fists had nearly been powerful enough to send him over the edge. The whistling of a shepherd nearby had pulled him back, a lilting Irish tune that he'd never heard before and hadn't heard since. He had given the astonished man nearly all the money in his pockets, keeping only enough to get him to Belfast and passage from there to England.

He wanted to tell her that the only reason he had gone to Anastasia Balashova's soiree that evening months earlier was that the courtesan was as noted for the general entertainment she provided as the private. He had gone to hear the music Madame Balashova always had. It had been Purcell that night. He thought he still occasionally heard strains of the composer's *Tempest* when he was inside Nell.

He didn't know if he would ever find the right moment to tell her any of those things. Perhaps once they were back in Ireland. There would be time then, and maybe a place—by the standing stone at the headland or on a dolmen capstone. He would hold on to these thoughts until he could give them to her.

By then he would have discovered a way to be with her, to be inside her, without needing her. Without allowing her to slip any deeper inside him.

The concert ended soon after. Two by two, the guests filed into the grand dining room for a late supper. Trevor held Nell off to the side. They had received too many cold glances upon arriving; he didn't want to subject her to more. The duke and duchess had been nearly gracious. They loved their son and had—reluctantly, Trevor expected—extended the invitation. But even their cool acceptance and the much more forthright support of Oriel and his wife was not quite enough to soften the hard eyes of the elite guests. Those who didn't know much of Trevor seemed to know too much about Nell, and the other way about.

The presence of the Ballyclares and Killones had been the bitter icing on an unappealing cake. Ballyclare had winced as he'd passed Trevor. Lady Killone had gone stony-faced at the sight of Nell; her son had merely looked speculative. *Ginger arse,* Trevor had thought, the man's expression chafing.

"Let's go home," he murmured to her, as the very matron who had given him his sad introduction to Beethoven swept by without acknowledging them at all.

"Can we?" She sounded so wistful that he nearly smiled. "I do not wish to insult the Oriels. They have been very kind."

"They have been meddling," he replied without rancor. "They'll understand."

Neither did. Isobel roundly scolded them for disappointing her. "I had so looked forward to having anoth . . . having a chat with Lady St. Wulfstan. I rather think we will find we have much in common. Shame on you, Trevor, for dragging her off!"

Her husband was more succinct when he pulled Trevor to the side. "Are you *trying* to get yourself shot?" he hissed. "Wait for us. We'll see you home."

"And put you in the line of fire?" Trevor had forced a smile. "Once I might have done just that, but not now."

In the end, Oriel had insisted on having his parents' carriage readied. Nell protested, blushing in embarrassment at the inconvenience to her hosts. What, she had demanded, would they possibly think of such impertinence? Trevor, not in the least concerned with the Abergeles' opinion or convenience, had quietly thanked his friend, ignored his wife's questions as to why they were leaving through the garden, and hurried her home.

When it became obvious that he was not going to satisfy her curiosity, Nell lapsed into a silence that Trevor knew was something far more serious than a sulk.

Once upstairs, he stood by the fireplace and watched her remove her gloves and fold them neatly away in her dressing table. Then she carefully wrapped her necklace—the only piece of jewelry he had seen her wear, he realized, other than her wedding band—in a velvet cloth and put it away, too. She carried her shoes into her dressing room, where he knew she would place them in a tidy line with the rest. He was struck by the calm familiarity of her actions, as if nothing in their lives was anything other than what it should be.

The afternoon and evening had been almost eerily civil. Neither had mentioned the angry words they had spoken only a few hours earlier. Nor had they talked about Nell's impulsive act. Trevor hadn't had the words for it. But he had carried the twist of hair with him throughout the day. Even now it was coiled in his waistcoat pocket.

He crossed the room. "Nell."

"Hmm?" She appeared in the doorway of her dressing room, hair loose, nightgown draped over her arm.

"I . . ." He nearly snarled with frustration when the words still didn't come. So he turned to the safety of command. "I want you to promise that you won't leave me behind . . . I mean that you won't leave the house without me—for the time being."

"Oh, Trevor—"

"No. No questions."

She sighed. "Because you might choose not to answer them."

He snared her arm as she turned back to finish preparing for bed. Stability bedamned. For a few hours he would accept the fissures. "Nell . . . I . . . I need you tonight."

For a long moment he thought she was going to refuse him. Then she gave him a soft, quick smile that nearly melted him. "I'm glad," she whispered, and came into his arms.

CHAPTER 19

The park was nearly empty at nine the following morning. A solitary man with his spaniel was walking on the far side of the lake, a corps of horse guards trotted briskly toward the Mall, and a trio of giggling, gaudily dressed girls hurried away from Carlton House. Nell could only imagine whom they had been entertaining all night. She silently and fervently wished them some happiness in the years ahead. She doubted many others would.

There was no one else in sight on the lush lawns or among the tree-shaded paths. Nell felt conspicuous standing in the center of the park, so she made her way down to the little lake. A family of ducks spied her from the tiny island in the middle of the water and splashed noisily as they cast off for shore. She had nothing to give them. She spread her empty hands in apology. The mother duck, quickly comprehending that there was no food to be had there, quacked irritably and herded her family away.

"Mrs. Nolan."

Nell turned to find the duke standing a few yards away. He looked tired, she thought, worn down. There were weary lines around his mouth and his cravat, fresh though it no doubt was, appeared slightly wilted. But he held himself rigidly upright, chest out and chin

up, defiant and determined. In that instant, Nell thought
he looked very much like his father.

"Oh, I do beg your pardon," he said coolly. "I
should have said 'Lady St. Wulfstan.' "

Nell sighed. She hadn't come to fight. "Good
morning, Your Grace. Thank you for agreeing to meet
with me."

It was the first time she had addressed him as such
and his eyes narrowed. "If you think to charm me out
of my suit—"

"I hardly think I could," Nell interrupted gently,
"so I have no plans even to try." She walked up the
rise from the lake and gestured to a path that wound
through a copse of elm trees. "Shall we walk? What I
have to say won't take long."

He stalked off and Nell hurried to keep up with
him. "Say your piece, madam. I find this situation
distasteful."

"I'm sure you do." It was cold in the shade and Nell
shivered despite the spencer she had donned. "I wish
to speak to you about your father."

"Do you indeed? Fancy that."

"This would have pained him terribly, you know."

"Am I meant to feel bad about that?" Clonegal
snapped. "You and he made your bed, madam. I
imagine it's uncomfortably cold to lie in now."

Nell bit her lip. She hadn't expected this to be easy,
but she had never been good at handling others' well-
fueled anger. This time was no exception. "There
were so many things he intended—"

"Witless old fool! I don't care how sound of mind
he was, madam, and neither will the courts. You did
nothing for him, but give him delusions of invinci-
bility. You—"

"Held him while he died."

Clonegal hissed out a breath, but ceased his diatribe.

"Do you know what he was thinking of in those final moments?" Nell asked.

"Having the last laugh, no doubt," was the bitter reply.

"He was thinking of you. Yours was the last name he spoke."

Sebastian. I used to bounce him . . . on . . . my . . . knees.

Nell felt the familiar knot of sorrow high in her chest, felt tears rising. She blinked them back. "He was a good man, Your Grace. A wonderful man."

Clonegal grunted. "A matter of opinion and yours, Mrs. Nolan, doesn't count for a great deal. Now I expect you are going to tell me that this wonderful man wanted you to have the house and money."

"No, that isn't at all what I am going to say." Nell drew a deep breath. "I am going to say that I know another wonderful man whose father went to his grave hating him, hating him with a passion that had turned to violence. I don't know if the father is at peace, but the son has none. He carries his father's hatred with him . . . like a scar . . . that will never go away."

She resisted the urge to fumble in her pocket for a handkerchief. Instead, she let the tears fall, not caring if the duke saw. She was crying for Trevor. It wasn't much; it certainly wasn't of any use, but it was something she could do for him.

She swallowed, then continued, "I know a woman; there is nothing wonderful about her, but she has endeavored to do some good in her life and no harm. Her father hated her and his hatred drove her into a life not meant for her—one she struggled to manage. He died without a farewell or a blessing, or any small gesture to tell her that his loathing had diminished over the years. And she will carry that with her forever."

"I hardly see—"

Nell swiped once at her cheeks, then stopped and turned to face him. "Anger can last forever if it isn't met—somewhere—with compassion."

Clonegal stared down at her, face hard. "And what am I supposed to do with this little tale of woe? Forgive my father for his anger? For hating me?"

"He loved you."

"Say prayers for his cold soul and . . . What was that?"

"Your father loved you," Nell repeated. "A great deal. He didn't know where the rift began. He took responsibility for it; he knew he was not the best of fathers. But he didn't know how to mend things." She drew two papers from her skirt pocket and handed him the first, a sealed letter. "He bade me give this to you when I thought the time was right. I left it in London when I was gone, thinking I could just have it sent. I wouldn't have felt right doing that, but I had no idea when I would return and . . . Well, I am fulfilling my promise now."

Clonegal turned the letter over and over in his hands but didn't open it. "Have you read this?" he demanded harshly.

Nell wished she could lie for his pride and for his father's memory. She couldn't. It would be wrong to mislead him here, and he would probably figure it out as soon as he opened the missive and saw the hand in which it was written. "I wrote it." She sighed. "In the end, he could not hold a pen long enough to do more than sign his name. He dictated and I wrote. But for what it's worth, Your Grace, I have no intention of ever repeating the contents to anyone. Now, this is the other matter."

He took the second paper. "What is this?"

"It is the deed to the house."

"*What?*"

Nell smiled sadly at him. "I don't want it. It was a comfort to me after your father's death, sitting in chairs he had occupied, reading his favorite books. But I never intended to stay. Here is the key. You are free to take possession anytime that suits you."

She held out the heavy key. He accepted it wordlessly. "I have taken only my personal belongings," she informed him, "and some books. None is of any value except sentimental, but I will give you an accounting if you wish. I . . . I would like the painting, the Turner seascape. You will probably say no just to spite me, but I had to ask. I wouldn't just take it."

"Mrs. Nolan," he began harshly. "Lady St. Wulfstan—"

"That is all I needed to say, Your Grace." The sorrow was threatening to overcome her, and she wanted to be long gone from his presence when it did. "Good-bye. May you be . . . happy with what you have."

She walked quickly away down the path. She allowed the tears to fall unchecked and they coursed down her cheeks, cool in the morning air. She thought of her duke, of his sad eyes and tender smile as he'd said what he needed to his absent son, and choked out a ragged sob.

If I could have one wish, Sebastian, it would be for an hour when we were somehow unable to form a spiteful word to cast at one another. Then I would beg your

*forgiveness and you would tell me you understood—
even if you didn't really, and everything would be well
in the world . . .*

Her tears continued to fall during nearly the entire
walk back to the house. Nell cried for the kind, ailing
man who hadn't been able to touch his son, for herself, for her husband. She attracted a few curious
glances as she went, but she didn't care. Only when
she turned the corner of Curzon Street did she slow.
She found her handkerchief and carefully dried her
cheeks, blew her nose. If she had time, she would
splash some cold water on her cheeks before facing
Trevor. She didn't want him to see her like this.

She wanted to be smiling, even if he wasn't, when
they spoke. She would slide into his arms, hold him
tightly whether or not he held her back, and ask him
to take her home to Ireland. Just that. He would open
his arms and heart and pain to her if he wished to, but
she wouldn't ask. All she wanted was to return to
Connemara, and everything would be right in the
world.

A sleek town coach was sitting outside the house, its
door open. Nell could just see the toe of a man's boot.
A rather rough-looking groom stepped around the
door as she approached. "The gentleman would like a
word with you, m'lady," he grunted.

Nell sighed. It appeared Trevor had been correct.
The men were returning for Mrs. Nolan. Drawing
herself upright, hoping she appeared far more cool
and distant than she was feeling, she marched toward
the door. "I cannot imagine we have anything to—"
she began as she reached it.

The rest was lost to a muffled cry as the footman
shoved her hard from behind, knocking her onto the
floor of the carriage. As she pushed herself up on her

hands, he seized her feet, sending her facedown again
and all the way into the vehicle. The door slammed
against the soles of her boots. Immediately, the driver
shouted to the horses, cracked his whip, and they
rolled off quickly down the street. A hand fisted
roughly in her hair.

"What on earth do you think you are . . ."

Nell never finished her question. In looking up,
she'd come nose to point with a lethal-looking knife
blade.

Trevor paced the library angrily. He had been very
clear on the matter. Nell wasn't to have left the house
without him. And she had agreed. But she had been
gone when he awakened and the staff had no idea
where she'd gone, only that she had left on foot
around eight o'clock. It was now nearly noon.

Each time the door knocker had gone, Trevor had
launched himself into the hall. So far he had turned
away three sly-eyed newspaper reporters and heard
the demands of a half dozen creditors. Everyone in
London seemed to know that the St. Wulfstans had returned to Town. He had not been polite with any of
them. The reporters hadn't crossed the threshold. The
merchants had been forced to face him across the
daunting length of the library. He knew Nell paid her
bills immediately and had left London with no debts
outstanding. These bills being thrust upon him were
for nothing more than the running of a quiet house
while she was gone. Coal, milk, foodstuffs for the staff
of the Davies Street house.

"Please understand, my lord," the oily coal merchant had whined. "With the news being what it is,
'twas only natural that I would be concerned for my
interests. If your lordship would but guarantee that

future bills will be paid by yourself, I will gladly continue to deliver . . ."

Trevor had tossed a handful of coins at the man and shoved him out the door. As he did with all the others, he informed this one in no uncertain terms that the St. Wulfstans would be using other vendors in the future. He'd almost come to like Macauley when he'd seen the old retainer usher several of the visitors into the street by the backs of their coats.

The irony of the situation didn't escape him. These people wanted only to hear that the viscount would handle the viscountess's debts should she find herself out of a fortune. Ordinarily Trevor would have commended himself on having done so very well at keeping his financial circumstances a secret. As it was, he was too preoccupied with his wife's absence to gloat over anything.

Noon passed. Trevor was chafing with impatience. By one, impatience had turned to annoyance. Behind that, fear lurked. He ruthlessly quashed it and called for his hat. He was just thundering down the stairs, ready to bang down Anastasia Balashova's door, the Oriels', Berry's shop—any place she could possibly be—when the door knocker clacked again. He shouldered Macauley out of the way and flung the door open. A boy stood there, no more than ten, looking ready to wet himself at the sight of the hulking man in the doorway.

"What is it?" Trevor growled.

The boy flinched, then held out a carefully tied paper parcel. "F—for 'is lordship."

Trevor seized the parcel. His name was written in elegant script across the front. "Who sent you?" he demanded as he tore away the string and attacked the end of the paper.

"A b-big bloke"—the boy swallowed audibly—"tho' not 'alf as big as you. Stopped 'is carriage in the Mall, gave me a shillin' to deliver this. Said I'd get more 'ere."

Trevor growled as he fished in his pocket for another shilling. It disappeared into a grubby little fist. The rest of the boy disappeared just as quickly. Before Trevor could reach out to stop him, he'd hared off down the street and vanished around the corner. Cursing, Trevor stepped back into the house. Macauley was gaping, wide-eyed, at his feet.

"What is it, damnit?" Trevor snapped. The butler pointed a palsied finger. "Oh. Oh, hell."

There on the marble floor where it had fallen from the parcel was a long skein of dark blond hair, bound with what looked like a lady's bootlace.

Trevor's hand went immediately to his waistcoat pocket. His fingertips brushed the thick coil he'd tucked there several hours earlier. Silently, heart pounding, he drew it out, then bent to pick up the skein from the floor. There was no question about it. They'd been clipped from the same head.

"Oh, dear God. Nell." He ripped the parcel all the way open and tore out the single sheet of paper. All that was on it was a street and number and the words *Come alone*.

Less than five minutes later he was in a hack, speeding toward the Thames. The journey seemed to take forever. By the time the hack turned down the last street, Trevor was nearly howling in frustration. He jumped down before the carriage had rolled to a halt and left it behind as he stalked down the street, reading the numbers under his breath. He found the place easily, a darkened facade in a row of the same.

There was no one in sight in either direction; everything was eerily silent. He approached the door slowly. He wanted to run, to burst through it with a mighty kick. But years of military experience had honed his instincts and his behavior. He paused outside the door, drawing the gun he'd remembered to bring from his pocket. He cocked it, then tapped softly on the warped wood. There was no answer. He rapped again, harder this time, and the door swung slowly inward. Every muscle tensed and ready, he took a single step inside.

The room was dark; all of the windows had been boarded shut. But he could see enough to know it was empty. There was no one there, nor anything for a man to hide behind. A door across the room was opened a few inches. Moving slowly, gun at the ready, Trevor headed for it.

Beyond was a dark hallway with several closed doors along one wall. Trevor inched along, back to the opposite wall. "Nell!" he called softly. If someone had been waiting for him, they knew he was here. There was no element of surprise to ruin.

There was no answer. Cursing under his breath, he kicked open the first door and saw nothing but empty darkness. Then, just as he'd kicked in the second, there was a thump from the front room and he was plunged into darkness.

Idiot! was his only thought before a hard object connected solidly with the side of his head.

"Trevor."
Nell's voice drifted gently to his ears.
"Trevor!"
He grunted as something slapped at his cheek, then

again. "Stop!" he growled, then hissed as his head pounded in protest. "Ow, dammit."

"Oh, thank God."

"Nell?" He couldn't see anything in the blackness overhead. But he could smell her, the sweet, subtle scent of honey.

"I'm right here." Her hand stroked down his cheek.

"So you are. Have you any idea where here is?"

"A cellar of some sort. The walls are cold and slimy." She shuddered above him. "There are no windows and only the one door. I checked as soon as they left me here."

"They?"

"Two men. I've never seen either of them before. I think there was a third, but one of the others shoved a sack over my head, so I'm not certain. Can you sit up?"

He did, with a groan. Her helping hands weren't helping. It wasn't just his head that hurt. He felt bruised all the way to his toes. "Nothing broken."

"Thank God," she said again. "I was so frightened. You didn't move for such a long time."

He winced as he rubbed at his very sore chin. "Christ, I feel as if someone went at me with a mace."

"They hurled you down the stairs," Nell informed him just before she threw herself against his aching chest.

He sighed and wrapped his arms around her. "Well, that would explain it. Are you hurt?" He felt her shake her head. "Thank God," he echoed her fervent words. Then he buried his face in her hair. "Remind me once we're out of here to paddle you soundly for scaring the hell out of me."

"Scaring *you*?" she gasped. "When you were lying so completely still, I thought . . ." She held him tighter. "What is happening?"

He didn't have a satisfactory answer to give her. "Someone is sending us a very pointed message." Before she could speak, he demanded, "Where did you go this morning?"

"St. James's Park. I . . . I went to meet Tullow . . . Clonegal."

Trevor's chest constricted painfully. "Why?"

He wasn't certain what he'd expected her to say, but his relief was palpable when she replied,

"To give him the house, of course. And to pass on a message from his father."

"What was that?"

"It doesn't matter. It was a promise I made and now I've kept it." She pulled away to sit beside him. "Who, Trevor? Who put us here?"

Trevor tensed as a scraping sound reached his ears. "I have no idea, sweetheart, but I have a feeling we're about to find out," he muttered, as door hinges creaked above.

CHAPTER 20

At first all that was visible was the blinding light of a lantern. A disembodied voice—cultured and feminine—spoke from behind it. "I wasn't certain you would follow my orders, St. Wulfstan. One never knows with your sort." Then the lamp was lowered and a face appeared.

Nell's eyes widened in disbelief. "My God," she whispered. "Why?"

Lady Killone tilted her faded blond head toward the younger woman as she descended the stairs. "Why what, Lady St. Wulfstan? Why did your husband come for you? Guilt, perhaps. Affection. Stupidity." Her too-bright gaze sharpened. "Or are you asking me why I want him dead? He knows the answer to that one. Don't you, you vile bastard? Ah, ah!"

Trevor had come up in a blur of motion, but he went completely still when Lady Killone lifted a pistol from her side. The barrel slowly swung from his chest to point directly at Nell. "Your speed in arriving leads me to believe that you are fond of your whore, St. Wulfstan. So should you think of attacking me, I would not advise it. I will shoot her right between the eyes while you watch. My late husband wasn't good for much of anything, but he was a master marksman and he taught me to shoot."

Nell's mind was whirling. She'd barely absorbed the fact that this woman, whom she scarcely knew, had used her as bait to bring Trevor here. She couldn't even begin to get her mind around the fact that Lady Killone claimed to want Trevor dead—and appeared entirely ready to shoot her in the process. What she did know with complete certainty was that the lady was entirely serious on all counts. The mad eyes and deathly calm voice left no room for doubt.

Nell had ample experience with anger; none with madness. The closest she had ever come was her zealot father. She had learned at a very early age that the only way to connect with him at all was to encourage him to talk about himself. She had no idea if it would work now, but she had to try. Lady Killone was swinging the gun slowly, almost lazily, back and forth between her and Trevor, forefinger crooked firmly around the trigger.

"My lady," Nell began as she rose slowly to her feet. The barrel swung back to point at her. "I do not understand any of this—"

"And I do not care," came the tart retort.

Nell drew a breath, dragged her eyes away from the black mouth of the gun barrel, and continued as if Lady Killone hadn't interrupted. "Will you explain it to me, please?"

From the corner of her eye, she saw Trevor inching toward the center of the room in order, she thought, to put his body between her and the pistol. She silently begged him to stop. And suddenly he did, freezing in place when Lady Killone turned her fevered gaze back to him. "So you haven't told her? Curious. Well, go ahead, bastard viscount. Tell your whore viscountess why you deserve to die. I find myself feeling generous.

Tell her. She has a right to know, I suppose, as she must die with you."

"I rather think *I* have a right to know as well," Trevor said evenly. His own calm was impressive. Nell watched him move another inch and wanted to scream at him not to be so foolish. "Have I injured you, madam?"

"The fact that you have to ask is an insult in itself, but hardly surprises me. You have lived your life as vulgarly as you began it."

Nell saw Trevor stiffen. He was nearly between her and Lady Killone now. "That isn't what you hate about me, is it, madam?" he demanded. Nell bit her lip. The older woman now had the gun leveled directly at Trevor's chest. "What you hate is that you know you made me . . . what I am. Did he blame you for his straying? Do you blame yourself?"

Lady Killone hissed out a sharp breath. Nell caught hers. Trevor had what he wanted; the gun was no longer pointed at Nell. Why, she wondered frantically, did he continue to antagonize the woman holding it?

"How dare you?" Lady Killone spat. "How *dare* you speak such words to me? You, spawned by one whore and now ready to spawn with another. It will not be."

Slowly she set the lantern on the step by her feet and brought her second hand up to steady the pistol.

"No!" Nell's cry had both Trevor and Lady Killone's heads jerking toward her. She stepped forward, agilely ducked the arm Trevor thrust out and slipped in front of him. She wouldn't have it. She wouldn't have him protecting her at the risk of his own life. "Lady Killone, please . . ."

"Go ahead. Beg for his life. It might amuse me." The woman's smile sent a chill down Nell's spine.

"What do you think you could possibly say that would make a difference? Don't you know that you are both dead already?"

They died, the pair of them . . . before their hearts stopped beating.

Nell blinked. She knew she was missing something vital, something just beyond the edges of her comprehension.

The pair of them . . . hearts stopped beating.

She groped behind her for Trevor's hand and felt it close reassuringly around hers for an instant before he firmly tucked her behind him.

"Let her go," he said gruffly to the woman above. "She isn't a part of this."

Lady Killone clucked her tongue. "She married you."

"For the title. Nothing more. She doesn't care what you do to me—"

"Enough. How stupid do you think I am, St. Wulfstan? I am not as unobservant as one might think, considering the circumstances. It took me more than thirty years, but I finally saw him in you. I might never have known, not for sure. Always wondered . . . always suspected, but never known.

"Remember this as you draw your last cursed breath," Lady Killone continued, voice tight. "You will die today because you smiled at a whore." She jerked her chin toward Nell. "At the opera. I saw it, not your familiar debauched smirk, but a real smile. It was *his* smile. And I knew. After all these years of suspicion, I knew. And I couldn't bear it any longer, the thought of seeing you about Society. I won't live with that."

There was a click and Nell tensed, waiting for the explosion. It didn't come. She watched, mind whirling and knees weak as Lady Killone lowered the gun to her side. She felt Trevor's taut muscles, hard as rock beneath her hand.

"Surprised, are you? No, I am not going to shoot you, St. Wulfstan. I am not going to shoot either of you. I wouldn't dream of it." Lady Killone smiled her chill smile. "I put a portion of my late husband's money to that use. I thought it apt that he pay for your demise. You shouldn't have long to wait. The men I hired have no qualms about killing you, St. Wulfstan—despite the fact that they haven't had much success at it thus far—but they're arguing over which will be the one to dispatch your wife. I told them she was nothing more than a whore, but scruples come in the oddest places. Good-bye, and may you rot in hell."

Trevor lunged, but it was too late. Lady Killone slammed the door closed behind her. He heard the heavy thud of the bolt. Cursing, he bent and felt for the knife in his boot. It wasn't much, but it was a chance . . .

Lady Killone had left the lamp, and he turned back to find Nell staring at him, hands clasped tightly at her waist. She didn't look frightened, although he knew she must be.

"Don't look at me like that," he growled.

"Like what?"

"Like your heart is irreparably splintered. It's how you looked the first time I saw you."

He couldn't bear the thought that it would be the same the last time he saw her.

She merely tilted her head and studied him through sad, fathomless eyes. "Why didn't you tell me?"

"Tell you what?"

"That Lord Killone is your father."

The words smacked him like fists. To learn at last—

this way—from a madwoman. "Because I didn't know myself until today."

"But you knew it wasn't the man who raised you. Oh, Trevor, how awful. I don't think I could have borne it."

He winced. "I didn't tell you because I didn't know, and because I was convinced you would respond . . . just as you are."

"Trevor—"

"Ah, the irony of it." He forced a twisted smile. "Are you disgusted, Nell? You the minister's daughter, wrongly labeled a whore. There is something positively biblical about it."

"Oh, *Trevor*—"

"Despise me if you will. I'll survive it." He laughed harshly. "I suppose that depends on what comes through this door." Trevor stared into Nell's pale, heartbreakingly beloved face, his heart thudding a defeated beat. "Well, say something."

"I love you."

"*What?*" He hadn't heard her correctly. He couldn't have.

"I love you," she repeated calmly, simply. Then she walked toward him, hands outstretched. "With all that I am. For precisely what you are."

"I am—"

"The bravest, kindest man I have ever known." When he made no move to take her hands, she cupped them around his jaw. "When I said I couldn't have borne the knowledge, I meant that I don't think I could have stood my father's cruelty, knowing there was another man out there, perhaps a truly good man who might have loved me. Oh, my darling, I've always known you were strong, but I don't think I realized just how strong until today."

"Nell . . ." He tried to jerk away when she tenderly ran her fingertips over the horrible line of his scar. "Nell, don't."

"Don't what? Don't touch you? Please don't ask that of me. Don't love you? It's far too late for me to stop doing that." She went up onto her toes and placed a feather-soft kiss on his mouth. "If you'll let me, even if you won't, I'll love you for the rest of my life."

For an instant, it didn't matter that the rest of their lives might amount to nothing more than minutes. "You were wrong, old man," he growled under his breath. "My God, you were wrong." Then he was crushing her to him, holding her so tightly that he could feel the beat of her heart. Her arms came around him, certain and strong. "Nell," he murmured, lips against her hair, "I don't know if I have the words for you—"

"Shh. I'm not asking for them. I don't expect them."

"You should."

She shook her head. "That isn't the way it works. It doesn't matter how much you care for me. Or how little."

"What nonsense—"

"Trevor." She lifted her face, flushed and beautiful with her emotions. "We don't survive on how much we are loved, my darling. We do it by how much we love. It's that simple."

And in that moment, he knew. Her feelings for him—for the rest of his life, for he would certainly let her love him—would keep him solid and grounded and strong. But it was his love for her that would have him rising in the morning, every morning, just so he could see her face.

"Ah, Nell." He felt the slow, satisfied smile spreading. "So very sensible. And so very, very foolish."

"Am I?" Her own smile dimmed slightly.

"Mmm. You want so little, expect so little. But don't you *want*? Don't you care, even a little, about your value to me?"

"Oh ... no. I know I have value to you. It doesn't ..." He heard her sigh, a single, small sound. "Yes. Of course I want. Of course I do. But it doesn't—"

"You are my heart, Nell."

"I ... I am?"

"My heart, my rock. The very best part of me." He stared down at her, willing her to understand that and all the things for which he didn't have words—yet.

The first tear slid down her cheek, just as the bolt on the other side of the door creaked.

Trevor was ready. He kissed Nell once, hard, for love and luck, then thrust her away from him. He was damned if he was going to die now, not when he had finally found someone who would mourn him— someone he could not bear to leave behind. He leapt to the top of the stairs and kicked the lantern to the floor, shattering the glass and plunging the cellar back into darkness. Then he crouched, knife ready in his fist.

He lunged at the first sound of the door grating open. Hitting it with his shoulder, he felt it strike someone on the other side, heard the thud of a body meeting the floor. In a heartbeat, he'd burst into the hallway and thrown himself on the supine figure there. He turned his wrist, ready to drive the knife home.

And found himself eye to familiar cobalt eye with Stephen Killone.

"Ah, hell," he cursed.

The other man smiled despite the knife point pressing against the underside of his jaw. "Dare I hope you are opposed to fratricide?"

"Beggin' y'er pardon, m'lord . . ."

Trevor looked up and was shocked to see Macauley standing there, lantern in one hand, ancient pistol in the other. He had the latter pointed steadily at two thugs who were lying facedown on the dusty floor several feet away, hands linked behind their heads.

"Ye might want to let t'young gentleman up," he suggested. " 'E says 'e's kin."

"Mac?" Nell's face appeared through the doorway. "What on earth are you doing here?"

"Getting' ye out o' another scrape, I'd say," was the terse response. The butler jerked his stubbly chin at Trevor. "Went flyin' out o' t'house like a bat from 'ell. Thought I'd best make use o' the paper 'e left behind an' follow."

Nell looked completely confused, but she nodded. "And Lord Killone?"

Trevor pushed himself to his feet, all the while keeping a close eye on Killone's hands. He still wasn't certain they were empty. As if reading his mind, the other man eased himself into sitting position and thrust his fingers into his ginger hair. "She actually had me waiting for her in the carriage down the street. Said she was performing a charitable act. God, what a fool I am. I never once thought she would resort to this," he said quietly. "I don't expect it will mean much, but I'm so very sorry."

"You knew," Trevor grunted.

"That my mother was trying to kill you? No. Nor was I certain of the other, but I wondered." Killone looked up, smiled faintly. "I cannot believe I am the only one who ever noticed how much you resemble my father. Perhaps it was that his hair was as red as mine. Or perhaps people simply don't see what they don't wish to. I . . . wished to."

"You expect me to believe this little *denouement* delights you."

Killone shook his head. "I don't, and there is no way of proving it to you, I suppose."

Behind them, Macauley cleared his throat. " 'E went at the door like a demon, m'lord."

"She looked so unlike herself when she returned. I made her tell me. I . . . she is in the carriage, with my footman attending her."

Trevor stared down into the other man's eyes for a long moment. All he saw was simple honesty—and hope. Sighing, he extended a hand to help Killone to his feet. "I don't know if I want a brother."

"I'm sorry for that. But I understand. My mother . . . God. I don't know what to say about that. I suppose her hatred for my father . . . our father turned to madness finally. I know I have no right to ask for your mercy . . ."

Trevor felt Nell's hand, gentle on his back. He silenced the other man with a raised hand. "Will she try again?"

"What?" Killone blinked at him.

"We're going back to Ireland, for good, I hope. Will she try to harm us there?"

Killone shook his head. "I can make certain she doesn't. I have cousins in the Americas who will take her in. Will that do?"

Trevor nodded. For the first time in a great many years, he felt no unease, no anger or desperation lurking in the back of his mind. All he felt was a sudden bone-weariness, and a peace he knew he would have to accept slowly. It was more than he had ever imagined. More, he feared, than he deserved.

Killone turned to Nell. "I believe my comment about your father distressed you when last we met." He sighed. "It was not my intention. You see, I believe we met years ago, Lady St. Wulfstan. You wouldn't recall the occasion. You were but a child, but I could not have forgotten your eyes . . . And your father dined with us a few times through the years. I thought . . . I thought it right to mention the connection, but . . ." He spread his hands with a sad grimace. Then he turned back to Trevor. "You don't have to see me again if you don't wish to. I will make the necessary arrangements."

Trevor nodded. He wasn't ready to make any decisions just yet that didn't involve Nell and a warm bath. He looked down when she slipped her hand into his. "Let's go home," she said softly.

They had just stepped into the waning sunlight when the shot rang out. Nell screamed; Trevor spun to see if she had been hit. But she was standing, a bit wobbly but unhurt, one hand pressed to her mouth. Behind him, Killone, too, was unharmed, and Trevor could see Macauley and his two prisoners—the pair of them still on their bellies—through the door.

For a long moment, no one moved. Then Killone gasped, "Oh, dear God," and leapt toward his carriage, which stood nearby.

His footman stopped him before he reached it, holding him back from the scene inside. Trevor wrapped an arm around Nell when she buried her face in his shirt. One gloved hand, bloodied now, hung limply out the carriage door. The gun that had fallen from it rested on the ground below.

An hour later, when the two felons had been taken away by the authorities and Lady Killone's body had been quietly removed, Trevor approached her son.

Stephen sat on the step of a silent warehouse, head in his hands. He looked up when Trevor reached him, patent grief in his eyes. "It sounds appalling—it *is* appalling—but I suppose it's better this way. She's at peace, so can you be."

Trevor crouched down in front of him. "And you?"

"I certainly don't blame you, if that is what you're asking."

"It wasn't."

"Ah. Well." Killone gave a lopsided smile. "I'll mourn her in my own way. She was my mother. Perhaps I'll eventually be able to live with myself for feeling some relief. And I'll go on. I might reopen the house in Clare. Could you . . . would you consider coming to visit?"

Trevor sighed. "I don't know."

"I understand. But the invitation stands."

Trevor left him there and joined a very subdued Nell in the waiting hack. He immediately tucked her close to his side, thinking how very easy it would be to hold her like this forever, thigh to thigh, her arm twined with his.

Eventually she broke the silence. "Back there," she said quietly, "you told some absent person that he was wrong. Your father?" When Trevor nodded, she pressed, "Wrong about what?"

Trevor remembered the lash of the whip, the thud of Richard's boots against his ribs, the screamed words. But none of it mattered any longer. "He cursed me, told me I would never in my life have a woman's love."

There was a long pause, then Nell murmured, "He was wrong."

"He was wrong." Trevor pressed his lips to her temple, closed his eyes in mute thanks. Then, "I have done some terrible things, Nell. I—"

"I don't care."

"I don't think you understand—"

"I don't care," she repeated firmly. Then, gently, "If you wish to tell me about them another time, I will listen, but hear me well: Nothing you say will change how I feel about you. Nothing, ever."

Trevor felt the tears rising in his eyes. And let them fall. "You humble me, Nell."

"I don't mean to," was her soft reply.

"No. No, you wouldn't." He drew a shaky breath. "Promise me you will never leave me."

"Cross my heart," she said.

They arrived home to find a large paper-wrapped parcel bearing Nell's name in the foyer. She smiled, a potent mixture of sorrow and joy, at the sight of it. When she made no move to remove the paper, Trevor demanded, "You know what it is?"

"Yes, I think I do."

"Well, then, open it."

She shook her head. "Later."

"Nell . . ." When she shrugged and gestured for him to go ahead, he tore the paper away. It was a painting, a small seascape that he knew he'd seen before. "What is this?"

"It is a Turner. Lady Oriel believes he will be very famous someday." She pulled a folded paper from the frame. Trevor read over her shoulder.

Lady St. Wulfstan.
  It is a paltry thing I do here, showing my immense gratitude with another man's gift. Forgive me that. Forgive me.

                                      Your servant,
                                      Clonegal

Trevor saw the tears in his wife's eyes. They tore at him, even as he knew they weren't from sorrow.

"Nell."

"Hmm?"

"What can *I* give you?" he asked her, his voice low and ragged. "Ask for my life and it's yours."

Her lips curved, a smile that wrapped around his heart. "Oh, my love. You've given me yourself. You've given me the moon. And I didn't even have to ask. What more could any woman possibly desire?"

County Clare, Ireland, three weeks later

Nell waited quietly by the graveyard's low stone wall and watched her husband. He stood tall and powerful in the soft dusk, hat in hand, in front of the stone that read *Killone*. Nell had no idea what words he had for the man who rested there, but she imagined they were peaceful ones.

She could never have dreamed of the past few weeks, could never in her most secret, desperately romantic moments have imagined the joy Trevor brought her. They'd left London quickly and quietly. Indefinitely. He'd held her hand in his as they drove from the city and had touched her—some part of him on some part of her, even if only his fingertips on her sleeve or his gaze warm on her face—nearly every moment since.

Some nights, limbs tangled with hers, he talked about his life. The dark seemed to make it easier for him. Nell knew there was a great deal he didn't say, the harsh and brutal details he wanted to spare her. Still, she'd cried more than once for him, held him while he shook with the pain of memory and later while he slept. She talked about the years at Horgan's and the ones after. He held her while she cried, and while she slept.

He told her of his love, daily. And kissed her into dizzy silence every time she tried to return the words. "It doesn't matter," he teased her. She knew better. She knew how very much her love mattered to him; he'd had so little in his life. And she was just as secure in his emotions, even if he was still occasionally bemused by them. He would just have to grow accustomed to being moonstruck, she thought with a smile. If ever two drifting souls deserved each other, it was theirs, and rational thought had absolutely nothing to do with it.

Trevor was taking her home now and he seemed to grow more relaxed with each mile that brought them closer to Connemara. He had wanted to make this stop in Clare on their way. He had taken her to the towering Cliffs of Mohr nearby, where they had stood high above the sea and shouted greetings to Mannanán MacLír. He had shown her the stark beauty of the Burren, where the deep layers of limestone beneath their feet appeared to have been tunneled by a thousand ancient worms. They had stretched out together on the Poulnabrone dolmen and counted the stars. And today, as they prepared to travel northward toward Galway, they had stopped at this little stone-ringed cemetery.

Trevor glanced over at her then and her heart skipped, as it always did, at the simple sight of him. He said something to his father's headstone, then stalked across the hard earth. He didn't slow as he approached Nell, merely swept her off her feet and carried her to the waiting carriage. "You could arouse a dead man with those eyes," he murmured against her lips as he lifted her onto the seat.

"Charming thought," she teased as she kissed him back.

"Ah, well, I have plenty of those. I'll share one or two in Ennis tonight." He scooped a small satchel off the floor of the carriage. "Don't go anywhere. I'll be back."

Nell scooted to the window and watched as he strode back into the graveyard. He drew something she couldn't see from the satchel and placed it on the earth at the base of the Killone marker. He gave a jaunty bow, settled his hat back on his head, and returned. Nell could hear him whistling as he came around the rear of the carriage. He was still whistling, a merry West County tune, as he dropped into the seat beside her and hauled her into his lap.

"What was that you left?" she asked as they rolled away.

"Didn't you recognize it?"

"I couldn't see it." More curious now, she prodded him in the ribs. "Well?"

"It was your little coffer."

"My . . . No. Not the one Annie gave me."

He grinned. "The very one."

Stunned, too mortified to consider the significance, Nell gasped, "Stop the carriage! We must go back. You cannot leave such a thing there. It's . . . it's sacrilege."

"Hardly." Trevor grasped her chin between thumb and forefinger and held her face so she was looking straight into his eyes. They were warm and wicked. "Do you really want it back, Nell?"

Belatedly she realized what he had done. Her heart swelled with love, and with the hope she had so painfully tucked away. "No," she whispered. "No. I don't want it back."

"I should think not. Now, can you think of a better place for me to leave it?"

Bested, Nell couldn't hide her smile. "No, I confess I cannot."

"*Sin a bhfuil*," he said decisively.

And that, indeed, was that. Nell gave a silent *thank-you* to the slow-rising moon as they drove away.

On sale now!

*In Regency England, there is a very thin line
between love and hate . . .*

ENTWINED
by *Emma Jensen*

Nathan Oriel returns to London society a great military
hero of the Peninsular Campaign and a most eligible
bachelor. Unbeknownst to the rest of the world, Nathan
has been blinded and has only one goal in mind—to
uncover the traitor responsible for the death of his comrades and for his injury. He shares his secret with only one
person, the headstrong and beautiful Isobel MacLeod,
who agrees to serve as his "eyes" and help him unmask the
traitor in their midst. This unlikely duo can barely stand
each other's company—or so they think—until they find
themselves falling deeply in love, a love threatened by
an unknown enemy with murder and betrayal in his
heart.

Published by Ivy Books.
Available in your local bookstore.

They were forbidden to love.
But together they have…

FALLEN
by Emma Jensen

Gabriel Loudon, a special agent to the British army, was always one step ahead of Napoleon's troops—until a vital mission went tragically wrong. Now he has one last chance to redeem himself. His orders: expose an elusive French spy hiding on an isolated island off the coast of Scotland. What he doesn't expect to find there is another fallen angel.

When her scandalous love affair with a young Englishman ends, Maggie MacLeod retreats to the safety of her beloved, remote home. Alone on the cliffs of Skye, she can surrender to romantic dreams of a true love that will never be. Until a mysterious stranger invades her seclusion, awakening her senses and threatening everything she cherishes—especially her splintered heart. . . .

Published by Ivy Books.
Available in bookstores everywhere.

Gaelen Foley has become one of the hottest new writers in romance, enticing her readers with bold love stories that burn with emotional intensity. Now don't miss the next two books in the Knight Miscellany series, about the dangerous, irresistible twins of the Knight family who return from the Napoleonic wars, one a hot-blooded warrior, the other a cool, cunning spy...

Please turn the page for more details about the Knight twins...

LORD OF FIRE
by Gaelen Foley

No one in London suspects that Lord Lucien Knight is England's most cunning spy, an officer who has sacrificed his soul for his country. Now an unexpected intruder has invaded his fortress of sin, jeopardizing his carefully laid plans—and igniting his deepest desires.

Beautiful, innocent, Alice Montague finds herself at the mercy of scandalous Lord Lucien. But as he begins his slow seduction to corrupt her virtue, Alice glimpses a man tormented by his own choices, a man who promises her nothing except his undeniable passion. . . .

Published by Ivy Books.
Available in your local bookstore.

LORD OF ICE
by Gaelen Foley

Damien Knight, the earl of Winterley, is proud, aloof, and tormented by memories of war. Though living in seclusion, he is named guardian to a fellow officer's ward. Instead of the young homeless waif he was expecting, however, Miranda FitzHubert is a stunning, passionate beauty who invades his sanctuary and forces him back into society. Struggling to maintain honor and self-control, Damien now faces an even greater threat: desire.

In bookstores February 2002!